**GIFT OF THE
CLAYTON COMMUNITY
LIBRARY FOUNDATION**

ONE SUMMER

WITHDRAWN

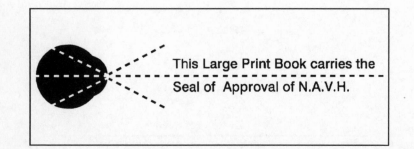

This Large Print Book carries the
Seal of Approval of N.A.V.H.

A SHELTER BAY NOVEL

ONE SUMMER

JOANN ROSS

THORNDIKE PRESS

A part of Gale, Cengage Learning

GALE
CENGAGE Learning®

Detroit • New York • San Francisco • New Haven, Conn • Waterville, Maine • London

GALE
CENGAGE Learning·

Copyright © The Ross Family Trust, 2011.
Thorndike Press, a part of Gale, Cengage Learning.

ALL RIGHTS RESERVED
This is a work of fiction. Names, characters, places, and incidents either are the product of the author's imagination or are used fictitiously, and any resemblance to actual persons, living or dead, business establishments, events, or locales is entirely coincidental.
The publisher does not have any control over and does not assume any responsibility for author or third-party websites or their content.
Thorndike Press® Large Print Romance.
The text of this Large Print edition is unabridged.
Other aspects of the book may vary from the original edition.
Set in 16 pt. Plantin.

LIBRARY OF CONGRESS CATALOGING-IN-PUBLICATION DATA

Ross, JoAnn.
    One summer : a Shelton Bay novel / by JoAnn Ross. — Large print ed.
        p. cm. — (Thorndike Press large print romance)
    ISBN-13: 978-1-4104-4361-8(hardcover)
    ISBN-10: 1-4104-4361-2(hardcover)
    1. United States. Navy. SEALs—Fiction. 2. Photojournalists—Fiction. 3. Women veterinarians—Fiction. 4. Summer—Fiction. 5. Large type books.
    I. Title.
PS3568.O843485O64 2011
813'.54—dc23   2011035069

Published in 2011 by arrangement with NAL Signet, a member of Penguin Group (USA) Inc.

Printed in the United States of America
1 2 3 4 5 6 7 15 14 13 12 11

Again, to all the men and women
of the U.S. military —
and their families — for their
service and sacrifice.

To Natasha Stowe Gebhardt
for her friendship.

And, as always, to Jay,
as we begin yet another new
exciting adventure together.

ACKNOWLEDGMENTS

With heartfelt appreciation once again to the fabulous team at NAL, who makes writing such a joy — this time, especially designer Mimi Bark for my beautiful cover!

With my enduring gratitude to the Empress of Lunches — my agent and friend, Robin Rue. And her super assistant (and debut author!), Beth Miller.

Thanks to former Vanity Fair lingerie designer Jearlean Petrey Stowe for coming up with the perfect name for Shelter Bay's lingerie boutique.

And finally, a huge shout-out to the members of the Portland, Oregon/Vancouver, Washington, chapter of Project Linus, along with the thousands of volunteers nationwide, for the very special work they do to comfort children by providing security through blankets. To learn more about the organization and how you can help, go to www.projectlinusoregon.org, or nationally, www.projectlinus.org.

1

After having spent more than a decade in war zones and other hot spots around the globe, Gabriel St. James was an expert at zeroing in on a shot.

Even when that target was in a bustling crowd of people, as this one was.

Unlike most people on the planet, Gabriel hated weddings. Although there were those in the military who'd called his ability to nail the perfect shot preternatural, and he was more than capable of lowering his cone of silence to shut out the bedlam of merry-making, weddings were just a screwup waiting to happen.

There were too many people. Too many variables. Too many chances for someone to stumble between him and his target.

But against his better judgment, he'd signed on to this mission solely because of loyalty. When you'd been in the trenches with a guy, when you had become even closer than blood brothers, you owed him.

Simple as that.

Semper Fi.

The bride and groom were dancing. Twirling around the floor like a couple on top of a wedding cake come to life. He was looking down at her in a besotted, goofy way that suggested if he dropped dead at that moment, he'd die a happy man.

She was smiling up at him as if she felt the same way.

Damn. Gabe really hated to see another one bite the dust.

Not that it was any of his business. This was a mission. Same as any other.

Yeah, right.

He narrowed his field of vision, cutting out the musicians, the guests, the wedding party. Then further.

Gone was the bride's fairylike, frothy white lace princess dress. And the groom's snazzy military uniform with the shiny brass buttons and colorful field of service ribbons.

He'd closed his focus down to two faces, which were about to be frozen in time.

Gabe took a deep breath, the way Marine sniper scouts were taught to do before taking a shot. Steadied his heartbeat.

Put his finger on the trigger.

Because he was a professional, and because they were lost in their own lovey-dovey world, neither the bride nor the groom noticed him.

Or his camera.

"You know," a woman's voice behind him said, "you *are* allowed to enjoy yourself at a wedding."

"I happen to be working."

He tilted the Nikon to portrait and took a vertical shot. God. Was a dip the most clichéd photo ever?

But the bride had been very specific about what the bride wanted, and apparently big tough Marine Cole Douchett wasn't about to deny her anything her little heart desired. In fact, Gabe's former battle buddy was so besotted, Gabe wouldn't have been surprised if when he printed the photos, little pink hearts would show up dancing around their heads.

"I've noticed. You're very diligent."

When she paused, as if expecting him to comment, Gabe remained silent, hoping she'd go away. She didn't. Nor did her scent, which reminded him of a summer meadow blooming with lavender and wildflowers.

"You're not like any other wedding photographer I've met," she said conversationally.

11

"Thank God for that." Oh, hell. Not the garter shot. Why didn't they just take him out and shoot him so he could get this day over with? "Met a lot of wedding photographers, have you?"

He'd taken an oath to follow fellow Marines through the gates of hell, if necessary. Gabe had never envisioned that might someday include wedding duty.

"Quite a few, actually."

Cole was now kneeling in front of the chair and had begun stripping the bit of pink and white lace from the bride's thigh. The new Mrs. Cole Douchett did have dynamite legs — he'd give her that.

"What are you? A wedding planner or something?" He hadn't met one at last night's rehearsal dinner, but then again, after taking the obligatory shots, he'd gone back to the campground, where he'd spent the night in his RV with a beer and a ball game.

"No. I've just been in a lot of wedding parties the past few years. They seem contagious. Weddings, that is."

"I guess they're like the flu." Cole was taking the garter off with his teeth. Was that even allowed in mixed company with children present? Apparently so, since, by their hoots and cheers, the spectators all appeared to be enjoying the show immensely.

"Always a bridesmaid?" he asked. The damn fragrant cloud, more aura than perfume, was surrounding them. Even as he fought against it, Gabe found himself being drawn to it.

"Not always. I've done the white tulle thing." She paused again. He thought he heard a sigh. "It didn't work out."

"Sorry about that."

"So was I. For a time. But then I decided I was mostly upset because I really hate failing at anything."

"Join the club."

Since she apparently wasn't going to go away, after he captured the garter toss for posterity, Gabe finally lowered his camera and glanced over at her.

She was tall. Lean, but not in a skinny, Hollywood actress way. The pale yellow sleeveless dress that skimmed her body revealed well-toned arms and defined thighs that looked as if she'd spent a lot of time doing PT. Sleek dark hair was pulled back in a tidy tail that fell just below her shoulders, and if he'd been a portrait photographer, which he damn well wasn't, or possessed a romantic bent, which he didn't, her cool green eyes might remind him of a primeval rain forest. "If you're not a wedding planner or a bridesmaid, what are you?"

"A vet."

That got his attention. Momentarily forgetting the show going on, he narrowed his gaze and gave her a longer, more judicial perusal. "Which branch?"

"Excuse me?"

"What branch of the military were you in?"

"Oh!" Intelligent eyes lit up as comprehension dawned. "Sorry. My mistake. I'm not former military. I'm a *veterinarian*-type vet. Small animals. Dogs, cats, and birds, mostly. Along with the occasional reptile. Just anything that can be qualified as a family pet."

"Sounds interesting." *Oh, oorah. They're moving on to the bouquet toss.*

"I like it." She followed his gaze. "Well, I guess I'd better let you get back to work."

It had been a very long time since Gabe had endured any sort of casual conversation. Longer since he'd talked at any length with any woman other than his agent. His social skills had definitely gotten rusty.

As he watched the woman whose name he hadn't bothered to ask for walk away, he felt a twinge of regret.

Then shook it off as the bride prepared

14

for the damn requisite bouquet toss.

A clutch of women had gathered around like basketball players getting braced for a jump shot. The brunette, he noticed, showed a distinct lack of interest as she skirted the crowd.

Click. Gabe shot the bouquet as it left the laughing bride's hand.

Click. Shot it again as it arced through the air.

Although the new Mrs. Cole Douchett didn't even come to her husband's shoulder, the woman had a hell of an arm on her. The lilies tied up in purple ribbon went flying through the air, over the waiting women's outstretched hands, and smacked against the front of the vet's yellow dress.

Acting on instinct, she caught hold of it. Her expression, visible in Gabe's lens, was that of someone who'd just caught a live grenade.

As if sensing him watching her, she glanced toward him.

And *click!* Was instantly captured.

She rolled her expressive eyes, then smiled in a way that had him thinking things. Hot, sweaty things. Things he had no business thinking.

But that didn't stop him from imagining shooting her naked. Lying in the middle of

15

tangled sheets. Or maybe on a blanket in a mountain meadow, looking flushed and satisfied.

Don't go there.

He was just trying to convince himself that walking across the room and attempting to pick her up would be the mother of all boneheaded moves, when the wedding party moved on to the pyramid of cupcakes that the bride had chosen instead of a traditional wedding cake.

At the same time, the vet tossed the bouquet back into the clutch of eager females, wagged her fingers at him, and, slender hips swaying on a pair of ice-pick heels that matched her dress, walked out the door. And out of his life.

Or so he thought.

2

Harborview Veterinary Clinic was, as its name suggested, on Harborview Drive. Housed in a turreted, gingerbread-encrusted Victorian with a wide, wrap-around front porch that spoke of the opulence and optimism of a bygone era, it not only boasted one of the best views of the blue-green water of Shelter Bay's harbor; it came with a colorful history, having once served as the town's bordello.

After it had sat vacant and fallen into disrepair over decades, its next incarnation had been an inn, with a sea-themed lobby and restaurant on the first floor and rooms on the second. Its illicit past had given it a certain naughty cachet that kept rooms filled with honeymooners and others seeking romance.

Still, slow-paced coastal living wasn't for everyone, so the inn changed hands several times. Fortunately for Charity Tiernan, the former owners had been eager to return to the more bustling Seattle and put it on the market just as she had begun looking for a place to set up her practice.

She'd told herself, not quite truthfully, that her move west had nothing to do with her calling off the lavish ceremony the *Chicago Sun-Times* had dubbed the Wedding of the Year ten minutes before she was due to walk down the aisle.

Unsurprisingly, her breakup with Ethan Douglas — the groom-to-be and former *Forbes* magazine "most eligible bachelor" — had been the talk of the city.

While packing up wedding presents to return, she'd paused while rewrapping a stained-and sea-glass sun catcher depicting the harbor and bridge at Shelter Bay. A gift from Lucas Chaffee, the stepbrother her serial-marrying mother had brought into her life, the sun catcher had reminded her of a halcyon vacation she'd spent with her mother and that season's husband — an architect from Portland — on the Oregon coast.

Those six weeks had been, she'd realized as she'd held the colorful gift in her hand, the first time she'd actually felt free to totally be herself. She ran barefoot on the beach, she didn't worry about whether her hair was properly combed, and instead of using little-lady manners with a nanny, she devoured hot dogs and s'mores cooked over a campfire, crabs fresh from the boats boiled right on the dock, and taffy from a white paper bag after being enthralled watching it pulled in the candy-store window.

Shelter Bay had been the closest thing to paradise Charity had ever known. Which was why she'd always intended to return. But then her mother had — no surprise — divorced Lucas' father, severing her connection to the small coastal community.

Or so she'd thought.

But, as she'd sat on the floor, surrounded by the gifts wrapped in gold and silver paper from Chicago's most chichi stores, an idea hit. It was so sudden and so bright, she'd nearly looked up over her head for the light-bulb.

The moment she'd seen the house listed on the online real estate site, she'd wanted it. She spent hours watching the virtual tour, imagining herself living and working beneath the roof that, from the photos, definitely would need to be replaced.

Flying west to tour the house in person only strengthened her resolve. A previous owner had put in soundproofing between the floors to keep guests from being disturbed, which she took as another sign she was destined to live here because it would allow her to set up her clinic on the first floor, and turn the second into living quarters.

She changed the exterior paint from a foggy gray to a sunny yellow with gleaming white trim and window boxes to exude a more positive vibe. Adirondack chairs on the wraparound front porch with a view of the boats chugging in and out of the harbor provided an additional, outdoor waiting room on nice days.

Eighteen months since arriving in town, she'd put the quick pace of the Windy City behind her and settled in, reveling in the way people would wave as she passed them on the street, and how everyone knew everyone's name. And everyone else's business, which she reminded herself was a small price to pay to live in paradise. Just walking down the street made her feel like that happy, carefree girl she'd once been.

"So, how's our girl doing?" she asked as she entered the front door, which opened onto the foyer.

To the left was one of two waiting rooms, while the right doorway led into what had once been a guest parlor — where, in earlier times, men from fishing fleets and logging camps had selected their ladies of the evening — and was now her reception area. Her own dog, a one-hundred-pound Great Pyrenees ironically named Peanut by its former owner, thumped his fluffy white tail in greeting. Then stood up as the aroma of baked goods rising from the box Charity was carrying reached his nose.

The girl in question was an elderly stray English bulldog, who'd been found both emaciated and pregnant, fighting with gulls over scraps from a beach waste barrel she'd apparently tipped over, searching for food. Although birth was usually a natural process in dogs, just as with humans, some pregnancies were high risk. This happened to be one of them.

"Amie says she's ready to pop," the gray-haired woman behind the desk said, seconding what the vet assistant's text message had already told her.

The sixty-something receptionist had walked in looking for a job a month before the clinic's opening, while Charity was painting the waiting area a soft sea blue meant to soothe both patients and their owners. A recent divorcée, she'd been looking for a day job to support her painting, which had just begun to be shown in a local gallery.

She and Charity had immediately clicked and Charity had hired her on the spot. Janet proved to be a gem as she organized files, including setting up a bookkeeping system more efficient than the one the high-priced accountant had set up in Chicago. And if that weren't enough, she'd turned her talents to painting murals on the wall behind her counter and in the waiting rooms and hallway.

"So the text message she sent me said. I come bearing goodies." Charity placed the pink box with *Take the Cake* written in tasteful script onto the counter. The baker, who'd become a friend, had sent along some leftovers from the reception.

"There goes my diet." The pleasingly plump woman sighed as she snagged a dark, decadent chocolate cupcake topped with milk chocolate frosting and chocolate shavings. "And any chance I have for burn-up-the-sheets sex with George Clooney."

"Life's filled with trade-offs." Laughing, Charity plucked a tropical-island cake with pineapple-coconut frosting from the box for herself and a chocolate topped with peanut butter frosting for her assistant. After tossing Peanut a liver snap, she headed back into the surgical area.

"How are we doing?" she asked her assistant.

"I've done all the blood work, shaved and sterilized the surgical area, and as soon as you said you were on your way, I gave her an injection to relax her, so as soon as you put in her breathing tube, she'll be good to go."

Amie Bayaa's gaze narrowed as she focused in on the cupcake Charity was holding out to her. "Of course, a couple more minutes isn't going to make that much of a difference." She snatched the cake and took a huge bite. "So," she asked around a mouthful of chocolate as Charity kicked off the foot-killing spiked heels she'd foolishly allowed Amie and Janet to convince her to buy, "how did the wedding go?"

"Everyone was having a great time when I left." She exchanged the dress, which the women had convinced her she also had to buy for the occasion, for a pair of blue scrubs in a dog-bone print.

"Sorry to have to pull you away from the festivities."

"No problem." Charity nearly wept with relief as she slid her aching feet into a pair of sunshine yellow Crocs. Until today she couldn't remember the last time she'd worn heels. "Weddings aren't my favorite thing, anyway. I just felt I owed the Douchett family for taking two homeless dogs off our hands."

"As if anyone could say no to you when you're in full steamroller mode. Did you get to meet the hottie Marine?"

"There were a bunch of Marines there." Standing out like a blizzard in July with their high and tight haircuts. "And most were hot."

"I'm talking about the wedding photographer."

"That photographer's a Marine?"

"Former, though my gung ho gunnery sergeant dad would tell you there's no such thing as a *former* Marine. Apparently Gabriel St. James is an old battle buddy of Cole's. A war photojournalist."

"Taking wedding photos is a long way from taking war photos."

No wonder he'd been in such a rotten mood. And she wouldn't exactly call him hot. His face — all sharp angles and lean hollows — was too harsh to be conventionally handsome and the jagged white scar slicing through one dark brow added a vaguely menacing appearance. His deeply hooded eyes, the color of January rain, revealed both arrogance and chilly remoteness. Except for when he was looking

24

through the lens, they were never still, constantly tracking the room.

Her former fiancé had been handsome. Handsome, rich, pedantic. Yet she'd foolishly convinced herself that the fact that he could be rigid and, yes, even boring was a trait in his favor. Sure, he didn't make her feel all gooey inside, and their lovemaking hadn't exactly rocked the earth on its axis, but having watched her parents chase after passion with disastrous results, Charity had viewed her and Ethan's lack of passion as another positive.

She'd realized at an early age that a long and lasting marriage — which was what she'd always dreamed of — wasn't built solely on sex, but on shared interests, respect, and trust. Which was why she'd talked herself into believing that Ethan was her type.

She'd been wrong about that.

But that didn't mean that Gabriel St. James, with a glower that could probably melt an enemy's bullets before they had the chance to hit him, *was.*

"The wedding gig is definitely beneath his talent level," Amie said as Charity's thoughts drifted to that moment, right after that damn bouquet had fallen into her hands and their eyes had met, when she'd felt an unmistakable zing. *Definitely not your type.* "I may be a 'Kumbaya'-singing Native American pacifist," her assistant continued, "but that guy's photos are the bomb."

Charity snapped on a pair of purple latex gloves. "You've seen them?"

"He's got a coffee-table book on sale down at Tidal Wave Books." Amie swallowed the rest of the cupcake and scrubbed her own hands. "There are also two copies in the window. One showing the back cover with a knee-weakening hot picture in Marine battle gear. Apparently he's hot in more ways than looks. His photos have been in papers all over the world, including the *New York Times.* He's even won a Pulitzer."

"And you know this how?"

"Jeez, Charity." Fluorescent magenta-hued bangs ruffled as Amie blew out a frustrated breath. "Even if I hadn't read the cover bio, Amber, at the Grateful Bread, told Edna, at the sheriff's office, who told Hannah, at Fresh Fields market, who told Brianna, at Cut Loose, who did the bridal party's hair for the wedding, who told me while I was getting these streaks put in yesterday. The guy's been the main topic of conversation ever since he hit town two days ago."

"Main topic of gossip, you mean." Having

landed in the eye of a gossip hurricane, Charity went out of her way to avoid listening to any herself.

"True, but in case you haven't noticed, Shelter Bay isn't exactly the big city, like Chicago. Gossip is major entertainment around here."

"They gossip in Chicago, too."

"Oops. Sorry. I didn't mean to bring up bad memories."

"The wedding already did that. And you know what?"

"What?"

"I realized I no longer care."

It was true. She'd come to that conclusion even before getting that unexpected sexual zing from the Marine turned wedding photographer.

When she'd first arrived in Shelter Bay, being the new flavor in town, she'd been asked out by several local men. Since males tended to outnumber women in town, many would've definitely been considered eligible bachelors, if she'd been interested. Which, having been so recently burned by someone she'd trusted, she hadn't been.

Eighteen months later, she still received her share of invitations. In the beginning, she'd been so busy refurbishing this house and building a practice, she'd barely had time to sleep or eat, let alone consider any type of social life.

But the debacle that was to have been her wedding day was nearly two years ago. Doing some quick mental math, Charity realized she'd been going to bed alone for 610 nights. And waking up alone — unless you counted Peanut, who slept on the floor at the foot of her bed — for 611 mornings.

Not that she was counting. But perhaps it was time to rethink her dating moratorium.

When her mind drifted back to Gabriel St. James, she tacked on a caveat.

With someone safe.

If she was going to dive back into the dating pool, Charity preferred to stay in shallow waters. Getting involved with that Marine would be like skinny-dipping with a great white shark.

3

Trust Cole Douchett not to have a typical wedding, Gabe thought as he drove away from Bon Temps, the Cajun dance hall and restaurant where the event had been held.

Although details were still sketchy, from what Gabe had been able to piece together, Cole's brother Sax had been working with Shelter Bay's sheriff on a pair of cold cases involving past murders in town. When they received a call informing them that a consulting former FBI agent had discovered evidence pointing to the killer's identity, the two had raced away from the reception to apprehend the suspect.

Cole had assured Gabe that he wouldn't mind his going along on the chase, since he'd probably be able to catch some shots he could sell to the press, but Gabe had assured him in return that he was through with taking pictures of anything that might involve weapons.

So he'd stayed around until the happy couple had left the party in a hail of birdseed. Having tried the marriage thing once before, Gabe had no intention of repeating the experience. Still, he had to admit that the expression on Cole's face, as they'd driven off to catch a flight in Portland for a Hawaiian honeymoon, had been that of a lucky bastard who'd just won the Powerball jackpot, World Poker Championship, and Super Bowl all on the same day.

Having witnessed some of the hell Cole had experienced as an elite Recon Marine, Gabe figured he deserved to be the happiest guy in the whole USA. And no one would bring the motto "Honor, Courage, Commitment" into a marriage better.

But now that he'd done his duty, he was grateful to escape the crowd of wedding guests. He'd always been a loner. In fact, his former wife had — in her "Dear Gabriel" letter informing him that she was divorcing him — accused him of being a cold, distant island unto himself.

Gabe hadn't been able to disagree.

Which was why he shunned the fame and fortune his agent kept insisting could be his if he'd just be a little more open to editorial suggestion about warming up his photos. Not by color, but viewpoint.

He supposed that having grown up in a home that was about as far away from the idyllic Waltons as you could get might have contributed to him not seeing the world as both his editor and his agent assured him others did. His view was, admittedly, harsher, colder than others might see with the naked eye.

Whether they were taken in the midst of a battle, or displaying smiles lighting up the battle-weary faces of troops who didn't look old enough to shave handing out Beanie Babies to Iraqi children, the photos remained detached, showing none of the photographer's personal view of his subjects.

And yet for some reason they touched emotional chords. Not just with the military, who'd made him a photojournalist after seeing the shots he took during the battle of Fallujah, but with the editors at the *New York Times,* who'd first started featuring his work.

His photos had gone on to be collected in a book published by USNI, the U.S. Naval Institute. Then two books. Then three. Since they'd been taken while he'd been in the Marines, he didn't receive any royalties, but he hadn't joined the service to get rich. Nor had he taken his photos with money in mind.

His mission, as he'd seen it, had been to tell the truth. To be a witness to war. And he'd been damn good at his job. Unfortunately, after eighteen straight months in Iraq and Afghanistan, he'd returned to the States with an unexpected and annoying case of PTSD.

It hadn't been enough to have him in danger of going off on a shooting rage. Or feel suicidal. Nor had he turned to alcohol or drugs for relief. He'd just shut down, clamped the lid on his emotions even tighter.

When his tour of duty came to an end, he'd opted out of reenlisting. After stepping back into civilian life, he'd intended to take at least a year away from his camera. Unfortunately, two weeks into that plan, he'd discovered that when he wasn't working, nightmares and flashbacks attacked with a vengeance.

When his agent (and who the hell ever suspected a guy from a small South Carolina Lowcountry town would end up with a high-powered New York City agent?) suggested he do a pictorial study of American life during wartime, to contrast with the more involved home-front behavior during the Vietnam and World War II eras, he'd agreed.

Not only could he use the money; even more appealing was that the work didn't involve actually interacting with people.

He'd bought a motor home and a Jeep to pull behind it, then started out in Maine, where he'd photographed fishermen clad in plaid shirts and ball caps protesting low lobster prices. He shot a coal miner in Pennsylvania, face and hands as black as tar, smoking a cigarette after a long day belowground, and a young couple exchanging vows on a Florida beach, while black clouds, heralding an oncoming hurricane, roiled behind them.

After months on the road, he'd wandered his way though the continental states, not having any preplanned itinerary, just going wherever the mood moved him. Which was definitely out of his comfort zone after all the years of planning a mission to the nth degree.

Oregon was his forty-seventh state, and he couldn't deny that, with the exception of the wedding photos, so far it was his favorite, with its scenic contrasts of high desert ranching country, orchards and rolling farmland, soaring, snowcapped mountains, lush vineyards, fishing harbors, and rugged coast.

He was on his way to his next stop — Washington. Then the plan was to head up to Alaska before the snow started falling, then finally park the motor home and fly to Hawaii to wrap up the project.

A few miles out of town, he pulled the rig over onto a scenic overlook. While he had no interest in postcard scenic shots of lighthouses and sunsets, down below, on the beach, a group of senior citizens was climbing off a tour bus. All were wearing name tags and were dutifully walking — in perfect step, as if they were shouting out cadences in their heads — in dual lines.

The rigid uniformity of their behavior in such a wild, untamed place interested him enough that he took out his camera, snapped on the long lens, and was about to shoot when an old beater Ford Econoline came pulling up from the other direction.

Damn. One thing Gabe hated about taking photos in the civilian world was that unlike in war zones, where both troops and locals were trying to stay alive, he'd often draw an audience. People always wanted to ask questions and compare cameras, and, God help him, in this age of digital, often insisted on showing the snapshots they'd taken.

He lowered his cone of silence, but for some reason, the inner alarm system that had kept him and his fellow Marines alive on more than one occasion kicked into full alert mode. Even the hair on his arms rose.

Assuring himself it was merely the coastal breeze blowing in from the ocean, he regained focus and lifted his camera just as the door to the van opened.

He snapped quickly, instinctively, without bothering with f-stops and focus, before whoever had stopped could interrupt. But instead of a person, a small ball of black fur was thrown out.

It rolled, like a hedgehog, right up to the stone wall, which kept it from going over the cliff.

"Hey!" he yelled.

The van door closed and the car took off with a squeal of wheels and the acrid burning scent of rubber.

Unfortunately, the black ball, which turned out to be a dog, managed to scramble back on its feet and damned if it didn't race after the van with amazing speed, considering its size.

The driver of the van swerved.

Now Gabe was running, as well.

The van ran over the dog, amazingly seeming not to hit it. But something — the collar? — caught on the underside of the vehicle, dragging the animal a good ten feet before it finally dropped off with a sickening thud.

Undeterred and showing a determination far beyond its size, the small black dog scrambled to its feet and raced after the van as it sped away.

Concerned it was going to get run over in the busy tourist traffic, Gabe sprinted after it, scooping it up under his arm like a football.

"Hey, buddy," he said as the dog wiggled to get free, "it's going to be okay."

Maybe it was something in his voice. Maybe it was because the dog realized the impossibility of catching the van, which had disappeared around a tight S curve. Maybe it was just flat-out tired of running.

Because it looked up at Gabe through a tangle of matted fur, huge round eyes like marbles, as if to say, "Well? Now what do we do?"

4

While Charity never took any surgery for granted, some admittedly were dicier than others. Which was why, as she walked into the operating room she'd painted an uplifting buttercup color that filled the room with sunshine on the cloudiest of Oregon coast days, she was grateful that she'd spared no expense in this part of the building.

Raiding her savings account, she'd sprung for a hydraulic heated table along with a troweled-on epoxy-quartz floor that made cleanup easier. Unlike surgeons who operated on humans — with several assistants, separate anesthesiologists, extra nurses on standby to give IV fluids — veterinarians were, by necessity, highly skilled at successfully making do with what little they might have.

Sort of, Charity considered, her mind uncharacteristically drifting back to the wedding photographer, the way Marines were reported to be.

Unlike the windowless box she'd operated in back at the large, multivet clinic in Chicago, this room boasted large windows that offered a view of the emerald green exercise lawn and contemplation garden she'd had the landscaper create.

Not only did the plants, waterfall, and koi pond make a restful place to eat lunch; the garden also provided serenity for stressed-out owners and animals. Especially those owners with beloved pets facing euthanasia. Which, on nice days, could actually be done outside amid so much soothing nature.

So, although her surgical unit might not compare with those depicted on *ER* and *Grey's Anatomy,* it was her dream clinic. She couldn't imagine ever leaving it, or Shelter Bay.

A recent Oregon State University graduate, Amie was learning the ropes of the business while waiting to get into veterinarian school. What many people didn't realize was that since there were only twenty-seven vet schools in the country, acceptance was actually more difficult than getting into medical school. This was also her assistant's first time to witness a C-section. Charity hoped she'd look back on it with excitement, rather than regret.

"Bulldogs have, unfortunately, been bred to have large blocky heads." Although the dog was already floating on soft clouds of calming anesthetic, Charity patted the patient's huge head to give it an encouraging rub before sticking the IV needle into the shaved spot of her front leg, which would allow her to administer anesthesia before inserting the breathing tube. Efficient as always, Amie had already hung the bags of fluids on the metal rack.

"That's what makes them look so cool," her assistant said.

"It definitely gives them their individuality, but the downside is that bulldog puppies' big heads are more likely to get stuck. Which is why C-sections are the safest way to deliver."

Charity felt a flash of anger at whatever cretin had abandoned the poor pregnant dog. Then tamped it down because she needed a cool head. "Anesthesia for this surgery is tricky, because we want muscle relaxation and don't want the mama to experience pain, but on the other hand, the goal is to get the babies out fast before they absorb too much from their mother's blood."

"Plus, you want the mom to be awake as quickly as possible, so she can nurse."

Charity shot her assistant a rewarding smile. "You've been studying up."

"I told you I aced my GRE."

Grades and test scores were one thing. But empathy for both the animals and the people who owned them — something Amie displayed on a daily basis — was equally important.

"You're going to be a great vet."

"Tell that to the dean. Maybe he'll move me up the list to get into vet school."

"I wish I had some influence. But most of us go through the same thing. Which maybe is a good thing, because it gives us time to really consider if the job's right for us."

"I've known since I was five and began bandaging my stuffed animals that I wanted to be a vet. But if I have to wait, working with you is turning out to be a bonus and it sure beats dealing blackjack at the casino. Not only am I going to have a head start when I finally get into the classroom — you've taught me so much about the human side of being a vet. Watching you interact with people has made me even more sure of my decision."

"Thanks. I appreciate that."

It was also good to hear because even with what Charity was paying her, Amie would be leaving school with huge debts. Loving her work would make them easier to pay off. Not that student loans had been a problem for Charity, thanks to an inheritance from her maternal grandfather. But she'd watched so many classmates struggle.

Although Amie's mother was a doctor and her father a lawyer, both had chosen to live on the Siletz reservation and were active in the community. Her mother was a member of the tribal council and her father did legal work for the casino and lobbied for Native American rights. Which didn't earn either of them what they could have made if they'd moved to private-sector jobs in the city. But they'd obviously passed down the values of dedication to vocation, along with personal responsibility, to their daughter.

"It wasn't sucking up," Amie said.

"I know." Charity switched to a safer gas anesthetic. "But, hey, if you're going to suck up, who better to suck up to than your boss?"

They both laughed at that idea.

Since the radiography had shown six puppies, all fortunately alive, Charity needed to move swiftly. Not making matters easier was the fact that the mother was a "golden paws" dog — too elderly to be safely giving birth.

She opened the extended abdomen. "First

thing is to inspect the uterus for tears, or adhesions. And make sure we're not dealing with infection or other problems."

She stepped aside to let Amie view the open cavity.

"Looks good to me," the assistant said with a confidence that would serve her well in her own practice someday.

Maybe they'd even become partners down the road, once Amie got her DVM. The slower pace here on the remote Oregon coast had Charity seriously considering a less workaholic lifestyle that allowed more time for pleasure. Like roasting marshmallows over a campfire on the beach. Hiking in the forest. She loved sitting on her front porch and watching the sailboats skim across the waters of the bay. Maybe she'd take up sailing.

The idea was appealing. But at the moment, she had a job to do.

"Okay. Here we go." She pulled the Y-shaped uterus, which was filled with pups packed in rows along the horns.

"That is so cool." Amie looked as awestruck as Charity herself had been the first time she'd seen the squirming fetuses eager to come into the world.

"It never fails to amaze me," Charity agreed.

She made a slit in the wall and began extracting the puppies, one by one. Amie quickly took each one away, cleared their airways, and stimulated them in a warmed box filled with blankets. Before long, the sextuplets were squirming, breathing, and mewling.

After spaying the dog to avoid future pregnancies, Charity stitched up the long line on the already deflated abdomen.

"Not exactly a bikini scar," she told the sedated bulldog. "But you did get a nice tummy tuck out of the deal."

One danger of a cesarean was that the dog could be groggy and accidentally lie down on a pup and suffocate it. Since the sedative Charity had chosen was designed to leave the system quickly, soon she, Amie, and Janet were standing over the box, watching, as the mother, whom Janet had named Winnie, nursed her hungry babies.

"It's a miracle," Amie said on a long, happy sigh.

"Absolutely," Charity and Janet agreed. Charity was also relieved that the dog's maternal instincts were so strong. Another problem with forgoing a natural birth was that occasionally, not understanding how those puppies got there, a mother dog might not accept them. Fortunately, that was not the case this time.

"Next up, finding Winnie a home," Charity said.

She'd already managed to place the puppies, one of which was going to Sax Douchett's fiancée's young son as a surprise birthday present. But elderly dogs were always more of a problem.

"Sofia De Luca was in earlier with Rosemary," Janet revealed.

The upbeat mood in the room plunged at that announcement. Sofia was an elderly widowed gardener who'd searched the world to create one of the most extensive herb gardens in the Pacific Northwest, if not the country. Although her Lavender Hill Farm was routinely featured in gardening, cooking, and lifestyle magazines, she appeared to have never let the glowing reviews go to her head. Rosemary was her golden retriever, whom Charity had recently diagnosed with metastatic cancer.

"How was she?"

"Sofia or Rosemary?"

"Both." Sofia De Luca was the most optimistic person Charity had ever met. Despite suffering the tragedies of losing her daughter and son-in-law in a plane crash and, more recently, her husband to cancer, she still managed to maintain an optimistic enthusiasm for life. Along with the energy of a woman half her age. But Charity also knew the emotional toll a terminal pet could have on its owner.

"Sofia seems resigned. Rosemary's thin, losing fur, coughing, and urinated on the floor without seeming to realize she'd done it. But that didn't stop her from greeting Peanut with a tail wag and a good sniffing. Which Sofia took as a sign the dog's still got a few more days in her."

"Sofia's a wise, thoughtful woman. She'll make the decision when the time's right."

"I know," Amie agreed. "Which is why I sent her home with another packet of those pain meds you prescribed."

"Good call." Although the golden's unrelenting good nature kept her from revealing signs of discomfort, Charity knew she had to be experiencing it.

Charity glanced over at the pups, eagerly suckling on their patient mom, who appeared to have been through this before.

"Sofia and Winnie have a lot in common," she considered. "They've both been through a lot and landed on their feet." Four feet in the bulldog's case.

"And neither one is young," Janet pointed out.

Another point in matching them up.

Early on in her practice, Charity had discovered that often the elderly, especially those without family, worried about taking on the responsibility of a younger pet they might end up leaving behind.

"It's going to be a while before the pups are weaned and Winnie's on her own. Which gives us time to think about suggesting an adoption. But it's definitely something to keep in mind."

The C-section taken care of, Charity stayed downstairs to monitor Winnie and her newborns after Amie and Janet left for the day.

She thought about Winnie. And Sofia. And poor sweet Rosemary, whose time on earth was growing short.

Life and death. Wasn't that the circle of life that Charity had chosen to constantly live with?

Looking down at the temporarily blind and deaf puppies instinctively snuggling up to their mother for warmth and comfort, Charity felt a distant tug she couldn't quite define.

5

The mutt was a mess. Not only filthy, with fur tangled into mats, but probably flea-ridden, as well. Which meant that putting him into his rig would probably end up giving the fleas a whole new home.

But after he'd lived with the nasty sand fleas in Afghanistan and Iraq, it wouldn't be anything new. Plus, he still had a jar of Combat-Ready Balm no Marine stationed in what had to be the holy land of sand fleas was ever without.

Not knowing the name of the vet he'd talked with briefly at the wedding, Gabe did a GPS search for the nearest clinic. Then, making a U-turn, he followed the automated female voice's instructions back into Shelter Bay.

The clinic, which, from the outside, looked more like a Victorian bed-and-breakfast, was located at the far end of the harbor. A simple white wooden sign read

HARBORVIEW VETERINARY CLINIC, DR.
CHARITY TIERNAN, DVM, DAVSAB.

Gabe left the dog in the motor home, in
case the office was closed, and walked up
the steps to the wide front porch. The white
Adirondack chairs next to potted flowers
added to the B and B look and offered a
spectacular view of the harbor. According
to the hours posted on the front window,
which had been brightened with a colorful
glass sun catcher, the clinic was closed. But
below that, a note invited people to ring the
bell after hours.

So he did.

Less than a minute later, the door opened.
And hot damn, there she was. The woman
from the wedding.

She'd undone the clip holding her dark
hair back, allowing it to fall loose over her
shoulders. She'd also changed into a pair of
pink and purple striped pajama bottoms
and an oversized T-shirt that read, *I Sleep
with Dogs.* A huge animal, which looked
more like a polar bear than a dog, stood by
her side. Not growling or bristling, but it
was obvious he was there to protect his
mistress.

"Well, hello," she greeted him. "This is a
surprise."

"It's not what you think," he heard himself saying.

"And that would be?"

"It's not a booty call." Where the hell did that come from? Oh, yeah. He definitely needed to hone his communication skills.

"Okay." She could have at least appeared a bit disappointed as she folded her arms. "Since I doubt you're here to sell me wedding photos, why are you standing on my porch at this time of night?" Her tone and the sparkle that lit up her green eyes suggested she was laughing at him. Which was definitely not something Gabe was accustomed to.

"I've got this dog."

"Good for you. Dogs are some of my favorite people." She absently patted her own beast's massive head as she glanced past him at the rig.

"Well, it's not *my* dog. I picked it up."

"It's a stray?"

"I'd say so. Given that its owner dumped it out on the coast road."

She sighed. The light dimmed in her eyes. "That happens all too often, unfortunately. But how did you know I ran a shelter?"

"I didn't. He's hurt. My GPS kicked up this address for the nearest vet."

"Hurt?" The same way a convoy might

react to an IED explosion, she switched into immediate, full professional alert. Her gaze snapped back to the rig. "How badly?"

"Nothing's broken. At least I don't think so. But he's got one helluva case of road rash from being dragged beneath the van."

"Can you bring him in?"

"Sure. I doubt he weighs in at ten pounds."

"Poor thing." She shook her head. "I'll fix up an exam room while you fetch him."

The dog was sitting right where he'd left him, on the passenger seat. Marble-round brown eyes gazed at Gabe as if the dog was patiently waiting for him to make things right, while an underbite showed a row of bottom teeth that under any other situation might have been comical. One of the teeth was chipped. Amazingly, considering what he'd been through, he thumped a fuzzy tail on the leather upholstery.

"Don't get any ideas," Gabe warned as he scooped up the ball of filthy fur. "Just because I did the Good Samaritan thing doesn't mean there's any room in my life for a dog." As it was held against Gabe's chest, the mutt lifted its front paws to his shoulders and licked his cheek. "Not going to work," Gabe said as he carried it into the building.

The inside of the clinic was as bright and cheery as the outside. The wall of the reception area boasted a mural, jewel-toned fish swam in a saltwater aquarium, and painted signs above the two doorways leading off the main room designated separate cat and dog waiting rooms. Snapshots of dogs of various sizes and breeds up for adoption were tacked onto a bulletin board, like the FBI's most-wanted criminals on a post office wall.

"Aw." The vet took the dog from him and stroked its filthy head. "Poor baby, you've had a rough time of it, haven't you, sweetie boy?"

The huge white dog was gone. Gabe guessed she'd put it away just in case it might scare the mutt. Or eat it for a night-time snack.

She carried her patient down a short hallway, painted with more colorful animal-themed murals, to an examination room.

"You're right on the money," she said after weighing him. "Nine pounds, at least a pound of which is probably fur. He looks like a Shih Tzu mix beneath that mess, which means he could use a bit more weight on him."

As the dog sat patiently on the scale, as if waiting for whatever might happen next, she held out her hand. "We haven't been formally introduced. I'm Charity Tiernan."

"Yeah, I got that from your sign." Her grip was firm, her slender hand soft. "Gabe St. James."

"I know *that* from your book."

"You've seen it?"

"No. But it comes highly recommended by my assistant. I'd planned on checking it out at the bookstore tomorrow morning."

Gabe had never really given much thought to the people who bought his books. But for some reason he liked the idea of this woman looking at his work. At least, he figured, given her career, she wouldn't be put off by the bloody scenes that had been part of his life for more than a decade.

She hadn't taken her hand back. It felt like silk and smelled like the tropics, probably from some lotion she'd rubbed into it before he'd shown up, but that didn't stop the little zing that had him thinking about lying with her on a sun-drenched beach, feeling those hands touch him all over. And him doing the same thing to her.

He felt her pulse do a skip dance at the base of her thumb and realized she'd felt it, too.

"Well." She stepped back and snapped on a pair of latex gloves.

She'd looked both intelligent and sexy at the wedding. When she'd opened the door, she'd looked soft, slightly tousled, and approachable. Now she somehow managed to look both nurturing and briskly professional at the same time.

The dog, having more guts than he would've expected, proved surprisingly stoic during her examination. But it did keep those huge, beseeching eyes on Gabe, as if with a need to make sure he, too, wasn't going to bail.

"You're right," she said finally. "Although I want to take a couple X-rays, given the trauma he would've suffered by being dragged beneath a vehicle, I can't find anything broken.

"He does, however, have ticks, and those fur mats are risking infection, because they irritate his skin." She brushed aside a tangle and showed him the red rough skin beneath. "It's more than ugly — it can become a bad cycle. The skin itches from the mats, so the dog licks it, then the hair sticks, and causes more irritation and seepage, so the dog licks again. We'll need to demat him, then put some antibiotic on the sores, road scrapes, those other burns."

"Other burns?"

"Here." She brushed aside some of the

tangled fur. "And here." Another spot. "And here. These small round circles."

"Shit." Gabe had seen his share of horrors. Been smack in the middle of them all too often. But as he identified those red blisters, his stomach turned. "Those look like they're from a lit cigarette."

"Probably. Unfortunately, again not so uncommon." When she stroked the dog's head, it licked her gloved hand.

"How do you do it?" he asked.

"Do what?" She took a syringe and needle from a cabinet.

"Stay so cool and not get furious at a crime like this?"

"I *am* furious." A quick, sharp whip in her voice underscored her claim. "And after years of working with animals, I've never understood the human mind-set that allows abuse." She injected the mutt, who didn't emit so much as a whimper. It might look like a sissy dog, but beneath that mass of fur, it was proving to be as tough as any Marine. "I also run a no-kill shelter, and believe me, it's all too easy to become cynical about people if you allow yourself to be."

She took a deep breath. Pulled off the gloves and ran one of those silky hands through her hair. He watched her gather up her composure, which had shown signs of fraying. So, the lady had some heat inside. *Interesting.*

"But instead of dwelling on my anger, I try to concentrate on my job, which is caring for animals who don't have anyone else to care for them. I realized while I was still in vet school that it's a waste of time trying to comprehend how anyone could purposefully torture a sweetie like this. What we need to do now is do our best to make up for past behavior and offer this little guy the future he deserves."

"I couldn't be that forgiving." Although Gabe knew veterans who'd managed to successfully compartmentalize their lives, he doubted he could ever get to the point where he could forgive those bastards who'd done their best to kill him. And who'd killed so many fellow Marines.

"It's an ongoing effort. Some days are admittedly easier than others. Today I attended a wedding of two people who are obviously madly in love, ate a cupcake that was to die for, and delivered six puppies. The pups and the mother probably would've died if Bernard Douchett hadn't found her rummaging through a trash can on the beach and brought her to me. So I was in a pretty good mood when you showed up at my door." Her smile was like sunshine breaking through a dismal coastal rain. "Which helps."

"So, what are you going to do now?"

"Bathe him, give him a tick and flea dip, treat any skin irritation and wounds, give him a clipping to get rid of those mats and make him more presentable, and feed him a decent meal. I'll also want to insert a microchip, give him a rabies injection, and, of course, neuter him."

Gabe's testicles pulled up tight.

"Do you know, every time I say that to a man, he gets the same look on his face that you have right now?"

"Maybe it's because most guys have this thing about keeping their nuts."

"Don't worry." Her tone was dry, but he could hear the repressed laughter in it. "Yours are safe. There are enough unwanted dogs in the world. This guy doesn't need to be contributing to that population explosion. He'll never know the difference and have fewer health problems as he gets older. That antibiotic I gave him will last ten days. If he shows any signs of infection, I'll give him a second dose. That'll save you from having to try to get him to take pills."

"Me?"

"You're not going to keep him?"

"I don't have any room for a dog."

"It's a large motor home. And he's a small dog."

"Well, yeah, but I was talking about my lifestyle. I never stay anywhere more than a few days."

"Do you have any idea how many full-time RVers there are in this country? And how many travel with pets?"

"Haven't a clue." Gabe didn't really give a damn, either.

"Neither do I," she admitted. "But there's a bunch, because we get a lot of tourists in Shelter Bay. I treat their pets occasionally as they pass through. Most people enjoy their company."

"I'm not most people."

"Wow, now, there's a news flash. Being above average intelligence, I've already figured that out for myself. How many Marines take wedding photos, after all?"

"So you know I'm a Marine?"

"I told you, my assistant told me about your book," she reminded him. "Apparently you're the talk of the town. And extremely talented. Which makes me wonder what had you taking on a wedding gig. Not that wedding photography might not be a lovely career, but it's quite a major subject leap from war photos."

"Cole was in my unit."

"Ah." She nodded. "The *Semper Fi* thing."

"Yeah."

Her eyes lit up. He could see himself reflected in them. "That's sweet."

"News flash, back atcha, Doc — Marines don't exactly consider *sweet* a compliment. As for the mutt, I just did what anyone would do under the same circumstances. But I definitely wasn't signing up for any long-term commitment."

"You're a male," she murmured, as she wet a paper towel and washed some crusty guck from the dog's eyes. "Which, I suppose, means that commitment isn't exactly in your DNA."

"I don't know about all males." He'd done the till-death-do-us-part vows once before and that sure as hell hadn't worked out. Since then, he'd decided marriage wasn't in the cards. At least not for him. "But Cole was sure as hell looking poleaxed at the wedding."

She smiled again. "He was, wasn't he?" Her expression immediately sobered. *Contrasts.* "Look, this little guy needs to spend the night here anyway, so I can clean him up and observe him to make sure there isn't anything internal going on I may have missed. So, why don't you sleep on it, and let me know your decision tomorrow?"

"I don't need to wait until tomorrow to make a decision. The dog's no longer my problem." He reached into his pocket and pulled out his billfold. "Let me pay you what you think it'll cost, plus some overtime for interrupting your evening, and we'll be square."

"If only it were that easy. I mentioned the shelter."

"Yeah."

"Well, it is, at the moment, at full capacity. And I've currently used up my list of foster parents."

"But you could keep him until you found someone to take him on. He's probably cute enough, under all that dirt and hair, to find him a home."

"He's going to need more attention than I can give him. I'm afraid a prior commitment's going to have me a bit overextended for the next few weeks."

Dr. Charity Tiernan sure as hell wasn't proving to be a pushover. Gabe found himself wishing Cole's brother Sax were here. When he turned on the charm, the former SEAL had a smooth way about him that had most women agreeing to just about anything. Apparently Kara Conway, Shelter Bay's sheriff, had proved a tougher nut to crack than most, but from seeing them together at the wedding, swaying so close they were nearly making love on the dance floor, it appeared Sax Douchett had won her over.

She scooped the dog off the metal table and shoved it at him. "At least hold him for a sec while I go check the crate situation," she said. Although he figured it was a dare, Gabe wasn't willing to bet the dog's neck — which it could break if it fell — on it. Which gave him no choice but to take it from her.

She was gone longer than a "sec." Every Marine had a clock in his head, and Gabe figured she was pushing on five minutes when she finally returned. It was a good ploy, given that the dog had literally put its muddy paws around his neck again and was happily licking his face while its tail wagged to beat the band. Damned if the two of them weren't ganging up on him. But a guy who'd survived war zones wasn't going to be taken down that easily.

"As I said, we're full up," she announced. *Surprise, surprise.* "I was considering getting down one of the travel crates I use to take animals out to the shelter for him to spend the night in, but the poor little guy's been through enough. After I dip him, he might as well come upstairs with me."

"You live here?"

"It's a big place. It used to be a bed-and-breakfast, and when I saw it online, I fell in love. And the commute's a lot better than the one I had in Chicago."

"You're not a local?" Genuine and easygoing, she seemed to fit here, as if she'd been born to the place.

"No. I've only lived in Shelter Bay about eighteen months. But I visited once while growing up. My mother was married to an Oregon architect for a while and I have a stepbrother who's currently in the military, whom I'm close to. So, when I started looking for a change in scenery, and a place to put down roots, well, this town, where I spent the best summer vacation of my life, just felt right."

After giving up on that fanciful idea of having a little woman waiting for him at home, Gabe had decided roots tied a person down. But he also understood that his was probably a minority opinion.

"Well, I've already taken up enough of your time." If he was to be perfectly honest, he'd like to take up more, which was all the more reason to leave. *Now.*

He put the nine pounds of matted black fur back onto the table. "If you'll just tell me how much I owe you."

"I'm afraid I can't do that."

"Why not?"

"Because I have no idea what I may find after I bathe and clip him. He might have skin disease, more road rash, even ringworm. And he might need more tests."

"Why don't you make an estimate?" Gabe suggested. He pulled out a stack of twenties he'd picked up that morning at the gas station ATM. "Here's three hundred. I'll call tomorrow, and if it's more than that, I'll send the rest."

When she didn't immediately respond, Gabe wondered if she was worried about getting stiffed on her fee.

"You really should give the little guy a fair chance," she said. "See how he cleans up before you reject him."

"I'm sure he'll look just dandy. But I'm not in the market for a dog. And if I were, a foo-foo dust mop of a canine would be the last breed on my list."

The dog sitting on its haunches, looking up at him with a ridiculously adoring gaze, was about as far from a manly dog as Gabe could have imagined.

"I'm surprised." She looked him straight in the eye as she patted the mutt's head. "I wouldn't have expected a big bad Marine to have masculinity issues."

"Low blow, Doc." She was doing it again. Laughing at him. He should have been annoyed, but for some reason he'd think about later, Gabe wasn't. "And way off the mark."

She lifted her chin. "Prove it."

"How?"

"By taking him home tomorrow. Just for a test run. There's no need to do any in-depth personality testing, because he's already proven himself to be amazingly easygoing. We're only talking one day. If he still hasn't won you over after he's cleaned up, then no harm, no foul." She shrugged. "What can it hurt?"

Hell. Gabe had been up against Taliban fighters who weren't as tenacious as Dr. Charity Tiernan.

"I've got work to do tomorrow."

"You're not going to shoot that many photographs in the middle of the day." When he arched a brow, surprised she'd know that, she shrugged again. "Both my parents just happen to be serial marriers. One of my stepfathers is Peter Gillette."

Although he might have spent most of the last years out of the country, even Gabe recognized the name. Gillette was, hands down, the most famous photographer of the rich and famous in the world. Gabe had attended a show of his at the Philadelphia

Museum of Art while he'd been shooting in Pennsylvania, and had appreciated the way the photographer managed to reveal the individual behind the glamorous facade. Which sometimes, to the more judicial eye, wasn't that flattering.

"He's a genius." Gabe had always believed in giving credit where credit was due.

"So they say. He was my mother's fourth husband. They met when he did a photo shoot at our home for *Town & Country* magazine. When they were married, he used to let me sit in his darkroom while he developed his photos, which was cool." She paused. "You probably use digital."

"Yeah. I started out using film, but digital's faster when you want to get the photos out of a war zone fast. Besides, there were a lot of guys who liked having copies to send home to families."

"That's nice."

Gabe shrugged. Like *sweet, nice* wasn't a word he was accustomed to being used to describe him.

"People, if they think about it at all, believe military photographers exist to take photos of medal ceremonies, or document wars. Which are both part of the job. But I always thought of it as capturing moments in history."

"There's a difference between document-ing a war and capturing history?"

"I never thought about the fact that I was filming battles. What interested me was showing troops coping as best as they can in conditions civilians couldn't imagine in their worst nightmares."

"Yet in order to capture those historic mo-ments, you had to take as many risks and suffer the same hardships they experienced."

Gabe shrugged. "I was a Marine first. A photographer second. Though," he admit-ted, "after Fallujah, I started carrying a helluva lot more rounds of ammunition."

He hadn't realized he'd smiled until she said, "You should do that more often."

"What?"

"Smile. It makes you look . . . well, less threatening."

"Are you threatened by me?"

"No." She tilted her head and studied him. "Should I be?"

He gave her a hard, level look. "Probably. An ex told me I was the angriest man she'd ever known. Shortly before she left me."

"I'm sorry. But perhaps she needed an excuse to do what she already wanted to do for her own reasons."

The walls of the room had begun closing in on him. Gabe felt on the verge of suffocating. "And maybe she was right." His curt tone declared the topic closed.

Her hand absently stroked the dog's head as her verdant green eyes swept over him, making him feel as if he was being examined. Which, of course, he was.

"And maybe," she suggested mildly, "you're being too hard on yourself."

"And you know this how?"

"I realize some people might consider it overly simplistic, but I tend to judge people by the way they treat children and animals." She glanced down at the dog, who wagged his tail, then back up at him. "You interrupted your plans and intervened to possibly save this little guy's life today. That is not exactly the behavior of an angry man."

Not knowing how to respond to that analysis, Gabe said nothing.

6

Reading had brought Adèle Douchett a great deal of pleasure for more than six decades, first in childhood, serving as a magic carpet to carry her away to lands far from her isolated Louisiana bayou home, and later serving as a much-needed bit of brightness during the long, gloomy Oregon coast winters. But she'd been reading the same page now for what seemed like hours, and as soon as she'd finish a line, it would be as if her memory were a soap bubble that would immediately pop. So she'd begin again. And again.

The sound of the clock on the wall seemed inordinately loud. And slow. *Click . . . Click . . . Click . . .*

Finally giving up, she decided to turn to knitting more clothing for Harbor Home, a shelter for victims of domestic abuse. Only to discover that she'd forgotten to buy the yarn she'd been planning to use for a sweater.

"It's not as if you don't have plenty of other yarn," she muttered as she looked at the baskets overflowing with colorful balls in a rainbow of hues on the shelves her husband had built for her in their bedroom. "Just use something else."

The only problem was, she'd had her heart set on "Peace Pink," a soft pastel shade she thought was not only a soothing color but also appropriate, since the women and children living at Harbor Home had definitely gone there seeking not just safety but peace.

Unfortunately, her son and her daughter-in-law, with whom she lived, had gone into Tillamook to buy supplies for their bait shop. And her husband was out at sea with their grandson. A group of insurance men from Eugene who'd won a fishing trip in a sales contest had chartered Cole's boat. Since she knew her Bernard still missed his days as a commercial fisherman, she'd merrily waved him off this morning, promising that she'd stay home while he was gone.

As much as she loved her family, she was looking forward to a little alone time. She was also getting weary of their hovering over her as if she were an infant. She was seventy-four years old. She might not have traveled the world, as her three grandsons had done while in the military, and perhaps her memory wasn't as sharp as it had been when she'd been younger, but she wasn't ready for the old folks' home, yet.

She'd been living in Shelter Bay for fifty-four years. Although the town had experienced changes over time, much had stayed the same as it had been when she'd first arrived as a young bride after Hurricane Audrey had devastated the Louisiana bayou and shut down the shrimping business for a time. Figuring that crabbing wouldn't be all that different, her husband, Bernard, had packed what was left of their belongings in his old Ford pickup, and brought her here to Oregon.

Adèle had gotten a job working as a companion and housekeeper for Sylvia Blackwell, the widow of a timber baron, who'd opened her eyes to a larger world. Sylvia had not only shared tales of her travels; the wealthy woman had a vast library in the cliff house that she'd encouraged Adèle to use.

"It's not as if I just fell off a crab boat," Adèle reminded herself.

What she'd done was fall down the stairs at the house her grandson was now living in, hitting her head when she'd reached the bottom. Dr. Conway, who was not only a very bright neurologist but also the mother of the young woman with whom her grandson Sax was obviously in love, had diagnosed her with a form of dementia. That had been the bad news. The good news was that unlike "normal" dementia, she shouldn't get worse, and might even get better. But any recovery would, Dr. Conway had said, take time.

Unfortunately, unlike her husband, Adèle had never been known for her patience.

She looked up at the clock. It wasn't yet noon. She had plenty of time to walk the few blocks to the Knitting Nook and be back before the rest of the family returned. They'd never even know she left the house.

And maybe she'd stop at Take the Cake and pick up some of those coconut-lemon cupcakes she'd become so fond of since Cole's fiancée had brought them home from the wedding-cake tasting.

"See?" she said to herself. "Your memory can't be that bad. You remember those." Of course that might be because they were the best dessert she'd ever tasted. Although the sun was shining through the clouds, it was misting, a light, silvery rain that around these parts was known as "liquid sunshine." Slipping on a hooded sweater she'd knit in a soft and airy purple fingerling yarn that accented her dark eyes, she fetched her pocketbook and left the house.

The mist hadn't kept anyone indoors. This was, after all, the Oregon coast, where rain was to be expected. Tourists crowded the sidewalks, many carrying containers of crab from the takeaway shops, eating ice-cream cones, or digging into white bags of saltwater taffy. Along with its fishing fleet, Shelter Bay survived on tourism, so it was good to see the local shops doing a brisk business.

The harbor came alive every morning at sunrise, boats chugging out in search of lingcod, rockfish, along with trophy salmon, halibut, tuna, and Dungeness crab during the seasons. And then there were those taking tourists out to visit the pod of whales that lived in the waters just offshore.

The air was tinged with the scent of salt and faraway places; sea lions lounged on docks, barking to one another; a gull swooped down and grabbed up a crab nearly half his size. Unable to hang on to it, he dropped it onto the rocks, where it was quickly attacked by more opportunistic gulls.

Having been brought up in the steamy Southern bayou, Adèle had admittedly taken a while to get used to life in the

Pacific Northwest, but now, after all these decades, she couldn't imagine living anywhere else.

The Knitting Nook was less than half a mile away. She'd been there so many times, she could probably make the walk in her sleep. She strolled along Harbor Boulevard, turned right on Sea Stack Road, left on Parkside Drive, and up the hill, where the bronze statue of a young woman looking out to sea, waiting for her fisherman husband's return, was the centerpiece of an emerald green expanse of grass. The gardens were in full bloom, the glossy-leafed azaleas boasting a dazzling display of red, pink, yellow, and orange bushes that reminded her of a summer sunset over the ocean.

A group of children were scrambling over a crayon-colored jungle gym while their mothers, clad in hooded rain parkas, sat chatting on a fir green bench. One of the mothers, a stroller by her side, saw Adèle and waved. Although Adèle didn't recognize her, she smiled and waved back.

Then, continued on her quest.

For . . . what?

She froze in her tracks.

It's not that difficult. She took a deep breath that was meant to soothe and clear her mind. It didn't. *Just think back to what you*

72

were doing when you decided to leave the house.

Her mind, which was beginning to panic, was blank.

Surely she couldn't have been gone for very long. Shelter Bay wasn't that large. And she'd walked over every inch of it during her time living here. So if she knew where she was headed, she'd know why she'd gone out.

But even if she knew what she'd left the house to get, it wouldn't help her. Because as she looked around in a slow circle, taking in the tidy row of shops and houses with their colorful wind socks blowing in the sea breeze, the gleaming white pillar of a lighthouse flashing its light, as it did every day and night, the iron bridge over the bay, connecting the town to the coast, she had absolutely no idea where she was.

Calm down.

The trick, she'd learned, was not to get flustered. Which was difficult to do with her heart racing and her blood pounding in her ears.

She took another deep breath. Then another. *In.* The sound of the foghorn from the Shelter Bay lighthouse tolled its warning. *Out.*

Again. *In. Out.*

73

Her legs had turned wobbly. Afraid they'd crumble beneath her, she began half walking, half stumbling along, convinced that if she just kept moving forward, something, someone, would look familiar and her world would be back in its usual calm place.

The clouds covered the sun and although it was June, the temperature began to drop. One thing about this part of the country — if you didn't like the weather, all you had to do was wait ten minutes and it would change.

See. Adèle experienced a glimmer of optimism. *You remember that old saying.* So, surely she'd figured out where she was. And how to get home again. Because whatever she'd gone out for no longer seemed all that important.

She sank down on a blue bench and clasped her hands tightly together. Despite the chill, beads of sweat formed on her forehead and at the nape of her neck. If she hadn't already passed through the change, she'd think she was having a hot flash.

Gulls trailed a blue fishing boat, their strident squalls sounding unnaturally loud. The iron bay bridge began to tilt as her head spun.

Afraid she was going to create a scene by passing out, she closed her eyes. Felt the pain as her fingernails dug into the backs of her hands, even as she welcomed it because it was a tattered link with reality.

"Mrs. Douchett?"

The soft voice made her jump. Her eyes flew open. Startled, she looked up and saw a lovely young woman standing in front of the bench. Her hair was pulled back in a tail beneath a red baseball cap and her eyes were filled with concern.

"I'm sorry." Adèle wiped her damp brow and tried to place a name to the somewhat familiar face. "I'm afraid I don't —"

"I'm Charity Tiernan," the woman said.

Prayers of faith, hope, and charity were a standard childhood morning routine when Adèle was growing up. And didn't 1 Corinthians 13:13 read, "And now there remain faith, hope, and charity, these three: but the greatest of these is charity"?

If she could remember all that, why did she have no idea who this person was?

"*Dr.* Tiernan," the woman clarified gently. "I'm a veterinarian."

Relief flooded over her as recognition dawned. "You're the one Maureen and Lucien got their new dog from." Her son and her daughter-in-law had adopted their coonhound, Laffitte, from the veterinarian's no-kill shelter after their previous hound had died.

"That would be me."

"You also put their other Laffitte to sleep."

"Again, me." Her gentle eyes turned a little sad at that, reminding Adèle that her son and daughter-in-law had told her the veterinarian had made the emotionally painful process soothing and even dignified. "Are you feeling all right?" she asked. "Do you need help?"

It was hard to admit failings to anyone. Let alone a person she barely knew. But Adèle felt safe with Charity Tiernan. Also, she had no idea how long she'd been gone. She certainly didn't want Bernard to return home and discover her missing. Wouldn't that upset everyone?

"I'm afraid I'm lost," she said. She drew in a deep breath and decided to go for it. "And a little confused."

Usually people got a serious, worried look on their faces whenever she'd reluctantly admit to that. But the vet surprised her by laughing.

"Aren't we all from time to time?"

The young woman shifted the bag she was carrying in her right hand to her left. The bag was white, with the name *Tidal Wave Books* printed over a big blue wave.

"Were you here to buy a book?" Charity

76

Tiernan asked.

Adèle thought about that. She'd bought a great many books at the store over the years. But . . .

"I don't think so." She felt the sting of tears welling up in her eyes. "I don't remember."

She liked that the veterinarian didn't fuss over her, but merely said matter-of-factly, "I'd never remember a thing if I didn't make lists. Then I usually forget and leave the list at home, which isn't all that much help. So, since my shopping is done, and whatever you were out to get probably isn't all that important anyway, what would you say to stopping by Take the Cake on the way home for some coffee and —"

"I was going to have a cupcake." The memory hit like a bolt of lightning from the lowering sky. "Lemon coconut."

"One of my favorite kinds, although lately I've gotten hooked on the tropical island. It's like a Hawaii vacation in a cake."

After flashing her a dazzling smile that warmed even as it reassured, Charity Tiernan took out her cell phone, scrolled through her list, and said, "I'll call the Douchetts and tell them we're having a girls' day out and you'll be home in a while."

Adèle nearly wept with relief. "Thank you."

The phone call was brief, to the point, and mentioned no facts about how the veterinarian had found her in an embarrassing state of confusion. As the young woman gently braced her arm, Adèle remembered that Take the Cake was on Harborview, just three blocks from Lucien and Maureen's bait shop.

While the veterinarian chattered merrily about the weather and the book she'd bought — a photo book by that Marine who'd been taking pictures at Adèle's grandson's wedding — Adèle thought that once again Corinthians had gotten it right — the greatest of these was Charity.

Her eldest grandson was now happily married. Sax, her middle one, after giving his mother more than a few gray hairs over the years, was engaged. Which left the youngest, J.T., who was currently serving in Afghanistan. But even Marines couldn't fight all the time. Maybe she should suggest her daughter-in-law invite Dr. Charity Tiernan to J.T.'s welcome-home party.

The matchmaking fantasy had Adèle smiling as they walked together down the hill toward the bay.

7

The military, which couldn't exist without acronyms, had one that Gabe thought fit this damn dog situation perfectly: *Whiskey Tango Foxtrot.* What the Fuck.

After separating from the Marines, he'd taken off without any plans in mind other than to wander the country he'd been away from for seemingly forever and take his photos as they occurred to him. The plan was to *have* no plans.

Which was why the dangerously appealing Dr. Charity Tiernan didn't fit into the scheme. She was, he determined, the empress of planning. How else could she have gotten through veterinary school and managed to run both a clinic and a shelter? And wasn't she already planning to hook him up for life with that mutt?

"Like that's going to happen."

Gabe didn't have room in his life for any damn dog. And especially not for any vet, even if she did smell like temptation and have him thinking things he had no business thinking.

Gabe had trudged through the hellhole of Iraq, across the mountains of Afghanistan in both blizzards and sandstorms that had pitted his night-vision goggles. He'd sweated in jungles and fought night hand-to-hand combat in countries most Americans would never have heard of, let alone been able to find on a map.

He'd had bad guys trying to kill him more times than he could count. And, in turn, though his job was technically to take photos, there'd been firefights when he'd killed more than he wanted to think about counting. Admittedly, he'd always felt himself invincible when viewing the most deadly firefight through the lens of his Nikon. But never, in all his years, had he run across anyone who represented more danger than Shelter Bay's vet.

She had him remembering a time when he'd believed anything was possible. When he'd thought that sometimes, for a very chosen few, life really could have a happily forever-after ending, like those TV movie matinees his mother used to watch every afternoon.

There'd been something between Dr.

Charity Tiernan and him. More than a spark. Something deeper. Something that, if he had any sense, would have him running for the hills.

With the exception of his ill-fated, short-lived marriage, Gabe had always considered himself a sensible man.

So the thing to do, he decided the morning after dropping the mutt at the clinic, was to write the veterinarian a generous check, then get the hell out of Dodge.

8

Take the Cake was, as the last time Adèle had visited with Bernard, doing a brisk business. And no wonder, the way the aroma of baking pastries was wafting out onto the street. The bakery was more than just a place to buy cupcakes. It had become a gathering place for locals, with its pretty white wrought iron tables inside and out, and what the owner was promoting as the best coffee in town. A fact with which Adèle, who still made hers the old-fashioned Louisiana way, with chicory, couldn't argue.

As luck would have it, a couple vacated one of the tables on the front patio just as Adèle and Charity Tiernan arrived.

Also fortuitously, the sun had made its way through the clouds, burning away the mist. After suggesting Adèle sit down, the vet went inside and placed their orders.

"I love this bakery," she said when she returned outside to the table. "I can see why

Kelli chose cupcakes for her wedding."

"They were certainly popular," Adèle agreed as the day flashed back with blessed clarity. "You caught the bouquet."

"I didn't exactly have a choice, since it smashed against my chest," the vet said with a wry smile as she peeled back the yellow paper on a cupcake topped with a seashell executed in buttercream. Adèle's lemon coconut was adorned with a yellow rose. Along with the fabulous taste, Adèle admired the pretty blond baker's attention to detail. It was the same sort of perfection she aimed for in her own work, whether it was serving as a housekeeper when she'd been a younger woman, painting as she used to love to do while living in the coast house, or, these past years, knitting.

"You didn't exactly look thrilled," Adèle said, remembering.

"I'm not the least bit superstitious, so I've never believed that old saying about the woman who catches the bouquet's destined to be the next married." Charity licked a bit of coconut/pineapple cream cheese frosting off her thumb. "Still, I'm not sure marriage is in the cards for me."

"Why not?"

Adèle had discovered that one of the advantages of getting older was that you didn't have to beat around the bush. You could flat out say things and ask questions that might be considered out of line for a younger person. She'd always spoken her mind, but there'd been a time when she would have been subtler.

Now, as she entered the twilight of her years, she'd come to the conclusion that there really wasn't any point in wasting time with tact.

"I'm all for the idea in theory, but I'm starting to wonder if I lack a marriage gene. My parents have each been married so many times, I've given up trying to keep track of anniversaries."

"Just because they behave like butterflies, flitting from flower to flower, doesn't mean you're destined to. After all, you were engaged once. And called it off at the altar, from the way I heard it told."

Adèle cringed inwardly when she heard those words escape uncensored. Direct was one thing, but that comment had bordered on rude. Something she'd always prided herself on never being. But more and more often, especially since her fall, she'd found herself saying her thoughts out loud. There were times she worried about that, but Sofia De Luca, who'd been her closest friend for decades, had assured her that she did the same thing, even more often since her husband died. And wasn't Sofia the most down-to-earth, commonsense person Adèle had ever met?

If she was bothered by the idea of having her private life fodder for Shelter Bay's gossip line, the young woman didn't show it. Instead, she merely shrugged.

"It wasn't exactly at the altar," she said mildly. "Actually, I called it off a few minutes before the ceremony. But after the entire church was filled with guests."

"That must have been difficult." And, Adèle considered, brave. She wasn't certain she would've had the courage to disappoint so many people. Then again, it had been a moot point, since she'd adored her Bernard.

"You'd think so, wouldn't you?" Charity took a bite of cake. "Looking back on it, I think I was in a state of shock, because I walked down the aisle myself, which caused a bit of a stir —"

"I can see how that would get everyone's attention," Adèle agreed.

"The buzz sounded like a hive of hornets. Not that I was hearing all that well, anyway. You know how when you hold a shell up to your ear, you can hear the ocean?"

"Of course."

"That's pretty much the sound roaring

inside my head. Anyway, I went to the front of the church, explained in what my mother later assured me was a calm and collected tone that the ceremony was off, but since the banquet room, food, and drink had already been paid for, I hoped people would stay and enjoy the party."

"Everyone enjoys a party. Did you attend?"

"No." This time Adèle thought she caught just a hint of a shadow in those pretty forest green eyes. "Though I did snag the four-hundred-dollar bottle of bubbly my fiancé insisted on getting for the wedding toast."

"Gracious, that's a great deal of money for a bottle of wine. Even champagne."

"That's what I said at the time when Ethan — that was his name — insisted on it. Especially since although my taste buds know pastry, I'm no expert on wine. But at least I didn't have to share it with him." Her sunshine-bright smile burned the shadow from her eyes. "I woke up with the mother of all hangovers, but figure it was a small price to pay for escaping a miserable marriage."

"Absolutely."

For not the first time Adèle thought how fortunate she was to have met her Bernard while home on summer vacation from convent school. Suddenly the idea of becoming a nun had definitely paled in comparison with marrying the handsome young fisherman and having his babies. He was, decades later, not only the love of her life but her best friend.

And speaking of her husband . . .

Her memory might be failing her, but the one thing the accident hadn't been able to change was her absolute awareness of her husband. She looked up and there he was, walking toward her with that ambling, wide-legged gait of a man who'd spent most of his life on fishing boats, backlit by a shimmering rainbow that was arcing over the harbor.

He might be in his seventies, but his shoulders were still wide, stretching the seams of his denim work shirt. His arms were well muscled from years of hauling in crab pots, his stride long and strong.

She might be in her seventies, but that didn't stop her heart from doing its familiar tumble at the sight of him. Then she suffered a pang when she viewed the naked concern in his gaze.

"I'm fine," she assured him before he could start in on how she'd promised never to leave the house alone since that damn fall.

Sometimes she felt more like a child than a wife. Especially since they'd moved in with their son and daughter-in-law, and while family was special, there were times when Adèle missed the privacy they'd once shared.

Not that they'd had all that much reason for privacy, given that he'd been treating her like a piece of the delicate crystal they'd never been able to afford. Which had been fine with her, since to her mind knickknacks were just more things that required dusting.

She stood up as he reached the table and was immediately enveloped in a bear hug. She couldn't tell which of them was trembling. Probably both.

He put her a little away from him. The trouble in his eyes eased. "So," he said, as if she hadn't probably scared him half to death, "how are the cupcakes?"

"Same as always," Adèle said. "Mouthwateringly wonderful. Would you like one?"

"I wouldn't turn down a red velvet," he said, with that touch of sexy Cajun patois he hadn't left behind in Louisiana. "Maybe I should pick up a box of assorted for the kids while I'm here."

"I'll get them," Charity said, practically jumping up from the table. Adèle couldn't decide whether the vet was that eager to

88

help or just wanted to escape and give them a private moment.

"That'd be real nice of you." He reached into his pocket. Charity hesitated as he held out the bill; then watching her carefully, Adèle could tell the younger woman was afraid to risk offending him by offering to treat.

"She's a lovely girl," Adèle said as they watched her go back into the bakery.

"Not going to get any disagreement there." He turned a chair around, straddled it, and touched his hand to her cheek. "How are you, *chère?* Honestly," he tacked on before she could lie and assure him she was as fine as a fiddle.

"I had a few nerve-racking moments." After fifty-plus years of marriage she knew he'd spot a prevarication. "But they passed."

"You were lucky the vet was there to help."

"I know." She blew out a breath. "It just gets so blasted frustrating."

"I can understand that. Bein' how you've always been an independent female."

"A trait you weren't always so wild about, in the beginning," she reminded him.

"I was young. And stupid. And had been brought up to believe a man was supposed to be the boss of the family."

And hadn't everyone she'd known back

89

then? "But you changed."

"Got smart," he corrected with that grin that could still make her weak in the knees. "We're both hardheaded, independent cusses, Del, darlin'. Which is why I know, as well as anyone could, how you feel since that accident. But Dr. Conway said you'll probably continue to get better."

"I know. It's just taking so long." There were times, like today, when she felt as if she had a big red *D* for *dementia* stamped on her forehead.

He linked their fingers together. Lifted their hands and pressed his lips against the back of her hand, which wasn't nearly as smooth and pale as the first time he'd held it. "Independent and impatient."

Unlike him, who appeared to have been born with the patience of Job. Accustomed to always being on the go, Adèle had long ago decided that she'd go crazy within a week of being a professional fisherman.

"It's hard," she said, "always needing to ask someone to go with me when I want to leave the house."

"Being with you has never been a hardship, Del."

She laughed as another memory suddenly flashed back. Yarn! She'd been on her way to buy yarn. "Why don't you say that after our trip to the Knitting Nook?"

"I'd sure enough rather hang out at Mac's Boat Shop," he said honestly. "But if that's what you want, that's what you're going to get."

"You're a good man, Bernard Douchett." It was her turn to pat his weathered cheek. "Which is why I married you."

He looked around, to make sure no one was listening, then leaned close, his lips at her ear. "And here I've always thought you married me for the sex."

This time her laugh was bold and free and banished the last of the clouds caused by her earlier fear. "Well, there is that."

9

"They are so sweet together," Charity said as she and Sedona Sullivan watched the elderly couple through the front window.

"If I ever found a man I thought would still look at me like that after fifty years of marriage, I'd marry him on the spot," the baker said as she tied the pink box shut with her signature Take the Cake ivory ribbon.

"Do you think they even exist anymore?"

"I like to believe so." Sedona sighed a bit as Bernard Douchett lifted his wife's hand to his lips. "Then again, since my parents have been together for thirty-five years, I suspect I'm probably more of an optimist than a lot of women."

Like a woman whose marriage collapsed moments before the vows, Charity suspected Sedona was thinking but was kind enough not to say. The truth was, despite her parents' track record, and her own debacle in Chicago, she was encouraged by

Sedona's parents and the Douchetts.

"Tell Mr. Douchett it's on the house," Sedona said when Charity held out the bill. "And don't let him argue. That wedding has already brought me so much business I'm having to hire extra help."

"Guess that means you're still too busy to take on a dog."

"Absolutely. Dogs need walks. Attention. Something I'm in short supply of these days."

"I totally understand."

"Damn. I've been practicing my carefully thought-out argument against pet ownership since we talked at the wedding. And now it's totally wasted."

"I'd never push an animal on anyone that wouldn't be a good fit. And I can see you've got too much on your plate right now to give attention to a shelter dog. Especially since they often come with issues. Though, I do have a suggestion."

Sedona arched a blond brow. "Why am I not surprised?"

"How about a cat?"

"Oh, I don't know . . ."

When her voice drifted off, Charity pounced, just like the cat she had in mind might after a fat mouse. "I took in this Persian the other day," she said. "An IT computer programmer and father of three was just transferred to Hawaii."

"Lucky them."

"Lucky that they're going to spend the next two years in paradise. Not so lucky they just adopted a kitten a month ago who won't have time to qualify for a prequarantine pass."

"Meaning?"

"Meaning that when it lands in Honolulu, it'll have to spend one hundred and twenty days in a cage."

"Which, needless to say, they don't want it to have to do."

"Apparently the kids started crying at the very idea."

"Understandable. I grew up with pets that were part of the family."

"As well they should be. The thing is, the dad really can't turn down this opportunity. Especially since a lot of guys in his department are being laid off. Which is how the kitten ended up back with me."

"And now you're looking for a new home."

"Good guess."

"It's hardly a guess since everyone in town knows to cross the street when they see you coming."

Charity laughed with Sedona. It wasn't

exactly the truth. But she knew she had a reputation for being tenacious when it came to placing the animals she took in.

"A Persian's easy," she said, pressing her case. "Think of them as the couch potatoes of the cat world."

"They also look as if they have high-maintenance coats."

"Just a little combing every couple days will keep them free from matting. You can do it while you watch TV. Besides, it gives you a warm body to cuddle with. Until you find that perfect man."

"I'll think about it." Sedona held out the box. "Now please get out of my shop before I end up with a menagerie."

Knowing when not to push, Charity took the box, but exchanged it for a business card. "Call me," she said. "It's really a sweetheart." Pressing just a bit more, she pulled a photo out of her purse. "See? Isn't she pretty?"

Who could resist those wide blue eyes set in the middle of that sweet, flat white face?

"She is cute," Sedona allowed.

"With the best personality ever. Persians are much more of a lap breed than a lot of cats. She wouldn't mind you being gone during the day, but she'll just eat up any attention you want to give her when you get home."

"I test recipes at night a lot."

Even as the baker made yet another excuse, Charity, who'd run into tougher cases — like Marine Gabriel St. James — could hear the crashing sound as barricades began tumbling. Block by block.

"You could always put a little bed in the kitchen so she could keep you company. When the breed was brought back to Europe from Persia along with silk, jewels, and spices in the seventeenth century, they were viewed as status symbols."

"I'm not much for jewels and silks. Though I do like spices."

"Just consider it," Charity advised. "Though I've got to warn you, she's going to go fast. The only reason I haven't put her on the weekend TV *Adopt a Best Friend* spot or her photo up on the shelter Web site is that I wanted you to have a chance to see her first. Because I honestly believe you'd be a perfect match."

Sedona's only response was a long sigh. But she did glance down at the five-by-seven glossy Charity had left on the counter.

Her duty done, at least for now, Charity carried the box of cupcakes outside to the Douchetts, wished them both a lovely afternoon, then continued home, looking forward to the opportunity to spend a quiet summer afternoon on her front porch with a pitcher of lemonade and Gabriel St. James' photography book she'd bought at Tidal Wave Books before running into Adèle Douchett.

10

Salem, Oregon

It seemed to fifteen-year-old Johnny Harper that he'd spent his entire life packing. Every few weeks — or, if he was lucky, his travel reprieve could last as much as a couple of months — his mother would come into his bedroom, shake him awake, and tell him to grab whatever he could, and off he, his mother, and his sister would go, one step ahead of the landlord and the sheriff who were on their way to throw them out of their rented house or apartment.

Even during those times they'd settle down for a while, he spent much of his time waiting for his mom to come home. Sometimes she'd just stay away overnight. Other times she'd disappear for two or three days. Not knowing that every four-year-old didn't heat up his own SpaghettiOs on a propane camp stove because the electricity had been turned off, for a long time Johnny hadn't realized that his life could have been differ-ent. Towns, houses, even people, all were a vague blur in his mind. But there were some that stuck out more often than others, replaying over and over, like a bad dream.

One was from his fifth birthday, two years before his sister, Angel, had been born and before they'd both ended up in foster care. This time his mother had sneaked him out of a window in the middle of the night to escape whatever bad guys were chasing her. Then, pausing only for fitful naps at rest stops along the way, and buying junk food from the vending machines, she'd driven nearly nonstop from West Virginia to a desolate spot in the Nevada desert where the only things breaking up the barren landscape were rocks, wind-beaten Joshua trees, and a lonely scattering of single-wide trailers.

One of the trailers, rusting on its flattened wheels, belonged to his grandmother, who'd stayed on after her husband, a man too fond of the bottle and slot machines, had died from a rattlesnake bite. Being that the grandfather Johnny had never met had been passed out on the dirt in front of his bat-tered pickup at the time of the reptile at-tack, he hadn't, the coroner had assured the stoic widow, even known what hit him. Or, more accurately, *bit* him.

Johnny's carrot red hair and freckles earned him the usual taunts from the other kids, who'd also laughed at his southern Appalachian accent and called him a cracker hillbilly. But that didn't stop them from showing up for his birthday party after his grandmother promised there'd be cake.

It was the first time he'd ever had a birthday party, which should have been cool, but experience had taught him that something was going to happen to ruin it. Especially since his mother hadn't come back from a sudden trip to Las Vegas. Johnny suspected she was looking for medicine to help turn off the voices that whispered threats in her ear.

Or maybe the voices had stayed quiet long enough for her to remember it was his birthday and she'd gone to get him a present. What she couldn't understand was that all Johnny wanted — all he'd *ever* wanted — was a normal life like other kids had.

His grandmother had picked up the cake at the grocery store this morning. It was a chocolate sheet cake covered in bright pink frosting, which only gave the kids something else to laugh about. She'd bought it at a discount from the mistake rack because the name of the person the cake had been made for had been misspelled. Being a practical woman and, as she was always telling him, needing to pinch her pennies, she'd replaced the pink plastic princess with two of his Hot Wheels cars.

Then, assuring him no one would notice, she'd rubbed out the pink script *Debbie* with a kitchen knife, which had left a big smear in the middle of the cake. In the middle of the smear, she'd stuck six striped candles.

"Five for how many years you've been alive," she'd told him. "And one more to grow on."

Despite the laughter over the Barbie pink cake, the party wasn't too bad, although he wished the desert sand would open up and swallow him when his grandmother brought out a surprise — a pin-the-tail-on-the-donkey game she'd gotten at the Goodwill. Johnny knew she meant well, but he was still dying inside when all the kids started asking why they couldn't just play a video game.

"You do have one, don't you?" Kyle Conners had challenged. The smirk on his fat face told Johnny that he already knew the answer to that question.

Johnny was about to lie and claim it had

broken just before everyone showed up, when the metal door burst open and his mother arrived home, bringing with her a charged energy that caused his gut to clench. He could practically see the energy sparking around her, like the heat lightning that had flashed over the ocean that summer they lived in Jacksonville, Florida.

"Let's get this celebration for my baby boy started!" She flashed her most brilliant smile at the kids sitting around the card table they used as a kitchen table.

"About time," his grandmother muttered as she pulled a pack of the matches she used to light the stove from the kitchen drawer. She struck a match against the rough strip, causing a flame to spark to life.

A hush came over the room as she lit one candle, then another until all six were blazing merrily.

"Make a wish!" his mother demanded.

"Make a wish!" all the kids shouted.

Johnny closed his eyes and wished the same thing he did every morning when he first woke up and every night, right before he fell asleep.

Please let my mom just be normal. Like other kids' moms.

He took a deep breath.

Then blew.

And blew.

The flames continued to flicker.

Trying again, he drew in a deeper breath, then blew it out on a huge puff of air.

But the flames still burned.

"Weenie," Kyle said, laughing at him. The others, following their leader, echoed the taunt.

Unable to figure out what was happening (though he later realized they were trick candles), Johnny sucked in another breath, all the way to his lungs. Then let it out.

Although this time the flames bent sideways, they continued to burn as steadily as the sun.

How hard could it be to blow out six tiny candles? Johnny was trying to figure out what he was doing wrong when his mother screeched like some monster from a horror movie was chasing her.

"You can't have him!"

As all the kids turned toward her, eyes bugging out of their heads, mouths wide open, she snatched up the plastic pitcher of cherry Kool-Aid from the table and dumped it over Johnny's head.

The bloodred liquid flowed over his shoulders, onto the cake, finally dousing the six small flames.

"Don't worry, darling." She dropped to

her knees into a puddle of Kool-Aid surrounding his chair and gathered him into
her arms, pressing his face against the soft
cushion of her breasts. "I won't let that bad
old devil burn you alive."

While the other kids were caught between
laughter and shock, Johnny had known that
his wish would not be coming true.

Pushing down the long-ago painful
memory, he'd just shoved his underwear
into the duffel bag that probably had more
mileage on it than the space shuttle when
there was a knock at his door.

"May I come in?" the voice on the other
side asked.

"Sure." Like he had a choice? None of the
temporary homes he'd lived in over the
years had ever had a lock on his bedroom
door. Which Johnny figured said a lot about
how much people trusted him.

"So, are you ready for tomorrow?"

This foster mother, who was married to a
cop, was actually kind of cool. She'd told
him right off the bat that if he was looking
to get adopted, he'd be disappointed, because her mission in life was to provide
temporary homes for as many children as
she possibly could. But if he followed the
rules, didn't skip school, stayed out of
fights, and didn't do drugs or steal, he'd

find her a fair person.

Which she'd turned out to be.

"Yeah. I guess." He'd already been told he wouldn't be coming back here. Such was life in the revolving door of the system.

"You're going to have a great time," she said encouragingly.

He muttered something she apparently decided to take as agreement. Which it so wasn't.

Johnny hated everything about camp. The matching T-shirts everyone had to wear, the stupid games, all the forced fun where everyone had to fake having a great time.

But Camp Rainbow, held at a lake near Shelter Bay, one of those boring shit-ass coast towns, was the one time during the year he got to see his baby sister.

Which was why, only for Angel, he was willing to suck it up and pretend to be a normal kid.

11

Despite her volunteer work writing letters and sending monthly care packages to deployed troops, Charity had never really given a great deal of thought to the details of war. Obviously, she knew it was dangerous. And that the desert was hot and hostile, and that just driving down the street could be an invitation to a violent death.

Like everyone else in America, she'd seen clips of battles on the nightly news. Seen names of those lost in battle printed in the paper. But, living in Shelter Bay, where even the name of the town signified peace, she'd never put a face to those names. Or experienced the emotional jolt she got as she turned the oversized pages of *Semper Fi.*

Some, at first glance, depicted humorous situations, such as Iraqis dressed as Disney characters celebrating the end of Ramadan at an outside restaurant. Her smile immediately faded as the next page showed a young boy, no older than five, atop a Ferris wheel. Wearing a pair of Mickey Mouse ears atop his head, he was pointing a toy gun down at a U.S. Marine who was searching the trunk of a car for weapons.

In another photo, a preteen girl in a blue shawl and a woman — whom Charity took to be her mother — hidden from head to toe in a voluminous canary yellow burka stood side by side as the girl tossed bright orange poppies into a mass grave.

Even more unsettling was the total lack of photographer involvement in the photos. If Gabriel St. James had an opinion of the discordant scenes he was documenting — and surely, she thought as her attention was riveted by the sight of a Marine, his face bloodied, carrying a burned child from a firebombed mosque, he must have — he didn't reveal it. Instead he allowed — no, she corrected, *required* — the viewer to form his or her own opinion.

Which, in an odd way, made the photos all the more personal as she found herself imagining being there, in those faraway places, and in those frozen moments in time.

The ice in the lemonade she'd made with fresh lemons melted as the drink went ignored. Even as she grew more and more discomforted by the photos — one heart-breaking one of Marines with tears leaving trails in the dust on their faces as they gathered for a memorial to lost teammates in front of a trio of rifles stuck in the sand, helmets on top, boots that would never again be worn — she could not look away.

Which was why she was grateful when Peanut, who'd been lying in a sunbeam at her feet, suddenly stirred. He didn't growl — that wasn't in his nature — but he was definitely in full guard-dog mode as the car stopped in front of the house.

She'd been expecting St. James. After all, even if he didn't want the little black dog who'd spent the night curled at the foot of her bed, he'd already shown he cared about its welfare. Surely he wouldn't leave town without checking to see how it was. Also, she doubted he was the kind of man who'd run out on a bill.

But it was not the former Marine who climbed out of the car and waved.

"Brace yourself," she murmured to the dog as she put the book down on the table and stood up to greet her mother. "Typhoon Amanda has arrived."

"Darling!" Amanda Tiernan Jacobs Chaffee Gillette Rodzianko Templeton came running up the steps in a swirl of scarlet silk. Her skyscraper stilettos, fashioned in a flowered-print fabric, were even higher than the ones that Amie and Janet had forced onto Charity for yesterday's wedding. "Thank God you're home!"

She swooped down on her daughter, gathering her into her arms as if it had been forever, not merely six months, since they'd last seen each other. Which had been at her mother's first-anniversary bash at the waterfront home on the shores of Seattle's Lake Washington that Amanda shared with her sixth — and, she swore, final — husband.

"Good to see you, too, Mom." Charity was enveloped in a cloud of lavender, rosewood, and bergamot. Husbands may come and go, but her mother's signature scent had remained her one constant.

"How are you?" As she stepped a bit away to put distance between herself and the suffocating cloud, Peanut sneezed loudly.

"Oh, darling." Amanda collapsed onto one of the porch chairs with a languid grace Charity had given up trying to emulate by her tenth birthday. "I'm devastated. Though I'm not even sure that begins to cover this situation."

She opened an iconic quilted ivory Chanel clutch and pulled out a lace-trimmed handkerchief. Not only was she the only woman Charity knew who didn't lug around a huge tote — "Why ruin the look of an outfit when there's always a man to carry the extras?" Amanda had often pointed out — she might be the last person on the planet to actually own a lifetime supply of monogrammed hankies. Being a practical woman, despite her excesses, she'd stuck with a single embroidered initial.

"I'm sorry." Charity braced herself for the storm she sensed coming.

"So am I." The wail, rising high enough to risk shattering every window in the house, made even poor Peanut flinch.

"I'm guessing this is something about . . ."

Charity paused, trying to think of her new stepfather's first name. There'd been so many of them. It wasn't that her mother was a bad woman. Actually, she was old-fashioned enough to believe that if you wanted to sleep with a man, then you should love him. And if you loved him, well, it only made sense to marry him.

"Bentley?"

"Benton," her mother corrected on a sniff as she dabbed her wet and shiny eyes. "And yes, I'm afraid our marriage is over."

"I'm sorry," Charity repeated.

"But not surprised."

Her mother might be a diva, but she wasn't unintelligent. Only, it seemed, in matters of the heart. She'd always lived with a wild, reckless, the-world-might-end-at-any-moment abandon when it came to love.

"Actually, I am. I thought, when I met him, that he seemed a good match."

Meaning he was wealthy enough to be able to supply her mother with all the creature comforts she'd grown up accustomed to, while being as sober and steady as a judge. Which, ironically, he was. He'd also, from what Charity had witnessed during the weekend of the anniversary party, managed to unearth a more natural woman inside the drama queen.

Charity had been stunned by the sight of her mother wearing white jeans and a T-shirt that read, *Women love men who love boats because they're already used to high maintenance.* Not only that, she'd laughed as her hair had blown free in the wind during a sunset cruise on Puget Sound aboard the judge's 1930s wooden Chris-Craft runabout.

"I thought we were a perfect match, too. I foolishly believed that after having wed so many frogs, I'd finally found my prince." She wiped at her cheeks with the backs of her manicured hands, looking for all the world like a heartbroken six-year-old. "Not that your father was a frog, darling," she tacked on quickly.

"I know what you meant." Dylan Tiernan, a renowned plastic surgeon to the stars, who'd even for a time had his own television program, had many fine attributes. Unfortunately, monogamy wasn't one of them.

"We haven't been apart one night since we got married."

"I hadn't realized that." She tried to imagine the down-to-earth outdoorsman judge sitting in the front row at New York fashion week. Tried to imagine her mother not being there. Both ideas proved a stretch.

"It's true. Life's been so perfect, there really isn't anyone I'd rather be with." Her mother sniffled into the handkerchief. "Believe it or not, although Helga — you remember her, darling, our Swiss cook — does the weekly shopping, we've even gone to the farmers' market together on occasion."

"That's sweet." And coincidentally, exactly the type of marriage she'd always wanted herself.

"You'd think so, wouldn't you? He even goes clothes shopping with me." She frowned as she plucked at the red silk. "The saleswomen at Neiman Marcus and Nordstrom adore him because whenever I can't decide between two outfits, he insists I buy both."

"No woman's going to complain about that."

"I certainly wasn't about to. One of the problems with marrying such highly successful men is that none of them, until Benton, ever put me at the center of their lives. Which is why, when he said he had to attend some judicial conference on Maui, and that it was going to be all work, so wives weren't invited, I decided to put a little love note into his suitcase to surprise him when he unpacked."

"That's a nice gesture." Charity still couldn't see what the problem was.

"A gesture the horrid man damn well doesn't deserve." The tears began to flow again. Not the ones for show Charity had grown accustomed to, but real ones that streamed down her mother's face, leaving trails of mascara on her porcelain-smooth cheeks. "You'll never guess what I found."

Given that husband number five — who'd claimed to be a Russian count descended from the czars — had turned out to have a penchant for wearing women's underwear, Charity was afraid to ask.

"I don't know. Why don't you tell me?" As if a herd of wild horses could stop her.

"V–V–Viagra."

Oops. "Oh."

"It's not as if our sex hasn't been off the charts." Amanda recovered enough to toss her shoulder-length auburn hair. A redhead by both temperament and nature, she'd kept it the same rich color it had been all Charity's life. "And he's always been amazingly inventive. That is, until suffering that little episode a few months ago."

"Episode?"

"An MI."

"Your husband had a myocardial infarction? And you didn't think to call me?"

"He wanted to keep it private. And he assured me it wasn't all that serious."

"Mom, any heart attack is serious." Surely the judge's doctor had given the couple a list of post-MI instructions?

Her mother's spine stiffened. "I'm well aware of the seriousness, dear. But he's been walking along the lakeshore every day. And not only was he back on the bench in only a few weeks, but apparently he's healthy enough to go traipsing off to Maui with some bimbo."

"You don't know that he's with any bimbo." Though, granted, taking a sexual enhancement drug along on a business trip

114

while his wife remained at home was suspicious.

"We haven't had sex since he got home from the hospital," Amanda said, revealing yet more information about her sex life that Charity could've lived without. "Even though the doctor assured us both that it's safe. I also went online to get a second opinion. Actually, I found several physician Web sites all saying exactly the same thing."

"An MI, even a small one, is undoubtedly a sobering event, Mom. Benton could be depressed, or afraid of having a full-blown heart attack, or —"

"And of course, having one at some hotel thousands of miles from home — not to mention away from your wife — makes perfect sense," Amanda said dryly.

"Good point." And one Charity hated admitting, since she had truly hoped that this time her mother had found the happiness that had eluded her for so many years. "What did he say when you asked him about it?"

"I didn't."

"What? Why not?"

"Because if I brought it up, I'd have to yell at him. And then, although he's supposed to be avoiding stress, I just know we'd get into a fight if I let out all this emotion churning inside me." Her beringed hand trembled as she dragged it through her hair. More tears glistened in her eyes. "And despite being absolutely furious at him right now, I'd never forgive myself if I killed him."

Charity understood her mother's fear. Still, avoiding such a serious subject wasn't going to solve the situation, either.

She was trying to think of something, anything, to say that might prove helpful or encouraging when the black Jeep she'd last seen being towed behind Gabriel St. James' motor home pulled up behind Amanda's rental car.

A slogan Charity had seen on a poster in the local recruiting-office window instantly came to mind: *The Marines have landed; the situation is well in hand.*

12

She wasn't alone. Which, Gabe decided as he climbed out of the Jeep, was a good thing. With any luck, he could pay whatever he owed for the mutt's care and escape before she started pressuring him to take it with him.

It wasn't that he didn't like dogs. Not only had he always wanted one growing up; his unit had worked with a German shepherd in Iraq that had a nose for sniffing out IEDs and a jones for jerky. Which had worked out well for all of them.

But a dog would mean responsibility and commitment. And a dog who'd been through what that one had suffered would undoubtedly come with issues.

Like you don't?

Which was entirely the point. He'd long ago decided that staying emotionally detached allowed him to control at least his life in a crazed world where innocent people could be blown to smithereens in a marketplace, or burned out of their homes and murdered by religious differences gone amok.

Despite his one slip into a marriage that should have been declared dead at the altar, he'd always made it a point to steer clear of any women seeking a future. And with the exception of one CNN war correspondent who'd filleted him with words that would've earned her network one hell of an FCC fine if she'd said them on the air, he and his lovers always parted, if not exactly friends, at least without rancor.

The polar bear the vet was passing off as a dog stood up as he approached. That it was guarding its owner was obvious. Fortunately, it appeared to have remembered meeting him and didn't regard him to be a threat.

Charity stood up, as well. She was wearing a white T-shirt that read *Real Doctors Treat More Than One Species,* faded jeans, and white sneakers with red baseball stitching. Her hair was back in its tidy tail beneath a New York Yankees baseball cap.

She and the older woman sitting beside her were a study in contrasts. The woman's silk dress was a brilliant scarlet and her shoes looked designer and probably cost as much as his first car. Her makeup must've been shellacked or something, because the sea mist in the air appeared to have no effect on it.

"Mr. St. James," Charity Tiernan greeted him warmly.

"My *father* was Mr. St. James. I'm Gabe."

"Gabe," she agreed with a nod. "You're here for your dog."

"No." He folded his arms. "I'm here to pay you for whatever medical services you performed on that stray I brought to you."

She opened her mouth, probably prepared to argue, when the other woman, who'd been studying him as if he were a piece of jewelry she was considering buying, suddenly said, "Are you *the* Gabriel St. James? The amazingly talented war photojournalist?"

"I was a Marine photojournalist." He braced for the inevitable questions about how it felt to be in a battle. Or the eye-shifting thing that suggested fear of him breaking out in a rampaging case of PTSD at any moment. "Now I'm just a photographer."

"A brilliant one, according to a former husband." A Volkswagen-sized diamond flashed on her finger as she fluffed her wavy, dark red hair. "You may have heard of him.

119

Peter Gillette?"

"Of course. I've admired his work." Which was true, even though Gabe would rather be taken prisoner by terrorists than cater to the egos of celebrity clients. "You must be Charity's mother."

"Why, yes. I am." She shot a glance between him and her daughter. "I'm surprised Charity mentioned me." Clever green eyes sharpened as they lasered back to him. "You two must be close." Her voice went up a little on the end of the statement, turning it into a question.

"We were discussing his latest book," Charity jumped in. It was the second time he'd seen her actually flustered. The first had been the moment that bridal bouquet had landed against the front of her dress, forcing her to catch it. "Peter's name came up."

"Peter was a photojournalist in the Vietnam War," the woman whose name he'd yet to catch offered. "For *Stars and Stripes*."

"That's quite a career change."

It was, he realized, also much like what Charity had mentioned about his taking wedding photos. Then again, his being at that ceremony had been a special case — a favor for a buddy. Gillette had actually chosen a jet-set life among celebrities.

"That's what I thought," she agreed. "Though he did occasionally say taking war photos was easier. And at times even less dangerous." Somehow she managed to frown without furrowing her forehead. "Come to think of it, that was the only thing he ever said about those years."

"Some people prefer not to rehash it." And wasn't he one of those?

"I suppose so." She held out a hand tipped in nails as red as her dress. "I'm Amanda Templeton."

This obviously high-maintenance female might appear the antithesis of her daughter, yet as he took the slender hand she offered, he recognized it as a twin of the one who'd handled his dog on the exam table.

The dog, dammit. It wasn't *his* dog, and if he had anything to say about it, and he did, it never would be.

"Nice to meet you," he responded.

"It's delightful to meet you. In fact, I think I'll go inside and call Peter right away and tell him I've met you." She reclaimed her hand and turned toward her daughter. "We can bring my things in from the car later."

"Things?"

Okay. Count that as three times he'd seen Dr. Charity Tiernan flustered. This time she looked on the verge of panic.

"Well, darling, I have to stay *somewhere.*"

"What's wrong with your house?"

"I don't want to be there when — and if — Benton calls."

"That's what voice messaging is for. So you can screen calls."

"But you know me, Charity. I have absolutely no self-control. At least when it comes to my husbands. I'd pick up the phone and the next thing, we'd be in a terrible argument because I wouldn't be able to hold back how upset I am." She shook her auburn head. "No. I need time to plot a strategy."

"How about asking him straight out what he's up to?"

"Oh, I couldn't do that. It's obvious you've never been married, darling." Color flooded into her cheeks. "I'm sorry, that was thoughtless."

"It's okay."

"Still, obviously it's a sore point, after what happened, and —"

"Mom." The daughter's tone was soft, yet firm. "I *said* it's okay."

The older woman shot another of those appraising looks back and forth between her daughter and Gabe. "Aaah." She stretched the word out. "I see. Well, then, I'd best let you two get down to business."

122

She flashed a dazzling smile at Gabe, then hugged her daughter, whispering something into Charity's ear. What it was, he couldn't tell, but from the way the vet's spine beneath that T-shirt stiffened, Gabe suspected she was less than thrilled.

"I'm sorry about that," she said after her mother had gone into the house, shutting the screen door behind her.

"What? That I met your mother? Or that she called my work brilliant? Which, given who the quote came from, would have a lot of photographers calling their publicist trying to figure out how to use it on the front of a book."

"A lot of photographers, perhaps." Charity tilted her head. Studied him in that deep, serious way she had. "But not you."

"No. Not me. Taking photos is my job. Like some guys are plumbers. Others catch fish for a living. I like that I can make a living, be my own boss, and having grown up with a dad who spent more time on welfare than he did on the job, I'm grateful for the work."

Damn. Why in the world had he told her that? Like most children of alcoholics, Gabe had learned early on to keep secrets. After he'd brought home a kid after school to work on a magnetism project for fourth-grade science class, only to find his mother passed out on the couch, he'd quit risking having friends over to his house. Which, in turn, meant that he didn't have that many friends.

That had suited him just fine, especially after he'd discovered photography in high school and learned that he actually preferred life as seen through the lens of a camera, where he could adjust it — with film speed and aperture openings — the way he liked it. Rather than the way it might be in reality.

The military might have changed the focus of his viewpoint, bringing gritty, unblinking realism into his photos that had earned him a measure of fame. But he'd held on to one tenet from his childhood: He never, *ever* talked about his family.

Even Cole Douchett, who was the closest thing to a friend that Gabe had ever had, knew only that his parents had died in an accident when he'd been in college. During some of his and Cole's darkest hours together — when it wasn't certain either of them would make it out alive — while the other Marine had talked openly and fondly about *his* family, Gabe had seen no reason to share the details of his own life. Which, as far as he was concerned, had begun when he'd shown up at Parris Island, where he'd acquired a new family consisting of jarheads like him.

"I think we're all grateful for work these days," she said mildly. Although he suspected she was curious about him, as he admittedly was about her, Gabe was grateful she didn't press. "The shelter's been getting way too many animals whose owners can no longer afford to care for them, or have to give them up because they've lost their homes and are moving to apartments."

She sighed, then said, "I'll go get your dog for you."

Gabe opened his mouth to insist yet again that it was not *his* dog, but she'd disappeared into the house before he could get the words out.

Oh, yeah. The lady was quick. And smart.

And, he reminded himself, dangerous. Because, as he'd lain awake long into the night, he'd found himself thinking about things he'd stopped allowing himself to think about years ago.

And wanting things he had no business wanting.

13

After having been the topic of so much gossip herself, there was no way Charity was going to pry into Gabriel St. James' past. But it wasn't so much what he said — after all, how many people had actually experienced a Beaver Cleaver childhood? It was the way he'd looked as if he'd pulled the pin on a hand grenade that made her realize that he hadn't meant to offer her even a small glimpse into his past life. Which she could both understand and respect.

But that didn't mean she wasn't curious.

"You've got a complicated daddy," she told the dog as she scooped him up from her bed, where he'd settled into the throw pillows for a well-deserved nap. "He isn't going to be the easiest guy to win over. But I have every faith you'll pull it off."

If the wag of his fluffy tail and the happy swipe of his tongue on her face were any indication, the dog agreed.

"It's obvious you two have a lot in common," she said, continuing her pep talk as she carried him down the stairs, "since you're both survivors. And tough." After all, how many nine-pound dogs could be abused and dragged beneath a van and still come out of the situation with their sweet temperament intact? "And you know what? I think he needs you every bit as much as you need him."

Even though he wasn't prepared to admit it. Which might be because he wasn't ready to admit it to himself. She suspected when you spent so many years in war, you learned never to show weakness. And it wasn't merely warriors who'd developed that instinct that probably went back to caveman times. An instinct humans definitely shared with other animals.

She'd once treated a formerly feral calico cat who'd gone months hiding a broken leg that had healed crookedly on its own. Fortunately, after surgery and recuperation, it was doing fine, spending its days in the window of Tidal Wave Books, basking in the sun and the admiration of passersby and customers.

This little guy and the hard-edged, granite-eyed Marine would be good for each other. Which was why she was so determined to match them up.

"Who are you kidding?" she muttered to herself.

The truth was while she really did believe that the match would benefit both of them, she just wanted to keep Gabriel St. James in town a little longer. Not forever. She could recognize a rover when she met one. But just long enough to explore these unsettling, exciting feelings he'd stirred.

Charity had lived thirty-one years without experiencing a single sexual fantasy — unless you counted imagining herself as Amy March being courted by Christian Bale's breathtakingly handsome Laurie, but that daydream had remained as sweetly mild as the *Little Women* movie on which it had been based.

Last night's dream of the Marine's dark hands leaving a trail of sparks over her breasts, her stomach, the crease of her thighs, his mouth hot and hungry between her legs, had definitely not been G-rated.

He was waiting on the porch when she came out.

Before he could object that he didn't want the damn dog, as she knew he intended to, she simply shoved it up against his broad chest. As the ball of freshly shampooed fluffy black fur lifted its front paws to his

128

shoulders, she backed away, giving him no choice but to grab hold.

"Good try," he acknowledged her ploy as a pink tongue came out, and even with the inflatable "comfort collar" designed to keep him from bothering his wounds and neutering stitches, the little dog managed to lick the Marine's face. "But I'm still not in the market for a dog."

"So you say." She folded her arms so he couldn't shove it back at her. "Personally I think the two of you are a perfect match. And whether you want to admit it or not, you need him as much as he needs you."

"And you know this how?"

"I bought your book this morning. *Semper Fi.*" She gestured to where it still sat on the table between two of the chairs. "My stepfather's right. You're very talented."

"Thanks. But what does you buying my book have to do with pushing a homeless dog on me?"

"He won't be homeless if you take him."

"Hell, in case you've forgotten, I don't *have* a home."

"Of course you do. It's merely on wheels at the moment. Dogs are very adaptable. Much more so than cats. He'll fit right in. Besides you can't travel forever."

"Want to bet?"

Although she'd carefully planned out her argument ahead of time, after looking through his photos, that curt question momentarily threw her off track. "You don't have any place to go home to?"

"Nope. Haven't ever felt the need for one."

"I spent most of my life moving around whenever my mother remarried," she offered. "Although it was admittedly difficult being the new girl in school all the time, by the third husband, it had pretty much become the norm."

She'd grown up. Moved on with her life and was happy with who and where she was. But when just remembering how desperately she'd yearned for some stability caused a familiar ache inside, she absently reached out and scratched the dog's head. "But I've discovered since moving here that finding a place where I can finally put down roots is proving hugely satisfying."

Gabe shrugged. "Roots can tie you down."

"Well, that's certainly a different viewpoint," she said mildly. "What about your family?"

"I don't have one. How much do I owe you?"

And wasn't he quick to change the subject? Oh yes, Charity thought. There was a story there.

She hadn't realized, since moving to Shelter Bay, how much people in small towns got caught up in one another's lives. The same way everyone knew about her debacle of a failed wedding (though not the reason, which she'd shared only with Sedona), she knew intimate details of their lives.

Such as the fact Mary Beth Addison, after a year of trying to get pregnant, had begun buying chaste tree berry and wild yam from Sofia De Luca in hopes of increasing her fertility. Despite having a degree in accounting from Willamette University, and possessing a CPA certification, cake baker Sedona Sullivan had grown up living what, to Charity, sounded like a halcyon existence on a commune in Arizona's Red Rock country, for which she was named.

And then there was poor Adèle Douchett's unfortunate fall, which had left her with dementia, and Kara Conway falling in love with Sax Douchett, her dead husband's high school friend, and . . .

"Excuse me?" Dragging her mind from her neighbors, she realized Gabe had asked her a question.

"How much do I owe you?"

"Oh. I'm not sure, off the top of my head.

Why don't you come inside and I'll get the paperwork." She went back into the house, leaving him to follow. With the dog, which she'd still avoided taking back.

Retrieving the forms, she began clicking away on a desktop calculator. "Well, there's the tick dip, and the exam, and since we have to assume he hasn't had any vaccinations, I went ahead and did those. The rabies tag is on his collar." Which was a lovely red tartan she thought contrasted well with his dark fur and gave him a bit of a rakish look.

He frowned at the collar. "Didn't you have anything plainer?"

Yes! One didn't get that particular about a collar for a dog he didn't intend to keep.

"I'm sorry." She flashed him her sweetest smile. "But we're all out of the manly black-leather-with-steel-studs model."

She tapped some more. "And the antibiotic. And the cream for his burns, and medication to prevent heartworm, which is, unfortunately, all too common, and —"

"It's a damn good thing I *don't* have a house," he cut her off. "Because it's sounding as if I'd have to mortgage it to pay your bill."

Okay. That barb hit home. She tossed up her chin. "My rates are actually less than a lot of vets along the coast. And much less than in the cities."

"I wasn't challenging your prices," he said mildly. "Just pointing out that owning a dog isn't cheap."

"No. But much of this is a onetime charge. Besides, look at it this way — having a dog will save you money on doctor bills."

"And how, exactly, do you figure that?"

He did not, she noted, point out yet again that he had no intention of having a dog.

"There's a growing body of scientific evidence supporting the theory that pets are beneficial to people in a multitude of physical ways. Not only did researchers at the State University of New York at Buffalo find that pet ownership is better than medication for lowering blood pressure under stress situations, other studies at UCLA found that having a pet corresponds to overall better health and fewer medical visits. As many as twenty-one percent fewer trips to the doctor."

"I haven't been to a doctor since my pre-separation exam when I left the military."

"Well, you never know. Think of him as a preventative measure. Also, moving around as much as you do, you probably don't have much chance to interact with people."

"That's actually one of the *best* parts of

moving around as much as I do."

He wasn't making it easy on her. Fortunately, Charity enjoyed a challenge.

"There have been bunches of other studies showing loneliness reduces fruit-fly life spans and increases the chances of mice developing diabetes."

"Guess it's a good thing I'm not a fruit fly or a mouse." Balancing the dog on his hip, he pulled out his wallet and handed her a credit card. "Besides, you can be surrounded by people and still be lonely."

"Got me there." She ran the card and handed him the receipt to sign. "Which goes along with another study that suggests just the mental perception of isolation is enough to cause adverse effects in humans, including cardiovascular disease, obesity, and weakening of the immune system."

He scrawled his name on the paper, took his card back. But he hadn't yet put down the dog. "You have an endless supply of those, don't you?"

"I wouldn't say endless. But I did recently read that they've also had success using companion dogs to treat veterans suffering from PTSD."

"What make you think I've got PTSD problems?"

"Oh, I wasn't referring to you." But he

had answered just a bit too swiftly. Almost defensively. "Merely repeating what I'd read."

"Well, for the record, I don't."

"Good for you."

They fell silent as they looked across the counter at each other. Meanwhile, the dog continued to gaze up at him like a religious pilgrim looking into the face of his god.

"If you'd just keep him for a couple days. While I try to find him a family," she said.

"Two days."

"Oh, that's great. Thanks. I promise you won't regret —"

"Two days," he repeated. "If you haven't found anyone by then, you're getting him back."

"Two days is better than nothing. And maybe you'll just find that you won't want to give him back."

"Don't bet your practice on that, Doc. Is the food any good at the Sea Mist?"

Surprised by the sudden change in subject, but not wanting to say anything that might have him changing his mind about taking the Shih Tzu with him, Charity said, "It's great, actually. And the view from the patio is one of the best in town."

"Great. I'll pick you up at eight."

"What?" Was he actually asking her out

135

on a date?

"Dinner. You." He pointed at her. "Me." At himself. "Together."

He *was* talking date. "I can't." But, heaven help her, she wanted to. Even as common sense warned against it. "My mother," she reminded him, with a glance toward the stairs Amanda had disappeared up.

"She's an adult. She can't spend a few hours on her own?"

"Of course. But as you probably caught on, from her refusal to face her telephone, she's here because of a personal problem we need to talk about. I can't just run off and desert her."

He considered that while rubbing a dented jaw broad enough to park his motor home on. "Tomorrow," he countered.

"Okay," she said.

He nodded as if he hadn't expected any other outcome. She should have been annoyed by his male arrogance, yet for some reason, Charity wasn't.

He paused at the door, the dog still under his arm like a sack of potatoes. "I hope things work out for your mom."

And with that, he was gone. Leaving Charity with no choice but to go upstairs and face her mother.

14

Bon Temps was the type of Cajun restaurant/bar/dance hall that one could expect to find down in the Louisiana bayou. Established by Cole Douchett's parents, it had been refurbished and was now run by Cole's brother Sax.

Mardi Gras masks hung on walls the color of boiled crawfish, and colorful beads, like those thrown from parade floats, had been strung between the light fixtures. But the best thing was the aroma that hit the minute a customer walked in the door.

It was the middle of the day, not exactly rush hour anywhere in sleepy Shelter Bay, yet the tables were filled. Two old men, former fishermen, judging from their weathered skin, were sitting by the window overlooking the harbor, nursing beers and eating their way through a mountain of scarlet crawfish. Another guy was playing pool at a table on the far side of the room.

"So," Sax said as Gabe took a stool at the bar, "I see she got you, too." He pushed a bowl of bar mix toward Gabe.

"Who would that be?" Gabe took a bite of what the younger Douchett brother called Cajun devil peanuts. Which fit, since the things were as scorching hot as hell.

"The vet. Charity Tiernan."

"Word gets around fast."

"That it does," Sax agreed. "Of course, the mutt sitting in the passenger seat of your Jeep did give me a clue. You want the regular?"

Not accustomed to being anyplace long enough to have a "regular," Gabe said, "Why don't you surprise me?"

"You gonna eat?"

"Thought I'd have an oyster po'boy."

"Got just the thing." Sax reached into the cooler and brought out a bottle. "Rogue's Captain Sig's Northwestern Ale goes great with fish," he said. "And it'll cool those flames burning your tongue."

"You saying I can't handle some damn peanuts?"

"*Cher,* you may be a Marine, but you're not Cajun."

The malty ale, deep red in color, went down smooth and did soothe the flames. But Gabe wasn't about to admit that to a damn Navy frogman.

"I'm only keeping the mutt for a couple days. While she finds someone to take him off her hands."

"She's good at that," Sax said as he whipped an egg, dropped an oyster into the egg, then coated it with a mix of cornmeal, flour, and seasoning. "Haven't seen anyone who can say no to the woman when she sets her mind to something." While the oyster sizzled in the deep fryer, he spread mayo on one side of a baguette, some sort of red sauce on the other.

"She's like a damn pit bull," Gabe complained. "What's that stuff?"

"Come-Back sauce." Sax piled layers of shredded lettuce, tomato slices, and pickles on the bun. "It's an old secret family recipe my *grand-mère* came up with. It's the chili pepper that gives it a kick." He pulled the golden brown oyster out of the fryer, layered it on top of the dressings, and tossed on some thick-cut fries.

"This is a test, isn't it?" Gabe asked as he eyed the plate Sax put in front of him.

"What it is is the best sandwich you've ever tasted."

It sure smelled great. As the flavors exploded on his tongue, Gabe decided it tasted even better than it smelled. "Okay," he said around a mouthful of deep-fried seasoned oyster. "You're not going to get any argument from me about that."

"It's the Come-Back sauce," Sax said with a grin. "Gets them every time. I'm thinkin' of bottling the stuff and selling it to tourists. Maybe even set up shop on the Internet."

He left from behind the bar to deliver the check to an elderly couple wearing matching blue *I went whale watching in Shelter Bay* T-shirts. The woman, who appeared to be at least in her eighties, giggled like a schoolgirl at something Sax said. Oh, yeah, the guy definitely had a knack with women. Which had Gabe wondering if he'd ever turned that smooth charm toward the town's veterinarian before hooking up with the sheriff.

"So," he asked, when Sax came back with a handful of bills, "what do you know about her?"

"Who?" He put the bills into an old-fashioned metal box.

"Charity Tiernan."

"Not much."

"Did you know her that summer she spent here when she was a kid?"

"Nah. It's a small town, but summers here, as you can see, bring in a lot of strang-

140

ers. Besides, she and her stepbrother were rich and wouldn't have been likely to hang out with guys like Cole and me." He rubbed the bar down with a towel. "But here's a small-world thing. I ended up serving with him downrange."

"He was a SEAL?"

"A medic. The best I ever worked with. He was like a walking trauma center. If any military from anywhere in the world had better medical supplies, you know that somehow Chaffee was going to get his hands on it."

"He ever talk about her?"

"Not that I recall." He lifted a dark brow. "You sound like you're interested."

Gabe shrugged. "She's not my type."

"Sure. Not many guys are going to be attracted to a long, smooth drink of water with legs up to her shoulders, forest green eyes, a heart as big as all outdoors, and brains, to boot."

"I wasn't talking about her looks. Or her brains. It's the heart thing. The woman has marriage, two-point-five kids, and a picket fence written all over her. Hell, she even *has* a damn picket fence."

"So do I." It was Sax's turn to shrug. "It came with my house."

A huge white cliff house with a million-

141

dollar view, Gabe remembered. He'd gone there with Cole a couple nights before the wedding and spent some time sitting out on the porch, drinking beer and sharing war stories. The kind of down and dirty guy stuff you didn't share with civilians.

"My point" — Gabe tilted the neck of the bottle toward the other man — "is that she's not a one-night-stand type of woman." The thing to do was to get back into military mode and practice some serious strategic avoidance.

"My guess would be you're right about that. My other guess is that she's got enough going for her, a guy, were he interested, hypothetically speaking, might want to stick around for a while. See how things played out."

"I've got a contract." Gabe polished off the Sig's Ale. "Once I'm done shooting scenes here, I'm moving on to Washington."

"You going to settle down there?"

Gabe saw where he was going with this. "No."

"Then there wouldn't be anything keeping you from coming back. After you're done shooting your pictures." Sax took away the empty beer bottle and replaced it with a nonalcoholic brew. With an eye to detail Gabe figured SEALs, like Marines, needed, he'd obviously noticed that his brother's war buddy was a one-beer guy.

"I'm also not into commitment."

"Which is why you've got that dog sitting in the front seat of your rig."

Gabe followed Douchett's gaze out the window, where the mutt was waiting patiently for its rescuer to return.

"I'm just taking it off her hands for a couple days. Until she can find someone to adopt it."

The other man's deep, rumbling laugh drew the attention of every woman in the joint. "Good luck with that."

15

Amanda jumped on Charity the moment she entered the guest room her mother had commandeered.

"Darling," she said as she snapped her phone shut, "I was just telling Peter the exciting news about you dating *the* Gabriel St. James!"

"I'm not dating him."

"You're going out to dinner."

"You were listening?"

"The window was open." Appearing unconcerned at having been caught eavesdropping, Amanda waved airily toward the windows framed with white gauze curtains. "And I do think you were very wise not to accept his invitation for tonight. It's always good tactics to make a man wait."

"It wasn't a tactic. It was the truth. We need to talk."

"I don't know what about."

"How about the fact that you left your

husband without even discussing the reason with him?"

Oh, God, her mother was tearing up again. "You know how I dislike conflict."

"Perhaps some things — and some men — are worth fighting for."

"And Ethan wasn't?"

For someone who so loved being at the center of attention, her mother was an expert at turning the spotlight in a different direction when it suited her purpose.

"No. Ethan definitely wasn't."

"I didn't think so, either. I also thought you were incredibly courageous, doing what you did. When you did it."

Charity shrugged. "It seemed a better idea than going through with the ceremony, only to end up getting divorced six weeks later." She belatedly realized how that sounded. "I'm sorry, I didn't mean —"

"I know. My record on marriage is right up there with Liz Taylor's. Which is why I'm so angry. I really did believe I'd chosen a life partner this time."

"I believed that, too." It was the truth. "I also believe that you owe it to Benton to discuss it with him. There may be a simple explanation."

"Such as?"

"I've no idea. But things aren't always

145

what they appear on the surface."

"True." Amanda sighed heavily. "But I need time. . . . Meanwhile," she said, perking up considerably, "what are you planning to wear on your date with that handsome young man?"

Charity was about to repeat that it was not a *date,* merely dinner, when something her mother said sidetracked her. "You think he's handsome?"

"Absolutely. Don't you?"

"Not like Brad Pitt handsome." She thought about the harshly hewn scarred face, the heavily hooded, shuttered eyes, the too-broad chin, which hinted at an overdose of testosterone. "Compelling, maybe." And wasn't that the understatement of the year?

"He reminds me of your father. When we first met."

"Really?" Her father was George Clooney/ Cary Grant smooth. Nothing like Gabriel St. James.

"Oh, that's right. You only know him from after he'd had a lot of work done."

"My father had work done? Plastic-surgery-type work? Why?"

"Darling, give it some thought. Although he's always spent several weeks every year performing free and admirable reconstructive surgery for children in Third World countries, your father's driving career goal was to be *the* surgeon to the stars. Which would have been very difficult to do if he hadn't been Hollywood handsome himself. So he had some surgery to fit the image he needed to project to the public.

"When I married him, while he was in his final year of surgical residency, he had a scar much like Gabriel's. But his ran up the side of his face. Apparently he'd gotten it while serving in Vietnam."

"Wait a minute." Charity held up a hand. "My father was in Vietnam? And I never heard a single, solitary word about it?"

"Your father was drafted," Amanda said. "But he was much like Peter in that he never talked about the war, either. Then or now. But as a matter of fact, he was a medic who did three tours there. That's how he put himself through medical school."

Charity was honestly floored. "Is there anything else you're keeping from me?"

"Charity, dear." Her mother could have been talking to a six-year-old. "We all have secrets. Even you, I suspect. Besides, your father's story wasn't mine to tell."

"*He* could have told me." Was she actually pouting? She *never* pouted. That was her mother's forte.

"I suspect he'd put it behind him because

it was too painful to dwell on." Amanda's eyes sharpened. "Something I'd imagine you could identify with."

She had her there. After all, Charity never had shared with her mother the total story of why she'd called off the wedding.

It was also time to turn the focus away from herself. "When's Benton coming home?"

"I've no idea. He told me he'd be gone for a week. Then again, why should I believe anything the man says? But, whatever his schedule, if he wants to speak with me, he's going to have to come here. Because I'm not setting foot back in that house until he explains his behavior."

Oh joy.

Her mother brushed her hands together, as if ridding herself of a particularly vexing problem, and said, "So, what are you going to wear for your dinner with Gabriel?"

"I hadn't given it any thought."

"I passed the Sea Mist on the way here. It looks lovely."

The brown-shingled building on the bay was, indeed, lovely, with every table facing the harbor, and patio seating that proved popular on sunny days. "It is. But it's not dressy, like a lot of places in Seattle." She could see her mother's plan, like a freight

148

train barreling toward her.

"Well, still, you'll want to look your best. Do you even own a dress?"

"Of course I do. Really," Charity insisted when Amanda arched an auburn brow. She saw no point in mentioning that she'd donated all her city clothes, most of which she'd bought in a futile attempt to live up to her fiancé's family's lofty social standards, to Goodwill and Bottomless Closet, a charity that helped needy women get back on their feet by providing professional-looking clothing for job interviews.

"Let me see."

Feeling thirteen years old again, when her mother had dragged her shopping for a respectable confirmation dress, Charity led her to her bedroom, opened the closet, and took out the yellow sheath she'd bought to wear to Cole and Kelli's wedding at Bon Temps.

"Not bad," Amanda allowed. "Actually it's quite lovely and the color, while I'd certainly never attempt it, flatters your coloring."

Charity's relief at having escaped a shopping trip to Portland or Eugene was short-lived.

"Of course," her mother tacked on, "it's far too formal for a first date."

149

"It's not a date," Charity insisted yet again.

Ignoring that claim, Amanda's appraising gaze swept over her. "Fortunately, we're nearly the same size. I have a lovely gauze skirt with an off-the-shoulder peasant blouse that would suit the occasion perfectly. And it's a greenish blue watercolor silk that would bring out your eyes."

What was it with so many people suddenly wanting to dress her up as if she were their own personal Barbie doll?

"I'm not the gauzy-skirt type," she pointed out, running her palms down her jeans. "And didn't peasant blouses go out with flower children?"

"They're back. And surely you didn't plan to wear something like that?" Her mother's frown told Charity exactly what she thought of her usual uniform of jeans, T-shirt, and sneakers.

"I'm a vet. I don't need to dress up to operate on dogs and cats."

"I doubt you'll have any reason to perform surgery on any animals at the Sea Mist," Amanda countered. "What about a compromise? Wear a nice pair of white jeans with my top. That would look lovely with a seaglass and silver necklace."

"One problem. I don't own any white

jeans. They tend to show blood."

"If you're trying to shock me, Charity, it isn't going to work. I was, after all, married to a surgeon who brought home videos of his work to study. Finding a nice pair of dressy jeans shouldn't be difficult. We'll go shopping tomorrow."

"I have work tomorrow."

"You also have to eat. We'll shop on your lunch hour. Didn't I see a boutique near that cute bakery?"

"Yes, the Dancing Deer Two. It's run by two elderly women who recently moved down here from Washington, but, really, Mother —"

"Darling." The tone was familiar. She was about to get the full diva assault. "Did I not explain that my entire life is crumbling around me and I'm about to be surrounded by little more than the ruins of yet another failed romance?"

"Let's hope it's not that fatal," Charity suggested mildly.

"From your lips to God's ears. Still." She sighed. Dabbed at her eyes again. "I'm in desperate need of some retail therapy. And since I doubt there's anything for sale here in this quaint little burg I'd feel comfortable wearing, the next best thing is to go shopping for you."

When her mother actually seemed to brighten up at the prospect, Charity realized she was sunk. What could it hurt? She'd survived the shopping for the dress she'd worn to the wedding, hadn't she? Then again, that had been easier. She'd merely called ahead and explained what she needed, and one of the owners of the boutique had it waiting for her on a rack behind the counter. It had been like having her own personal shopper.

"Please, darling." Oh, that little tremor in the dulcet tones was good.

Charity had long ago accepted the fact that somehow she'd missed inheriting her mother's fashionista gene. It wasn't that she didn't try while she was in high school. Not only wanting to win her mother's approval, on those rare summer visits to her father in Los Angeles — where all the girls seemed to be blond and tanned, and looked as if they'd shown up from the *Clueless* and *Legally Blonde* departments of central casting — wanting desperately to fit in, she'd pore over *Seventeen* and *YM* and watch every episode of *Beverly Hills, 90210,* trying to decode the secret of what to wear. And, even more important, what *not* to wear.

But fashion, she discovered to her dismay, never stayed static. Even as she tried to feel comfortable in floaty flowered prairie dresses worn with cowboy boots, the characters would suddenly switch to baby-doll dresses, bike shorts, and combat boots.

The acid-washed-jeans days were more comfortable, though she never added all the chains and midriff-baring tops. But when two of the actresses fell into a grunge stage, which made them appear to be channeling Nirvana, Charity threw up her hands and accepted the fact that her personal fashion style would always be "pre-makeover."

She'd known Gabriel St. James was dangerous from the moment she'd first met him, but Charity never could've imagined, in a million years, exactly what danger he represented.

"I'm not getting out of this, am I?" Her mother might have the matrimonial behavior of a butterfly, but she'd never given up on her goal of turning her daughter into something less than a fashion emergency.

"Absolutely not."

"I didn't think so." She'd also, given a choice, rather be tick dipped. But if it got her mother out of her diva funk, which was threatening to spiral downward . . .

A pod of white-winged pelicans flew past the window, headed out toward sea. Charity wished she could fly away with them.

16

The next morning Gabe discovered that while it might look like a walking mop, the foo-foo dog proved to be a chick magnet. Since he was planning to drive up the coast to Astoria, he wanted to make sure the mutt did its business before leaving town for the day.

Bad enough he was stuck with it. Worse that it had insisted on sleeping with him. He'd tried being firm, putting it back onto the floor every time it jumped up on the bed. But when he'd locked it outside the bedroom, it had added door scratching to whining until he finally decided he had two choices.

Shoot it.

Or give in.

Which was why he woke up with big brown eyes looking directly into his.

He fed it some of the kibbles the vet had provided, then put on the leash — which was red to match that plaid collar Charity Tiernan had put on it — and took it, along with a handful of paper towels and an empty plastic grocery bag, down to the beach.

Where what should have been a brisk, goal-oriented mile-long walk on a foggy coastal morning looked destined to take forever as seemingly everyone in Shelter Bay had to stop to pet the mutt. Many also complimented him on his wedding photos, which Cole's overly efficient bride had already managed to post on their wedding Web site from her Hawaii honeymoon suite. He'd never liked talking about his work, which he figured spoke for itself. And he damn well didn't want to be known for clichéd wedding shots. But for Cole and Kelli Douchett's sake, he forced a smile and nodded at what he hoped were appropriate times.

Kids flew kites, splashed noisily in the surf, and built sand castles while protective parents hovered nearby, eyes constantly searching for impending danger, which was as foreign to Gabe, having grown up without supervision, as Afghanistan had been.

Dogs ran up and down the beach, to the edge of the water, then back again, their barks drowned out by the low roar of the waves and carried off by the breeze. Rather than straining at his leash to join them, the mutt pressed even closer to Gabe's leg, glancing up every few steps to make sure he was still there.

Adèle Douchett and her husband, Bernard, walked along the tide line, holding hands like newlyweds. Every so often she'd bend down and pick up a shell, which he'd put in a bag he was carrying in his free hand. Watching them, Gabe felt an odd stir of something that felt almost like envy. Then immediately, ruthlessly, tamped it down.

Pelicans flew in formation, low over the surf, looking for fish, while seagulls whirled, their raucous screeching disturbing the morning peace.

One gull dropped a crab near Gabe's feet. Although the mutt looked interested, he didn't try to gulp it down. Which couldn't be said for the other gulls, who landed on the sand in a frantic flurry of wings. Squawking wildly, they fought over the hapless crab like countries battling over a piece of land. The squabble was noisy and chaotic. A lot like war. Since he always had his camera with him, Gabe paused for a moment to capture the scene, thinking he might use it as a visual metaphor.

Several women were drawn to the dog, many making it all too clear that they were available. Feigning innocence, he continued to ignore the less-than-subtle invitations and forged on with his mission.

The sheriff, with whom Sax was seriously involved, drove by on the packed wet sand, patrolling the beach. She waved merrily at Gabe, rolled down her window, and paused to talk with him, her engine idling.

"Ha!" she said. "I see Shelter Bay's most tenacious veterinarian did get to you, too."

"I'm only keeping him a couple days," he said, telling her what he'd told the SEAL. "Until she can find him a home."

The laugh that bubbled out of Kara Conway was a direct contrast to the severity of her khaki uniform. "Good luck with that," she said, echoing Sax. Waggling her fingers again, she continued driving.

"No one frigging believes me," he grumbled at the dog, who'd begun digging for sand crabs during the brief conversation. He tugged on the leash, pulling the mutt from the hole he'd nearly disappeared into.

"Terrific. Now if I don't hose you off, I'm going to have wet sand everywhere." Including his bed and couch, because he had not a single doubt the mutt would find the most comfortable spot to hang out in while Gabe was looking for shots in hilly Astoria.

The mutt's only response was a wild wag of its ridiculously fluffy tail.

"Oh, isn't he cute!" a voice behind him said.

Bracing himself for yet another feminine come-on, Gabe turned and immediately recognized the baker from the wedding. Summer? Sierra? Some New Agey name.

"Sedona Sullivan," she helped him out. "We met at the wedding."

"You're the cupcake baker."

She laughed as she looked down at the pink T-shirt boasting a trio of colorful cupcakes with the Take the Cake logo. "What was your first clue?"

"Good advertising ploy," he said. She looked as tasty as one of her cakes, with that pink shirt, white shorts, running shoes, and sassy blond hair. Just a few days ago Gabe would have been interested. Even yesterday he might have gone for it. Until another female with silky dark hair and mermaid green eyes had gotten, not just into his mind, but under his skin.

"It's a lot easier to run in than wearing a sandwich board," she agreed cheerfully. She bent down and ruffled the dog's ears. "Though I'm probably going to have to rethink the design because I'm toying with the idea of adding pies to the menu."

"Never met anyone who didn't like pie."

"That's exactly what I was thinking. What's this darling's name?"

"I don't have any idea. . . . He's not mine," he responded to her quizzical look. "I just took him off the vet's hands for a couple days until she can find him a home."

She stood up and laughed just as Sax and the sheriff had. "I know the feeling. She's got a homeless cat with my name on it. It's like trying not to get run over by a bull-dozer."

"Or an Abrams tank."

She glanced down at the dog again. "You know the old saying 'Resistance is futile'?"

"From *Star Trek.*"

"Exactly." She laughed again and ran a hand through her windblown hair. "Maybe Charity's actually a Borg in vet's clothing."

Although he wasn't attracted to her, at least not in the same way he was to Charity, Gabe liked the baker with the sort-of hippie name. He also realized that he was actually starting to enjoy himself for the first time in a very long while.

"I guess that means we could be in danger of assimilation."

"Or more likely in danger of becoming pet owners." She sighed dramatically, then glanced down at her watch. "Gotta run. My assistant's watching over things, but having been an accountant in a previous life, I'm a huge control freak, so it's hard letting go.

"Besides, we open in thirty minutes, and I still have to run home and shower." She patted his arm in a friendly, nonflirtatious way. "Good luck!" she said, unknowingly echoing Shelter Bay's sheriff.

"You, too." Gabe watched her run off toward the steps leading to the top of the cliff. And even as he admired the way her long, athletic legs ate up the sand, he had the feeling she was right.

Resistance undoubtedly was futile. Unless he dumped the dog over the vet's fence and skipped town in the middle of the night — which even he wasn't bastard enough to do — if he didn't strengthen his resolve, he could be sunk.

17

The Dancing Deer Dress Shoppe Two had been established by identical twin sisters who'd moved down from Coldwater Cove, Washington. In their mid-eighties, they'd decided to retire and sold their popular Dancing Deer Dress Shoppe to a former software designer who'd escaped city life in Seattle.

They'd watched daytime TV, baked, and puttered around in their gardens for exactly six weeks when they realized they'd made a big mistake.

"We missed chatting with the people," Doris Anderson had explained at their grand-opening party.

"And helping them find the perfect outfit," Dottie had chirped in.

However, a deal was a deal, and the shop was no longer theirs.

"We could have opened up a second shop," Dottie had said.

"But that wouldn't have been fair to that lovely young woman who bought our business," Doris had said.

"So," Dottie had explained, "since Harold and Hayden have always been up for new adventures and love ocean fishing, they agreed to move down here so we could begin again." Harold and Hayden were also identical twins. The couples had been married for nearly sixty years, an idea that seemed both impossible and wonderful to Charity.

Chatty, personable, and very good at their business, before they'd been in town a month, they'd become fixtures and their store was more than merely a place to buy clothing, but also, like Take the Cake, a convivial gathering place for Shelter Bay's women. They'd even recently begun a weekly book club at the shop.

After being introduced to Amanda, the sisters fluttered around like eager birds, gathering up clothing from display racks throughout the store. Doris, who preferred earth tones in her own wardrobe, chose navy blue, brown, and olive green, while Dottie, who could often be found in brilliant scarlet or hot pink, dived into the bright hues and floral prints.

"This must be a special occasion," Dottie

said as she handed Charity a coral cardigan sweater printed with seashells.

"You don't buy that many clothes," Doris agreed, adding a pair of slim bark brown slacks to the clothing building up on the white louvered door of the dressing cubicle.

"Not that we're complaining," Dottie, whose personality was as bright as her choice in clothing, said quickly.

"Of course not." Doris added a taupe blouse that complemented the color of the slacks. "After all, you certainly don't need to dress up for work. And since you don't have any social life to speak of —"

"Sister," Dottie broke in. "You're going to hurt Charity's feelings."

Doris tossed up both chins. "I was talking, Sister."

"I realize that." Dottie patted Charity's arm. "But we don't want to get personal. Though," she admitted, "I won't deny being curious."

"She has a dinner date," Amanda informed them as she riffled through a woven basket of bangle bracelets. For the moment, at least, the cloud of depression had appeared to lift and her mother was in full shopping mode.

"A date!" Both sisters spoke at once.

"Oh, that's so exciting!" Dottie said.

"You're finally moving on from that terrible, unfortunate incident."

"Sister!" This time it was Doris' turn to criticize. "Talk about getting personal!"

"It's all right." Charity reached for the handle to the dressing room. Although she'd never enjoyed shopping, certainly not the way her mother did, trying on all those clothes suddenly seemed like a very good idea, if only to escape this conversation. "It's not as if my calling off my wedding isn't pretty much the worst-kept secret in town."

"I never believed the groom-to-be was good enough for her," Amanda revealed. "And he was certainly way too stuffy."

"Really?" Both sisters leaned toward her mother, eyes as bright as those of curious birds.

"Well, if you'll all excuse me." Shooting her mother a stern, warning look, Charity snatched the hangers from the door and made her escape.

On the other side of the door, she could hear Amanda deftly moving the conversation back to a safe topic as she set the twins to finding the perfect jewelry.

Sighing, she decided to begin with the white jeans her mother had added to the mix. They fit perfectly. As usual, Amanda's eye for fashion was unerring.

Although it was unlike anything she'd ever worn in Chicago, or here, Charity's eye was drawn past the maze of colors to a white sleeveless shirt with tuxedo pleating in the front.

She tried it on. And immediately fell in love. Except for one thing . . .

She walked out of the dressing room to find all three women waiting expectantly.

"Oh, it's perfect!" Dottie clapped her hands.

"A bit impractical, being all white," Doris pointed out what Charity had already considered. "But at least it's machine washable. And it does looks wonderful on you."

"It shows off your arms," Amanda said. "Which most women would kill to have. It's also very summery, while keeping to your own tailored style."

Until that moment, Charity hadn't even realized she *had* a style.

"I feel a bit like a nurse," she said. "From back when they wore white uniforms, sensible shoes, and perky caps." She wasn't old enough to remember those days, but she'd seen movies. Including *One Flew Over the Cuckoo's Nest.*

Terrific. She was going on her first date in nearly two years looking like Nurse Ratched.

"You just need color," Amanda said.

165

"To brighten it up," Dottie agreed.

"But not too much," Doris cautioned.

Diving back into the baskets again, Amanda came up with a necklace made of silver chains studded with green and blue sea glass. And a wide, plastic, blue cuff bracelet. Dottie, returning to a rack in the window, retrieved the twin of the seashell cardigan, this time in sea blue.

Doris, going along with the flow, managed to put aside her own tastes and came up with a pair of flat silver sandals.

"Perfect," they all said on happy sighs as they viewed the final result.

Charity couldn't argue. She looked crisp and summery, and, she considered, like the kind of woman Gabriel St. James would appreciate. Although she barely knew him, from the way he was resisting disrupting his life with that poor stray dog, she suspected he wasn't one to go for the ultrafeminine, high-maintenance type.

"It is nice." She turned around in the three-way mirror, noticing what she hadn't been able to see in the single wall-length one in the dressing room. There were silvery crystal designs on both back pockets of the jeans. "Though I'm not sure these crystals on my butt aren't overkill."

"Not overkill at all. Merely the payoff for

all those squats you've obviously been do-ing," her mother said.

"When you're manhandling animals who don't always want to go where you'd like them to, you have to stay in shape."

"And isn't it fortunate you have?" Dottie said. "Because those look fabulous on you." She sighed and turned toward her sister. "Remember when we had bottoms like that?"

"Vaguely," Doris said on a sigh of her own.

The way they were all looking at her, as if they'd placed all their own memories and romantic hopes on both her outfit and her upcoming date, made Charity decide the time had come to leave.

Unsurprisingly, her mother insisted on paying. Since Charity's practice and her shelter costs ate up all her income, as well as digging into the small inheritance that had allowed her to buy the Victorian house in the first place, she wasn't about to argue.

Besides, her mother had always enjoyed giving her gifts. Charity had often thought it was her way of trying to make up for the unstable home life she'd provided her only child.

"Oh!" Dottie said as Doris ran the credit card. "I nearly forgot to give you one of these." She held out a brightly colored paper flyer.

Charity read the announcement. "A clothing exchange?"

"We started it for prom. Since the economy's been down, we invited all the girls at the high school to bring in their old dresses and did a swap. It was grand fun."

"And, more important," Doris said, "everyone went home with a new dress. For no cost."

"What a lovely idea. Though it doesn't seem as if it would help your business," Amanda said.

"Oh, we're part of the community now." As so often happened, the twins didn't seem to realize they'd spoken in unison. "What's good for Shelter Bay is good for us."

"We'll get more business once the economy turns around," Dottie said. "Meanwhile, we're doing fine. And everyone had such a grand time, we've decided to extend the idea to the adults. We're having a party next week."

"Sedona Sullivan's providing cupcakes for the refreshments," Doris said. "Maureen Douchett's bringing her sweet tea and Sofia's giving away pots of herbs. You know how she's always trying to get people to plant their own gardens."

"That sounds like a nice evening," Charity said, thinking that she doubted, except for the yellow dress she'd worn to the wedding, and this new outfit, she had a thing in her closet any woman in Shelter Bay would want to swap for.

"We were hoping you'd come," Dottie said.

"Oh, I don't —"

"We thought you could bring some of those kittens or puppies," Doris said.

"In case there's anyone left in town you haven't talked into adopting one," Dottie tacked on.

Charity laughed at that. Hadn't the sisters adopted a pair of elderly Siamese cats? Unsurprisingly, Doris had chosen the brown chocolate point, while Dottie had gone for the lavender point.

And both Harold and Hayden had gone home from the shelter with older dogs — Harold with a taffy-colored cocker, Hayden with a graying Jack Russell terrier.

She might not have clothes to donate, but no way was she going to resist an opportunity to tell people about the importance of neutering their pets and invite those who might be thinking about getting a pet to come visit the special ones she had at her shelter. Dogs and cats who, in her view, weren't victims to be pitied but heroes for surviving the odds.

"You're on," she said.

18

Johnny's grandmother had told him that his mother, Crystal, had always been excitable and given to big dreams. But she hadn't been flat-out crazy until her first baby girl — born three years before Johnny — had died of SIDS, which his grandmother had explained was short for *sudden infant death syndrome.*

According to the story as it had been told to him, after finding the baby lifeless in her little pink onesie, his mother had sunk into the depths of despair, crying and staying in bed and being so miserable that her husband, unable to take so much sorrow any longer, had run off with her best friend.

But even that hadn't been enough to get her out of bed.

As his mother had related to his grandmother, she'd been crying buckets of tears into the pillow when a deep voice had spoken to her, rumbling like thunder in the dark. The voice, which his mother claimed to have belonged to God, explained that she was being used as a pawn in an apocalyptic battle between good and evil. And that although she'd be blessed with more children, she'd have to fight the demons to protect them. Which she'd done with a vengeance, even locking him in the closet whenever she left the house.

Later, his baby sister, Angel, had been locked in with him.

Although weeks, sometimes even months, might go by when life would be fairly normal, eventually she'd go off her meds again and other voices — belonging to saints and archangels — would warn her that her children were being hunted by evil people who were only waiting for her to drop her guard. During these times, she'd go without sleep for days, keeping him and Angel locked in whatever room they were living in at the time, pacing the floor, forgetting to bathe or eat, or feed her son and daughter. Which was when Johnny had begun teaching himself to cook.

Unfortunately, while she might have tried to protect her children against demons, Crystal was a great deal more lax about the men in her life. Although Johnny didn't really believe in demon possession, he'd got-

172

ten an up-close and personal introduction to evil when he was nine. After bouncing around the country, including Phoenix, Las Vegas, freezing his butt off during an icy winter in Minnesota, back to West Virginia, then Texas, it seemed they might actually be settling down in Salem, Oregon, long enough for him to spend an entire year in one school, when his mama brought home Uncle Buck.

Buck had been a mean, red-faced man with a bulging gut, thick hairy arms, and big hands. Hands that could make you see stars or wield a belt that would leave Johnny's butt with red marks for a day.

"Spare the rod, spoil the child" had been his excuse, though it didn't take Johnny long to realize that Buck was just a bully with a mean streak, which was made even worse by his liking for whiskey.

When Buck started beating up on Crystal, Johnny had tried to stop him, only to end up with a broken arm for his efforts. On the way to the emergency room, his mother had instructed him to say he'd fallen off his bike, because if the doctor knew what had really happened, then he'd have to report it and the police would come and take Buck away.

"But that would be a *good* thing," he'd said.

"People can be dangerous," she'd answered, telling him nothing he hadn't figured out for himself. "But sometimes, you're better off with the devil you know. Besides, you know how hard it is for me to keep a job. Without Buck's paycheck, we could end up living on the street. Or living out of this car again."

Although his arm hurt like the dickens and he hated the idea of Buck's big hands touching his mom, most of all Johnny hated living out of the car. With his wrinkled clothes always smelling like the take-out burgers and fries they were forced to live on, along with his hair and freckles, and being small for his age, he might as well go to school with a big red bull's-eye on his back.

So he'd lied to the doctors and the nurses, even though he could tell one nurse didn't believe him. But he'd stuck to his story and protected his mother in the only way he knew how.

A few weeks later, Buck had come home from the bar drunk and meaner than usual. It had been the worst night of Johnny's life. A long, scary night that finally ended when a police SWAT sniper shot Buck dead.

But not before Buck had stabbed Crystal with his switchblade knife. Although his mother had survived the wound, she'd been committed, against her will, to the state mental hospital.

The lady from DHS sent Johnny and Angel to live with his grandmother, who'd finally left Nevada and moved to Oregon. She was living in a downtown Portland apartment, working as a waitress in a river-front fish restaurant.

Looking back on it now, with the additional wisdom of his fifteen years, Johnny realized that his grandmother, who'd still been a young woman herself, wasn't all that wild about having two kids dumped in her lap. Especially a redheaded boy who spent most of his time angry, and the rest getting in fights.

He'd been sitting in class, trying to figure out the complexities of long division, when one of the mothers who volunteered in the school office came into the class and handed a note to the teacher.

They exchanged a few words. Then, when the teacher's gaze landed straight as an arrow on him, both women's faces serious and sad at the same time, Johnny knew this wasn't going to be good.

He left the classroom to a buzz of conversation. The kids were all wearing smirks. He'd seen that look before, too.

The hallway seemed a mile long as he

walked down it with the pretty blond woman who smelled like flowers. As soon as he entered the principal's office, he recognized the other woman sitting there immediately. She was the same one who'd come to the house after Buck had been shot. The one who'd taken Angel and him to his grandmother's house, with only their clothes on their backs, in the middle of the night.

"I'm afraid your grandmother has turned you back in to Social Services." The woman's tone, while not unkind, was also brisk, as if she told kids stuff like this every day. Which Johnny figured she probably did. "She says you're a problem child. That she can't handle you."

He looked over at the principal, Mrs. Ferguson, who had begun writing something that must have been really important because she wouldn't meet his eye.

"Mrs. Ferguson says that you've been getting in fights."

He speared an accusing look at the principal, who continued to write.

"It's all in your records," the social worker said in defense of the still-silent principal.

"Kids pick on me. So I fight back."

"You gave" — she opened the manila folder she was holding — "Tyler Young a

176

black eye. And broke his nose."

When he'd felt the satisfying crunch of bone beneath his fist, Johnny had, for the first time, understood a little of what Buck must've felt. The big difference was Buck had been a bully.

While *he* was standing up to bullies.

"He called my mother a crazy, nutcase whore."

Principal Ferguson's cheeks reddened a bit at that. Johnny knew she didn't tolerate bad words in her school. Tough. If she'd really cared, she would have called to her office all the kids who threw even worse words at him like a shower of stones every day and written all those words down in *their* permanent records.

A really bad thought occurred to him. "Did she turn in Angel, too?"

The social worker nodded. "Yes."

That hadn't made sense to Johnny then. And six years later, it still didn't. Okay, so maybe he *was* a "problem child." But his sister was an angel. Or as close to one as you were ever going to find here on earth. But it hadn't mattered, because their grandmother had dumped her, too.

And it was all his fault. If only he'd behaved better. If only he hadn't gotten into fights, and had cleaned his room, and not sassed his grandmother when she complained about having two brats dumped on her, Angel would still have a home.

As he left the office, the principal finally spoke. "Johnny." He glanced back over his shoulder. "I'm sorry."

Using his fists wasn't the only thing Johnny had learned from Buck.

He'd flipped her the bird. Then hadn't looked back.

He and Angel had spent the next six years bouncing from home to home. He'd always known it was his bad attitude that had kept him from being adopted. Not that he wanted to be placed in a permanent home. Because his mom was coming back and he knew that if he wasn't waiting for her, something terrible could happen.

But he'd never been able to figure out why no one wanted his sister. Especially since they'd been separated the entire time. So why should his behavior have anything to do with Angel?

The question had remained a puzzle until a year ago, when a bitch of a foster parent even more wicked than that bad witch in *The Wizard of Oz* had told him that no one would ever adopt either Johnny or Angel because no one trusted their blood history.

"No one knows who either of your fathers

were," she'd said. "And according to your records and the police report, your mother's a mental mess."

Which was, unfortunately, true. But that didn't keep him from feeling guilty. Maybe if he'd just loved his mother a little harder, taken better care of his sister so she wouldn't have to worry so much, they'd still be a family.

Not all his foster parents had been like old Wicked Witch of the West. Some were kind, and a few even treated him the same way they did their own children, even inviting him to call them Mom.

But he couldn't do it because they weren't his mother. His mother was out there. Somewhere. And she'd always told Johnny that whatever happened — that whoever took him away from her and kept them apart — she would always be his mother. His only mom.

So, refusing to forget her, as so many adults advised, forgiving her for past painful behaviors he understood were out of her control whenever her damaged mind burst its boundaries, he'd steadfastly waited for her to come back. Which, in his heart, he knew would probably never happen. But that didn't keep him from hoping.

And waiting.

While his mother's face and the scent of her jasmine perfume followed him like a shadow, from placement to placement.

Like a ghost.

19

Time might be slower on the coast, but this was ridiculous, Charity thought as she looked up at the paw-shaped wall clock for the umpteenth time. Having just assured a nervous cat owner that it wouldn't die after scarfing down an entire pork chop it'd snatched from the countertop, she was counting the hours before the Marine was due to show up at the house.

You're behaving like a teenager before a first date. It was ridiculous to be so nervous. It was, after all, just dinner.

Yeah, and how many times do you buy a new outfit to nuke a Lean Cuisine spaghetti Alfredo?

"Good point," she muttered.

"Did you say something?" Amie glanced up from stocking the supply cabinet.

"Just talking to myself."

"I do that all the time," Janet, who'd come back to announce a new patient, offered. "I figure as long as I answer, I'm okay." She handed Charity the patient's color-coded file. "It's when I start ignoring myself I may be in trouble."

"You've been jittery all day," Amie accused.

"I have not." It was a lie. But only a small white one.

"You've reminded me of a blind cat in a room full of rocking chairs," Janet jumped in.

"I'll bet it's the date," Amie said knowingly.

Janet nodded. "I was thinking the same thing."

"It's not a date." The denial sounded as false as when she'd tried it out on herself. "Simply dinner."

"A dinner you bought a new outfit for," Janet pointed out.

"And did your nails."

When both women's eyes zeroed in on Charity's fingernails, she was tempted to put her hands behind her back to hide them from view. "It's clear polish."

"True. Which is a shame, because if I had your long fingers, I'd want to show them off," said Amie, who was currently wearing a sky blue color on her own short nails.

"But they're not chipped like they usually

182

are," Janet said, proving to have the eye of an eagle, which probably served her well when painting landscapes. "And you shaped them."

"Jeez." Charity opened the file, determined to move the topic away from her. "It's not as if I go around town looking like a bag woman."

"Of course you don't, dear," Janet said. "It's just that it's been obvious that you're anxious about something. Since the day's been so quiet —"

"Don't say that!" Amie and Charity immediately cut the older woman off. If there was one thing every veterinarian knew, it was that the surest way to invite chaos was to state out loud how quiet things were.

"Sorry!" Janet covered her mouth with her hand.

Too late. A second later the bell on the door jangled. Then jangled again. And, as the receptionist bustled out to start triaging their patients, yet again.

Amie and Charity exchanged a resigned look. The deluge had begun.

20

Kara Conway was sitting out on the porch of Sax Douchett's cliff house — which she and her son, Trey, had moved into — sipping a glass of wine and watching the early-evening sunlight dance on the waves. Although winters might admittedly be gray and wet here on the coast, summers were heaven.

"I saw your brother's friend today," she said as she rocked on the porch swing with the man she'd fallen in love with.

"What friend was that?" he asked idly as he sipped on a beer and played with the strands of hair hugging the nape of her neck.

"The one from the wedding. The photographer."

"Gabe St. James."

"That's him. He was walking on the beach."

"Taking pictures?" Now he was nuzzling her neck, which made it really difficult to concentrate. With Trey on a sleepover and Bon Temps closed on Monday evenings, Kara knew exactly what Sax had in mind. The same thing she'd been planning, which was why she'd stopped by the Oh So Fancy lingerie boutique and picked up a pretty rose pink silk and lace camisole and tap pants, which she was currently wearing under her jeans and T-shirt as a sexy surprise.

"No." She tilted her head back, allowing his lips access to her throat. "He had a dog."

"I know. I saw it sitting in the front seat of the Jeep when he stopped by Bon Temps yesterday. But I couldn't tell what kind it was."

"I've no idea." Just when things had begun to get interesting, she'd managed to sidetrack them. Reminding herself that they had all night, Kara took another sip of wine. "Some little black thing. Maybe part Shih Tzu, with some poodle in it."

He threw back his head and laughed. "You're kidding."

"No. He said he was just keeping it overnight until Charity can find it a home."

He laughed again, the deep rich sound slipping beneath her skin and warming her from the inside out, as it always did. "That's what he told me. I also told him good luck with that."

"Once again we're on the same wave-length."

He'd always been able to read her mind. Even back when they'd been in high school. Giving up on the seduction part of the evening for now, she leaned her head on his shoulder and watched the fishing boats chug along the horizon, nets trailing behind them.

"I think there may be something going on between them," Sax said. "More than her trying to place another dog."

"Did he say that?"

"It was more what he *didn't* say. And the way he didn't say it."

Kara frowned. "I don't know if that would be such a good idea."

"Why not? They're both single and un-committed."

"She's had a sex moratorium since she called off her wedding."

"Really?"

"Really."

"Damn if it isn't true. Men don't stand a chance because women *do* tell each other everything."

"Female bonding and sharing information is cultural, going back to the beginning of time. It was important to keep the com-munity together while the men were out hunting woolly mammoths. And it's not like males don't tell each other stuff. I refuse to believe that you only talk sports over those poker games and fishing trips.

"My point," she stressed, holding up a finger as he opened his mouth to argue, "is that if Charity's going to get back on that particular horse, so to speak, perhaps she ought to start out with an easier one."

"One who's already been broke."

"So to speak."

"I was celibate until you came to town."

"So Kelli told me."

"What? How the hell did the woman who's now my sister-in-law know that?"

"Cole told her. And she told me."

"Like it was any of her damn business," he muttered.

"You had a reputation back in the day," Kara reminded him. "I think she just wanted to reassure me that you'd changed. Settled down."

"Cole shouldn't have told her. We only talked about sex once. In generalities, when we were discussing fixing up Bon Temps and he told me I should get laid."

"Which you did." She pressed a kiss against his frowning lips, then snuggled closer again. "But you were different. You were ready for a relationship when you came back to town."

"I'm not sure about that. But I sure as hell was ready for you." He pressed a kiss against the top of her head. "As for Charity, unless she has plans to open up a vet clinic in a convent, it makes sense that after nearly two years she'd be ready to get back on the horse. Or, mixing metaphors, the bike. Since I always figured sex is a lot like riding a bike. Once you figure out how to do it, it just comes back naturally."

"Which certainly seemed to be true for you."

"Why, thank you, *chère*." He put his fingers beneath her chin, tipped her head up, and touched his lips to hers, creating the slow, familiar smoldering stir she figured she'd still be feeling when they were a hundred.

"But, as I said, he just doesn't seem right for her. Not when there are so many other nice, easier men in town."

"Maybe she doesn't want easy. Maybe after all this time going without, she isn't interested in training wheels. You turned out to have a thing for bad boys. Ever think she might want to take a walk on the wild side?"

"You're not the same rebel you were in high school," she reminded him. Though he still had enough of that bad-boy flare to keep things interesting.

"True enough."

"So," she mused, "I suppose it's true that opposites attract."

"Works in our case," he agreed.

"But I don't know." She shook her head. "He just seems so intense. I like to think that I'm a pretty good judge of people —"

"You are. Which is undoubtedly important in the cop business."

"It is." And often could make the difference between life and death. Something her late husband had, tragically, found out the hard way. "And from the vibes I was getting from your Marine friend, just in that short time, I worry that the two of them together could be a lot like nitroglycerin and a flamethrower."

"They're grown-ups. They'll be okay. And speaking of flames."

He kissed her again. Longer, deeper. Skimmed a wicked hand from her shoulder down to her thigh.

"What would you say," he murmured against her mouth, "to going back in and setting some sheets on fire?"

Reminding herself that Sax was right, that Charity was a grown woman who'd had the guts to call off a wedding at the last minute, while guests were waiting for her to walk down the aisle, Kara put the problem aside for a time as she twined her arms around his neck.

"I'd say you just read my mind."

21

Although she'd experienced some tense moments during her career — such as the time a bullmastiff had plunked his huge butt down on her porch and refused to enter the clinic until she'd lured him in with a particularly smelly treat — Charity was not accustomed to feeling nervous.

"It's just dinner," she repeated yet again as she smoothed lotion into her skin after the shower she'd taken to wash off the kennel/hospital smell, then spritzed on the matching scent.

Which is why you're using that outrageously expensive perfume, a little voice in the back of her head piped up. *Which, until the wedding, had been sitting on the counter for the past six months.*

It had been a Christmas gift from her father, who, like her mother, tended toward excess. A trait that appeared to have escaped her. The fact that the name was written on the label in real gold leaf had been enough to make her put it aside, waiting for a special occasion.

Not that this was a special occasion.

After all, if she didn't use it, it would dry up. Or evaporate. She was only being frugal.

Okay. That was a lie. The truth was, like it or not, this *was* a date. She couldn't try to insist that it was about placing another homeless dog. She had, after all, managed to find homes for dozens of animals since coming to Shelter Bay and none of those cases had involved dinner. Well, except for a few meals at the Douchetts' home, but that had evolved much more into friendship than business.

Still, it wasn't as if she hadn't gone on plenty of dates over the years. Doing some quick math, she realized she'd been dating for seventeen years. Well, technically fifteen, taking into account her recent two years' moratorium. But that still worked out to more years of going on dates than she'd been alive when she first went to the Spring Fling dance with Charlie McMann her junior year of high school.

So why was she even more nervous now than she'd been back then?

Maybe because she was out of practice?

Or more likely because Charlie, who was

currently a pharmacist in Reno, was no Gabriel St. James. Charlie had been sweet, shy, and absolutely harmless.

Again, unlike the Marine, who was due to arrive in less than an hour. She suspected, given his years in the military, he'd be punctual.

She was already running late, thanks to the insanity that had ended her day: a case with a cat she'd diagnosed with diabetes, which required explaining to the upset owner how to inject the prescribed insulin; a routine dental exam on a cat that had ended up in surgery for two extractions; a Lab that had been shedding too much even for summer, and that she'd diagnosed with heartworm, contracted because the owner, a laid-off mill worker, hadn't been able to afford to buy the preventative medicine; and yet another unexpected surgery to remove a Hot Wheels fire truck from a Dalmatian's stomach. Since the surgery wasn't life threatening, she'd allowed herself to laugh with the owner once the metal truck had been retrieved.

Just thinking of the irony now took a bit of the edge off.

She was smiling when her mother appeared in the doorway. "You're not going to pull your hair back like that, are you?"

Amanda asked with obvious disapproval.

"It can be breezy at the harbor." She fastened it at the nape of her neck with a silver clip.

"Loose is sexier."

"Then I'm on the right track. Because I'm not going for sexy."

"Well, isn't that the waste of a date?"

"I fail to see how having strands of hair stuck to my lipstick could be considered sexy."

"You have a point." Her mother fluffed her own perfectly coiffed hair that always made her look as if she'd just walked out of a chichi salon. "Though that would call attention to your mouth."

"I don't want to call attention to my mouth. I don't want to call attention to any part of my body. In fact, I'd just as soon stay home."

"Too late," her mother said as the doorbell rang downstairs with a peal of chimes. "I'll go let him in."

Damn. She might be out of practice when it came to dating, but Gabriel St. James was even worse than she. What was he doing arriving thirty minutes early?

She threw on her new outfit, quickly slipped into the sandals, and was on her way down the stairs when she met her mother, who was on her way back up.

"It's not him," Amanda said. "There's a woman waiting in the foyer. With what I'm guessing, from her expression and red-rimmed eyes, is a serious problem."

Charity had learned early on in her career that most vets, especially ones in small towns that didn't have an after-hours emergency clinic, were on call twenty-four hours a day. Another important reason to love the work, she thought as she walked into the clinic.

Sofia De Luca was sitting on the love seat in the foyer, Rosemary lying at her feet. Sofia's face was blotchy and her eyes were, indeed, red-rimmed. Although the dog obviously lacked strength, Rosemary managed a welcoming thump of her tail. A young man Charity recognized as one of Sofia's gardeners was standing by the door, looking as if he'd rather be anywhere else.

"It's time," the older woman said, pushing herself to her feet. "Rosemary told me."

To anyone who'd not grown so close to a beloved animal, that statement might have sounded foolish. But Charity had witnessed this situation too many times to not totally believe it.

She placed a hand on Sofia's arm. "I'm so sorry. But if it's any consolation, I believe you're doing the right thing."

It was always hard to euthanize any pet. But Rosemary had a dreadful long-term prognosis. Perhaps, by increasing the medications and with constant care, they'd be able to eke out a few more weeks. But her suffering, as well as such a long good-bye, would be painful not only for the dog but for its owner.

"Well, it's not as if we didn't all know it was coming." Sofia sighed wearily and for the first time since Charity had met the herb-farm owner, she looked every bit of her seventy-plus years. "And she's been trying like the dickens to stay with me, but I realized this afternoon, when she could barely lift her head, that she was ready to let go." She glanced over at the silent young man. "Fortunately, Benny was working late, transplanting some lavender, and offered to carry her to the car. Then into here."

Charity offered him a slight smile. "Thank you."

"I was glad to do it." Red flooded into his already ruddy cheeks as he apparently realized how that might sound. "I mean, I'm not glad about Rosemary dying. That's really a bummer. But I'm glad I was there to help."

"We know, dear," Sofia said soothingly.

She managed a wobbly, encouraging smile of her own toward the young man.

"You didn't have to come into town." Charity had assured Sofia that when the time came, she'd be willing to make a house call.

"We wanted to." The smile faltered as she bent down and rubbed Rosemary's ears. "Rosemary does so love to ride in the truck, I thought she'd enjoy one more spin around the harbor. She perked up a bit at the sound of the gulls." Her voice cracked a bit on that part. "She's always enjoyed chasing them. I picked her up a crab cake at the Crab Shack, which is another of her favorite treats. She managed a little bite, but I suspect that was partly to please me."

"She's always loved you."

"She was my husband's dog," the older woman said. "I didn't really want another after our beloved cocker, Peggy, passed on. But Joe convinced me that the house was too quiet with just the two of us." She rubbed an age-spotted hand over the top of the dog's head. "He was right. Rosemary brought so much joy and energy back into our lives, I don't know what I would have done without her when he got the cancer."

She sighed. "And then it caught her, too."

"I'm so sorry."

"You're not the only one." She drew in a deep breath. Squared shoulders clad in a denim shirt. Her eyes, shiny with unshed tears, met Charity's. "We'd best get on with it."

Charity led the trio out to the contemplative garden, then instructed Benny to lay Rosemary onto the lawn, which still carried the sweet scent from this morning's mowing. When Sofia sat down beside her, the dog put her head into the woman's lap.

"I'll be back in a couple minutes," she said, wanting to give Sofia and her beloved companion one last private moment to say good-bye.

Benny, who followed her back into the clinic, was more than happy to wait while Charity performed what was always the most difficult part of her profession.

The dog's death was swift, peaceful, and merciful, and although Charity knew it may have been merely a trick of the light, she thought she viewed the life leave Rosemary's eyes an instant before she administered the injection.

"She's already somewhere else," Sofia said with what sounded like relief, despite the grief lining her face. Charity had seen such conflicted emotions too many times.

"Eating crab cakes," Charity said.

"And terrorizing gulls." Sofia chuckled even as the tears began to flow.

The prearranged plan was to leave the dog's remains with Charity, who'd arrange for cremation, then bring the ashes in the simple wooden urn back to the farm. Charity gave the woman a hug.

"Stay as long as you need," she said.

"Thank you." The elderly woman's words caught a bit on the lump in her throat.

Charity went back inside and waited.

After she'd come inside and thanked Charity, then said good-bye, Benny walked her out to the truck, then returned to carry the dog into the room where Charity would finish the job. Although she could have taken care of that herself, she understood it was something he wanted to do for his employer. And friend.

Standing on the porch, Charity watched the two of them drive away.

What Sofia didn't know was that Charity always took a clay paw-print cast of each animal she euthanized. In this case, there'd be a memory of Rosemary in the garden of Lavender Hill Farm, where she'd walked with Sofia for so many years.

The dog had lost a great deal of weight in the past weeks. Enough that Charity was able to lift its body in the freezer, where it would stay until the crematorium employee picked it up tomorrow.

Feeling the weight of the world on her shoulders, even knowing they'd done the right thing, she scrubbed up, then went into the kennel, where she found Winnie nursing her pups, who were happily suckling away.

"We'll give it a few days," she said, patting the bulldog's broad head. "Maybe a few weeks. Then I'll take you out to the farm to visit and see how you two get along on your first date."

Damn, she'd totally forgotten about her date with the Marine. Looking down at the grass stains on her new white jeans from sitting on the lawn with Sofia and Rosemary, she realized she'd have to change clothes.

"Maybe it's a sign," she muttered as she crossed the foyer, headed toward the stairs to go back up to her apartment. "That this damn date wasn't meant to be."

"Good try," a deep voice shattered her introspection. "But you're not getting off the hook that easily."

There, standing in front of her, not quite physically blocking her way, but large enough that she'd have to dodge around him, was Gabriel St. James. She thought she saw a glimpse of something — empathy, sympathy? — in eyes the color of rain. Then, like a flash of lightning out at sea, it was gone, leaving them cool and remote.

"I'm sorry." The surprising thing was, she meant it. "But I've had a really, really bad day, and —"

"All the more reason to get out of here for a while. I imagine, as convenient as it might be, there's also a downside to living above the store, so to speak."

That was true. But . . .

"I'd be lousy company."

"Believe me, your idea of what constitutes a good dinner companion definitely changes after you've sat on your helmet eating MREs hunkered down beneath a rocky ledge in the Afghan mountains with a team of Marines. Besides, you have to eat."

"I'm a mess." She ran her hand down her thighs and wondered if she smelled of clinic and death rather than the expensive perfume she'd spritzed on earlier. Then wished she didn't care.

He tilted his head. "Are you always this hard on yourself?"

"Not hard. Truthful."

"You look terrific. Though sad."

"I lost a patient."

"So your mother told me when she called."

"She called you?"

"To explain that you might be a bit delayed. And not exactly up for going out in public."

"Oh." Charity knew her mother wasn't nearly as shallow as she might appear. But she hadn't realized empathy was one of her traits.

"Which is why I stopped by the Crab Shack and picked up something to go. I also brought dinner for your mother."

Okay. *That* was thoughtful.

"It wouldn't hurt you to get out of here. Get some fresh air. I thought we'd go to the beach. Have dinner, share some conversation, clear your head."

"And unbreak my heart?"

"That's probably not possible. A loss is a loss, whether you're talking about a person or an animal," he said. "But fresh sea air, fresh crab, and a little wine might ease the pain. Just a bit."

Something occurred to her. "Where's your dog?" Surely he wouldn't have given it away? Or worse yet, taken it to one of those horrid kill shelters in one of the nearby towns?

"Upstairs with your mother. She offered to dog sit when she called. Last I saw, she was using pieces of fried shrimp to try to

202

teach him to do a high five."

A laugh burst out of her at the mental image of her socialite mother, clad in silk lounging pajamas, eating greasy fried seafood with her nightly martini while trying to teach a rescued Shih Tzu a trick.

"See." The smile that split his harshly hewn face was all the more warming because it was so rare. "It's already working. Run up and change into something that can handle the beach. Since the mutt seems to be surviving without me okay, I'll wait here."

She hesitated. Considered her options, then realized he was right. Some time out on the beach, breathing in the bracing scent of salt water and fir trees, was probably just what she needed.

"I'll be right back down."

He nodded. "I'll be here."

Of that, Charity had not a single doubt.

22

Charity didn't talk much as they crossed the bridge over the harbor to the coast. Which was fine with Gabe. After all these months alone, he'd gotten accustomed to silence. He could tell that the death of one of her patients was weighing on her, though. Her face was pale and her eyes, shiny with unshed tears, showed traces of strain and sorrow. The bright energy that had first garnered his unwilling attention seemed dimmed. Like a candle snuffed out by a coastal wind.

"She was a golden retriever," she said, finally breaking the silence.

"Great dogs."

She nodded, though she continued to look out the passenger window, her attention on a seagull perched atop a wooden piling. She'd changed into a pair of well-worn jeans and a loose cotton blouse printed in swirling sea colors that looked as if she might be channeling the Age of Aquarius. "Her owner's been through a lot, but she's definitely one tough cookie. Still, it had to have been horribly difficult."

"For both of you."

"As I said at Cole and Kelli's wedding, I don't like to fail."

"Name me one person who does."

"Point taken. The dog, Rosemary, had cancer." She shook her head. "We could have gone the chemo and radiation route, but —"

"It only would've bought a bit more time," he guessed.

"Exactly. Fortunately, it wasn't my call to make. Rosemary was twelve years old, which is a good run for a golden. Especially since their cancer rate comes in around sixty percent."

"I'm no veterinarian, but that sounds high."

"It is, relatively."

"Yet we all — dogs and people — have a one hundred percent rate of dying." Didn't he know that firsthand, having seen so much death himself? The dog's name belatedly sank in. "Are you talking about Sofia De Luca's dog?"

"Yes." She glanced over at him, obviously surprised. "Do you know Sofia?"

"I stopped to take some photos at a farmers' market on the town square the morning I arrived in town. Sofia was there with her herbs and invited me out to Lavender Hill Farm."

"She loves to spread her gospel of healthy eating."

"Fed me the best cedar-grilled salmon I've ever eaten on top of fresh greens. I nearly proposed on the spot."

Gabe found himself liking that he could make Charity smile.

"That's sweet."

"I told you —"

"Yes, I know." She brushed away his planned complaint. "Marines aren't sweet. Or nice. But maybe Shelter Bay's beginning to get to you. I've certainly changed since moving here."

"Next you'll be telling me there's something in the water."

"You wouldn't be the first person to suggest that."

It was his turn to shrug. "Whatever. I didn't spend much time with Rosemary, but she seemed like a great dog."

"She was one of the best I've ever known. Although I wasn't living in town then, she was there for Sofia's husband's cancer. It was as if Rosemary sensed Sofia's grief. She didn't leave her side for days. Even during the memorial service they held in the garden pavilion out at the farm."

"And no doubt you already have a replacement in mind."

"Not a *replacement.* A pet's not like a microwave or TV. They're not replaceable. Though there *is* this golden-paws bulldog that came in the other day. The one I had to leave the wedding for. She just had pups."

"Golden paws being old?"

"Got it in one. It's a term used for harder-to-place elderly rescued dogs."

She was good. Not just shoving animals into whichever home she could find, but making sensible matches. Not that he belonged with the fluff ball she was trying to push onto him, but, hey, no one was perfect.

"Makes sense," he said. "Being no spring chicken herself, Sofia won't have to worry as much about leaving a dog behind when her time comes."

"That isn't exactly the way I'd put it. But yes. That's what I was thinking. . . . Would you mind if I rolled down the window?"

"Be my guest. I would've myself, but most women I've met — outside the ones in the military — seem to worry about their hair. Especially on dates."

"I'm not most women."

He shot her a look. "Believe me, I've already figured that out for myself."

"And about this being a date —"

"It's more than just dinner. And we both know it." Hadn't he tried to convince himself that he'd only asked her out to save himself from having to nuke yet another frozen dinner in the motor home's microwave?

"My mother's already driven that point home," she said dryly. "But here's the thing. Would you mind if we just sort of ignored the first-date idea and pretend this is our second one?"

"Sure." Although he hadn't originally had any intention of sticking around once the wedding was over, Gabe liked the idea there'd be another. "Why?"

"Because I have this terrible habit of going too far on a first date. So, I'd like to avoid that problem tonight."

The same way he could make her smile, she could make him laugh. Gabe liked that about her. Especially since he knew it was a bald-faced lie she'd told to lighten the mood. Of course, liking it as much as he did also had his nerves tangling like kelp.

"It's a deal," he agreed even as he reminded himself yet again that this was the type of woman a man should care about.

The type you didn't just enjoy for the moment, then move on. "Though I'll probably be kicking myself when I'm forced to spend the night alone in the motor home."

"You won't be alone. You'll have your dog."

"Don't remind me."

He turned onto a narrow, sandy road, then stopped when he got to the edge of the beach, which stretched out in both directions like a sun-gilded ribbon of golden sand. It was also completely deserted. Which wouldn't be unusual most of the year, but this was high tourist season, when visitors flocked to Shelter Bay.

"How did you find this place?"

"Cole and Sax brought me here a couple nights before the rehearsal dinner for a three-guy bachelor party."

"That's pretty low-key for a bachelor party."

"We're not kids anymore. I suspect we've all done enough wild and crazy stuff to last us a lifetime."

"And after fighting wars, you're ready for mellow?"

"That, too," Gabe agreed.

He didn't want to talk about war. Didn't want to think about it. He'd done his duty, put in his time, and moved on. One thing

209

he'd always been good at was moving on. Which had been a large part of the appeal of the military.

"Apparently their family used to hang here a lot while they were growing up."

He decided not to mention the guys sharing that they'd also used it as a make-out place. Instead he pointed to a graying wooden picnic table. "Their grandfather built that table when they were kids."

"And it's still standing here. See, that's one of the things I love about this town. The sense of family continuity. I especially love Bernard Douchett, not just because he's a sweet man, but because he obviously adores his wife."

"Cole's dad is the same way about his mom." The way they'd slow-danced at the wedding together had shown that somehow they'd managed to keep the spark alive.

"I know. That's so special." She leaned back in the leather seat, closed her eyes, and took a deep breath of the salt-and-seaweed-scented breeze. "This is also a really great place."

"After your mother called earlier, I decided it might fit the bill."

"It's perfect." Until this smile finally brought the sparkle back into her eyes, Gabe hadn't been aware he'd been missing it. "Thank you."

Because he suddenly wanted, with an almost painful need, to touch his mouth to those smiling lips — and that was just for starters — he pulled back behind the internal stone wall he'd spent a lifetime constructing.

"No problem. Jake, at the Crab Shack, threw in some plates and stuff. I'll get them out of the back."

Coward. As he escaped the Jeep, Gabe assured himself that he was not retreating. Merely, as General O. P. Smith had said about the First Marine Division's retreat from Chosin Reservoir during the Korean War, "advancing in a different direction."

23

The local Dungeness crab was excellent as always. It was also messy. Fortunately Jake, the Crab Shack's owner, had thrown in a newspaper, which Gabe used to cover the table, then held down with beach rocks. Jake had also included plenty of wet wipes.

Instead of being boiled, the crabs had been roasted in a garlic-butter sauce. Their bright orange shells were crispy and brittle, the meat tender, juicy, and incredibly rich.

"Oh, my God," Charity moaned. "I could marry and live happily ever after with this crab."

"Sax assured me it was the next-best thing to his cooking. But Bon Temps is closed today."

"Sax's seafood Cajun cooking is fabulous and everyone in town is really grateful he reopened Bon Temps. But I'm not sure I'm ready to rate this second place." She dipped a chunk of the crunchy bread into the sauce that was good enough to inhale through a straw. "I'm going to have to call a tie."

It definitely wasn't a polite, first-date sort of meal. There was no way to eat it without getting messy, and she was undoubtedly going to ruin this peasant blouse her mother had managed to push on her after declaring everything else in her closet unacceptable. But Charity couldn't deny that breaking apart the butter-drenched crab and eating with her hands was proving hugely sensual. It reminded her of the erotic banquet seduction in *Tom Jones.*

"So," he said as he scooped up some crunchy coleslaw with one of the white plastic spoons Jake had tossed into the bag, "it doesn't sound like you've had it before."

"I love crab and I've ordered Jake's takeout sandwiches and salads before. But an entire crab just didn't seem like something to eat by myself."

"Hard to believe that the guys in this town are so boneheaded they haven't taken you there."

"Because guys consider eating greasy stuff with your hands a form of foreplay?"

"Got me there," he said easily.

"I've been asked. I just haven't felt like accepting."

"Why not?" He unwrapped two pieces of

corn. Which were — surprise, surprise — also drenched in butter.

Even though she could feel her arteries clogging just looking at the grilled corn, Charity couldn't resist taking a bite. Yep. She was definitely going to have to spend an extra thirty minutes on the treadmill tomorrow morning to even make a dent in this meal.

"I took sort of a moratorium on dating when I moved here." She wiped some butter from the corner of her mouth and watched his eyes darken. She'd been right. The man *was* dangerous.

"How's that working for you?"

"Actually, just fine. Starting a practice, along with opening the shelter, takes a great deal of time and energy. I'm not sure I'd have any left for personal life."

"Yet you're here with me."

"Good point."

"So." He braced his elbows on the table, put that chin with its sexy cleft on his linked fingers, and studied her with slow, silent interest.

Even as his expression remained neutral, as he continued his scrutiny, Charity was uncomfortably aware of the sharp intelligence lurking in his heavily hooded eyes.

"So?" she challenged as her nerves began to tangle.

"So, why, exactly, did you call off your wedding?"

"I realize that I've provided a great deal of gossip since moving here, but no one actually knows *which* of us called it off."

"It wouldn't have been him."

She gave him her coolest look. The one she'd given that horrid reporter just as she'd been preparing to walk down the aisle. "Because?"

"Because any man who'd let you get away would have to not only be an idiot but a eunuch, to boot."

She felt the damning tinge of color rise in her cheeks. Which was ridiculous. Because she *never* blushed. Jake must have put some hot spices in with the crab's butter garlic sauce.

"I suppose I'll take that as a compliment."

"Good. Because that's how I meant it."

Charity wasn't ashamed at what had happened. The entire mess, after all, hadn't been her fault. But she couldn't help being a little embarrassed by the way she'd so misjudged Ethan.

"Did you love him?"

"Who?" She pushed the foam carton of cabbage and shredded carrots toward him.

"Would you care for some more coleslaw?"

"I'm fine, thanks. Good diversionary try, though."

"Why would you even care?"

He shrugged. "Beats me. But I seem to, so why don't you humor me?"

What could it hurt? He exuded too many loner vibes to be the type of guy who'd hang out down at the VFW and gossip about her life. Besides, he was going to be leaving town any day. Whom could he tell?

"I thought I did. At least I tried."

"And now?"

"Nope." She dug a bit of crab out of a leg with a claw. "Not even a little bit."

"But you were going to marry him."

"You realize that if you're going to keep talking about this, there's going to be a quid pro quo. I'm going to get to ask you questions. Which is, as I seem to recall, what people actually do on dates. Share likes. Dislikes. Favorite movies. Books. Sometimes, even deep, dark secrets."

"I don't have any deep dark secrets."

"Liar." She pointed the orange claw at him. "Everyone has secrets."

"Maybe that's why they're called *secrets*. Because people don't share them."

"Yet you keep asking me about something I'm not comfortable with sharing."

"Touché." He polished off the beer he'd brought along with a split of wine for her. "So, here's another one that may be easier. Why did you become a vet? Were you one of those kids who had lots of pets roaming around your house you'd play doctor to?"

"You've met my mother. What do you think?"

"Good point. So I guess you put Band-Aids on your stuffed animals instead of playing Barbie?"

"Actually, you're describing my assistant, Amie. I decided on this career path while going to boarding school in Connecticut. The school required community service, so, on a whim, because I'd never been allowed a pet, I signed up to help one afternoon a week and Saturday mornings at a local animal shelter. I was hooked the first day. Though the number of animals they had to put down every week broke my heart. So, I decided I'd become a vet and open a no-kill shelter."

"Good for you." He pulled another bottle from the cooler. The fact that he'd switched to a nonalcoholic Kaliber might be a clue to one of his secrets. Or perhaps he was just being cautious because he was driving. "It must feel good to set a goal and succeed at it."

"I could say the same thing about you."

"Unless it involves a mission, I'm not much on setting goals."

"Which brings me to the question I've been wanting to ask," Charity said. "What are your plans?"

"Immediate? Or long-term?"

She felt a little prick of annoyance at how he'd dodged what should have been a simple enough question, but hadn't she done exactly the same thing when he'd brought up her wedding? "Immediate."

He shrugged. "With the exception of the save-the-date e-mail I got about Cole's wedding, I've spent the past year not making plans. Just driving around the country, taking photos."

"You've spent an entire year moving from place to place?"

"Yep."

"What about your family?" Okay, so admittedly that was prying.

"I told you, I don't have any."

"None?" Charity might have more stepparents than the average person, but the idea of having no one was unfathomable to her.

"None."

"That's sad."

"That depends on the family. Getting

218

back to your original question, although the Marines have sent me all over the globe, somehow I've missed the Pacific Northwest. It's turning out to be a nice part of the country, so now that I'm here, I may as well stick around and take some more photos."

If she hadn't already come up with a plan for Gabriel St. James, Charity would have been appalled at the little burst of pleasure she felt at finding out that he wasn't on his way out of Shelter Bay.

Despite ignoring her mother's urging to leave her hair loose, she felt the breeze coming off the ocean nevertheless cause some strands to flutter onto her face. When Gabe reached across the table to tuck them behind her ear, his gaze turned intense. Unwavering.

"Getting back to your marriage," he said.

Damn. He was just going to keep it up until she told him something. And it wasn't as if what had happened had been *her* fault. As Sedona kept telling her, her rat of a fiancé should be the one ashamed of himself.

"I was going to marry Ethan," she said. "That's his name. Ethan Douglas. He's an attorney at his father's international commodities-trading company in Chicago. And the definitive word is *was.* We're past tense. Over. Bygones."

"If it was that easy to get past, why did you take a sex moratorium?"

"I'm beginning to suspect the photography was just a cover," she said with an uncharacteristic flare of annoyance. "I'm getting the feeling you were actually an interrogator for military intelligence, because this is starting to feel like the third degree."

She waited for him to apologize. He didn't.

"Plus, although I may have forgotten a lot about dating, I *do* remember that talking about exes doesn't make for the most scintillating dinner conversation. So, since it's a lovely meal at a gorgeous location, I don't want to ruin the evening talking about it.

"All I'm going to say is that I spent my life watching my mother follow her heart instead of her head. With less-than-satisfactory results. So, after I got out of school, which had been all-consuming, and took a job in a large domestic-animal practice, I started thinking it might be nice to have someone to share my life with. But, unlike Mom, I opted to go with my head. Which, unfortunately, didn't work out. So now I'm in a holding pattern."

"Yet you're here. With me."

"Actually, I'll admit to an ulterior motive."

"You wouldn't get any resistance from me if that motive had anything to do with jumping my bones."

"I'm sorry." She gave him her sweetest smile. "I'm afraid not."

"Can't blame a guy for trying." He leaned back. Crossed his arms over that broad chest. If his body language meant anything, she wasn't in for an easy time. "So, what's your motive? Other than trying to convince me to keep the mutt?"

"Oh, that's already settled." She gave a breezy wave of her hand.

"And you would know this how?"

"Sedona, who runs Take the Cake, saw you with the dog on the beach today. And she wasn't the only one. Reports were that the two of you looked as if you've already bonded."

"Secondhand, hearsay reports," he pointed out.

"So they're false?"

"Not exactly. Let's just say that he's starting to grow on me. But" — he held up a hand, forestalling her saying how pleased she was about that — "on the outside chance I actually do decide to keep him, there's going to be a problem."

"What's that?"

"This is a fifty-state project. After I get done in Washington and Alaska, I'm going to finish up in Hawaii."

"Oh." She knew, of course, where he was going with that. Wasn't that why she'd ended up with the Persian she was trying to talk Sedona into adopting? "Well. It wouldn't be for that long, right?"

"Shouldn't be."

"Then I might be able to help out. Meanwhile, why don't we agree to jump off that bridge when we come to it?"

"Works for me. And your motive for eating crab on the beach with me is?"

"There's this camp."

"Camp." His expression was even less encouraging than his folded arms. However, having come up with the idea, which was even more perfect the more she'd thought about it, Charity doggedly forged on.

"A summer camp. At Rainbow Lake, just a couple miles out of town."

"I've been there. When I first arrived. But I didn't see any campers. Just tourists. Mostly families."

"That's because the camp doesn't officially start until tomorrow."

"It's a nice place. But I pretty much gave up sleeping on the ground when I left the Marines."

"The campers stay in one side of nice new duplex cabins," she said. "Most of the counselors bunk on the other side, though others, who are assigned to teach and run activities, have rooms with staff in the lodge. Volunteers usually drive in from town, except for one night when everyone has to get up really early for a canoe trip to the island to have a breakfast cookout, which is a lot of fun. There's this couple — Fred and Ethel Dalton —"

He arched the brow that had been sliced by that scar. "You're kidding, right?"

"No. Those are actually their real names. Anyway, they won the lottery a few years ago, quit their jobs, bought the lodge, and built the cabins. Since they'd also spent years as foster parents, they decided to establish a camp for foster siblings. Every summer, the kids get to spend two weeks with each other. What most people don't realize is that three out of every four foster siblings end up being separated."

Was it just her imagination? Or did the expression on his harshly hewn face soften, just a bit? "That's a rotten deal."

"Isn't it? Camp Rainbow is different from your typical summer camp. Along with the usual swimming, canoeing, and making s'mores, there are lots of activities to teach the kids problem solving, goal setting, effective communication, and cooperation."

"All disguised as fun."

"Exactly." She was pleased that he'd caught on so soon. It made her mission ever so much easier. "Campers bake bread, plant trees, even build shelters or lead an orientation expedition. The goal is to teach them elemental survival skills and wilderness training to build inner and outer strength."

"Now it's starting to sound a lot like boot camp."

She laughed at that comparison. And liked that he'd actually made a joke. Was he lightening up?

"Ethel's a child psychologist, or was until she retired, and Fred spent twenty-five years teaching geography and ecology at Coastal Community College. They're both active on environmental issues, so they're wonderful at helping the children experience a sense of connection to the earth, and everyone's importance in the greater scheme of things."

"Good for them."

"I volunteered last summer, and signed up again this year. I take shelter dogs out there, and the kids take care of them. It's good for the dogs because they get a ridiculous amount of love and attention. But it's good for the kids, too. Not only does it teach them responsibility — the dogs return all that attention with unconditional love. Something not many of them have known."

"I suppose they wouldn't have ended up in the foster system if they had."

Oh, yes. The man was definitely lightening up. His expression, and his entire demeanor, which had been guarded, had softened. Interesting that although he probably wouldn't readily admit it, he was a sucker for kids and animals. Which gave them something in common.

"So, I guess you want to take the mutt out to the camp for the kids to play with?" he asked.

"Oh, no! Well, I mean, you could always bring him along, but —"

"Wait. Just. A. Damn. Minute." So much for light and empathy. The rock-hard Marine who'd undoubtedly faced down death countless times was back. In spades. "Why would *I* be going out there?"

She leaned forward across the table to stress her point. "These kids have already had so much taken away from them. The one thing no one can take away is the special memories of their time together at camp. So, I was thinking, what better way to preserve memories than having photos of the experience?"

225

"Look, I can see that it's for a good cause. But just because I took some wedding photos for a friend doesn't mean I've sunk to shooting camper group shots that anyone, probably even Fred or Ethel, could handle."

"Oh, I'm not asking for that," she said quickly. Too quickly, Charity realized as that dark brow arched again. "Let me backtrack."

"That might be helpful. But the answer is still no."

"Would you just wait until you hear me out before you go back into ultimate Lone Ranger mode? Which, by the way, isn't all that appealing."

With a weary sigh, he waved her on.

"We don't need a professional photographer for the group shots. We all bring cameras, and although we're amateurs, we end up with photos for the kids to take home with them. So they can remember the good times."

"Makes sense. But I still don't see why you'd need me."

"Because it occurred to me that the photos would be even more meaningful if the kids were to take the pictures themselves."

"Again, that's not a bad idea. How many kids are you talking about?"

"About seventy-five, give or take a few. The number varies every year."

"That's a lot of cameras you're talking about."

She shrugged. "They're less expensive the more you buy. And I can afford it. My grandfather left me a bit of an inheritance."

Her mother's father had died on a solo around-the-world sailing trip when Amanda had been only twelve years old, but being both a wealthy and prudent man, he'd thought ahead to set up trust funds for any possible grandchildren. Which would be her. Charity had often thought that her mother's seemingly constant search for a man's love was, in large part, due to having lost her father at such a tender age.

Given that her grandmother had been widowed young, and her own mother's history, Charity had also wondered, on occasion, if the women in her family were marriage cursed.

"Still, that's generous of you."

"They're great kids. Though, I have to admit, the last day, as they all climb onto their separate buses, could break even the Grinch's heart."

She sighed. Then shook off that sad memory and concentrated on the positive.

"So, anyway, along with having the kids

work with the animals, we have different workshops. Last year Sedona taught a baking class. And Sax's grandmother taught the girls how to knit, and her husband, Bernard, taught chess and knot tying.

"An annual event is the dawn canoe trip I mentioned out to the island in the middle of the lake, where Fred shows all the kids how to cook their entire breakfast in a coffee can over a fire. Then, of course, there's skit night, and —"

"I've got the picture."

"You haven't even heard my plan."

"I don't need to. You've got a bunch of foster kids who spend most of the year away from their brothers and sisters. You're buying cameras so they can create scrapbook memories."

"Scrapbooks are on the agenda. There's a store in town, Memories on Main, whose owner's agreed to donate a bunch of paper, glue sticks, and other supplies."

Damn. As his eyes shuttered, Charity feared she was losing him.

Determined, she forged on. "But a lot of people are intimidated by even point-and-shoot cameras, which is why I thought, if you could perhaps just agree to donate a few hours teaching some basic techniques —"

"I'll think about it."

"You will?" She'd been so expecting yet another immediate refusal, her mind had been spinning forward, trying to think of the arguments she might use to persuade him. Having him suddenly agree to at least consider her idea threw her off track.

"Like I said, I'm not on any real schedule. The woman at the place I'm camped seems to like me —"

"Now, there's a surprise," Charity muttered, then, when she realized she'd spoken that thought out loud, found herself desperately wishing for the ground to open up beneath the table. There were, after all, the occasional earthquakes in this part of the country. Or even better, maybe they'd be hit by a tsunami.

He flashed her a wicked smile that had her thinking of the pirates that were rumored to have occasionally sailed off this coast. "She's ninety if she's a day." He paused a heartbeat. "Just in case you were jealous."

"I'm not. I was merely surprised, given that the Marine warrior glower you've perfected isn't exactly charming."

"Your mother seemed to like me okay."

"That's not exactly a ringing endorsement, since my mother isn't known for stellar judgment when it comes to men. And we're getting off track," she complained. "We were discussing the camp."

"And I said I'd think about it. Meanwhile, what would you say to packing up this stuff and walking off some of the dinner while I do?"

One of the few traits Charity shared with her mother was optimism that no matter how dark things could get, there was always a shiny lining lurking somewhere behind the storm clouds. All she needed was a bit more time. . . .

"Sounds like a plan."

24

Even as the setting sun cast a golden border of light around the clouds, a storm was gathering darkly on the horizon. Misty fog began to curl around their feet as they walked along the water's edge. Sandpipers skittered in and out of the frothy sea-foam; gulls whirled; the scents of salt and seaweed rode on the ocean breeze. In the distance, nearly swallowed up by the gray fog, the Shelter Bay lighthouse flashed its bright yellow warning.

There was not another person to be seen for miles. They could have been the only two people in the world.

Although the nightmares he'd suffered had mostly subsided once he'd gotten back to work, for the first time in as long as he could remember, Gabe felt both his mind and body begin to relax.

"This is nice," she said, unknowingly repeating his thoughts as they walked along damp sand strewn with rounded stones, bits of shiny quartz, seashells, and kelp.

"You're not going to get any argument from me."

A drizzling moisture — more than mist, not quite rain, and almost invisible to the eye — began to fall. After all the years living with the constant sand and dust in Iraq and Afghanistan that would embed itself into tents, trucks, and every pore in his body, the light rain felt clean, fresh, and cool.

"Want to go back?" He wasn't all that eager to, but felt obliged to ask.

"Why?"

"It's raining."

She laughed and lifted her face to the sky. "You're in Oregon. This is what natives call liquid sunshine. If you want to see *real* rain, you'll have to stick around a few months."

Her laugh affected him like sunshine. Linking their fingers together, he balanced her as she stepped over some slick, seaweed-draped rocks.

"My former fiancé comes from an old, established Chicago family," she said out of the blue. "Not only does it predate the Great Fire, Ethan can trace his family line all the way back to Stephen Douglas."

"Of the Lincoln-Douglas debates?"

"That would the be one."

"Guess they were also loaded?"

"That's putting it mildly. Their main business is international commodities trading, but they've got their fingers into just about any financial pie you can name. Banking, real estate, insurance. The wedding was at the chichi Oakbridge Polo Club. Where the Douglases have been members for all eighty years of its existence."

"I can't trace my family tree back eighty years." He'd never wanted to, either.

"Join the club." She bent over, picked up a variegated stone, and tossed it into the surf. Gabe suspected she was gathering her thoughts, trying, yet again, to decide how much to share.

"It wasn't that I didn't grow up without money," she continued. "My mother always said you can fall in love with a rich man as well as a poor one, and since you may have noticed that if you Google *high maintenance,* you'd get about a gazillion hits with her photo, their wealth didn't intimidate me. Nor did the fact that Ethan's father and uncles sat on boards of so many corporations. Thanks to Mom's liking the high life, I know how to play country-club games."

"Even though you don't like them."

"Hate them," she admitted. She looked

up at him. He could see the reflection of himself trapped in her rain-forest green eyes. "Be honest. Can you see me fitting in with the polo set?"

"Honestly?"

"I wouldn't have asked if I wanted you to lie."

"Okay, the truth is, I can see you fitting into whatever life you chose. Or whatever situation you landed in."

"Well." She seemed a bit surprised by that. And more than a little pleased. "Thank you."

"Like I said, it's the truth. But since you had family money, it couldn't have been that much of a stretch for you." Not enough of one to make her former fiancé's wealth an issue.

"Thanks to some wise investments my grandfather made, I've always been comfortable. But unlike my mother, I've never been into social cliques, or status, or any of that stuff. I hate the game playing, and while that's very nice of you to say you can imagine me fitting in anywhere, I'm honestly not very good at it. As Mrs. Douglas was always pointing out."

"Mrs. Douglas sounds like she was as much of an idiot as her son."

"Ethan graduated summa cum laude from

Princeton. Along with an MBA from Wharton business school and a Harvard law degree. That's what he does, mostly. Business law for the family firm."

"Good for Ethan." But the guy was still obviously an idiot for letting this woman get away.

"So, Mrs. Douglas — and no, I was never invited to call her by her first name, in case you were wondering — insisted I take etiquette training so I'd know which of about a gazillion forks to use for formal occasions. Did you know that the oyster fork is the only fork ever to be placed on the right side of a plate?"

"I didn't even know there was such a thing as an oyster fork."

"Neither did I. It does, however, go to the right of the spoons."

"I'll keep that in mind in case I ever encounter one at the Crab Shack."

"Good idea. Needless to say, I pretty much flunked the part of the test that covered the nuances of formalized behavior people like the Douglases live by."

"So why did you get engaged to the guy?"

"Believe me, I've spent a lot of time asking myself the same question. And it's complicated to explain, but looking back on it, I think one of the main reasons I accepted Ethan's proposal was that while he could admittedly be stuffy, I found the rock-solid stability of his family appealing."

"You wanted to set down roots." Another reason he should just stay the hell away from her.

Too late.

"Exactly."

"Which you've managed to do for yourself here in Shelter Bay. So it looks as if you didn't need your fiancé for that."

"True." She paused, as if trying to decide whether to tell him the entire story of how she'd become a runaway bride and ended up here on the edge of the continent, in Shelter Bay, Oregon.

He waited. If there was one thing both the Marines and photography had taught him, it was patience.

Finally, she shook her head. "As I said earlier, it's too lovely an evening to ruin it by talking about this," she said. When she shrugged, the blouse slipped off her shoulder, revealing enticingly smooth skin. "I've no idea why I brought the subject up again."

"Maybe because it still bugs you."

"I told you, I don't have any feelings for Ethan. What bugs me is making such a mistake."

"We all make mistakes. At least yours

wasn't fatal."

"Good point."

The tide was beginning to come in. Foamy waves lapped closer and closer toward the towering cliff. Out at sea, the setting sun created a gilded path that looked as if you could walk right out over the curve of the earth.

Turning back to avoid running out of room, they dodged around the blackened remains of a beach bonfire.

They were walking side by side in companionable silence when Gabe decided that maybe he wasn't in such a hurry to move on after all. It wasn't as if he had a hard deadline. He'd made that clear when he'd agreed to sign on to the project.

"I'll do it."

"What?" He'd surprised her again. When she slipped climbing over a wet, mossy driftwood log, he reacted instinctively, catching her as she nearly fell into his arms.

Oh, damn. As his hands bracketed her hips, Gabe told himself that he was only steadying her until she caught her balance again.

"I said I'll do it. The camp thing."

Her smile was blinding, like a sunset breaking through the quilted gray sky. "Oh, thank you! I promise you won't regret it."

Part of him, the part that had been determined to get out of Dodge before he found himself getting involved with this woman, already did.

"If you plan to print out those photos, you're going to need printers."

"I have two at my office. Since I'm having another vet from Depoe Bay fill in for me during the afternoons when I'm at the camp, I could take one of them. And I can probably round up more if I ask around."

"Don't bother. I've two large-format ones I'll bring with me."

"That's very thoughtful."

He shrugged. "I wasn't dumped on the system like the kids you get at your camp. My parents didn't die until my freshman year of college. But they weren't the easiest people to live with, so I pretty much ended up raising myself. I probably could've ended up going down a wrong and very rocky road if someone hadn't stuck a camera in my hand when I was fifteen. So I'm not going to turn down a chance to pay it forward."

"Okay. Despite the fact that you weren't exactly George Clooney suave when we first met at the wedding, I'm starting to like you, Gabriel St. James."

"Well, that's handy. Since I already like you back." Unable to resist, he skimmed his fingertips down her cheek.

Insane, the little voice of conscience, of sanity, shouted out from the far reaches of his mind. *It'd be sheer lunacy to get involved with this woman.*

True. But as noisy gulls wheeled overhead and the sun sank silently into the water, Gabe ignored it, lowered his head, and touched his mouth to hers. And in that instant knew, in what small part of his brain was still operating, that he was sunk.

She was so incredibly soft. As soft as the mist surrounding them. And he was so frigging, painfully hard.

Even as he knew the smart thing, the logical thing, the *safe* thing, to do would be to pull away, he drew her even closer.

Her breath caught. Then she opened her lips, inviting him to deepen the kiss. Which he did.

Her cool lips warmed. Her body, which had momentarily tensed when he'd captured her mouth, slowly relaxed.

Heat, already sparked, crackled, zigzagging back and forth between them like summer lightning.

He wanted her. Naked. Beneath him. Surrounding him.

The mist had beaded up on that honey-hued shoulder, creating a wild need to bite it. He doubted she'd object, because unless every instinct Gabe possessed had suddenly gone on the blink, which wouldn't be all that surprising since the intensity appeared to have short-circuited his brain, she wanted him, too.

As IEDs exploded inside him, Gabe knew that with the slightest effort — a stroke of the hand here, a touch of the lips where that pulse was beating beneath her jaw, some hot words whispered into her ear — he could be back at the motor home tangling the sheets with the lovely and luscious Dr. Charity Tiernan.

Just as he knew he shouldn't do it.

He slowly, reluctantly lifted his head.

She blinked. Slowly. Once. Then again. Desire swirled like a tempest in her eyes.

Hell. Talk about the road to hell being paved with the best intentions. . . .

He pressed his hand against the small of her back, fitting her even more solidly against his aching erection. "Again."

"Again," she agreed in a low, throaty voice that had Gabe understanding why ancient sailors had believed in mermaids. And why they'd allowed themselves to be lured into treacherous, storm-tossed waters.

This time his mouth came down hard. And ruthless.

There was a rushing, like the sea, in his ears. As she rose up on her toes, straining against him, he was hit by a wave of emotion that battered against the rigid self-control he'd begun acquiring early in life to escape repeating his father's mistakes. To keep his purpose.

Sweet.

Dr. Charity Tiernan was impossibly sweet. Kissing her was like a cool drink of water, or an icy beer after days spent crawling across scorching desert sands.

With heat curling deep in his belly, he slipped his hand beneath her blouse and felt her tremble, which sent a sense of power streaking through him. Although he didn't know all that much about her, Gabe suspected that the intelligent, confident veterinarian was not a woman to tremble for just any man. Yet she was trembling for him.

Encouraged, and unable to resist, he shaped her breast with his palm and felt the sigh beneath his mouth.

Damn. It would have been easier if she'd resisted. Or even held back, just a little. But instead, she'd thrown herself into the kiss, giving without hesitation.

Although he may have remained resolutely celibate during his travels across America, Gabe had not forgotten how it felt to have his body burn in response to a woman. He was accustomed to a woman's touch making his blood hot and he knew the ability of a woman's mouth to fog his mind.

But this was different.

Never had he experienced such hunger from a mere kiss. It battered at him with an intensity that bordered terrifyingly on need.

Which was why, with a very real regret, and ignoring her faint murmured protest, he lifted his head and backed away.

Silence descended.

"Well." She dropped her hands and took a deep breath that only drew his attention to those silky breasts he was still aching to lick. "That was . . . interesting."

"If *interesting* is as high as you're going to score it, I must have been doing it wrong."

"No." Another breath. "Actually, it was quite nice." She surprised him by smiling at that at the same time she held up her hand. "Sorry. Delete *nice.* But I'm certainly not going to complain."

"My ego thanks you."

"I do have one question, which I usually wouldn't ask at this point, but since it appears we're going to be spending the next two weeks together . . ."

Her voice trailed off as she seemed to be thinking of how to phrase the question.

"Shoot."

"Where exactly do we go from here?"

Talk about getting to the point. Although it would've been easier to lie, Gabe told the absolute truth. "I have no idea." Then, because it was also fact, he said, "I know I want you. A lot." And wasn't that an understatement? He was perilously close to begging.

She tilted her head. If she was still even the slightest bit shaken by the kiss that had rocked his world, she didn't show it. "You don't sound very happy about that."

"I'm not. I've always prided myself on my self-control."

Another smile. That touched her eyes and, God help him, had him on the edge of groveling. "Me, too. Which is why I suspect I pretty much know what you're feeling."

"I can't give you what you're looking for." He thought, since something was obviously happening between them, he ought to make that clear from the beginning.

"Oh?" As her warm gaze instantly frosted, he was surprised it hadn't turned the drizzle to sleet. She folded her arms. "And what would you think that might be?"

Intrigued by the way what he'd originally thought was innate and unrelenting sunshine could turn icy, Gabe shrugged.

"Pretty much what most women want. A house, white picket fence, two-point-five kids, a guy who comes home at six Monday through Friday, and coaches the kids' soccer games on Saturday."

Able to view himself with the same brutal lens he turned on the subjects of his photos, Gabe knew that he was too emotionally bankrupt to give her any of those things.

"Wow. Are all Marines such a throwback to the cavemen, or are you merely an exception?"

The ice in her eyes had turned, in a blink of one of those siren eyes, to humor. Instead of being annoyed at his purposefully exaggerated chauvinism, she appeared to be laughing at him. The same way she'd been when he'd first shown up at her door.

The weird thing was it only made her more appealing. Which could mean that it had definitely been too long since he'd gotten laid.

"Are you saying you don't want a family?"

"No. What I'm saying is that while I may not want to follow in my mother's Louboutins, my vision of what a family entails has actually graduated beyond *Father Knows Best.* And even if I had a sudden urge to morph into a Stepford Wife, which, for the record, I don't, just because I happen to

244

lock lips with someone doesn't necessarily mean that I'm looking for it to lead to a diamond ring and a walk down the aisle."

"What happened to that moratorium?"

"The moratorium was on *sex*. What you and I just shared was merely a kiss."

His skepticism must have shown on his face because she added, "Okay, it was a rock-the-world kiss that may have landed on my top ten kisses of all time if it'd continued for another few seconds. But surely you don't marry every woman you kiss?"

"Of course not."

"How about sex?"

"I'm a guy. Which means, in principle, I'm for it."

"I meant, do you have sex with every woman you kiss?"

He threw the question back at her. "Talk about the third degree. What do you think?"

"A lot of women go for men in uniforms."

And didn't he know that all too well? "And you don't?"

"We're talking about *you*."

Which was exactly what he was trying *not* to do. "No. I'm not saying I have sex with every damn woman I kiss." Frustrated, he rubbed the bridge of his nose. If he'd screwed up a mission as badly as this, he wouldn't have made it home to even be having this discussion. "I'm just trying to do the right thing here and warn you that this — whatever the hell it is — can't go anywhere."

"What makes you think I want it to? Am I attracted to you? Sure." She shrugged. "That should be obvious even to someone as clueless about women as you appear to be. But just because we admittedly seem to have chemistry doesn't mean that I'm suddenly smelling orange blossoms and looking for ever-afters. Or, for that matter, even looking to sleep with you, though I won't deny that there was a moment there when I was tempted. So what's the problem?"

The damn problem, which he wasn't willing to share with her, was that the sexy veterinarian with the skin of silk terrified him.

"Are you always this honest?"

"I'm afraid so," she admitted. "I deplore lies. And having watched too many of my mother's marriages fail due to lack of communication, I'm also a firm believer in getting things out into the open.

"Look," she suggested, placing a hand on his arm when he didn't immediately respond. "We're going to be spending a lot of time together." She paused. "Unless you've changed your mind about helping out at the camp?"

"No. Whatever else you might be thinking, I'm not the kind of guy to welsh on an agreement. The Marine code — honor, courage, commitment — isn't just words. It is, as we say in the corps, what you are in the dark. If I give my word, I damn well keep it."

She was studying him again. In that searching way of hers. Gabe felt her on the verge of saying something when an incoming wave suddenly rushed in, coming close to drenching them.

"I'm glad to hear that," she said. The moment had passed and she was back to the friendly, focused vet who'd opened the door to her pretty sunshine yellow house and tilted his world on its axis.

"We'd better be getting back before we end up stranded. Do you want to meet out there at the camp?" she asked conversationally as they headed back down the damp sand. "Or would you rather just stop by the house and we can drive out together? That way I can introduce you around.

"The first half day is mostly a getting-acquainted, laid-back type of deal, so I won't be taking the dogs out until we set up teams and figure out how many we need.

You can bring yours over to the clinic. We have a doggy day care and he'd probably love playing with others."

"Aren't you afraid I'll dump him on you and leave town?"

"Nope."

"You're that sure of yourself?"

"No." Her laughing gaze turned serious again for a moment. "I'm that sure of you."

Gabe had always been able to compartmentalize. Not only had it been imperative as a Marine on a mission; he'd developed the talent early, living with his parents. But the way she'd managed to continually switch gears not only impressed him; it also made him want to get to know her better. To start peeling away those layers he was discovering.

Of course, the safest and easiest thing would be to just keep as much distance from the woman as possible. But just as he'd never been a fan of *safe,* a lifetime of experience had taught Gabe not to trust easy.

"What time do you want me to show up?"

"The buses never arrive until noon. So why don't we make it around one? That way I can make sure everything's set at the clinic before we take off."

"Works for me."

"Super."

Her smile lit up the foggy dusk. Then she laced her fingers with his in a casual, uncalculated gesture as they continued back toward where he'd left the Jeep.

A mistake, he warned himself yet again. As he breathed in the seductive scent of flowers wafting on the sea air, Gabe vowed to remember that.

25

It would have been so easy, Charity thought as they drove toward Shelter Bay while a silvery rain beaded the windshield. He wanted her. She wanted him. They were both adults, after all. And even if she was looking for a happily ever after, which truthfully she was, *someday,* Gabriel St. James would be the last person she'd consider.

How far, she wondered, would things have gone if he hadn't had that surprising attack of conscience? It would have been so easy just to give in to instinct and take. And be taken.

But then what?

There were more important issues at stake than just scratching a sexual itch. She wasn't like her mother, following her heart, not even seeming to notice the destruction she was leaving behind in her wake. It had been Lucas, the stepbrother whose wedding gift had resulted in her coming to Shelter

Bay, who'd spelled things out for her when the marriage between his father and her mother had disintegrated just weeks after that Shelter Bay summer vacation.

She'd been nine. He'd been eleven, which, looking back on it, she realized wasn't nearly as adult as she'd viewed him at the time. He'd come into her bedroom, where she'd been sobbing her shattered heart out into her pillow, and told her that from what she'd told him about her mother's marital record, and from what he'd witnessed for himself, Charity was never going to have anything resembling a normal family life.

So she had two choices. She could spend the rest of her life eating worms and throwing herself pity parties, or she could suck it up and realize that the only person you could ever really depend on to make yourself happy, or fulfilled, was yourself.

Which was, he'd shared with her, something he'd learned to do when his little sister had died after a long battle with leukemia when he was in the third grade. The pain the family had suffered during those three years she'd been ill had mortally wounded his own parents' marriage. His mother had returned to her hometown in Colorado, leaving him with his father. Although he visited her during alternate Christmases and three weeks every summer, he'd never found any way to lighten the sorrow that seemed to have embedded itself into Janice Chaffee's every pore.

Looking back on it now, Charity realized how mature Lucas had been for his age. He'd been tall, his eyes the color of melted chocolate, his brown hair streaked by the summer sun. At the time he'd been the cutest boy she'd ever met, and although she would never have admitted it, she, along with every other girl in Shelter Bay, had a bit of a crush on him.

He'd also been the most caring, compassionate, and intelligent individual she'd ever met. Which was why, after he'd dried her eyes and shared a Milky Way bar with her, she'd decided to try to follow his advice.

Which she had over the years with varying success.

As much as she'd desperately hoped for a "normal" life, whatever that was, her parents' failed relationships, along with her own, lay behind her like flotsam littering the beach after a storm. Sometimes Charity wondered if she even knew *how* to be part of a couple. If she was even capable of figuring out what it took to create a family. After all, it wasn't like earning her DVM. For that, there'd been courses to study, exams to take, and grades that pointed toward potential success. Given the divorce rate, half the people who walked down the aisle every year could probably use some marriage training.

Perhaps she was one of those women destined to spend her life alone. With only dogs and cats for companions.

And wow, wasn't that a fun thought?

She'd assured herself that her sexual moratorium had been the logical thing to do. Didn't all the relationship columns and self-help books warn against rebound romances? Taking some time off, especially when she'd had so many things on her plate, made perfect sense.

She had, over the months, convinced herself of that.

But then Gabriel St. James had kissed her and she'd felt ice she hadn't even realized she'd built up around her heart cracking.

Instead of welcoming the sudden thaw, Charity was unnerved by it. Because — and, yes, it was a cliché of romantic movies and novels — she'd honestly never felt that way before.

Her mother had always been a drama queen, given to wide mood swings, her emotional pendulum never seeming to stay at calm center.

Charity, on the other had, had always been focused. Deliberate. Even when she'd accepted Ethan's proposal, and again when she'd called off the wedding, she liked to think she'd been behaving rationally. Reasonably.

There was nothing reasonable about the storm of emotions brought about by that shared kiss. She'd felt as if she were standing atop the edge of the cliff. One more step and she could have been flying.

Of course, you could just as easily fall crashing back to earth, she reminded herself.

The fog blowing in from the sea had thickened to a swirling white blanket that wrapped around the car windows. A stand of Douglas fir trees screened both sides of the winding roadway, making it seem as if they were driving through a narrow green alley.

"I was married," Gabriel said as they waited for the bridge, which had lifted for a ship to pass out to sea, to lower.

He had dropped that bombshell so unexpectedly, and so quietly, deep in introspection as she'd been, Charity wasn't certain she'd heard him correctly.

"Excuse me?"

"I was married."

"Oh." And wasn't that a scintillatingly

254

brilliant response? She tried again. "Are you now?"

"What?"

Oops. Apparently that wasn't any better, since he shot her a look that could blister the paint off a Humvee. The fact that he didn't answer immediately was another clue — along with the back-and-forth motion of his jaw — that he wasn't exactly pleased by her follow-up question.

She cleared her throat and tried not to feel intimidated. Which admittedly she was. Just a bit. While he might make his living taking photos, Gabriel St. James was a warrior. All the way to the bone.

"I asked —"

"I got that." His words were clipped, his eyes hard. "What I want to know is how you could possibly believe I'd even come on to you — kiss you, *touch* you, dammit — if I had a wife sitting at home somewhere."

"Some men might not find that an impediment."

She could have sworn she saw sparks shooting from those gunmetal gray eyes. "I'm not *some* men. Maybe you weren't listening when I mentioned that little detail about the Marine code about being who you are in the dark."

And wasn't that part of her problem?

255

Charity had been thinking — and dreaming — about what this particular Marine might be like in the dark since they'd first met.

"It's a great motto. But —"

"I said I *was* married," he cut her off again. "Past tense."

"I'm sorry."

She was sorry about his marriage failing, since she knew even the most cordial break-ups could be painful. But she was not sorry they were having this discussion, because it allowed her to peel back yet one more layer in the mystery that was Gabriel St. James.

"So was I."

"Since you brought it up, am I allowed to ask what happened?" *Hello, pot. This is kettle.* Although she hadn't offered up full disclosure herself, Charity was curious.

"It's not that unusual a story. I married a woman who fell for the snazzy uniform and the idea of a Marine husband. What she hadn't bargained for was being left alone for months at a time while that husband was deployed in war zones." His voice echoed, deep and rich in the intimacy created by the fog. "So she found someone else to keep her company."

"I'm sorry," she said again.

Didn't she know how that felt? Not that infidelity was why she'd broken off her

256

engagement. She also noticed that Gabriel had left out the reason he'd gotten married. He shrugged. "It worked out in the end. She's happy, living in San Diego, married to some guy who sells cars. BMWs. They have two kids — neither of which are mine in case you're wondering — and another one on the way."

Amazingly, he didn't seem to hold any grudges. Then again, perhaps he hadn't really cared. Maybe, a little voice in the back of her mind warned, he wasn't the type of man to care about any woman. Maybe he didn't have any family because he truly meant exactly what he'd said about not wanting one. Which, again, made him totally the wrong man for her.

"Did you love her?" She pressed a hand against her jittery stomach and realized she was holding her breath waiting for an answer.

"No."

Okay, that was a surprise. She'd honestly expected him to at least claim to have *thought* he'd loved the former Mrs. St. James. Or tried. The way she'd tried to love Ethan. It appeared he wasn't exaggerating about that Marine honor-code thing, which apparently also included a tenet about not lying.

"I guess, looking back, I just wanted to *be* married. To have someone waiting for me when I came back from deployment. Someone who cared whether I lived or died."

"You wanted a home."

This time the glance he slanted her way held more question than annoyance. She watched as he processed her comment.

"Yeah," he said finally. "I guess that might've been it." The bridge lowered.

"But you changed your mind."

Another pause. "I suppose I did." He glanced over at her again as they crossed over the harbor into town. "Believe me, I'm not carrying any baggage from the breakup. Things happen. There's an old saying that if the Marines wanted a guy to have a wife, they'd issue him one. It's probably close to the mark, since I sure as hell wasn't the only person in our unit to get a Dear John e-mail.

"I've moved on. The only reason I even brought the subject up is what you said about that quid pro quo deal. I'll admit I was kind of heavy-handed, the way I pushed you about your fiancé, so I figured I ought to be up-front with you."

"I appreciate that." Charity also wondered how much of the surprising revelation about his failed marriage had been his way of warning her, yet again, that he wasn't a guy looking for any forever-afters.

He nodded brusquely and turned his attention back to driving as the Jeep bumped over the railroad tracks, past the Douchetts' bait shop, then turned onto Harborview Drive.

Neither of them spoke the rest of the way back to the house.

26

"I hope you know what you're doing," Amanda said as Charity stood in the window watching Gabe and the still-unnamed Shih Tzu drive away.

The dog, whose ecstatic bark had risked shattering every piece of glass in the house, had literally leaped into its rescuer's arms the minute they'd walked in the door. Although he'd held on to keep it from bouncing off him, Charity would know Gabriel was really hooked when she heard him call the poor thing something other than *mutt* or *foo-foo dust mop*.

"About what?"

"About that Marine."

"Former Marine."

"I'm told there's no such thing." She came over and stood next to Charity, watching as the Jeep drove away. "He's a rolling stone, you know."

"I sort of figured that out from the fact

that his house has wheels." The red tail-lights, blurred by the rain, disappeared around the corner and back out of town. He'd told her the campground where he was staying was located on the ocean side of Shelter Bay. "But he's going to stay in town for the couple weeks to help out with the camp."

"Really?" Amanda glanced over at Charity, her eyes gleaming with feminine speculation. "He doesn't exactly seem like the camp-counselor type. I suspect his reason to stay in this admittedly charming little burg has a lot more to do with you than a bunch of foster kids."

The pitiful thing was, Charity hoped her mother was right for once about a man's intentions.

"He alluded to some not-all-that-pleasant family stuff growing up. I think he may identify with the kids."

"He's also attracted to you."

Amanda might be clueless when it came to marriage. But surely she must have picked up a lot of knowledge about male behavior over the course of all her marriages?

"He seems to be."

"And it's mutual."

"Yes." She wasn't about to try to deny it.

"And you don't exactly sound thrilled at that idea."

"I worry about you. That you'll have your heart broken."

The weird thing was that, despite her unconventional upbringing, despite her mother being a major diva, Charity knew that her mother truly did worry about her. She'd always been more like a girlfriend than a parent. There'd even been more than one occasion when Charity felt more like a big sister than a daughter. But the one thing she'd always known was that her mother loved her.

"I know what I'm doing." Besides, although she might treat animals, she'd taken enough anatomy to know that human hearts couldn't actually break from a failed love affair.

"Where have I heard that before?" Her mother tapped a scarlet nail against her cover-model perfect teeth. "Oh, I know. It's what I always tell you whenever I get engaged."

Charity laughed. "You know," she said, putting her arm around her mother's waist, "growing up, there were so many times I wished I had a normal family."

"There were many times growing up I wished I could give you a normal family."

Amanda sighed. "And I'm not dodging responsibility here, but I think it's also partly why I kept getting married. Instead of merely hooking up like people seem to do these days. You weren't the only one who wanted a normal family. Whatever *normal* is," she tacked on. "Do you believe that's even possible?"

Charity thought about the people she knew. From the stories Sofia told, while her marriage had been more adventurous than some, as she and her botanist husband had traveled the world searching for herbs and plants, their marriage had remained rock solid to the end.

Fred and Ethel were still obviously in love, as were Adèle and Bernard Douchett. And the sizzle between Sax Douchett's parents had been all too obvious at Cole's wedding.

"I think it is," she decided. At least she hoped so. "It's probably not easy. And I imagine you have to work at it." Surely the loss of a daughter, along with her husband's cancer, must have challenged Sofia's marriage. And she suspected Adèle's injury-caused dementia, which she'd learned about while getting her hair trimmed at Cut Loose, wasn't easy on either her or Bernard. "But yes, I believe it's possible."

"Which is why you're still yearning for an

idyllic all-American family of your own."

"*Yearn* may be putting it a bit too strongly, since I'm honestly happy where I am in my life right now. But yes." Charity couldn't deny it. "I know it sounds hopelessly outdated. And not the least bit feminist." She sighed. "But I do. Eventually. When the time's right."

"Well, then." Her mother leaned her head against Charity's shoulder. "I want it for you, too."

They stood there in companionable silence, looking out through the rain-streaked window as the Shelter Bay lighthouse atop the cliff on the other side of the bridge flashed its bright yellow warning.

27

It was raining as the buses began rolling into the Rainbow Lake Lodge parking lot. Having learned early on to keep his emotions to himself, Johnny put on his most sullen face and wrapped himself in the cloak of isolation that had protected him like a force field during all his years in the system. No one looking at him would guess how hard he was telling himself not to cry when Angel got off one of those buses.

She was coming in from Bend, which, being on the other side of the Cascade Mountains, made it as about as remote as if she'd been sent to the moon. He'd been promised they'd have a chance to meet so they could say their good-byes before she left Salem, where they'd both been living at the time, though in different homes. But the caseworker had lied — surprise, surprise — or just been incompetent, which was just as likely, and his sister had been driven out of the city in the middle of the night.

Fortunately, he knew a girl who worked an hour every afternoon in Angel's elementary school office, filing papers for business-class credit. She also, for some reason he'd never figured out, actually liked him, because it hadn't taken much — just a few desperate kisses beneath the bleachers and a promise of more to come — to get the girl to look up Angel's school transfer sheet, which had revealed her new address.

That had been the first and only time Johnny had run away. He'd wanted to lots of times, but no way was he going to desert his baby sister. Bad enough that, like him, she'd never known a father. But she'd also been a lot younger when their mother had been taken away, so she didn't have the survival skills he'd taught himself. Johnny was the only family Angel knew, which was why he'd promised himself that the minute he turned eighteen and got out of the system, he was going to get her back so they could be together all the time. Instead of the few-times-a-year picnics held so prospective parents could check the kids out to see whether there were any they might want to adopt.

As soon as he'd gotten off the Greyhound bus in Bend, he'd found himself facing a sheriff's deputy and a really unhappy case-worker. But showing she had some heart, she did let him visit his sister before she took him back to Salem. Not at the place where his sister was staying, but at a pancake house, where Angel had a strawberry waffle piled high with berries and whipped cream, while he ordered his usual favorite — blueberry pancakes — which tasted like cardboard. Then again, he figured nothing would've tasted good, the way he was feeling.

Thirty minutes later, after ignoring the sharp warning look from the caseworker, Johnny promised Angel he'd visit her again. Then he was sitting in the passenger seat of the official state car, headed back over the Cascades.

That had been nine long months ago. As he stood beneath the drizzling sky, Johnny zeroed in on every kid getting off each bus, watching for Angel's blond hair, which was as soft and pale as dandelion fluff.

Years spent in the system had taught him how to sense adults' moods, and he knew the various caseworkers who'd traveled with the kids to camp just wanted them all to line up and get inside so they could be sorted into proper groups. But the old couple who ran the place seemed to under-

267

stand what their campers were feeling, because they stubbornly allowed all the early arrivals to wait and watch for their sisters and brothers.

Impatience was making his skin itch. Johnny felt as if he'd been stung by a swarm of mosquitoes.

"She'll be here soon," Ethel, the camp owner, assured him. Round as an apple, with pink cheeks to match, she was the most optimistic person Johnny had ever met. But not that fake kind of cheeriness adults put on when they didn't know how to talk to kids. He'd figured out right away last year that she was the real deal.

"Maybe she missed the bus. Or got moved again. To a different home." Maybe she wasn't even in Oregon anymore. He and Angel had been moved to different towns over the years, but did the system allow them to be moved out of state? Or maybe she'd gotten adopted and no one had bothered to tell him because they thought he might run away again.

"No." Ethel shook her head. "Angel's on the list. Fred called a few minutes ago and checked to make sure."

He wasn't used to people actually going out of their way for him, so even something as simple as making a phone call caused a lump in Johnny's throat. Since he had no idea what to say to such an act of generosity, he just jammed his hands in his back pockets and kept looking down the treelined gravel road.

There were about twenty kids left. All standing with him, all waiting for the bus that probably wasn't coming. Although Johnny figured they had a lot in common, he didn't talk to any of them. Nor did they talk to him. Oh, yeah. He wasn't the only kid who'd developed a force field.

"There, see?" Ethel put her arm around Johnny's shoulder and hugged him against her fluffy side as the yellow bus, smaller than the earlier ones, turned the last corner and came into view. "Didn't I tell you?"

"She might not be on the bus."

She clucked her tongue. Not in a disapproving way, but he knew he'd disappointed her with his negativity. She might not be such a Mary Poppins if their situations were reversed. But he couldn't be mad at her. Not when she wore the aroma of oatmeal cookies, the way he'd always fantasized a grandmother should smell. Whenever he'd allow himself to think about such things, which wasn't very often, because remembering how his own grandmother had tossed Angel and him into the grinding wheels of the system only made him madder.

Then the red braking lights lit up, the accordion door opened with a squeal and a hiss, and five kids burst free of the bus, Angel among them.

She shrieked when she saw him standing there and, ignoring the caseworker who tried to grab her arm, ran straight toward Johnny, threw herself into his arms, and clung.

"I was so afraid you wouldn't be here," she said against his neck. "Some mean girls on the bus said you might not come."

"Never happen," he assured her.

"But what if you got adopted, like they said maybe happened?"

Like that was going to happen in this lifetime. "Then I'd make sure the family adopted you, too," he assured her, even though the first thing he'd learned about the system was that kids weren't in any position to control anything about their lives. "They may keep us apart. But they'll never separate us. We're a team."

"Like SpongeBob and Patrick Star," she said.

"Scooby-Doo and Shaggy," he said, putting her back on her feet. She'd grown since he'd last seen her. She also was beginning to look a lot like their mother.

"Ariel and Flounder."

"Frodo and Samwise." He continued the game.

Her small brow furrowed again. "Who are they?"

"They're hobbits. From *Lord of the Rings*."

"Oh, that's a movie, right?"

"And books." Johnny's favorites. He'd dragged them from placement to placement for the past three years. "But you're probably not ready for them yet. Though the movies are great. Maybe you could rent them."

"No." Curls bounced as she emphatically shook her head. "Mrs. Young — that's my new foster mother — doesn't let us watch movies. She says they invite the devil into your mind."

Johnny's jaw ached. Realizing he was clenching his teeth tight enough to break them, he took a deep breath. If he showed anger, they might send him away, blowing this once-a-year chance to be with his sister.

"I had foster parents like that when I was about your age," he said.

The husband had been a minister, the mother a professional foster parent. They were like Buck in that they believed in never sparing the rod. There were a bunch of kids, all fosters, all crowded into a small, stuffy

271

attic room in bunk beds.

One kid, who was six, used to cry like a baby into his hard, flat pillow every night. He also wet the bed. Although Johnny and one of the older girls used to try to get his sheets washed and dried before he'd be found out, whenever they were caught trying to cover up, all three of them would be punished.

There were still nights, when he was lying in the dark, that Johnny could hear the sound of the plastic under-sheet as the little kid had tossed and turned and cried.

"Do they ever hit you?"

"No." Another shake of the head. "They're mostly nice. A lot nicer than my last family. And we are allowed to watch some DVDs. Like *VeggieTales*. Oh!" She clapped her hands. "That's another team! Larry and Bob! Bob's a tomato and Larry's a cucumber, although sometimes people think he's a pickle.

"They tell adventure stories about the Bible. Mrs. Young says they're morality plays, whatever those are. They're really funny. I especially like the parts when Bob hates *what we learned today* and Silly Songs by Larry. This is my favorite song, because it has my name in it."

As they got into the line headed into the

lodge to get their name tags and cabin assignments, she began belting out "Pizza Angel," a stupidly silly song that seemed to be about Larry the cucumber impatiently waiting for a take-out pizza delivery. Which didn't make any sense to Johnny, but he was happy his sister appeared to be happy in this latest placement.

The check-in process was surprisingly fast and efficient, which made Johnny think that the state foster-care system would run a lot more smoothly if Fred and Ethel were in charge of things. They were given plastic name tags, two camp T-shirts, a camp debit card that allowed so much a day for extras, their room assignment, and a paper map to their cabin in under twenty minutes.

"There will be cookies in the community rec room here in the lodge in an hour," Ethel announced. "Where we'll introduce this year's staff and all get acquainted." Her smile, as her gaze swept over the campers, lit up her apple-cheeked face. "I don't know about you, but I'm so excited at what we have planned! This is going to be the best year ever!"

Johnny viewed the skepticism on many of the faces. It didn't take long for them to figure out that most of the time when adults said something like that, it was going to turn out to be a big fat lie. But he knew that Ethel believed what she was saying. And that unlike so many people who drifted in and out of the campers' lives, she really was going to try to give the kids a good time.

Last year, coming off a really bad placement, he hadn't bothered to try to enjoy himself and had spent much of the time brooding. It was only afterward he'd realized how much Angel had fretted about him, which had kept her from having the fun she deserved.

She was a year older, which meant she'd probably be even better at sensing his mood. So he'd have to go along with the program, even if he had to fake every minute of the next two weeks.

The log cabin their counselor led them to turned out to be one in a circle of five, set in the woods, close enough to the waterfall that he figured, once all the kids shut up, you might be able to hear the water pouring over the rocks at night. Two bedrooms and a shared bath connected to a main living room where wooden shelves were filled with books and puzzles and board games. A map that was a duplicate of the one they'd each been given and a bulletin board listing a schedule of daily events and meal menus were on the pine-paneled wall next to the door.

The other room had four kids in two sets of bunk beds. The oldest kid, who reeked of cigarette smoke, looked about Johnny's age, the youngest closest to Angel's age. Johnny knew, from last year, that Ethel would have goofy games planned for everyone to learn more about one another. Which was when he figured most every camper lied.

Their bunk beds were made of pine logs that matched the walls and covered with dark green sheets and blankets that had Indian designs on them. The window, with curtains that matched the blankets, looked out onto the forest.

"Are you going to take the top bed?" Angel asked.

"Yeah. Since I'm older, it makes sense."

"I like being up high. It would be like being in a tree house."

He started to say it could also be dangerous, then realized that although he might think of her as his baby sister, she wasn't really a baby any longer.

"Sure. It's yours."

Instead of looking excited and scrambling up the ladder to claim her bed, she just stood there, small white teeth worrying her bottom lip.

"What's the matter?"

"I thought maybe we could sleep together. Like we did last year."

He'd let her climb into his bunk after she'd claimed to be afraid of the dark. Although he hadn't wanted to delve into the problem, Johnny suspected that fear might have come from lingering memories of their mother locking them in the closet.

"You don't have to worry. I brought along a battery-operated night-light," he assured her.

"That's not it. I'm a big girl now." She tossed up a small, pointed chin. "I don't mind the dark anymore. I just like sleeping with you. The way we used to sleep with Mom in her bed."

To protect them from Satan, Johnny remembered. The problem was, they hadn't gotten all that much sleep, with his mother waking them up every few minutes all night long to make sure they hadn't been taken in their sleep like the sister they'd never known.

"I don't know if that's such a good idea."

"Why not?"

"Because, like you said, you're older than you were last year. So am I. And I don't know if it's right for us to be sleeping together anymore."

276

She stuck out her bottom lip in a pout he recognized too well. She was an expert at playing to his emotions, which was one more reason he couldn't figure out why she hadn't won herself a permanent home. He couldn't imagine any family not wanting Angel if she played her cute card.

"I don't know why not," she complained. "You're not going to have sex with me."

"What?" He realized he'd shouted when she flinched. *Damn.* Crouching down in front of her, he took both her narrow shoulders — clad in a pink Ariel T-shirt — in his hands. "I'm sorry, I didn't mean to yell."

"Th-th-that's okay." But it wasn't. He could see the tears swimming in her eyes.

"No. It's not. I was wrong." He took a deep breath and felt as if he'd just jumped into an ocean filled with man-eating sharks. "Where did you hear about people doing that?" He managed, just barely, to keep his tone from revealing the churning in his gut.

"From when I was at the Worths'." Her voice was small and trembled, which only multiplied his guilt. "In Salem, before they moved me to Bend."

Ice was running in his veins. At the same time he was sweating like he'd been running for hours across the desert, and there was a roaring in his ears, like a freight train.

"Did anyone there, at the Worths' house, ever touch you?"

"Mrs. Worth spanked me sometimes. For not cleaning up my room good enough, and not being fast enough getting ready for school, and once I broke a plate while I was doing the dinner dishes. That made her really mad because it was part of a set."

Okay. That was enough to make him hate his sister's foster mother with a white-hot flame that burned away the ice. But punishing Angel for an accident wasn't what he was worried about right now.

"I mean, did anyone touch you in a private place?"

"Oh." She shook her head. "Not *there*. She just spanked my bottom. And she slapped me on the face a couple times. Because I'd been bad."

Johnny was torn between fury that anyone would slap his baby sister and relief that she apparently hadn't been molested by some sick perv.

"So how do you know about . . ." Hell. He might think about sex most of the time lately, but Johnny couldn't say the word out loud to his baby sister. "Sleeping stuff?"

"Brandon — he's Mrs. Worth's son — used to sneak out of his room at night to

278

sleep with one of the older girls in our room. He was seventeen and Della — that was her name — was fourteen."

"He did that while you were there?" It wasn't uncommon. He'd witnessed the same thing himself more than once. He'd even had an older girl at one of the homes try to get him to have sex with her last year. But this was his sister, dammit! Who somehow seemed to have stayed openhearted and vulnerable, even after nearly a lifetime in the system.

"Uh-huh." Her voice was muffled as she pulled her pink shirt over her head and exchanged it for the official camp one, which depicted the lake and falls with a big rainbow arching over the scene.

"Della had the bunk below mine, and it was dark, so I never saw anything. I just heard them." She tugged the camp shirt over her stomach and smoothed it down. "Sex must hurt."

Hell. He was not prepared for this. "I think it's different when you're grown-up."

"Oh." She frowned. "I don't think I ever want to grow up if I have to have some boy putting his thing inside me. And one of the other girls said Brandon peed inside Della, which is how boys put babies inside girls." Her face scrunched up even more. "That

279

sounds really icky."

Okay. That was it. He was so over his head here, Johnny decided it was time to change the subject.

"Well, it's a long time away before you're a grown-up, so you don't have to worry about it now. How about we get unpacked, and then we go back over to the lodge?" he asked with a huge helping of fake enthusiasm.

"Okay." She'd always been so agreeable. Which, he feared, could also make her a target to creeps like Mrs. Worth's asshole son. "Do you think Dr. Tiernan will bring dogs this year?"

"Maybe."

"I hope so," she said brightly as she began pulling colorful T-shirts and shorts from her backpack. "They were my favorite part of camp. Next to being with you."

As she smiled up at him, Johnny vowed that somehow, whatever it took, he was going to keep his little sister safe.

28

Charity was out on the porch when Gabe showed up at the house. She was not alone. Her mother, looking as if she'd been shopping for safari wear on Rodeo Drive, was with her.

While Charity wore what appeared to be her usual uniform of jeans and T-shirt, this one reading *A Vet Is a Dog's Best Friend,* the older woman's khaki silk shirt sported little wooden-button-tabbed epaulets. Her fabric belt was a leopard print that matched the frames of her oversized sunglasses, and her cuffed shorts showed off legs that a woman half her age might have considered killing for.

Instead of going with more practical running shoes, as her daughter was wearing, she'd opted for the type of brass-studded brown leather sandals a gladiator might have worn. Her auburn hair had been pulled back into a ponytail that stuck through the

281

back of a black Prada baseball cap.

"Gabriel!" He was enveloped in a fragrant cloud as she hugged him, air-kissing both his cheeks. "It's so lovely to see you again!"

"Good to see you, too, Mrs. —" Damn. He'd forgotten which of her many husbands' names she was currently going by.

"Oh, call me Amanda, darling." She patted the side of his face as she backed away. "Having a handsome Marine call me Mrs. makes me feel like I'm ready for a nursing home."

"Hardly." Since she was not so subtly fishing for a compliment, he gave her a slow male perusal, from the top of her bright head down to her toes, tipped in a grass green lacquer, which Gabe thought looked kind of weird, but guessed must be in style since he doubted that this woman had ever had an unfashionable day in her life. "You look terrific."

"Thank you." She flashed a satisfied smile. "I do try. To be perfectly honest, I feel like moping beneath the covers and feeling sorry for myself, but decided that the least I could do, since I was in town, was to help lift the spirits of those poor children out at the camp."

"Sounds like a plan," he agreed, trying to imagine Charity's mother roasting marshmallows over a campfire.

"Mother's going to be doing makeovers," Charity revealed. "Here, let me take this little guy out to join the others."

She held out her hand for the leash. When their fingers brushed, Gabe felt a familiar zing. Damn. He was in danger of, as Cole used to like to say whenever one of their team would tumble into the lust pit, becoming toast.

It wasn't that he didn't trust Charity, which he did, but Gabe decided to go along with her, just to check out the other dogs in the day care. The mutt wasn't all that bright. What if he tried to pal up with some huge, bad-tempered dog that could eat him for lunch?

Which didn't turn out to be the case. The moment he was let into the yard, he took off racing across the emerald green grass toward the polar bear, who let out a huge *woof* in recognition and immediately fell over, like a tree chopped down by a logger's ax. And stayed that way, letting the bliss-crazed mutt jump all over him.

"They've made friends," Charity said what he could tell for himself. "The night he stayed with me. And Mom says that your dog wore Peanut out by insisting on wrestling for nearly an hour last night."

"He's got energy."

"And spunk," she agreed. "Which he'd have to have to survive all he appears to have been through."

Gabe couldn't disagree.

"So," he said, oddly feeling like a parent must feel the first day leaving a kid behind at kindergarten, as he walked with her back toward the house, "your mother's coming along?"

"Yeah, it was a surprise to me, too. And you don't have to worry," she assured him. "All the dogs have been personality tested before being allowed to join the group, but even if any other one did decide to bother your dog, Peanut would defend him."

"I wasn't worried."

"Of course you were. It's only normal for a pet lover. I feel the same way whenever I go on a trip and have to leave Peanut behind."

"*Pet lover* might be stretching it."

"But you're going to keep him?"

Gabe decided there was no longer any point in denying it. Not after the mutt had spent the night lying across his feet. "Might as well, since he doesn't take up that much room."

"I'm glad. Now he needs a name."

"What's wrong with *Dog?*"

"Nothing. But it should be more personal, don't you think?"

Like the dog would even know? "I haven't given it any thought."

"Well, you still have time. Though you'll want him to have a name to respond to when you take him to obedience training."

"You're kidding. It's not like he's a Doberman."

"All dogs should be taught to be good citizens. Besides, it'll give him confidence and teach him proper ways to behave around all different types of dogs. It'll also help keep all that natural exuberance from getting him into trouble."

Gabe couldn't see himself taking the mutt to a damn school, but since he'd be leaving town as soon as the camp ended, it wasn't as if she'd find out he let that part of his apparent pet-ownership duties slide.

"Did you ask your mother along?" he asked, changing the subject back to her mother.

"No." She sounded a bit puzzled, then stopped and let out a short laugh. "You thought I was bringing her along as protection, didn't you?"

"Do you feel you need protection?"

"There you go again." She let out a huff of breath. "Answering a question with another question. No, I do not feel as if I need protection. I'm a grown woman. Something my mother appears to have forgotten."

"Are you saying she doesn't like me?" If that was the case, the older woman was a damn good actress.

"Actually, although she hasn't said anything about her sudden decision to come out to the camp today, I think the problem is that she's afraid you'll break my heart. So I suspect she's coming along as a chaperone."

"I figured as much."

"I'm sorry. It's ridiculous, really. Treating me as if I'm sixteen. Especially since she mostly left me in the care of the private school and housekeepers when I *was* actually sixteen."

"Maybe she's trying to make up for lost years."

"Or more likely she's just feeling adrift, given that her marriage may be breaking up."

"That's tough."

"It always is. But usually she bounces back pretty quickly. This time . . ."

Her voice drifted off. They walked a bit more. The early-morning rain had stopped, dazzling the landscape in the golden light natives called a sun-shower. The floral aroma of the garden was tinged with spicier scents of fir trees and sea salt.

"This time?" he asked when she didn't finish her thought.

Charity sighed. "I think she's honestly feeling lost."

"Maybe she should just call her husband. So they can discuss the problem, whatever it is, like two adults."

She stopped again. Looked up at him. "How did you know — oh, I remember, you were here during the hysterics."

"I wouldn't exactly use the term *hysterics*." Having dodged more than a few thrown household items growing up, Gabe figured his own definition involved more cursing, holes in Sheetrock, and broken glass. "But she was fairly dramatic about whatever's happening."

"That's her MO. Things fall apart and she hides behind her diva persona until she recovers. But this just feels different."

"Maybe, if she hurts enough, for long enough, she'll pick up the phone."

"The trick is for her to let her guard down enough to feel the pain. Which is what brings us to today's camp expedition. I honestly cannot recall my mother ever camping in her life. Even the summer we

287

came here, whenever we could talk her into going down to the beach, she wore designer sundresses and wide-brimmed straw hats that were constantly blowing off, so Lucas and I would have to chase them down. Usually she stayed on the porch of the cottage, read books, and drank lemonade while Lucas' dad took us on sightseeing adventures."

"Since it sounds as if she's not exactly into communing with nature, if you give her enough time, she might just decide going back to her husband is preferable to playing Camper Barbie."

"One can only hope." She reached out, took his hand, and squeezed. "Thanks."

"For what?"

"For listening. I'm not used to having anyone to talk with about her without sounding as if I'm being judgmental, or making her out to be a bad mother. Which she really wasn't. Just, well, a bit careless and self-centered, I suppose."

"Feel free to share all you want. But believe me, she could be a lot worse."

"Believe *me,* I tell myself that on a regular basis."

It was one thing to want to drag Charity off to the nearest bed. Gabe found the spikes of lust encouraging, proof he hadn't left all feeling in the Afghan mountains. But what was more than a little unsettling was how much he just plain old *liked* her. He'd lived in a testosterone-driven world for so long; although there were women Marines, he'd never worked closely with any. So he'd never had a woman friend.

Until, just maybe, now.

Oh yeah. He was definitely toast.

29

Gabe was more patient than Charity would have expected, actually nodding and making vague comments at the appropriate moments as her mother, seated in back, chattered on nonstop about the scenery, the "darlingness" of the town, and how she'd come up with the "brilliant" idea to give all the girls at the camp makeovers in the first place.

"I was getting a shampoo and blowout at the local salon this morning," she said, "when Camille, who runs Cut Loose, said she does makeovers at the local nursing home. We were talking about what a lift it gives those women's morale, when it hit me. Why not do the same thing for the poor little foster girls?"

"Sounds like a great plan," he said.

Which was the same thing Charity had said when her mother had come home with all those bottles of nail polish. It would also, she considered, help take her mother's mind off her own domestic problems.

"Camille's going to meet me there to make the process go more quickly," Amanda said. "We're also doing tattoos."

"Tattoos?" Charity asked, alarmed.

"Don't worry, darling. They're only the temporary kind. Camille's stopping by Think Ink on her way out to the camp. Apparently they sell rub-on tattoos for people who don't want permanent ones, or who'd like to try out a design before they get it. She's going to get some for the boys, as well, so they won't feel left out. Though we do have one little problem."

She paused. Sighed.

"What would that be?" Charity asked, on cue.

"We're afraid the boys won't be willing to accept ink from two middle-aged women."

There was another longer, significant pause. Charity bit her lip to keep the laugh from escaping.

"You know," Gabe drawled, allowing that sexy hint of the South she'd heard in his voice before, "I'm beginning to understand where your daughter got her ability to talk everyone in the county into adopting a pet."

"Not *everyone,*" Charity corrected. "Only people I'm convinced would be a good fit."

"You don't have to get up on your high horse, sugar. I was merely pointing out that you're more your mother's daughter than some people might realize, at first glance."

Sugar?

"Thank you, Gabriel," Amanda gushed before Charity could challenge his statement. "That's such a lovely thought. . . . So, will you do it?"

Charity's momentary pique diminished when he laughed good-naturedly at her mother's question. "Do I have a choice?"

"Gabe's going to be pretty busy teaching photography, Mom," Charity said in an attempt to give him an escape route.

"That's okay." He shot a grin toward Amanda in the rearview mirror. "Seems only fair the girls not be the only ones getting ink. But I draw the line at doing manicures and pedicures."

"Oh, never fear, darling," Charity's mother said breezily. "Camille and I have those covered."

"You know," Amanda said as Gabe drove past quaint and cheery Cape Cod–style shops selling local crafts, along with galleries featuring coastal artists, "I'd forgotten how charming this little town is."

"It's picturesque, all right," Gabe agreed.

"According to Margie Bremerton, the

docent at the local historical museum, the town started out as a collection of fishing shanties scattered around a very modest railroad station," Charity said. "It became an actual town during the nineteen hundreds after a derailment on the Oregon-California border stopped all train traffic up the coast."

"What, everyone got off and stayed?" Gabe asked.

Although Charity knew he was joking, she enjoyed sharing the colorful history of her adopted home.

"Cute. But as it turns out, a private Pullman car on the train was fortuitously owned by a shirttail relative of Charles Crocker. Crocker was one of the founders of the Central Pacific Railroad, which became this western portion of the first transcontinental railroad."

The Coast Starlight, considered one of the most scenic routes in the country, from Seattle to Los Angeles, still ran through the heart of town.

"As history tells it, he'd suffered blinding headaches all of his life. So, when his manservant told him that the stationmaster mentioned that the native Indians and fishermen claimed the springs out at Rainbow Lake had miraculous curative powers, he sent him to get him a drink."

"Oh, I remember Duncan telling me that story during that summer vacation we spent here," Amanda said. "Ten minutes after drinking the water, the pain supposedly disappeared and the man's vision cleared."

"Clear enough to see he'd struck gold," Charity agreed.

"He bottled and sold the water," Gabe guessed.

"Oh, he had much bigger plans than that. Realizing the potential, within a year he'd built a grand hotel at the edge of town, the lodge, then, using his family ties to interest reporters at newspapers up and down the coast, started a promotional campaign touting the hot springs as a cure-all for just about everything, including headaches, gout, female disorders, and nervous conditions.

"Unfortunately, the hotel burned down in the 1930s, but a lot of the original buildings are still standing."

"Like your place."

"That's one of them. Though as you may have noticed, the rest of the Victorians were built higher up the hill."

"Charity's home was originally a brothel," Amanda volunteered. "Which is why it was built right across from the harbor. To make

294

it easy for the fishermen clients to visit."

"Interesting past," Gabe said, slanting Charity a wicked grin.

"I like to think so," she agreed mildly.

The two-lane road twisted like a snarled fishing line out to Rainbow Lake. Although it had stopped raining, the sky was the hue of tarnished silver. Sunbeams slanted though a green screen of Pacific silver fir, western hemlock, and majestic Douglas fir, laying down shimmering stripes of light across the pavement. The sound of moving water was everywhere as streams born in melting mountain glaciers fed the rivers running to the sea.

It was impossible not to be moved by such scenery. Charity couldn't help noticing that even her mother had fallen silent as she drank in the view.

The campers had already assembled in the main lodge when they arrived at the camp. At the cheer that went up when Ethel called her up to the microphone, Charity knew that last year's campers were already anticipating the dogs.

"It's good to see you all again," she said over the mike's squeal. Fred, the detail member of the Fred and Ethel team, leaped forward to make a few adjustments that had those kids who'd covered their ears lowering their hands. "How many of you are looking forward to the best year of camp ever?"

Another cheer went up. As she scanned the large timber-roofed room, she saw more than a few children remain silent, arms folded across their chests. Undaunted, determined to help lighten their attitude before their time together ended, she forged on.

"Fred and Ethel will be dividing everyone into teams for the dogs," she explained. "We've a few more campers this year, so we're going to make it so each cabin will adopt at least one dog."

There was a bit of grumbling about that, but Charity decided that the upside was it would force the campers to learn to work together as teams. Which was why she'd come up with the plan when Ethel had first called her with the increased numbers. Unfortunately, the downturn in the economy had led to more broken marriages and escalating abuse, which had resulted in more children entering the system.

And while the same problems had brought additional abandoned pets to the shelter, Charity would bring only ones she'd thoroughly behaviorally tested. As she had

Gabe's dog that first night it stayed with her.

"You may have noticed that I've brought a couple new people with me," she said. "This is my mother, Amanda." As she waved toward her mother, who gaily waved back, Charity decided that it was a good thing campers, staff, and volunteers all went solely by their first names. Because there was no way all her mother's last names would fit on the "Hello" tag she was actually wearing on the front of her silk shirt.

"She's going to be helping Camille, who runs the Cut Loose beauty salon and day spa, do makeovers."

The gasp of surprise was audible. Looks between the girl campers were exchanged and faces lit up as bright as the rainbow that often shimmered above the falls that had given the lake its name.

"So you guys won't feel left out, Gabe" — she gestured toward him — "has volunteered to do tattooing." She held up a hand as a roar of approval rocked the room. "They're temporary, though still way cool.

"Gabe's also a U.S. Marine photojournalist. He's going to be teaching everyone how to take super photos so you can leave with pictures of memories of all the good times you'll be having. And here's the best news

— you'll be able to take the cameras you'll be using home with you."

That definitely proved popular. Charity knew that many of the kids could carry all their personal belongings in a pillowcase. And some actually did. Just watching the amazed expressions — as if suddenly Santa had arrived in their midst — made her eyes fill.

"Sounds as if you scored a home run," Gabe said as Fred and Ethel began separating the campers into groups.

"That excitement wasn't about me. We always have way more women volunteers than men. Plus, being a Marine has to increase your appeal level. I don't know how to thank you."

Pewter eyes darkened as they roamed her face with the intimate impact of a caress. "I have a few suggestions along those lines. After we have that official first date we missed at the Sea Mist. You know the one. Where you go too far." His seductive Southern drawl slipped beneath her skin in a way that sent her nerves humming again.

"Maybe I'll hold you to that."

As they stood there, surrounded by the sea of excited campers, a now familiar awareness arced between them.

Gabe's gaze drifted to her lips and lingered, as if he was remembering their taste. His slow, rakish smile was as dangerous as it was impossible to resist. "Plan on it."

30

Damn, he wanted to kiss her. Right now, Gabe considered as desire curled in his gut and tension hovered between them like a live wire. He could just lower his head and take her mouth and —

What?

Nothing they could get away with here, in front of a bunch of homeless kids.

He tugged on a loose strand of hair that had escaped the confines of its clip, gave her the same hot smile more than one Marine groupie had assured him was irresistible, then turned and strolled over to the far side of the room where Fred had gathered all the boys next to a stone fireplace tall enough to stand in.

Camille had already given the older man the stick-on tattoos. He'd laid them out on a wooden trestle table. Among the more heavy-metal-type lightning bolts and skulls and the cartoon characters for the younger kids, Gabe recognized the same Marine anchor tattoo he wore on his chest.

The plan, as it was set up, was that he, Fred, and Bernard Douchett, Sax's grandfather, would each set up shop in a different corner of the room while the girls all left to wherever they were going to have their makeovers.

The kids would choose a tattoo, then get in line. Watching the two older men's obvious organizational skills, Gabe was not surprised to learn that Fred was former military — Army infantry — from the Vietnam era, while Bernard was a fellow jarhead who'd fought with the Fourth Marine Division in Korea.

The procedure went like clockwork. Gabe had inked half a dozen campers when a tall, gangly teenager, with dark-framed glasses and a shock of orange hair, stood in front of him.

"Where's yours?" Gabe asked.

The kid held out both arms. He had *Angel* on one forearm, *Mom* on the other. They'd definitely not been professionally done.

"Nice." Gabe nodded. "Did you ink them yourself?"

"Yeah. With a pen and a needle."

"I'll bet that hurt."

"Nah." The kid shrugged shoulders that

301

looked like wire hangers. "Didn't hurt at all. 'Cause I'm tough."

"You don't have to convince me," Gabe said mildly. "I imagine the system isn't for sissies."

"Hell, no."

Deciding this wasn't the time to get into proper language, Gabe instead asked, "Is *Angel* your girlfriend?"

"My sister," he mumbled.

"Guess she's off getting a makeover."

He shoved the carrot-colored hair that had fallen over his eyes out of the way and scowled at that idea. "She doesn't need any stupid makeover. She's only eight."

"I'm no expert on the female of the species, but it'd be my guess that most of them like getting fancied up."

"Maybe." The kid, whose name tag read JOHNNY, shoved his hands deep in the pockets of his thin jeans, raised his chin to a stubborn level, and shot Gabe a skeptical look. "Are you really a Marine?"

"Yeah. Well, I'm not active service anymore. But there's a saying in the corps that once a Marine, always a Marine."

Gabe knew that the corps still clung to him, ingrained in the way he stood, the way he moved, the way his experiences had set him apart from civilians. The same way

302

growing up with drunks had set him apart. He'd long ago come to the conclusion that some people were meant to fit in. He wasn't one of them.

"Did you kill anyone?"

And why was it everyone always eventually got around to asking that? Gabe wondered wearily. Most of the time, when asking, the questioners would be looking at him as if they expected him to go Rambo at any minute.

"I was in my share of battles. But since I was a combat photographer, most of the time I was taking photos."

"But did you kill anyone?"

Gabe had been lied to enough times that he'd always sworn he'd never lie himself unless his life, or the life of someone he cared about, was at risk. Which it wasn't.

"Yeah."

"Did you like it?"

"No." Gabe considered blowing the kid off, but he recognized him all too well. Except for the difference in their coloring, he could have been looking in a mirror nineteen years ago. "You sure you don't want a tattoo?"

Thin lips turned up in a sneer. "Stick-on ones are for little kids."

Gabe shrugged. "Your choice." He glanced

at the long line forming behind the teen. "That about it?"

The kid flushed, his ears turning bright red. "Yeah."

"Okay, then." Gabe kept his tone casual, matter-of-fact. "Guess I'll see you around for the photography class."

Another shrug. "Maybe."

The lost boy named Johnny turned and slunk away. With that false wall of bravado on the verge of crumbling, he reminded Gabe of a whipped dog. Of himself a very long time ago.

Hell. And isn't this a fine mess you've gotten yourself into?

31

Johnny didn't know why he'd even gotten in that fucking line in the first place. It wasn't like he wanted one of those stupid sticker tattoos. Okay, maybe the dragon ones were kind of neat. And he would have liked the skull if he hadn't known it would scare Angel. But part of him, the part that kept clinging to the idea that there really was a life after the system, had been thinking that maybe if he joined the military after graduation, then the state would consider him a responsible adult. Which would let him apply for custody of his sister.

Of course, if they sent him off to fight in some bum-fuck war, he wouldn't be able to take care of her himself while he was gone. But lots of Marines and soldiers were married and had kids. Which meant that maybe he could pay someone to be like a live-in nanny. It wasn't that he'd need whatever salary the military would pay him. If they covered his room and board — which they had to do, didn't they? — then he could just sign his paycheck over to Angel.

He'd wanted to ask that Marine how it worked. But as soon as he'd looked into those gray eyes, which outwardly seemed friendly enough, but looked as if they could see straight through him, all the questions he'd thought up while waiting for those other kids to get tattoos popped like a soap bubble.

He glanced back, watching as the Marine wiped a little kid's arm with alcohol, patted it dry, then applied a tattoo of the cowboy from *Toy Story.* The kid was beaming and his chest was so puffed up with fucking pride, he looked like he was about to float all the way up to the wooden rafters.

Which, for some stupid reason, as his fingers curled around the stupid anchor tattoo he'd stuck in his pocket, made Johnny want to cry.

32

Since she hadn't brought any animals today, Charity was drafted into doing makeovers. Which, although she wasn't nearly as handy with curling irons and polish as her mother and Camille, she found herself thoroughly enjoying. Not so much for herself, but for the pleasure it obviously gave the girls.

One especially captured her heart. The little blonde had talked a mile a minute, her pale blond Orphan Annie curls bouncing like springs as she'd accented her words with nods and shakes of her head. Angel Harper had been in and out of the system since she was a toddler, but somehow it hadn't seemed to leave any emotional scars on her. Yet.

And wasn't that the key? Charity thought as she sat in the passenger seat on the way home, barely listening to her mother rattling on about her day to Gabe, who'd slant Charity a questioning look every so often.

She knew he was wondering about her silence. Probably wondering if she'd changed her mind.

Which she hadn't. In fact, one of the reasons she didn't want to meet those all-seeing gray eyes was that he'd undoubtedly realize she was close to sitting on her hands to keep them from ripping open his shirt.

Which was why it was better not to think about it. At least not until later tonight.

But still, just the idea of him following through on his promise had her blood humming.

"Well," he said, as he pulled up in front of the house, "what time do you want me to pick you up?"

"The Sea Mist tends to have a rush from about five to seven," she said. "All the tourists and retirees like to eat early. How about seven thirty?"

"Works for me."

He got out of the car. Charity hopped out of the Jeep and was on the sidewalk before he could open the passenger door, but Amanda, accustomed to men's attention, waited, then climbed out, her hand laid lightly in his, with the grace of a princess exiting a royal coach.

"You'd be doing me a great favor if you let your sweet little dog stay with me again,"

Amanda volunteered. "He has such a way of lifting my spirits."

"I'd appreciate that," Gabe said. He gave Charity a long look rife with sexual promise. "See you in a couple hours, then."

"I'll be ready."

His grin was quick and wicked as sin. "I'm counting on it."

This time she didn't watch him leave. After checking with the fill-in vet and Amie, who were buttoning up after a fortunately uneventful day, and Janet, who reminded her that — damn — she'd scheduled a surgery for tomorrow morning, she raced up the stairs to the living quarters.

"I need something to wear," she called out to her mother.

"You're looking for a seduction dress. Something that will make Gabriel St. James swallow his tongue."

"That's a bit extreme. What I'm looking for is something besides jeans to wear to dinner."

Though, admittedly, whatever she unearthed in her mother's closet, she didn't intend to wear that long.

"What happened to wanting a forever after?" Amanda asked, even as she began delving into the guest room closet.

"I still want that." Charity yanked the T-shirt over her head. "I want a husband, kids, a house, and a dog. I've already got the house and the dog, so all I need is a husband to have kids with. But since I realize that I'm not likely to get that with Gabe, I've decided to settle for hot, no-strings, chandelier-swinging, mind-blowing sex."

"Hot, mind-blowing sex isn't exactly settling." Amanda pulled out a handful of dresses and tossed them onto the antique four-poster bed. "And your Marine certainly looks capable of providing it. But you've never been a no-strings type of person."

"Neither are you."

"True enough. Which would have saved me a great deal of heartache."

"Yet somehow you've managed to stay friends with all your exes."

"I have."

"So, looking at the bright side, you managed to enjoy the companionship, and probably hot, mind-blowing sex, with some really interesting, talented men."

Amanda paused, her hand over the top of a quilted jewelry bag. "Again, that's true."

"So it hasn't all been negative." Charity picked up one of the dresses.

"That's one of my personal favorites," her

mother volunteered. "The judge bought it for me at a little boutique during a trip to Santa Barbara."

The watercolor silk halter dress was the color of the sea, with a handkerchief hem that would flow seductively around her calves. It was wispy and romantic. And made Charity wonder where on earth her mother thought she'd wear such a dress in Shelter Bay.

"It's pretty. But so not me."

"And isn't that precisely the point? To push your boundaries?"

"Good point." She put aside another, a silk sheath in a bold, eye-popping leopard print. She might be ready to jump off the sex cliff, but she wasn't sure she'd be able to live up to the wildcat billing the dress advertised.

The third dress, a short, strapless cotton covered with tropical flowers on a dark background, shouted out, "Choose me!"

So she did. "This one."

Her mother nodded. "A perfect choice. I bought it before Benton informed me I wouldn't be going to Hawaii with him, so naturally I won't be able to wear it after what he's done. But it's such a cheerful print, and I thought it was perfect for you, so I brought it along."

"So why didn't you just show it to me first?" Comprehension hit. "Because you knew I'd have to reject some before I totally wrapped my mind around this."

"I'm not accusing you of being predictable, but —"

"But I am."

"Not always."

Charity knew her mother was referring to Ethan. Whom she so didn't even want to think about ever again. Let alone tonight.

"I'm going to take a bath."

"Do you need appropriate underthings?"

"Actually, believe it or not, I've got that covered."

Other women might buy shoes. Or expensive designer bags. Perfume. Or jewelry. Charity's sole indulgence was lingerie. Although she might be the only person who ever saw the expensive bits of lace and silk, there were times when she thought she was single-handedly keeping Oh So Fancy, Shelter Bay's lingerie boutique, in business.

"Good. Because anticipation is the key to romance. And I promise the man won't taste a bite of dinner wondering what you're wearing beneath that dress."

Charity was about to insist that this wasn't about romance. That it was merely sex. Amanda might be the world's expert at seducing males, but what Charity had in mind was a great deal more basic — she and Gabe both had an itch, so why not scratch it?

As she turned the water on in the tub, tossing in a handful of tropical-scented bath salts Janet and Amie had given her last Christmas, Charity wondered when she'd become such a liar.

What she wanted, with every fiber of her newly awakened being, was for Gabriel St. James to take one look at her and swallow his tongue.

33

He couldn't believe it. As he climbed the steps to Charity's porch, Gabe felt ridiculously like a pimply-faced kid on his way to his first prom. With the head cheerleader.

Biting back his anxiety, he rubbed his jaw, which he'd shaved for the second time today after getting back from the camp. Then took a deep breath meant to calm — it didn't — and rang the bell.

The door, with its leaded-glass fan insert, opened instantly, making him wonder if perhaps she'd been just as impatient waiting for him. But as he took in the sight of her, that question, along with any possibility of coherent thought, fled his mind as all the blood in his head flowed south.

"Hi." Her voice was breathless. As if she'd run down the stairs.

"Hi yourself."

He wondered if she had any idea what a vision she made, with her dark hair in that artful tousle atop her head. He thought he detected a touch of uncharacteristic makeup, but she'd applied it with such a light hand he couldn't tell if the soft color in her cheeks was due to cosmetics or emotion.

Instead of her usual jeans, she was wearing a strapless sundress that displayed her long curves and showgirl legs to mouthwatering advantage. The black cotton, brightened with a tropical print, hugged her body like a glove and made him wonder what she might be wearing beneath it.

"Thank you."

"For what?"

"Wearing that dress."

She skimmed a hand over her hip. "You can thank my mother." She reached into the front closet and took out a lacy summer cardigan. "It was originally hers."

"I'll do that." She looked like a tropical flower that had been transplanted to the foggy Oregon coast. He toyed with the seashell earring that dangled nearly to that bare, fragrant shoulder he had a sudden urge to nip. "When I bring you back home tomorrow morning."

Her forehead furrowed. "About that."

Reminding himself that she was allowed to change her mind, Gabe said, "I guess I was rushing."

"It's not that. It's just that my receptionist reminded me that I have a surgery scheduled for tomorrow. It's a simple spay and the vet who's filling in for me offered to do it, but the owner had an unfortunate veterinary experience when she was living in Corvallis, and it's taken me a while to earn her confidence, and —"

"And you feel responsible."

"Yes. I do."

"What time?"

"Nine. But I'll need to be back to the clinic by at least eight thirty."

"No problem." It wasn't as bad as he'd expected.

"Thanks."

"Hey, you're good at your work. And you care. And while I'll admit to being sidetracked from time to time by the fact that you're sexy as hell, I also admire your commitment."

"Well." She blew out an obviously relieved breath, which had him wondering if the former fiancé perhaps had problems with her not always being available for him. "I still appreciate your understanding."

As much as he wanted to believe that it was that simple — a dinner out, a roll in the sack, no strings, no ties, no promises,

316

Gabe still wasn't sure they were on the same page.

"I still have Washington to photograph," he said as they walked toward the Jeep. "Then I want to finish up in Alaska before the snow drives everyone inside."

"That's a good idea. Although I imagine the winter scenery is spectacular, your dog — which I really wish you'd name because I hate talking about him in such an impersonal way — has the kind of fur that clumps up really badly in snow."

Still not trusting his luck, he asked, "That's it?"

"You told me your traveling schedule. You also made it very clear that you're not interesting in long-term relationships. So we'll keep things simple."

"Simple."

"Simple," she repeated with the patience one might use when talking to a simple-minded kindergartner. "Believe me, I'm used to people in my life moving on. . . .

"There is one more thing," she tacked on as he opened the door and, with a palm to her elbow, since she was wearing a pair of strappy, barely there sandals, gave her a boost up into the high leather seat.

Ha! He knew it wasn't going to be that easy.

"And that would be?" He struggled not to swallow his tongue when the dress pulled even higher on those long smooth thighs as she settled into the leather bucket seat.

"It's important to me that you understand I don't have sex with just any hot guy who comes through town."

"I suppose I should be flattered."

"Absolutely. And I'm totally with the program. Except I'm not really into regrets. So, when you leave town, and again, I totally understand you plan to, I want it to be without regrets on either one of our parts."

He was about to assure her that wouldn't be a problem when a warning tolled in the back of his mind. He ignored it.

"Agreed."

"Well, then." She flashed a bright smile, then crossed her legs. "We'd better get to the Sea Mist before we lose our table. This is steamer night. Which is always popular."

Still thinking there had to be a catch — wasn't there always? — Gabe closed the door, walked around, climbed into his own seat, and found himself wishing for those days, before his time, and definitely before seat belt laws, when vehicles had bench front seats and girls snuggled up against a guy while he drove. Because as he drank in the scent of Hawaii emanating from her

buffed and polished flesh, the console
between them seemed to be a gap as wide
as the Grand Canyon.

"Where in the hell are you from?" He realized he'd asked the question out loud
when she laughed.

"That's a long story. I'm not sure we can
cover it in one night."

"The camp's just begun." He skimmed a
palm over her left thigh. "There'll be other
nights."

She covered his hand with hers.

"I'm counting on it."

34

The Sea Mist restaurant harkened back to the town's seafaring days. The paneled walls were stained a light blue-gray, designed to appear weathered by decades of wind and coastal storms. A mural of the Shelter Bay lighthouse covered one wall. Old black-and-white photos had been hung on the other walls, and over the arched doorway a carved wooden bust — a female figurehead of Rubenesque proportions, salvaged from the prow of some ancient ship — kept a watchful eye over diners.

The wooden tabletops glowed with the patina of years of lemon oil. The lighting was soft, flickering in shadowy corners. In the center of the table, a white candle glowed in a short brass seaman's lantern.

"Inside or out?" the hostess, clad in a black skirt and starched white shirt, asked.

Gabe looked down at Charity, inviting her to make the decision.

"Out." The sun set late this time of year, and outside the wall of glass facing the bay, the sapphire water sparkled as if it had been scattered with diamonds.

"The Pacific Northwest may arguably have the most gorgeous summers on the planet," she said as the young woman led them to an umbrella-topped table on a wooden deck perched over the water. "But I've learned that whenever blue skies show up, it's obligatory to celebrate." He felt a pang of loss as she slipped on the lacy sweater, covering up those bare shoulders. *Later.*

"I'm all for celebration." After pulling her chair out for her, because it seemed an eternity since he'd kissed her, he bent his head and touched his lips to hers.

The kiss was quick and light, but he'd felt her breath catch beneath his mouth.

"I don't know about the food here," he said as he sat down. "But the appetizer was certainly tasty."

Appealing color drifted into her cheeks again as the hostess tried, with scant success, to smother a laugh as she placed the menus in front of them, rattled off the specials, then left with their drink orders. A glass of sauvignon blanc for Charity, a Sam Adams for Gabe.

"You realize," Charity said, as she unfolded her napkin onto her lap, "everyone is now looking at us."

"News flash. Everyone was looking at us the minute you walked into the place in that dress."

"Only because it's not what they're used to seeing me wear."

"No. It's because you look tastier than anything on this menu." He glanced up from the menu in question and grinned. "And I'm the lucky SOB who actually got a sample."

"The entire town will be talking about that kiss by morning."

Having grown up in a small town himself, where his parents provided a great deal of grist for the local gossip mill, Gabe suspected she was right.

"Should I apologize?" He didn't want to cause any damage to her professional reputation. But it wasn't as if he'd stripped off that dress and taken her on top of the table. Which was what he really wanted to do.

"No." She smiled her thanks at the waitress who'd delivered their drinks, then, after offering them more time to decide on their choices, discreetly disappeared back into the building. "Actually, since calling off my wedding has been the main topic of gossip about me since I arrived in town, people will undoubtedly enjoy a change of subject."

Although she'd been living in town long enough to undoubtedly memorize the menu, she began to study it as if she'd be hit with a pop quiz at any moment. Sensing she was avoiding talking any more about her failed marriage, Gabe decided not to press.

They kept the conversation casual. About the weather — which, he'd discovered, could change from minute to minute on the coast — the campers, her work with the shelter.

Unlike many city restaurants he'd been to, where the staff seemed determined to turn over tables in under twenty minutes flat, the pace was leisurely, the mood relaxed.

Much, much later, as he signed the credit card charge, he was certain the meal was one of the best he'd ever eaten. But he couldn't remember tasting a thing because all his attention had been focused on Charity. And his plan for the rest of the night.

Over the clam chowder, he'd imagined slowly taking those pins from her hair and watching it tumble free over her bare shoulders. During the cedar-plank-smoked salmon he'd imagined the silky feel of her hair draped across his chest. His thighs.

And as he'd watched the white napkin she used to wipe away a bit of whipped cream that topped the fresh marionberries, myriad fantasies of other things he'd like to do with that whipped cream flashed through his mind. Although he might make a living in what his agent insisted on calling "the arts," Gabe had never thought of himself as a fanciful man.

Until now. As he allowed his fantasies to take flight, pictured himself drawing whipped cream circles on her breasts, then slowly licking them off, the surrounding sounds of conversation, cutlery clinking, and whale-watching boats chugging back into the harbor faded away. He could practically hear her soft, needy sighs. Her throaty moans.

The mental images became more and more vivid and erotic, forcing Gabe to grit his teeth and try to think of something, anything, that would allow him to walk out of the Sea Mist without giving the town an entirely new and definitely triple-X-rated topic to discuss.

35

Something was wrong. Except for his sister fretting when she'd first gotten off the bus, she'd been her typical chatterbox, upbeat self since arriving at the camp. Even when describing what, to him, didn't sound like that great a placement. Though, from what she'd said about the previous Salem one, it had to have been an improvement.

She'd been excited right before she'd dashed off to get in line with the other girls. But when she came back with the fairy tattoo on her thin upper arm, she looked about ready to cry.

"What's the matter?"

"Nothing."

She was looking down at the ground, scuffing at fir needles with the toe of her pink sandal.

"Hey." Johnny crouched down, put his finger beneath her chin, and lifted her miserable gaze to his. "What happened?"

"Nothing." She was a terrible liar. Probably because she hadn't had as much practice as he had.

"Angel —"

"Don't call me Angel." Thin shoulders beneath the Camp Rainbow T-shirt slumped. She looked as miserable as he'd ever seen her. "Angels are people who died and went to heaven. I don't want to be dead, so that's not my name anymore."

Where the hell had that come from? Just a few minutes ago, she'd been happily belting out the stupid angel pizza song, which was her favorite because she'd decided it was about her.

"Okay." Johnny wished, not for the first time in his life, that some superhero — Batman would be cool — would come racing up in the Batmobile and take care of things. Of course, with his fucking luck, he'd probably get Robin. "What's your new name?"

That stopped her for a minute. She tilted her head as she considered the problem.

"Jasmine," she decided. "She's my favorite Disney princess, because she's pretty and brave and has adventures."

She nodded as the idea sank in. "And she ran away from the palace when her father was going to make her marry a bad prince. Then almost got her hand cut off because she didn't know about money and gave an apple to a poor boy. But then Aladdin rescued her. And they fell in love."

She nodded again. This time with more enthusiasm, causing curls to bounce. "That's my new name — Jasmine."

Johnny blew out a relieved breath as the light came back into her eyes. Another crisis averted.

36

Although she certainly hadn't lived the life of a cloistered nun, well, at least until she'd broken up with Ethan, neither had Charity ever allowed herself to go to bed with a man she'd known only a few days.

Having lived through the wreckage that Amanda's quicksilver temperament and rash decisions had left in their wake, she'd worked to take a different life path.

She'd spent most of her life planning every deed, censoring every word, avoiding attention, and, until the day she'd thrown away months of wedding planning, avoiding confrontation.

She'd told herself she was happy living in Shelter Bay. Which was true. She loved the town, the people, the spectacular Pacific Northwest location. She'd made friends, and she had the satisfaction of knowing that every time she placed a homeless pet, she not only saved the animal's life but enriched the life of its owner.

But now, as Gabe drove back over the bridge toward the coast, Charity realized how much of a toll repressing her sensual self had taken on her. During dinner, although somehow they'd managed to keep a fairly coherent conversation going, every time his eyes, as watchful and hungry as a wolf's, looked at her as if he wanted to rip her dress off and ravish her right on the Sea Mist's patio, an insane part of her had been hoping he'd do exactly that.

Emotions, feelings, sensations, were all flooding over her, as if escaping from a breach in a stone dam.

The sky was darkening quickly. A first star winked brightly to life.

I wish . . .

What?

And wasn't that the problem?

She'd been outrageously attracted to Gabriel St. James the moment she'd spotted him, all serious glower and radiating testosterone as he'd taken those photos at Cole and Kelli's wedding. Which was why she'd made the effort to get past his shields. With less-than-encouraging results.

But then he'd shown up on her doorstep and if she'd believed in fate, which she didn't, she would have thought they'd been destined to meet. Especially since if Winnie had gone into labor ten minutes earlier, she would have left the reception without ever getting up the nerve to talk to the man.

It wasn't as if she were some moonstruck teenager. During the day, she'd managed to keep thoughts of him at bay as she'd focused on her work. On her patients and their often stressed-out owners.

But during the night . . . oh, that had been a different story altogether. He'd invaded her sleep, with carnal dreams of clothes ripping, and big strong hands bruising, and her crying out, begging for release, as he'd drive her higher and higher. But then, in the morning her damn alarm would go off, leaving her hot and bothered amid tangled sheets.

Maybe she was making a mistake, leaping into a sexual affair with him so soon. It wasn't as if he were offering her a future. And despite what he'd said about sticking around for the entire camp, what did she really know about him? Except for the obvious. That he was a rolling stone. A hot, unbelievably sexy rolling stone that could make her shiver all the way down to her toes with a mere look. And have her feel as if her bones were melting like a sand castle at high tide with his touch.

She deserved this, dammit! After a lifetime of behaving responsibly, of putting everyone else's needs ahead of her own, she deserved a hot summer fling.

And who better to have it with than a man who wouldn't be sticking around to complicate things once the earth turned, the leaves changed, and her comfortable, predictable life got back to normal?

37

The Hi-Tide campground was small, each site tucked away beneath the trees near the edge of the cliff.

"Wow." Pulled out of her introspection by the sight of the rising moon glistening on the waves, Charity caught her breath. "There are people who'd pay big bucks for this view."

"According to the owners, they've had offers to sell to developers with deep pockets over the years, but they grew up camping here when their parents owned it, and they want to keep it so other kids can experience the fun they had."

"That's nice."

"Yeah. I thought so when they told me about it." He leaned across the console and cupped his fingers around the nape of her neck. The pressure, while not painful, still made her tremble. Just a little, but she knew he'd felt it.

"You realize" — his deep voice caused her heart to thrum — "there's still time to change your mind." His eyes, silvered by moonshine, focused on hers. "But once you come inside, you're mine."

The claim of possession could have been either promise or threat. Since it echoed the dreams of ravishment that had tormented her sleep, Charity took his words as a hot, glorious, nerve-tangling promise.

But the common sense that had served her all her life made one last attempt to make itself heard.

"This is all happening so fast."

"Not fast enough. I wanted you the minute I saw you."

"I certainly couldn't tell. You were so caught up in your work."

"I had a job to do. And you, sugar, were a major distraction."

"I'm going to take that as a compliment."

"Good. Because it is. I almost went after you."

"I almost expected you to," she admitted.

"I should have. But the fact that I wanted to was even more reason to leave."

"But you didn't."

"I was on my way out of town when the dog got tossed from that van."

"Which brought you to me."

"Yeah. Which leaves me thinking that, just maybe, there are times when all the stars and planets are in the right place, the gods are generous, and two people meet and click right off the bat."

She tilted her head. He'd opened the moonroof on the Jeep during the drive from town, and she assured herself that it was the cooling breeze blowing in from the ocean, and not anticipation, that shivered over her bare skin.

"Do you honestly believe in fate?"

"I didn't. But since meeting you, I've got to admit that I'm rethinking the concept." He hit the button, closing the roof. "Especially the part about gods not taking kindly to people who reject their gifts."

"Well, I certainly wouldn't want to risk the wrath of the gods."

"Wise woman."

It was only a few feet to the door, but it seemed like a mile as Gabe resisted the urge to just scoop her off her feet and carry her to bed. And wouldn't that set tongues wagging? While he'd never been one to let gossip bother him, he also wouldn't be the one having to live with it.

One of the first things the military taught him was that a failure to plan was planning for failure. So he'd taken time to set the stage this morning before leaving for the camp. Just in case.

He'd changed the sheets, put fresh towels in the bath. He already had candles, for power outages, and a quick run to Sofia De Luca's Lavender Hill Farm had resulted in some sweet-smelling heirloom roses. She'd even provided a vase, something he hadn't thought of. Which definitely showed how long it had been since he'd thought about romance.

Mission accomplished.

She drew in a breath as she entered the bedroom and viewed the flowers, along with the bottle of champagne he'd set on ice next to two flute glasses he'd seen in one of the shop windows. Blue stemmed, they'd been hand painted with a coastal scene.

"Oh, you needn't have gone to so much trouble," she said. "I don't need all the romantic trappings."

"I know." He flipped a switch and sent slow, seductive music flowing out of the hidden speakers in the walls and ceiling. "But it seems I do." Flames sparked and began dancing as he took a match to the wicks of the white candles. "Besides, it occurred to me that the breaking of a two-year moratorium deserves more of a celebration than a quick roll in the sheets."

"I'm all for celebrations," she said mildly. She picked up the bottle of wine and studied it. "I don't know anything about wine. Especially champagne. But I do love the flowers on the bottle."

"I don't know all that much, either," he said. "But the guy at the market assured me this is a good label. And the flowers reminded me of you."

"Oh, that's lovely. Now I'm definitely going to have to taste it." She put the bottle back down on the built-in dresser and turned toward him. "Later."

She took a deep, ragged breath. "I'm sorry." He prepared for her to change her mind. "I really, really want this." Color drifted into her cheeks. "But it's not turning out to be as easy as I'd imagined it would be."

Gabe looped his arms lightly around her waist. "I'm not sure it should be all that easy." He'd sensed from the beginning that nothing about this woman was going to be the least bit simple.

But still he'd stayed.

He kissed her. A soft, satiny meeting of lips. A mingling of breath. Then slowly slid the sweater off her shoulders, folded it, and carefully placed it on a chair.

Then skimmed his fingertips along the

bare skin he'd been dying all night to touch, pleased by her slight shiver.

She was soft, but far from safe. Yet even knowing that, Gabe wanted her. Too much for comfort, too much for sanity. But like a man beguiled by a mythical siren, he lowered his mouth to hers once more and allowed himself to be bewitched.

He'd vowed to take things slowly. Carefully. And not just for her, but for himself. He wanted to savor this moment, to create a memory they could share even after he'd left Shelter Bay.

Scents. They rose from her warming flesh, surrounding him in a fragrant cloud. As he breathed them in, Gabe knew he'd never see flowers again without thinking of this woman.

Tastes. The honey taste of her lips, the sweet, moist sunshine taste of her throat beneath his lips lingered on his tongue, spun in his head.

Feelings bombarded him. Emotions too numerous to catalog rushed over him, until he felt as if he were drowning in them.

"I dreamed of this," she murmured as she slipped her hands beneath his shirt and ran them over his back. "I've been dreaming of you." She pressed her lips against his neck. "Wild, wanton, wonderful dreams."

Her breathless admission caused whatever blood that remained in Gabe's head to flow south. He pulled out the pins, as he'd been imagining doing during dinner. Then, tangling his hands in her hair, he kissed her hard and long. Needs flowed out of him and into her. Desire flowed out of her and into him.

Her body was soft and pliant, but he could feel the strength there, as well. She was forged steel in shimmering silk. Gabe found the combination impossible to resist.

Ever since he'd lost his virginity during a hot, sweaty, uncomfortable, and over-way-too-soon tumble in a Trans Am parked out in a Lowcountry marsh, Gabe had regarded the taking off of a woman's clothes as merely a necessary prelude to sex. But now, as he unzipped the dress, letting it drift to the floor, he realized that undressing Charity was as sensuous an experience as the heady tastes of her kisses.

And when he viewed her standing there, in only a strapless black scrap of lace, matching panties so skimpy she might as well not have bothered with them, and high-heeled sandals, Gabe was slammed by a punch of lust.

"You know how I thanked you for wearing that dress?"

A flush, the twin to that in her cheeks, bloomed on the crest of her breasts. "I seem to recall that."

"Well, that goes double for this." He rubbed his fingers along the lace, his knuckles brushing the rosy skin. Having always enjoyed contrasts, he liked discovering this sexy part of her personality that she kept hidden away. "Did I mention how hot you are?"

"I could say the same thing about you," she said. "But you're wearing way too many clothes."

She set to work on the buttons of his black shirt, folded it back, and pushed it off his shoulders, tossing it uncaringly onto a padded bench.

Her soft hands fluttered over his shoulders, moved down his chest, across the thick shrapnel scars dotting his torso beneath the globe and anchor tattoo.

"What's this?"

He shrugged. "A souvenir of a mission that didn't go entirely as planned."

"You're lucky it didn't hit your heart."

"I've always been lucky." Forcing a careless shrug, when his body wanted to tremble, he ran his hand down her hair. Gabe was feeling awkward and clumsy. No other woman had ever made him experience either reaction before. "Which you being here with me tonight proves."

Because thinking about war wasn't his favorite thing to do any time, but least of all when he was on the verge of taking a beautiful, sexy woman to bed, he kissed her again, a long, lazy exploration of tastes that had her lips parting on a throaty moan.

"Do you have any idea how much I want you?" He continued kissing his way down her throat, where her blood pulsed. Then lower.

"I want you, too." Her breath trembled out as his lips darkened the black lace. Her heart was beating like thunder beneath his mouth. "Probably more than I should."

It wasn't exactly what he'd wanted to hear.

But it was close enough.

For now.

The mattress sighed as he drew her down onto the bed. Rough, fumbling urgency took the place of well-honed skill as he whisked away the black lace barrier, then practically tore off his own clothes.

Their legs tangled and when she shifted beneath him, arching her back, then moving in a slow, rhythmic motion, Gabe had to grit his teeth to maintain control.

When he could have ravished, he sipped. When he could have taken, he forced himself to seduce.

He felt her tremble where his hands touched. And lingered. When he skimmed his mouth over heated skin, he tasted passion. And promise.

This was more than the simple need of a man for a woman. He wanted her.

He wanted her to feel sensations she'd never felt with any other man. And although he knew it was selfish and chauvinistic, he wanted to brand her with his mouth, his hands, so that whenever any other man touched her, she would feel *his* touch instead.

So that if any lips ever attempted to drink from hers, the tastes of Gabriel St. James would come between them.

And if she ever made love to that faceless, nameless male lurking somewhere in the murky shadows of her future, Charity would find her bed — and her body — already claimed by his presence.

Even as he knew that was impossible, it was imperative that she remember him — and this night — long after he'd gone. For the rest of her life.

As Gabe knew he'd remember her.

Mists, as soft and delicate as the fog drifting in from the sea, enveloped them. Time slowed. Then seemed to stop. There was no yesterday. No tomorrow. Only now.

He'd never met a woman as generous, as trusting, as Charity. No woman had ever loved him so patiently. So completely.

Gabe was no stranger to lust, but he'd never realized that a need this powerful could also be so quiet. So perfect.

Never had he been so patient. So careful.

Soft murmurs, quiet sighs. The warmth of flesh against flesh.

Drowning in her tenderness, murmuring her name like a prayer, he slipped into her.

She took him in, enfolding him.

"Oh," she breathed on a shimmering sigh.

Her hands glided over his shoulders, then tightened around him.

Her moon-gilded eyes looked up into his.

"Now," she said.

Thank God. "Now."

He began to move, his deep thrusts echoing the age-old rhythm of the surf pounding against the rocky cliff.

No longer pliant, she wrapped her long silk legs around him, and matched him, stroke for stroke. In and out. Again and again.

All the time Gabe never took his eyes from hers as he drove her up crest after tumultuous crest.

Muscles straining, his ragged breaths

threatening to rip his lungs apart, he gripped her hands as he sent them over the final wave, crashing down the other side, helpless to do anything but drown.

38

Charity lay with her cheek against Gabriel's chest, drinking in the musky scent of his skin and listening to the sound of the rain on the metal roof that added a counterpoint to the steady thudding of his heartbeat as it settled back to normal.

As for her own heart, she wasn't sure it would ever be the same.

She'd never given so freely, so openly of herself. And until tonight, she hadn't realized that she'd never wanted to. The simple truth was that sex had never been an overwhelming force in her life. She'd spent the past years getting through school, pouring her energies into her work, receiving satisfaction from her career.

She'd spent her entire life keeping her emotions on a tight rein, opting for practicality over passion, logic over love. Until now. Until making love with Gabriel St. James.

Not that she was in love. It was just sex.

Hot, mind-blowing sex, but she wasn't going to repeat her mother's mistake of confusing the two.

"You can accuse me of being repetitive," he murmured in a rough voice that caused a renewed little spike of desire. "But thank you."

Putting aside introspection for now, Charity laughed and trailed a finger down his chest and, since she was feeling more satisfied than she'd ever felt in her life, tried not to think about how he'd gotten those scars. His skin was no longer hot to the touch, but wonderfully warm and moist, emanating a musky scent that amazingly stimulated another little spike of desire.

"I made you sweat."

"You did a helluva lot more than that, sugar." He combed lazy fingers through her tousled hair.

"I never knew." She pressed her lips against his stomach and felt his muscles clench. "That it could be that way. That *I* could be that way." She rolled over on top of him. "Do you think it was a fluke?"

"No. I knew you'd be hot."

"Hot." An unfamiliar laugh, throaty with satisfaction, bubbled up from somewhere deep inside her. It was a stranger's laugh. A hot, sexy stranger's laugh.

"I was, wasn't I?" She began moving against him in a way designed to rekindle smoldering ashes. The way a hot, sexy woman would move when she was out to seduce a naked man.

"Absolutely."

"I want you." Her tongue made a wet swath along the seam of his mouth. "Again." She nipped at his lower lip. "And again. Because I'm not nearly done with you yet, Gabriel St. James."

"What if I can't live up to your expectations?" he asked as her fingers trailed down his chest.

"Don't worry." God, she loved his body! "I'll help you."

"Well, then." He sucked in a harsh breath as she lowered her head again and began following the trail with her mouth. "I guess we won't have any problem."

"That's exactly what I was thinking. And you don't have to worry." Charity laughed against his stomach. "I promise to respect you in the morning."

She'd been a little afraid it would be awkward. Afraid that, after making love all night long, she'd feel like a slut in the light of day. Afraid, although it was a cliché prob-

346

ably first invented by the morality police, he really might not respect her in the morning.

She was wrong. As she came out of his shower into the bedroom, wrapped in a thick brown towel, hair streaming over her shoulders, he greeted her with a kiss, and a cup of coffee.

She sank into the kiss as the mug warmed her hands and the steam rose between them.

"I have dry cereal and milk." He punctuated his words with featherlight kisses that skimmed across her mouth and up her cheek. "Or English muffins." Her other cheek. "Or I can make an omelet."

"Just coffee's fine."

He'd already showered and apparently made coffee while she'd been in that half-wake, half-sleep mode, basking in memories of the night that had lasted way into the morning. He was wearing jeans. Just jeans. Wranglers, from the leather label on that very fine butt.

"Didn't your mother ever tell you that breakfast is the most important meal of the day?"

"Have you not met my mother?" She didn't want to talk about Amanda. What Charity wanted was to lick his ripped dark chest.

"Good point." The hand that had created

347

such glorious havoc on her body all night long stroked her side, from shoulder to thigh.

"Besides, you don't have to go to any trouble."

Just as she'd never had anyone light candles and buy flowers as a prelude to lovemaking, the last person to cook for her had been one of a changing parade of housekeepers Amanda had hired to take care of anything remotely resembling a domestic chore.

"It's no trouble. I have to eat, so cooking for two isn't any big deal. Besides, you need to keep up your energy." His hand slipped beneath the towel to caress her bare leg.

"I have plans for you."

"Well, since you put it that way . . ." His touch was making her light-headed with remembrance. If it weren't for that scheduled surgery, she'd drag him back to bed and have her way with him. "I wouldn't turn down an English muffin."

"How about some Canadian bacon and an egg on it?"

Since Shelter Bay's governing and zoning council had successfully kept out franchise restaurants, Charity hadn't had an Egg Mc-Muffin in ages. And although she'd never been much of a breakfast eater, she seemed to have worked up an appetite. And surely last night had worked off about a gazillion calories.

"I've love one. If you're sure it's not too much trouble."

"I never say anything I don't mean." He brushed his lips against hers, the quick kiss ending too soon. Then left to let her get dressed.

Charity decided it was a sign of how much just one night could change a person's viewpoint when she didn't even worry about everyone in Shelter Bay seeing her coming home early in the morning in the same dress she'd worn to the Sea Mist last night.

She pulled back her hair to braid it, revealing a mark on her neck. There were probably others, she thought with a secret thrill. And with luck, there'd be a lot more.

She usually spent a few minutes every morning doing yoga, followed by a brief meditation. She'd found while going to vet school that not only did meditation help her deal with the stress of the job; it focused her mind on the day ahead. Since she was going to miss that this morning, she *had* to stop thinking about sex.

Easier said than done. Just looking at his bare back, as he stood in front of the three-burner cooktop, caused a now predictable spike in her hormones.

"Can I help?"

"I'm fine." He waved toward the dinette. "Sit."

"That's very good." She did as instructed. "You put just the right amount of command in that order without sounding overly stern. You and your dog will probably ace obedience training."

He made a noncommittal sound that she decided to take for agreement, although he still didn't seem all that enthusiastic about the idea. Deciding not to push, she changed the subject.

"This is really nice."

Since her mind definitely hadn't been on motor home decor when she'd arrived last night, she'd gotten only a fleeting glimpse of the combination living room/kitchen before they'd gone into the bedroom, but now she could see that it was a great deal more luxurious than she would have suspected.

The cabinets — including a built-in wall unit with a wide-screen TV — were maple, the countertops granite, the floor hardwood. Both the sink and the appliances were stainless steel. The upholstery was black leather.

"I like it." While Canadian bacon sizzled in one pan, he began frying three eggs in another.

"I guess I supposed it would be more like camping out."

"I spent enough years doing that. This was previously owned by a country singer who moved up to a bus." He put a muffin in the toaster. "Since the RV market apparently cratered with the rest of the economy, I got it at a fire-sale price."

"Lucky you."

"Funny." His gaze was warm as it turned back to her. "That's exactly what I was telling myself while you were in the shower. That I'm one lucky SOB."

Oh, no! As she found herself drowning in the depths of his eyes, Charity realized she'd lied. She didn't just want his body. She wanted his heart.

Might as well wish for the moon.

"So, what's the plan?" he asked as he warmed up her coffee.

"The plan?"

How could it have happened? How, when she wasn't looking, had she turned into her mother?

"To get all the dogs and gear out to the camp this afternoon?"

"Oh, that." Cooling relief flooded over her that he hadn't somehow read her mind. "I thought since you're going to be bringing out that printer, if you could, I'd let you also take the cameras and my printer. And, of course, your dog. I'll take the others, since I'll want them crated."

"Works for me." He put the plates on the table and sat down across from her. His legs were long, the table small enough that their knees touched. Charity knew she was sunk when even that physical contact caused a now familiar zing.

She knew, as his gray eyes darkened, that Gabe had felt it, too.

He wanted her again. Just as she wanted him.

The problem was, she wanted him too much.

No. The problem was that come summer's end, he was going to get into this motor home and drive away. From Shelter Bay. And her.

"What's wrong?"

"Nothing." She forced a reassuring smile that felt frozen on her face.

"You were a million miles away."

"Just planning ahead." This smile felt a little more natural. "It's what I do."

What she'd always done. Planned for the next stepfather, the next school, how to fit in as her mother had moved them around like a rolling stone.

She'd decided in her teens to become a veterinarian and she'd done everything to make that happen. Next she'd worked her way up from assistant veterinarian to being on staff at one of Chicago's best and biggest veterinary clinics. And then, after she'd set her mind to moving here, she'd gotten the house remodeled and the clinic established in record time.

A year later, she'd fulfilled her dream of opening up a shelter, but she was already thinking of ways she could draw other vets from other counties in, to create a network of shelters and volunteers willing to foster animals waiting for adoption.

Except for that halcyon summer here in Shelter Bay, Charity could not recall ever just living in the here and now. She'd learned not to dwell on the past, even as she was always looking toward tomorrow.

"I was also thinking," she murmured, "that there's a lot to be said for living in the moment. One day at a time."

He took her hand and lifted it to his smiling lips. "Sugar, you are playing my tune. Especially when the day's as perfect as this one."

39

The siren shattered the soft afternoon air. Blue and red lights flashed atop the sheriff department's cruiser.

"This is the tweriff," a voice instructed over the loudspeaker. "Come out with your handth up!" The order would've carried more weight if it hadn't been coming from a five-year-old pigtailed blonde with a lisp.

"I think you just might have won the Ms. Popularity contest," Gabe told Kara Conway as they watched the line of kids waiting for a chance to play with all the gear.

"Kids seem to love playing cops and robbers," she agreed. Her deputy, who didn't look much older than some of the kids themselves, appeared to be having just as much fun.

"Did you?" he asked.

"Sure. But although my dad was Shelter Bay's sheriff, I didn't consider going into law enforcement until after I'd gotten married."

He hadn't realized she'd been married before. Then again, most of the people he knew had been married. Some more than once. With the seeming exception of Charity, who'd stopped at the brink.

"I was widowed," she revealed.

"I'm sorry."

"So was I. The irony was that Jared, my husband, made it through two tours in Iraq, only to get killed during a domestic cop call."

"That's tough." And tragic, yet from what he'd witnessed at the wedding, and from her cheerful attitude the other day on the beach, he guessed she'd gotten over it.

"It was the darkest time of my life. But I was fortunate to have our son, which kept me from just crawling into bed and pulling the covers over my head for the rest of my life."

She sighed softly, then shook her head. "You know what they say about what doesn't kill you makes you stronger?"

"Roger that," Gabe agreed.

"It's true. Yet if all that hadn't happened, I wouldn't have ended up back here in Shelter Bay. With Sax."

By the way her face lit up when she said

Cole's brother's name, he could tell that what the two of them had was the real deal. It also made him wonder what secret the Douchett family had that the rest of the planet couldn't seem to figure out.

"I heard you and Charity had dinner at the Sea Mist last night." Her tone might be conversational, but he caught a question in the statement.

"You and probably everyone else."

She shrugged khaki-clad shoulders. "It's a small town. People talk. It actually makes my job a lot easier. . . ."

The way her voice trailed off made him suspect she'd been planning to say something else, and was debating whether to go for it. Since he'd seen her patrolling Harborview as he'd driven away from Charity's house this morning, he figured her arrival home hadn't gone unnoticed by those cop eyes, which, despite the way the sky had begun to cloud up, were currently hidden behind a pair of sunglasses.

"I bought your book," she said.

That wasn't what he was expecting.

"Thanks."

"I almost didn't because I wasn't sure I wanted to see what Jared had seen."

"I can understand that."

"But everyone was talking about it, so I

dropped by Tidal Wave Books yesterday and looked through it." She looked up at him, but he still couldn't see her eyes. Which was probably the point of those shades all cops seemed to wear. "You put me there. With those photos."

That was how he'd always viewed his mission. To be a witness to history. To shake people out of their indifference.

"Is that good? Or bad?"

He didn't mention that the photos, as graphic as they were, were only a fraction of what he'd seen and smelled and heard. Nor did he share that he lived with an entire library of violence and suffering in his head.

"I haven't quite decided. You did help me understand a lot of why he'd changed so much when he came back home after his last tour. I bought it to look through again, since Sax was downrange, too. I've decided to put it away for Trey, my son, when he's older. To help him know a bit more about his father."

"I'm flattered you believe my photos might help."

"They're very good." She folded her arms. "I especially like the way you somehow managed to keep your own feelings to yourself, leaving it up to the viewer to experience individual emotion. That must have been difficult."

Again, he heard the question.

"I guess it's a trick I developed." He had, after all, been keeping his feelings to himself for a very long time.

"Well, it worked."

Two kids, twins from the look of them, were climbing into the backseat behind the screen that separated prisoners from the driver of the patrol car.

"I also hear you've been traveling the country taking photographs for a new book," she said.

"You heard right."

"How long do you plan to stay here in town?"

Finally. There it was. "Is this where you tell me the town's not big enough for the two of us, Sheriff?" he asked mildly.

"Of course not." There was an edge to her tone that reminded him what Sax had said about her not having always been a small-town sheriff. She'd been a cop down in Oceanside and had even attended classes at the FBI Academy.

"Good. Because I'm not finished here."

"But when you are, you'll be moving on to the next state."

"Washington," he agreed absently as Charity, who'd been in the kitchen helping

Sedona Sullivan give a baking class, came out of the lodge. "Then Alaska. And finally Hawaii."

"Sounds ambitious. I've always fantasized about just taking off and seeing the country."

"It's been quite the trip."

He watched Charity scan the parking lot. When she spotted him, then waved and flashed that dazzling smile that could brighten the grayest of days, Gabe felt his heart shift, like the tectonic plates that were always moving and colliding here in America's part of the Ring of Fire.

"Charity moved here shortly before I returned home," Kara volunteered, following his gaze. "We've become good friends."

"She's definitely friendly."

"True. But here's the thing." She shoved her glasses up on the top of her head. Her gaze was hard, her tone all cop. "If you hurt her, I may have to shoot you."

She was joking. Right? She had to be. Strangers disappearing in outwardly friendly small towns that turned out to be harboring dark and dangerous secrets was just a fictional cliché.

"I'll keep that in mind," Gabe said as *Bad Day at Black Rock* flashed through his mind.

She nodded, the warning clear. "You do that."

40

"I could get used to this." Charity stretched happily, every muscle in her body feeling deliciously relaxed.

If word ever got out that an hour of great sex could accomplish more than a year's worth of yoga exercises, Seventh Heaven Yoga studio would shut down in a week.

"I already am," Gabe said.

She felt a tinge of loss when he left the rumpled bed, though watching him walk over to the dresser was certainly no hardship. She might not have seen all that many naked men in her life, but seriously doubted that there were many out there who had as hot and hard a body as Gabe had — and were so comfortable with it.

When he turned back around, he was holding his camera.

Quick, sharp panic sliced through her. "Oh, I don't think —"

"Don't think. And don't move."

"Gabriel." Feeling the flush of heat rising in her breasts, she went to cover them with the sheet. "I'm naked."

"Exactly. And you look incredible."

"But —" She folded her arms over the sheet, holding it tightly beneath her arms. "I can't pose for that kind of picture."

"I don't take *that* kind. This is art."

"Since when do you take art photos?"

"Since tonight. When I saw you looking all flushed and satisfied, bathed in starshine and candlelight." Uncommonly for the coast, the sky was clear tonight, allowing the light from a thousand whirling stars and a slice of crescent moon to flow in from the skylight above the bed.

His wicked smile faded just a shade. "Unless you don't trust me not to post pictures of you all over the Internet."

That idea was so outrageous that she let out a laugh on a short exhaled breath that had her relaxing. Just a bit.

"Of course I trust you."

"Good." He gently tugged the cooling sheet back down to where it had been gathered low on her hips. "Just lean back, relax, and let me do all the work." He skimmed a hand down her side, knuckles brushing against her warming skin as he adjusted the sheet to his liking.

"I'm not a model," she protested, even as the caress created a humming in her blood.

"No, you're a woman." He brushed her sex-tousled hair back over her shoulders, leaving her even more exposed. "A very sexy, very desirable, incredibly hot and luscious woman."

The way he was looking at her did make Charity feel hot. Sexy. Even, amazingly, wanton.

"You're just prejudiced."

"You bet." Framing her face between his palms, he bent his head and took her mouth, coaxing her back into the mists.

"Gabriel —"

Even as she felt herself succumbing, the cautious, logical part of Charity, who'd spent her entire life shying away from emotions like the ones that were threatening to swamp her, tried to make itself heard.

"Trust me," he murmured. Her eyes drifted shut as he lightly nipped at her bottom lip with his teeth. "I want to remember you like this."

She felt him move. Heard the click of a shutter.

"With stars in your eyes, and my name on your lips."

His words cut through the clouds in her mind, reminding her that their precious time together was slipping away, like beach sand though her fingers.

"Look at me, Charity."

Refusing to allow herself to cry, and not wanting to waste a single moment, Charity opened her eyes.

And her heart.

41

"Johnny!"

Jasmine, the girl formerly known as Angel, came running toward him, her bag of gathered shells banging against her tanned bare leg. It was their first trip to the beach this year, and she'd been as free and happy as Johnny had ever seen her.

Despite her earlier problems with those mean girls, she'd made friends with two sisters from Ashland, and instead of clinging to him, the way she had last summer, she'd spent much of the day with her new friends, building sand castles and collecting shells. Which would probably be stolen by some other kids her first week back, but since the sun was shining, the picnic lunch from some crab place had been so good, and his sister was behaving a lot like he figured kids who weren't stuck in the system would do at the coast, Johnny wasn't going to worry about that. Now.

"Guess what I found!"

"A shark?"

"No." She shook her head.

"Moby Dick?"

"What's that?"

"A whale."

"No." Another, more emphatic shake of the head.

"A pirate ship?"

"No. But it's almost as good." Her face split into a grin even brighter than the diamonds the sun was making on the water. She grabbed his hand with her free one. "Come see."

He walked with her about twenty yards down the beach, skirting around tangled green kelp and tide pools that were home to orange and blue starfish. The beach Fred and Ethel had taken them to was crescent shaped, curving around the Shelter Bay lighthouse cliff.

"You have to promise not to tell anyone," she said.

"I promise. How much farther?"

"It's right here!" She stopped in front of what appeared to be a cave. "It's Aladdin's cave!" she announced. She tugged on his hand. "Come see!"

In contrast to the sunny day, the cave carved into the cliff was as black as night.

As he came in from the light, it took John-ny's eyes a few seconds to adjust to the darkness. When they did, he saw what had his sister so excited.

"See!" She was spinning around, arms outstretched, like the tiny ballerina that had danced in a music box his mother had owned years ago. She'd wind the key and dance around their apartment the same way Angel was doing now. "It has diamonds on the walls."

From the geology lesson Fred had given some of the older kids earlier, Johnny knew the brilliant chips glinting from the walls and dark sand floor were actually quartz, garnet, and maybe gold, which was prob-ably fool's gold, since he figured all the real stuff had been dug out over the years.

"It's really cool," he said.

Which, even though those weren't dia-monds, was true.

"It's wonderful!" She hugged herself, as if trying to keep the joy from having her float-ing up to the sparkling ceiling. "Guess what I was thinking?"

"What?"

"That people could live here."

"Until the tide came in." Fred had also taught them about tide charts.

"There's a ledge." She pointed. "We could

stay up there until the tide went out. And we could fish and catch crabs and sell diamonds for money to get other things we needed. There's lots of room. It'd be just like camping out."

"It's something to think about," he said, not wanting to burst her bubble.

"We could live here," she said again, as if he couldn't fully grasp her wonderful idea. "Then you wouldn't have to go back to Salem, and I wouldn't have to go back to Bend. And Social Services would never know where to find us."

Oh, shit. Why didn't someone just take that fish-fillet knife Fred carried on his belt and slice his heart into pieces? It would probably hurt a lot less than this.

"It's a great idea," Johnny said. "But what about school?"

"You're ahead of me. You could teach me."

She'd apparently thought it through. In eight-year-old fantasy fashion.

"I think," he said slowly, "that if we ran away from camp, we'd get Fred and Ethel in a lot of trouble. Then they might have to close down the camp. Which would mean other kids wouldn't get to come anymore."

"Oh." Her lower lip came out. "That would be sad."

"Yeah."

"Though I wouldn't mind if those mean girls who were on the bus never got to come again."

"Have they been bothering you again?" Maybe he should talk to Ethel. Or maybe Charity, who was really nice. More than one kid had wished out loud that she could be their mother. And although it felt disloyal to his real mom, Johnny had secretly wished the same thing.

"Not too much. Nobody else likes them, anyway." She sighed. "I really thought it was a great idea."

"It was." He reached down and tousled her hair. "Maybe I can go to court to become an emancipated minor." He knew a kid who'd sued to do that last year. "Then I could get Social Services to let me be your guardian and we could move here to Shelter Bay and come down here all the time."

She perked up a little at that suggestion. "We could get rent money for an apartment from the diamonds."

"That's exactly what I was thinking." He took her hand, squeezed her fingers reassuringly. "Though we'd better leave them here for now. So no other campers will steal them."

"Good plan!"

Although it was too dark to clearly see her

face, he could hear the smile return to her voice.

The Marine was walking toward them, which gave Johnny the feeling that he'd watched them leave and he'd come to check up on them. Which felt kind of strange, since Johnny wasn't used to that many people caring what happened to him.

He wondered, since taking care of an eight-year-old's changing moods was honestly wearing him out, how their mother would ever be able to handle the job. Even if she did ever keep her promise to return.

Which caused the anxiety that had eased with this day trip to the beach to return to gnaw at his stomach again.

42

Charity linked her arm with Gabe's. "So, how are things going?"

"Okay. The kids seemed to like the cameras."

"Didn't they?" She beamed at the memory of all those smiling faces.

Even the tougher kids' facades had cracked a bit once Gabe had set them taking photos of their siblings during yesterday's beach trip.

"How did the dog training go?" he asked.

Although he would've enjoyed watching her work, Ethel had scheduled their sessions at the same time. Something Gabe had decided he was going to have to change. If he was going to be stuck here every afternoon, and it appeared he was, he fully intended to spend those afternoons with Charity.

Having discovered her penchant for sexy underwear, he was aching to know what she was wearing beneath those snug jeans and Camp Rainbow Kids T-shirt.

"It went really smoothly. Of course it helps that all the dogs have already been taught to do the basics like sit and stay, so we're mostly training the kids. Well, yours hasn't been to school yet, but he's really smart and picks things up really fast. Of course you may not ever get him back."

"Oh?" She smelled like vanilla, probably from the baking. Gabe had never realized, until now, that cupcakes could be an aphrodisiac.

"There's this little girl who's fallen in love with him. Her name's Angel, though for some reason, she seems to have decided to change her name to Jasmine, but believe me, she looks as if she's come from central casting to play the role of Zuzu in a remake of *It's a Wonderful Life.*"

That got his attention, which had been imagining spreading chocolate buttercream frosting over her lean, hot body, then slowly licking it off.

"Her brother's the redheaded kid, right? About fifteen?"

"Johnny." She tilted her head to look up at him. "And you called his age right on the money. How did you know that?"

"I saw his tattoo. It was one of those DIY

ones. One arm reads *Mom.* The other, *Angel.*"

"Oh. That's so sad."

"Yeah. It sucks. He asked me if I'd ever killed anyone."

"What did you tell him?"

"The truth. That I had and I hadn't liked it. We didn't exactly get off to a great start, but he showed up for the camera class."

"He probably wants to make sure his sister has photo memories of the summer to take home."

"Yeah. That's what I was thinking."

His fingers were itching with the urge to touch her. Just a hand to her hair. Or her face. But having already created enough of a public stir by showing up with her at the Sea Mist, he resisted the temptation.

"So, when can we blow this pop stand?"

"Feel free to leave any time."

"I meant us. You and me." He bent down, his lips next to her ear, and shared some of the things he'd been thinking about doing to her. With her.

"You're so bad." She laughed and lightly slapped his arm.

"I didn't hear you complaining last night." Which had, amazingly, been even better than their first night together.

She glanced around, as if looking for

eavesdroppers, then lowered her voice to something just a few decibels above a whisper and said, "And you won't tonight, either."

She checked her watch. "I need to retrieve the dogs. One of the volunteer counselors decided to set up an agility course. The kids and the dogs were all having a grand time when I got called away to play kitchen assistant to Sedona's Top Chef. Why don't I take them back to the house and meet you out at the campground?"

"Works for me. I'll pick up dinner."

"That'd be great." She watched as a car pulled into the parking lot and her mother got out. "Uh-oh." Amanda's hair was a very uncharacteristic mess. Mascara had streaked down her cheeks. "Hold that thought."

Gabe watched as she met her mother halfway. Her mother's hands were wildly fluttering in the air. She appeared to be talking a mile a minute even as Charity was obviously trying to get a word in edgewise.

Finally, Charity put her hands on the older woman's shoulders and said something to her. Then turned and walked back to him.

"I'm sorry," she said. "I'm going to have to take a rain check."

"What's wrong?"

"It's Benton. Her husband. Although she's really upset and not entirely making sense, I think he's gone missing."

43

"I don't understand it," Amanda wailed as she paced a patch in the hardwood floor. "Where could he be? How could he just take off without letting me know where he was going?"

"He left about a gazillion voice mails on your home phone," Charity pointed out.

"Not to apologize," she sniffed. "But to talk to me in that oh-so-reasonable tone, accusing me of trying him and convicting him on circumstantial evidence." She wiped the backs of her hands against her wet cheeks, looking for all the world like a heartbroken five-year-old. "Sometimes he talks just like a damn judge."

"Maybe because he *is* a judge," Charity said, looking over toward Gabe, who'd followed them back to the house.

"He's a liar and a cheat and if he isn't already an adulterer, it's probably only because I caught him before he had a chance to use that damn Viagra."

She was quickly working herself from heartbroken to injured party. Charity had watched this scene play out so many times she could probably write the script in her sleep.

"You said you didn't talk to him."

"I didn't." Amanda took the Kleenex Gabe handed her and gave him a watery smile. "Thank you, darling."

He just nodded. Charity suspected that getting involved with anyone else's personal family problems was the last thing he wanted to do.

"But he said —"

"He was in the air," Amanda broke in. "So I left a message on his cell telling him I'd found the damn blue pills and I was leaving him. And filing for divorce."

"You were going to file for divorce without letting him explain?"

"No. I wanted him to suffer. The way he'd made me suffer. Then grovel." Gabe handed her another Kleenex. She used it to dab at her eyes. Then stopped pacing in front of him. "You're a man. Tell me something."

He shot Charity a panicky look that suggested he'd rather face down a horde of Taliban armed with AK-47s than be dragged into this conversation.

"Mother." Although she doubted it would work, Charity tried for reason. "Gabriel doesn't even know Benton."

"He's a man," Amanda repeated on a flare of heat. She put her manicured hands on the hips of a purple gauze sundress. "And we need a man's point of view right now."

"I can't really speak for all men," Gabe said. "But I'll try."

"If you loved a woman, truly loved her, and had pledged a vow to love, honor, and cherish her, until death you do part, and then did something to break her heart, wouldn't you do anything to make amends?"

For not the first time since he'd come back to the house with Charity and her mother, Gabe wondered what the hell he'd thought he could do about this situation.

Until death you do part. He'd already tried that, and although neither he nor his ex died, when he'd first heard those words said, while standing in front of that Marine chaplain in that pretty white chapel at Camp Pendleton, they'd sounded ominously like a death sentence.

This was so above his pay grade.

"I think —"

"I mean," she overran what he'd been about to say, "wouldn't you be willing to crawl naked, down the main street of town, over broken glass, if that's what it took to get the woman you loved back?"

Gabe dearly hoped the judge — who may or may not have been cheating in Hawaii — wouldn't be held to that penance when he resurfaced, but understood how Charity's mother might not be thinking logically at the moment.

"I'd do whatever it took," he assured her.

"See?" The skirt swirled around her still-shapely calves as she spun back to her daughter. "If he really loved me and was innocent, he would've been on the first plane back home. Instead of staying down there with his slut bimbo."

"You don't know that's what he's doing. I understand how upsetting this is," Charity said, "but you're not exactly being fair to him, Mom."

"Like he was fair to me?" She tossed her auburn head as anger began to overcome her earlier distress. Gabe wouldn't have been surprised if she'd stamped a sandal-clad foot.

He could tell that Charity's patience was growing thin. In fact, it looked to be hanging by its last thread.

"Maybe you should call the police," he suggested.

"Oh, I wouldn't want to do that," Amanda said quickly. "He's a judge. He has a reputation to protect. I may want to kill him, but I certainly wouldn't want to injure his reputation. Especially since judges have to stand for election in Washington. I'd never forgive myself if I cost him a career he loves."

Gabe exchanged a look with Charity that told him they were thinking the same thing. That she might be furious and hurt, but there was still at least a spark of love there.

"I know some people at MCBH," he said. "That's the Marine base in Hawaii. Maybe I can find someone with connections who'll do some checking without raising flags."

"Oh, thank you!" When the older woman flung her arms around his neck and kissed his cheek, Charity rolled her eyes.

She was clinging like poison ivy. Taking hold of her waist, Gabe put her a little away from him.

"I can't promise anything."

"I understand." Even as she nodded, Gabe knew she was expecting him to solve her problem. Charity couldn't be more dissimilar from her high-maintenance mother if she'd tried. Which, he realized on a sudden burst of insight, she probably had.

"Why don't I give you two some mother-daughter time alone while I go back to the motor home and make some calls," he told them both. "I'll let you know if I find out anything."

"You're my hero," Amanda said with a watery smile.

This time Charity didn't roll her eyes. Merely mouthed *thank you* behind her mother's back.

She walked him to the door. "I really appreciate this," she said as they went out on the porch, the mutt trotting along between them, while the ridiculously named Peanut stuck to Charity's side.

"Like I told your mother, I can't promise anything."

"I totally understand and I'd be surprised if you do find any information. But you stopped the floodgates, at least for a while. And calmed the storm. Which I'm hugely grateful for." She went up on her toes and kissed him.

He put his hands on her waist. "I suppose sex on the front porch is frowned upon in Shelter Bay."

She looped her arms around his waist and rested her head on his shoulder. "I suspect Kara would have us in the slammer."

"Jailhouse sex." He tipped her head up and kissed her again. Longer. Deeper.

"Truly bad," she said on a laugh even as

her lips clung. "And you know what?"

"What?"

"I like that about you."

Gabe had never thought of himself as a greedy man. His wants and needs had been fairly basic. But as restless need pumped through him, he realized he'd been wrong. Because he wanted Charity in every way possible. For as long as possible.

"I'd better go," he said even as he imagined her sitting on his lap on one of those white Adirondack chairs, her long legs over the wide wooden armrests.

"I suppose so." With a deep sigh that assured him she shared his regret, she backed away and touched a fingertip to his lips. Lips that he knew would still be able to taste her long into the night he figured he was destined to spend alone.

"I really want to be with you tonight," she said, revealing that, once again, their thoughts were traveling the same path. "But —"

She glanced back over her shoulder, into the house.

"She's your mother. You need to take care of her."

"I know. And hey, that's so easy to do, in my spare time this evening I might as well cure cancer and achieve world peace."

He took hold of her hand, linked their fingers together, and tried not to notice that in this, too, they were a perfect fit.

"I have faith in you."

"That makes one of us." Her smile was quick, wry, and, he thought, a little sad.

Tenderness. As unaccustomed as he was to the feeling, it took Gabe a moment to recognize it. Another to realize it didn't terrorize him like he might have expected. It flowed through him like a river, and as much as he wanted her — and he did — right now he wished even more that he could cheer her up.

"I noticed a thrift store the other day while I was driving around town."

"People mostly use it as a recycle place. It does a pretty good business, since conservation's always been popular here and locals are pretty green-minded." He could tell she was a little confused by his change in subject. "Why?"

"Because I thought that maybe tomorrow we can stop by and pick up some cheap dishes."

"You need dishes?"

"I figured you might." He brushed his knuckles down her cheek, pleased as the soft color he'd come to count on bloomed.

"I hear throwing china's a good stress reliever."

She laughed at that, as he'd meant her to. "Thanks for the suggestion. I know an even better way to relieve stress, though."

The invitation was there. In her sultry tone, her gleaming eyes, the Mona Lisa smile teasing at the corners of her lips.

"All the more reason for me to get moving and get on with the mission." Having a goal was actually appealing after all these months of drifting and taking life as it came. "So we can get your mama back with her judge husband. And you back in my bed."

"From your lips," Charity agreed.

44

Maybe he couldn't run away, but Johnny had discovered years ago that running took away some of his frustration and anger. The bitch was that he'd been looking forward to being with Angel again for months. But now he was already dreading the morning when she was going to get on that damn bus that would take her across the mountains to Bend.

Impatient to get outside, but not wanting to leave the cabin until he heard the steady breathing that assured him she'd fallen asleep, he lay in bed, smelling the smoke drifting beneath the door from that other kid who ignored the no-smoking rule every night. No fan of rules himself, Johnny wasn't about to turn him in.

It had taken her an even longer time than usual to finally crash, because she'd rattled on about baking the cupcakes everyone had had for dessert at dinner, and the pictures she'd taken — every single one of ducks floating on the lake — and that goofy-looking little black dog she'd fallen in love with that she wished she could take home with her.

Yeah. Like that was going to happen. Even if the dog didn't already belong to the Marine, there was no way a foster kid would be able to keep a pet. The one thing you learned right away was to travel light.

There was a computer room in the lodge. Kids couldn't go online, probably because they didn't want the older boys looking at porn or the girls spending all their time inside talking with Facebook friends, but maybe he could ask the vet if she could look up some shopping places to see if there was a toy stuffed dog that looked kind of like the Marine's mutt. It wouldn't be exactly the same thing. But another thing you learned in the system was that life was all about settling for less than you wanted.

The sky was clear tonight and the moon-light lit up the trail around the lake nearly as clear as day. His running shoes pounded on the needle-covered dirt as he ran and ran and ran, trying to work off the anger and frustration that had been lurking just beneath his skin all day.

"It fucking isn't fair," he muttered as an

owl hooted somewhere in the treetops.

So, who told you life was going to be fair?

If it weren't for Angel, he'd just keep on running. Split and hitchhike up to Seattle. He'd heard there were lots of homeless kids who banded together up there. If the state insisted on breaking up his family, he could just make a new one.

He'd do it. Be gone tomorrow.

But he wouldn't, couldn't, leave his sister.

The Marine hadn't turned out to be as hard-assed as he looked. At least not with the kids. He'd complimented Angel on her ducks, and even suggested she might have a career as a wildlife photographer for *National Geographic,* which was totally bogus since foster kids were pretty much on a dead-end road, but she'd gotten so excited she'd gone racing off to take more.

Maybe he'd go ahead and ask the guy about joining the military, after all. What could it hurt?

He turned a corner, jumping over a log that had fallen across the path, then was forced to pull up short to keep from slamming into a woman who'd suddenly come out from behind some tall trees.

"Mom?" It had been five years since he'd last seen his mother. This woman's hair wasn't the bright yellow blond she'd had then, but the same brown as the deer he'd seen earlier browsing in the bushes near the lodge.

"Hello, my darling." She held out her arms.

Johnny had been dreaming of this day for years. Waiting for it. Even, sometimes, though God didn't seem to listen to kids like him, praying for it.

So why did it feel as if his shoes were suddenly bolted to the damn ground?

"Hi. Uh . . . what are you doing here?"

"Why, I've come to see you, of course." She slowly lowered her arms, which made him feel guilty. So, what else was new?

A court-ordered psychologist had once told him that he wore guilt like a ball and chain. He'd never thought of it that way before, but he'd decided maybe the shrink was right. Which hadn't changed anything. All it had done was give a name to that feeling constantly eating away at his stomach.

"How did you know I was here?"

"I went to the DHS office in Salem to schedule a meeting with you and your sister, and the woman told me you were away at a camp and I'd have to come back when it was over. So, I went to the library and used their computer to Google the camp." She held up her hands again, palms up. "So, here I am."

"But how did you get here?"

"Oh, that took a bit more doing." She smiled with her lips and with her eyes. She looked okay, Johnny thought. A lot better than last time when she'd shown up at his foster home, smelling of alcohol and with fresh needle tracks on her arms. "I got a job with the market in town that supplies the food to the camp. Mostly I stock shelves, but since today's my day off, I talked one of the drivers into letting me come along to help."

"That was . . ." Sneaky? Crazy? "Clever."

She winked. "The Lord works in mysterious ways."

Apparently his worry showed on his face because she quickly said, "Johnny, it's just an expression. You don't have to worry. I've been in rehab. I'm all better and I'm on my medication, which keeps me nice and level, and I even put a deposit down on a lovely apartment in Shelter Bay. As soon as you and Angel get out of camp, you're both going to come live with me, and we'll finally be a happy family again."

Johnny couldn't remember ever being a happy family. But he also wanted to believe her. "My caseworker didn't say anything about that."

"Oh, you know bureaucracies." She waved a hand. Her laugh sounded a little too brittle.

Johnny told himself she was probably just nervous. Hell, *he* was nervous. Although he'd been waiting for her to get her act straight for what seemed like forever, there was a really big part of him who was still that five-year-old kid with Kool-Aid dripping off his head and shoulders into a Barbie pink birthday cake.

"Yeah," he said. "I know them real well."

He couldn't quite keep the edge from his voice and worried that he might have hurt her feelings, but she nodded. "Then you know they move about as slow as molasses in January. But don't you worry, baby."

She ran a hand over the top of his head. Her fingers were stained, showing she still smoked. Which he figured made sense. One foster home he'd been in for six months his first year of middle school, the husband had been in AA and smoked like a chimney.

"By the time camp's over, I'll have jumped through all their legal hoops and everything will be just hunky-dory."

She glanced around, looking a little more nervous. Which sort of made sense. He figured a lot of people were probably afraid to be in the woods alone at night. What they didn't realize was that the dark could be just as dangerous in your own house.

"Well, I'd better be getting back before that truck leaves without me. I just wanted to touch base with you and let you know my exciting news." Her eyes got all shiny, which had his burning with tears he was trying to hold back, too. "I'm so happy."

He'd been here so many times before. And each time something had gone so wrong. But that didn't stop him from putting his arms around her. Which was when he realized that since the last time he'd seen her, he'd grown taller. Taller than her.

"I love you, baby." Her voice wavered, reminding him a lot of Angel, when she was trying not to cry.

"I love you, too, Mom." It was the total truth.

She was clinging to him. So tight Johnny was afraid he might suffocate. But he didn't want to push her away, so he stood there, and instead of feeling as happy as he'd thought he would, as happy as she said *she* was, Johnny desperately hoped she'd leave before Angel came looking for him.

He still loved her. He probably always would. But that didn't mean he trusted her. Not entirely. Not enough to let her near his sister.

At least not yet.

"You have to promise not to say anything to Angel," she said as she finally released him. "I want her to enjoy her time here at camp, and if she knew I was back, she might get it into her pretty head to want to leave early. And that might cause problems with those tight-assed bitches at DHS, who would probably accuse me of breaking the rules."

Which she was. The agency instructions had always been very clear from the first. No unsupervised visits.

He thought about Angel giggling with the closest thing to joy he'd seen in years as she'd shown off her duck pictures. And how she'd had that smudge of flour on her cheek from baking this afternoon. While the image of her happily carrying that black dog around flashed though his mind, Johnny said, "I promise."

Walking back to the cabin, he reran the brief conversation over and over again in his mind, reliving every word, every gesture, like putting them under one of those micro-scopes Fred had brought to camp to show them all the things living in the lake water.

His mother had always been a small woman, but when he hugged her, she felt — he searched for the word — *frail.* Was she

392

too thin? Had she been sick? She was wearing a sleeveless blouse and he couldn't see any new lines on her arms. But that didn't mean she wasn't taking pills. Not the ones she was supposed to take. But the ones she'd get on the street to help quiet the voices.

She promised that she was all better. That she'd been through rehab and had her life back on track.

And where had he heard that before?

As the moon rode across the night sky, Johnny lay on the top bunk, Angel snuggled up beside him, listening to the faint sigh of the wind in the towering trees outside the cabin and the sound of water rushing over the rocks. And although he knew that daring to wish for any normality was like spitting in the wind, he hoped it was true.

His mom had told him when Angel was born that he was the big brother now, the man of the family, and it was his responsibility to protect his sister. Which he'd promised to do.

Which hadn't always been easy. Like the time the social worker told him that Angel wasn't going to be his sister anymore. He hadn't understood how that could happen. Of course she was his sister. He'd been at the hospital with his grandmother when

Angel had been born.

But according to the woman, someone wanted to adopt Angel. He remembered her sounding surprised by that. So, legally, once the adoption was final, she'd have a brand-new name and belong to a new family.

That was the first time he'd run away. He'd gone to the house where she'd been living, where he'd been allowed to visit her once, on her last birthday. But when he arrived, it was already too late. She was gone.

He'd failed. Even worse, he'd worried what his mother would think when she came back and discovered that she had only one child, not two.

He'd felt like the worst son in the world. It was the first time he'd stopped talking, because what excuse could he give? How could he have let Angel and his mother down so badly? There were no words to make things better.

The police found him sleeping in an alley in Corvallis and took him back to DHS. Since he was considered a runaway threat, instead of placing him with another family, they'd put him into a group home, which was pretty much as close as he could get to going to jail without actually committing a crime that got him locked up in juvie.

Johnny hadn't cared. It was what he deserved.

But then, one day, after he'd been there about a month, he'd gotten called to the front office, where a new social worker told him that she'd gotten him a new placement. He hadn't cared about that, either. It wasn't as if any of them were really homes. One was pretty much the same as another.

But there was more. The social worker confided that things hadn't worked out as well as everyone had hoped with Angel. So she was back in foster care. Which meant she was his sister again.

The news was the next-best thing she could have told him. The best news would have been that their mom was okay and was waiting outside in the car to take them both away with her. Which she wasn't.

He'd asked the social worker if she knew where Angel was staying. She hadn't, but promised to check. She also promised to arrange a visit. Something that never happened, because shortly after that, the woman had moved on to other kids, and his new social worker claimed to know nothing about any visit.

And now their mom was back. And, if she was telling the truth, she was finally all better and she, Angel, and he were going to live together like normal people. Which was all he'd always wanted.

What he'd been waiting for what seemed like his entire life to happen.

So why did he feel like he was in one of those Halloween haunted houses, waiting for the zombie to leap out at him?

With his mind spinning like a leaf in one of those eddies below Rainbow Falls, Johnny failed to notice the faint scent of cigarette smoke drifting in from the cabin's living room, where Crystal Harper sat alone in the dark, sitting vigil over her children.

45

"I don't understand it." Amanda was back to pacing, making Charity glad the floor was hardwood, because she undoubtedly would have worn a path in any carpeting by now. "I'm not the guilty party in this situation. Why would Benton be punishing me like this?"

"What makes you think he's punishing you?"

"Surely you don't think it's merely a co-incidence that he disappeared from the face of the earth after I refuse to answer my phone?"

She shook her head as she looked out the window, over the harbor, toward the bridge leading to the coast. As if she could look across the vast blue Pacific to the Hawaiian Islands and spot her errant husband.

She suddenly went white as the sails on the boats docked at the marina. "I just had a horrible thought."

"What?" From her mother's pallor, Charity suspected she'd stopped thinking about herself long enough to focus on another possibility.

"What if he hasn't run off with the bimbo? What if something terrible has happened to him?"

"He checked out of his hotel room." Using his network of connections, Gabe had found a former Marine who was now a Maui cop, who'd checked out the judge's hotel. "The front-desk clerk said he'd appeared to be alone when he'd checked in. And there weren't any signs of violence," Charity reminded her.

"I believed we had such a good marriage," Amanda said for the umpteenth time. She seemed more bewildered than angry.

Charity couldn't blame her. Hadn't she felt the same way when she'd discovered how Ethan had betrayed her? So much of that day was still a blur. But she could definitely remember the pain.

"It looked that way to me." She crossed the room and smoothed her hands over her mother's shoulders. Even as they were slumped in discouragement, she could feel the boulderlike tangle of muscles beneath her fingertips.

A sailboat skimmed across the water, the

red, green, and white running lights reminding Charity a bit of Christmas. Which, in turn, had her wondering if Gabe would still be in Shelter Bay when December came around.

Fat chance of that.

Since he didn't have an actual home to return to, he'd probably spend the winter somewhere warm. Maybe South America. Or perhaps Costa Rica. She knew a vet who'd set up a practice in the capital city of San José and swore the country was paradise on earth. Maybe he'd head for the spun-sugar beaches of Mexico.

"We were going to sail around the world," Amanda said, dragging Charity's mind back from a mental video of Gabe drinking salt-rimmed margaritas and making love with some sexy señorita with flashing dark eyes who knew more ways to seduce a man than Charity could learn in a lifetime.

"I'm sorry. I was thinking of something. About your situation," she said, not quite truthfully. "What did you say?"

Surely she'd heard wrong. Her mother was the last person she'd imagine sailing around the world. Unless she was on a luxury yacht with a full crew doing all the work while she sipped mimosas and worked on her tan.

"When Benton retires from the bench, he intends to buy a blue-water sloop. We were planning to spend a year just sailing the globe."

"Is that something you'd really want to do?"

Her mother had a lifelong habit of taking on the characteristics she thought her husbands would want in a wife. But since they were often at direct odds with her own vibrant personality, it was little wonder the marriages hadn't worked out.

"I know it sounds absurd." Despite the seriousness of the situation, she managed a wry smile. "I certainly thought so when he brought it up the first night we went out to dinner. But until I went out on the boat with him, I'd forgotten how much I enjoyed sailing with my father."

Charity decided this was not the time to point out that the grandfather she'd never known had died on a trip much like the one Benton was suggesting.

"Since we've spent so much time on the water, I decided it sounded like a grand adventure," Amanda said.

"I can't deny that." Not one she'd be at all interested in, yet her mother had seemed different and far more carefree the day they'd all spent out on the boat.

"But now it's too late."

"No." Charity's own life might be in flux right now, but of this she was absolutely certain. "It's only too late if you don't tackle whatever problems the two of you might have. By having an adult conversation and seriously addressing the issues."

"It's difficult to address the issue if I can't find him," Amanda pointed out with a flare of her usual spirit, which Charity found encouraging.

"If you really want to make things work with your husband, then you should go for it."

Amanda lifted her chin. Renewed determination flashed in her eyes. "I intend to."

Then she sighed and looked out the window again at the boat skimming beneath the bridge. "But first I have to find him."

46

Gabe couldn't sleep. After calling Charity one last time to let her know that the Marine-turned-cop had tracked down a guy who'd sold the judge a thirty-six-foot sloop, which apparently had been his actual reason for flying to Hawaii in the first place, he'd lain awake, thinking about her fathomless green eyes, her silky skin, the soft little sounds she made while making love.

No. They hadn't been making love. It was sex. Okay, maybe it was the best sex he'd had in . . . well, forever . . . but it would be a mistake to read too much into it.

After all, she wasn't the only one who'd been celibate for way too long. It only made sense that they'd be explosive.

But it was more than just sex. He honestly liked her, and although they might seem like polar opposites, he realized they actually had more in common than even she might be willing to admit.

He liked being around her. Liked talking with her. Liked watching her with the dogs and kids, which had him picturing her in that rich, full family life she'd admitted she wanted here in Shelter Bay.

He could understand why she'd chosen the town. It was quiet, yet lively in its own way with all the interconnections between its residents. There'd been a time when Gabe would have considered such a lack of privacy intolerable. But viewing it as he might through the lens of his camera, watching the interactions of all the volunteers at the camp with the eye of a professional, uninvolved observer, he realized it was the way the community worked. The same way people would come together to help a fellow resident in need, they'd also feel free to engage in discussions of that same person's personal life. He figured those who'd chosen to live here considered it a reasonable trade-off.

However, although he was surprised to be actually enjoying his time here in Shelter Bay, his days with Charity, the kids at the camp, and even her mother, who might be a drama queen but whose intentions tended toward good, he'd leave it — and them — as he'd left other towns, and other people.

Moving on was what he did. Washington

was waiting for him — gleaming white ferryboats plying the waters of Puget Sound, glaciers and rain forests. All those Gore-Tex-wearing people drinking their lattes and chai teas.

Then there was Alaska — oil fields, more glistening glaciers, fishermen. Even after he finished up in the Aloha State, there was still a big wide world waiting for him to explore.

And if that nagging little voice in the back of his mind suggested that maybe he was running away from something, rather than running toward it, Gabe ignored it.

47

After tossing and turning, spending way too much of her night thinking about Gabriel, Charity dragged herself out of bed and, fortified with about a gallon of coffee nearly strong enough to stand a spoon up in, performed two surgeries — a Siamese cat spay and a Dalmatian's tooth cleaning.

After handing the clinic off to the afternoon fill-in vet, she was standing behind the reception counter, checking tomorrow's schedule, when Kelli and Cole walked in.

"You're back!" She came around the desk and hugged Kelli. "Wow, you're tan!"

The new bride smiled prettily and practically preened. "We got in last night. As for the tan, it's all that fabulous Hawaiian sun. I wish I could have bottled it to bring back with me."

"Considering that Oregonians tend to rust rather than tan, you could probably sell it and make a fortune," Charity said. "Especially come February. What can I do for you?"

"We're here to ask about adopting a puppy," Cole said.

"We want to start a family as soon as we can." Kelli beamed up at her new husband. The stars in her eyes told Charity that their honeymoon had been a smashing success. "Now that Cole's finally out of the service, we don't want to waste any more time."

"Kelli read that it's best to have a dog settle in before the baby arrives."

"I'd agree with that," Charity said. "Especially if you're set on a puppy, which is a lot of work. You're going to have to housebreak it, and train it not to chew up your furniture and shoes, and baby toys, and it's going to have to go out and be walked, and cleaned up after, and . . ."

"Gee." Kelli's previously dazzling smile faded in wattage. "It sounds as if you're trying to talk us out of the idea. But everyone knows you want to find every homeless animal in the county a home."

"I do," Charity said. "But I want it to be a forever-after home. If people take a pet home on a whim and it turns out not to be a good mix for them or their family, the poor dog gets into a boomerang situation. Which causes its confidence and social skills to drop, which makes it even more difficult to place. So, since the goal is to have the dog and its owners happy, it takes a little matchmaking."

Cole nodded. "That makes sense."

"Have you thought about what type of dog you'd like?"

"We were thinking something sort of medium-size," Cole said. "Maybe a Lab."

She laughed. "A Lab is only medium-size if you're comparing it to a Saint Bernard or Great Pyrenees like Peanut. But it's still a good choice and there's a reason Labs have become one of the most popular dogs in the country.

"They're sweet, extremely loyal, and super family dogs as long as you understand that they can also be pretty high energy and that it'll take two or three years of growing up before they approach that calm dog that's depicted lying in front of a fireplace on so many Christmas cards."

"We had a chocolate Lab when I was growing up," Kelli said. "So I know about their energy. Which is why I thought we'd get a head start before I get pregnant."

"That's wise," Charity said, her mind skimming through a roster of dogs currently staying in volunteer homes around the town. "What would you say to skipping a bit past the puppy stage? It just so happens that we have a four-year-old yellow Lab in foster care. Princess Leia's great with kids, and already housebroken and obedience trained."

"Princess Leia?" Cole looked less than pleased by that idea.

"Her foster mom's a big *Star Wars* fan." Charity also understood that the former Marine might not be wild about calling *Princess* in to dinner every night. "Of course you're free to change her name."

"Wouldn't that confuse her?"

"It could. But you could always shorten it to Leia."

"Oh, that's a pretty name," Kelli said, looking hopefully at her husband, who still didn't look entirely convinced.

"If she's so good, how did she end up in a shelter?" Cole asked.

"She was a stray who'd been scrounging for scraps on the beach. At first we were hoping she'd just gotten loose from her owners, but we put her on our Web site, and several others, and no one's shown up, which leads me to believe she was probably just dumped.

"She was underweight and had heart-worms when we rescued her. But she's all recovered and ready for her new home."

"That's horrible that anyone would just dump a defenseless animal."

"Unfortunately, it's happening more and more. But as a member of the AVSAB — for the American Veterinary Society of Animal Behavior — my goal is to improve the quality of life for all animals. Since that includes strengthening their bond with their owners, I'd never place a dog or cat in a situation I don't feel it's not well suited to."

Cole rubbed his jaw as he exchanged a look with his new wife. "What do you think, honey? I know you wanted a puppy —"

"Well, Charity does have a point." Kelli's forehead furrowed as she studied the posters of available dogs on the wall. "People say babies are really disruptive. Perhaps trying to train a puppy while bringing home a newborn might be more stressful." She focused in on the dog Charity had pointed out. "She looks sweet."

"Leia's a darling," Charity said, using the dog's name to personalize her. "And child-tested. Her foster mom has four kids. The youngest is a rambunctious boy toddler who climbs all over her and there've been no problems. She even gets along with the family's cat.

"Why don't we do this," she suggested. "Let me bring her by your house sometime in the next week or so. We can see how you think she'll fit in. Give her a trial run, so to speak."

"That's a good idea," Cole said.

"I'll cook dinner," Kelli said, seeming to like the proposal, as well.

"Oh, I wouldn't want you to have to go to all that trouble."

"Really, it's no trouble. Cole's mom has been teaching me how to cook some of his favorite meals, and I'd love a chance to try out a dinner on someone else besides my husband." She brightened at that idea. "You'll be our first guest as a married couple. How about this weekend? Are you free Sunday?"

"I'd have to check." If she was only going to have this brief stolen time with Gabe, Charity didn't want to waste a minute.

"Of course Gabe's invited, too."

"Word travels fast." They'd been back only a few hours, yet somehow Kelli had managed to hear that she and Gabe were a couple.

Charity knew her thoughts were written on her face when Kelli laughed. "Mary Chapman just happened to mention you when I was checking out with my groceries this morning. Then Amber at the Grateful Bread filled me in when I stopped to pick up some sourdough rolls and those scrumptious blueberry coffee beans they sell every summer. I have to admit I was surprised to hear Gabe was still in town, since he seemed as if he couldn't wait to leave after the wedding."

"He got sidetracked by a dog."

"Not just a dog, to hear both Mary and Amber tell it. And I have to say, I couldn't be happier. Gabe really needs someone in his life. And heavens, everyone's been waiting for you to give up that silly moratorium."

Everyone?

"You'll have to forgive my bride," Cole said. "Now that she's experienced the true bliss of matrimony with the perfect husband, she wants everyone else to get hitched."

Kelli didn't deny the accusation. "You can't blame me for wanting all my friends to be as happy as I am." She went up on her toes and kissed that allegedly perfect husband. It was only a quick peck, but Charity could feel the genuine affection between the couple.

Just as she experienced a little prick of something that felt too much like envy for comfort.

After putting off the dinner invitation for now, Charity set up a morning appointment

411

to bring the Lab over to their house one morning later that week.

That settled, she was preparing to leave when Amanda came downstairs dressed in her belted khaki shorts and a forest green twin set, the cardigan tied over her shoulders. Instead of the sandals she'd worn the day of the makeover, she was wearing an obviously new pair of snowy white sneakers.

"I've made a decision," she announced.

"Oh?" Charity asked carefully.

"You were right. About me always losing myself in my husbands."

"I don't remember saying that." Though she had admittedly thought it.

"I know. But I could hear it in your tone when you asked if I really wanted to sail around the world with Benton. Which I did. And still do," she admitted. "But since he seems to have sailed off without me, I've decided to make lemons out of lemonade —"

"I think it's the other way around," Charity murmured.

"Whatever." The diamond on her left hand flashed and caught the sunlight, splitting it into rainbows. "My point is that I might as well use this time wisely to start living my own life. Just in case I don't manage to salvage this marriage."

"That's very adult of you." And so not at all like her mother.

"Isn't it?" Amanda sighed. Then squared her shoulders, as if going into battle, and flashed a Cheshire cat smile as she put on a pair of oversized, rhinestone-studded, black-framed Chanel sunglasses that made her look a bit like a glitzy Jackie O. "Better late than never."

48

Las Vegas

Las Vegas' Fremont Street had, for many years, been most people's picture-postcard image of the city. It had also appeared in many movies, including a chase scene in the James Bond flick *Diamonds Are Forever.* Once known as Glitter Gulch, due to all the neon lights luring tourists into the casinos, the street fell onto hard times due to competition from the brighter, bigger, flashier Strip.

Just when it looked as if the giant neon cowboy towering over the street might be waving a final good-bye, Fremont Street was transformed into a pedestrian mall covered with the world's largest LED-screen canopy that flashed light shows over tourists' heads. Unfortunately, thanks to heaters and air conditioners keeping the street at a constant seventy degrees, it had also become a popular place for hookers to hang out.

Streets in Las Vegas had never grown old gracefully. Just a block off Glitter Gulch, the neighborhood turned dicey again. This area was not one Jack Craig had ever visited before. Nor did he ever intend to visit again. If he could help it.

A monsoon storm was threatening on the horizon. Jack could feel the electricity in the air. Taste it, along with the metallic sting of dread, on his tongue. The dark clouds boiling in from the western desert echoed the turmoil churning in his gut.

The detective agency was located on the second floor of a narrow building squeezed between a seedy souvenir store and a bail bondsman. The peeling walls, which could use a coat of paint, were lined with black metal files, the tops of which were piled high with dog-eared manila folders, lined yellow pads, and newspapers.

A portable TV attached to one wall with a metal bracket was tuned to a Chicago Cubs game. Apparently the curse of the goat was going strong, because the Cubs were losing to Washington fifteen to three.

Jack did not want to be here today. But if he wanted to have sex ever again in this lifetime, and he definitely did, he had no choice.

"Mr. O'Keefe?" he asked the man seated

behind the desk, who was eating from a white take-out container of Chinese food. Which explained the spicy aroma of kung pao shrimp pervading the office. Or maybe it was drifting up through the vents from the restaurant on the street level.

The guy looked up. "That's me. And you would be Jack Craig."

Jack inwardly cringed. With three car dealerships and commercials running around the clock on all the local television and radio stations, both his name and face were familiar.

He stood in the doorway, wondering, not for the first time, what he was doing even looking for Crystal Harper. The woman was nothing but trouble. She'd been, for six roller-coaster weeks, his own personal curse. A curse that once he'd managed to escape, he'd put entirely out of his mind.

Until he'd gotten the cockamamy idea to share his life story with his new wife.

"I am. But I'd like to keep this confidential." Which was why he hadn't asked his attorney for the name of a respectable detective.

"No problem. I get that a lot." The man's voice had a Midwestern flatness, which along with the framed aerial photo of Wrigley Field on his wall suggested that he, like

416

nearly everyone else in the city, had come from somewhere else. Many seeking a fresh start and the anonymity Jack would've given anything for today.

"So, what brings you all the way downtown?" O'Keefe asked, appearing unimpressed by Jack's local celebrity status. "Using my amazing detective powers of deduction, I'm guessing you're not here to sell me a car."

Jack glanced over at the single wooden chair on the visitors' side of the desk. "Would you mind if I sat down?"

"Oh, sure." The detective, such as he was, waved a chopstick at the chair. "Just put those papers anywhere."

This could well be, next to getting involved with the whacked-out woman in the first place, probably the worst decision Jack had ever made.

"It's a little complicated," he said as he carefully moved the jumbled stack of papers from the chair seat to the cluttered top of a low, horizontal filing cabinet.

"Most of my cases are. If they were easy, people wouldn't need me." O'Keefe stabbed another bite and gave Jack a long look as he chewed. "You want some lunch?" he asked around a mouthful of shrimp and vegetables. "The place downstairs delivers."

"No, thank you." Jack's stomach was already roiling from nerves. "There was this woman."

"My cases usually involve a woman." The detective looked up at the television again. Shook his head and sighed. "Damn goat."

Pointing a black remote at the screen, he turned off the game, put aside the carton of food, and gave Jack his full attention. Although the office might not inspire confidence, Jack viewed intelligence in the detective's dark eyes.

"Why don't you start at the beginning?" Daniel O'Keefe, owner and seemingly sole employee of O'Keefe and Associates Detective Agency, suggested. "Then we'll see what we can do to solve your problem."

Jack took a deep breath and thought back on the tears, threats, and recriminations he'd been treated to this morning instead of a proper breakfast. Then began the long, painful story from the beginning.

49

"Your Marine has an amazing amount of patience," Sedona said as she and Charity stood at the kitchen window of the lodge, watching the kids splashing in the lake.

"He's not my Marine."

"Tell that to someone who didn't see you driving home at dawn," said Kara, who'd ducked into the kitchen in search of a piece of the blackberry pie Sedona had shown up with for lunch.

Charity glanced around to make sure they were alone. "That's the trouble with a small town. You can't get away with anything."

"Tell me about it." Kara took a bite of pie. "Oh, yum. Okay, if I drop dead this minute, I'll die a happy woman. If more cops knew about this, the bottom would drop out of the doughnut business overnight."

"It's the cream cheese that puts it over the top," Sedona said. "Most people just use cornstarch or tapioca."

"It's definitely delicious," Charity said, eager for the change of topic. "The best pie I've ever eaten, and if your other recipes are anything like this, adding pies to your menu is definitely going to be a hit."

"Thank you," Sedona said. "And there's no point in trying to sidetrack the conversation, because it isn't going to work. Getting back to your Marine, I have to admit that perhaps it's because I grew up on a commune with parents who still keep copies of their police mug shots for war protesting in the family scrapbook, but I wouldn't have expected a warrior type to be so good with kids."

"Sax is great with Trey," Kara said, referring to her son. "And he was a SEAL, which is about as much of a warrior type as they come."

"Got me there," Sedona said easily.

"The kids do seem to love him," Charity said, watching as a pair of tweens strolled by in their two-piece swimming suits, trying out their flirting skills.

The girls especially had responded to Gabe, which was totally understandable. After all, he epitomized tall, dark, and dangerous. Yet the man inside that ripped body was definitely turning out to be more complex.

"How about you?" Kara asked as Peanut, wanting to join the fun, leaped into the water, causing a tidal wave of a splash.

"I'm attracted." She knew better than to try to lie to a woman who'd learned interrogation tactics at the FBI Academy.

"Who wouldn't be? He's nearly as luscious as this pie." Kara took another bite and sighed happily.

"You're engaged."

"True. And I adore Sax. But I'm not dead. And your Marine's the type of raw, dangerously compelling male a woman notices."

"It's just sex." She decided against pointing out yet again that he was not *her* Marine, since she suspected neither woman would believe her.

"And your point is?" Sedona asked.

Gabe's Shih Tzu, not to be outdone by his oversized BFF, followed Peanut into the lake. Then dog-paddled over to the little girl — Angel, Charity remembered — who'd been carrying him around like a stuffed toy since Gabe had first shown up at the camp with him.

"It can't go anywhere." She'd gone into this affair with her eyes wide open. No strings. No entanglements. No regrets.

"That's what I said in the beginning about

Sax," Kara said.

"And look how that turned out," Sedona pointed out.

"This is different," Charity argued. "Mine's a summer affair. That's all."

"Like *A Summer Place,*" Sedona said.

"Troy Donahue and Sandra Dee," Kara said approvingly. "And Kim Novak and William Holden slow dancing beneath those Japanese lanterns in *Picnic,* which is the best movie dance ever. Much hotter than *Dirty Dancing,* which was admittedly cool but, except for Patrick Swayze pulling Baby out of the corner, not all that romantic.

"Oh, and don't forget *Long Hot Summer.*" She looked out the window at Gabe, who was standing on the bank of the lake talking to Angel's brother. "Actually, now that I think about it, except for the difference in coloring, your Marine reminds me a bit of Newman's Ben Quick. More the charisma than the looks."

People who first saw the badge and gun belt would probably be surprised to learn that Kara was a romantic who had a weakness for fifties and sixties romances. Which was why, when it was her turn to choose the DVDs for their monthly girls' spa night at home, they usually ended up watching movies about star-crossed lovers who, after surviving myriad soap opera–type melodramatic challenges, ended up walking into the sunset to live happily ever after.

Except for last month's pick, *Splendor in the Grass,* where Warren Beatty's rejection gave poor teenage Natalie Wood a nervous breakdown.

"Real life isn't like the movies," she felt obliged to point out.

"Unfortunately," Kara and Sedona both said.

Charity couldn't argue.

50

Johnny was standing on the bank of the lake, snapping away with his new camera as Angel splashed her way through the beginners' swim test. Considering she hadn't even known how to float at the beginning of camp, and had been afraid of the water last year, this summer she'd leaped right in and seemed to be having a great time.

He'd been worried that his mother might come back, but so far, it had been five days since he'd seen her in the woods and she seemed to be staying away. Which he'd decided was a good thing because as much of a magpie as Angel was, if she knew Crystal was back, she would never have been able to keep the secret.

"Your sister's looking good out there," a familiar deep voice behind him offered. It was the Marine. Gabe, he'd said to call him, although since that seemed too weird, Johnny didn't take him up on it.

"Yeah. I think she's going to pass."

"With flying colors. She's taken to swimming like all those ducks she's been photographing."

"That was nice of you to say that about her pictures. She can't stop talking about how she's going to go to Africa and photograph lions when she grows up."

"Everyone needs a goal. And I wasn't being nice. It was the truth. The kid's got a good eye — she just may make it." He looked down at the camera Johnny was holding in his hand. "You're not so bad yourself. You capture moods more than a lot of pros I've worked with."

"Right." It was one thing to toss compliments to a little kid. But Johnny hadn't just fallen off the crab boat.

"Seriously. That one of your sister putting the necklace on my dog is close to professional quality."

Angel had made the necklace by stringing together wildflowers she'd picked from the butterfly garden Fred and Ethel had planted. The bright red and yellow flowers had shown up really well against the dog's black fur. Johnny had been pleased with the way he'd managed to capture the shot as the dog gazed up at his sister with what appeared to be adoration in those round brown eyes.

The compliment, which seemed genuine enough, shouldn't give him so much pleasure. But it did.

He shrugged, trying for nonchalance, as Angel dived off the board, disappeared beneath the water, then, just when Johnny started to worry, bobbed up like a cork. "Thanks."

"I was about your age the first time I picked up a camera."

"Really?"

"Yeah. It changed my life."

Johnny wasn't comfortable talking with anyone about Angel or his life. But he also wasn't used to people talking to him like they actually cared about him and what he had to say. And he was curious.

"How?"

"It's a kinda long story. I didn't exactly come from a stable home. My parents were both drunks."

Johnny knew something about having a parent who drank. "That's tough."

"Yeah. It was. I wasted a lot of years being angry."

And couldn't Johnny identify with that?

"I used to run, too. Like you do. Sometimes it helped. Sometimes it didn't."

Johnny was surprised the guy had been

watching him. Then wondered why.

"How about you?" Gabe asked. "Does it help?"

"Maybe I just run because I like it."

It was Gabe's turn to shrug. Damned if the kid's wall wasn't thick and high. Which made sense since he'd undoubtedly spent a lifetime building it. It wouldn't be easy to break through any time soon. Probably not even in the length of time left. But although Gabe was sure all the campers came with their own compelling stories, there was something about this particular teenager that tugged at him. Enough that he'd never be able to forgive himself if he didn't try.

"Whatever works," he said with studied nonchalance. "Anyway, I used to get in trouble a lot. Mostly for fighting. I was one of those tough kids who was perfectly balanced." He paused, waiting until the kid finally caved and looked up at him. "I had a chip on both shoulders."

Okay. So much for that try. The teen didn't even crack a smile.

Undaunted, Gabe forged on. "I got in trouble with the police once."

That drew another sideways glance.

"I was out with some older kids, which, I want to point out, is no excuse. Because I knew what we were doing was wrong. We got drunk, hot-wired a golf cart, and drove it all around the greens at the country club."

He didn't add that while he'd been down on his knees, puking his guts out into the toilet of the small-town two-cell Lowcountry jail, he'd wondered what the hell his parents liked about liquor and vowed never to follow his parents down that dead-end alcoholic path.

"Fortunately, since one of the kids' dad was a lawyer, he pulled some strings and we got off with paying restitution and community service. Even better for me, the sheriff's brother-in-law was the newspaper editor, who needed someone to photograph that night's high school football game after his sports reporter moved on to a job in Charleston. The guy stuck this old thirty-five-millimeter camera in my hand and told me to go out, and if I got anything decent, he'd pay me for each shot he used."

It was only much later that Gabe realized how fortunate he'd been. The other two kids' parents had simply written the checks to pay their share of the damage. Which his parents were too financially strapped to do, even if they'd been inclined to get him off the hook. Which they hadn't been.

But his life, which had been on the road

to some serious trouble, took a 180-degree turn.

"Seems I had a knack for it. And I liked being able to freeze time in that single frame. I went through six rolls of thirty-six exposures on that first Friday night game.

"Maybe the guy thought I had talent, or maybe he just wanted to save film, but he started teaching me how to bracket my shots, and how to choose how to tell the story, and how to select the image that would make the most impact."

"Like you were telling us today. About how if your picture wasn't good enough, you aren't close enough."

"Yeah. Which I got from Robert Capa, who covered five wars and really knew what he was talking about. Anyway, this editor who introduced me to photography worked for a weekly that was part of a syndicate of small-town papers scattered throughout the South. So, pretty soon I was picking up some extra cash taking other shots for them." He'd used some of the money he'd earned to buy a police scanner, which had paid for itself the first month.

"I went to college and spent two years majoring in photography, but by then I'd already been getting paid for my work for three years and didn't want to waste time.

I'd already decided I wanted to be a war photographer because it sounded dangerous. Since I was young, green, and wanted adventure, and figured the uniform would impress girls, I joined the Marines."

"So, did it? Impress the girls?"

Ha. He'd finally hit on something the kid was really interested in. Gabe grinned. "Yeah." Wanting to focus on the positive, he didn't see any reason to mention that hadn't always turned out to be a good thing.

"Were you afraid? Being in war?"

"Sure. But fear's not important. It's how you manage it that matters."

Johnny Harper thought about that for a long, silent time.

Then, *damn,* just when Gabe thought he might be going to share something personal, or ask something important, his sister came running up to him, waving a blue ribbon over her wet blond curls and calling out, "Did you see me floating, Johnny? On my back?"

"I sure did." As the teen bent down to scoop her up, soaking the front of his shirt and jeans, the moment was lost.

For now.

51

Jack Craig had practiced what he was going to say over and over again on the drive here from his two-million-dollar Seven Hills golf course home. But now the words stuck like a stone in his throat.

Where the hell to begin?

"I got married last year."

"Yeah. I don't read the social columns, but I saw something about that on the business page. So, did your ex really take you to the cleaners in that divorce?"

"I believe she left me enough to pay your fee." Jack glanced around the office, as if pointing out that the guy hadn't exactly set up shop in the Bellagio.

He was seriously considering walking out the door, but knew that he wouldn't have a moment's peace unless he "cowboyed up," as his Texas-born oil-heiress wife put it, and did what needed to be done.

"There've been other women in my life,

431

of course," he stated. "Before my wife."

Three wives now, but who was counting? Their lawyers, who'd soaked him for alimony every time. If Jack thought about how many cars he had to sell every day before he began to make a profit, he'd never get out of bed.

"Why don't you tell me something that would surprise me?" O'Keefe suggested dryly.

"One in particular. Several years ago."

"And she's surfaced to cause you a problem."

"No. Well, not directly." *Time to just spit it out.* "We had a close relationship."

"*Close* meaning you fucked her."

"Yes."

"And now she's threatening to make trouble with your wife?"

"No. I doubt she even knows I'm married." Christ, he was making a mess of this. "But my wife knows about *her.*"

"So? You're, what, fifty years old?"

"Fifty-eight." A year-round tan, racquetball three times a week, and a personal trainer kept him looking younger than his years.

"So, it's not like she expected you not to have a life before you married her."

"Of course not." Jack's fingers clenched

432

so tightly his knuckles ached. "She recently discovered she can't have children. It's some kind of female problem," he said, briskly brushing aside any unpleasant medical details he hadn't wanted to know himself. And which weren't pertinent to the situation.

"That's tough. I guess she wants a kid?"

"Yes. She's somewhat younger than me." Twenty-eight years younger, which might have been a mistake, since he'd thought he was done raising kids. "We were talking about adoption, but she's big on blood ties. Which is when I screwed up."

It was her fault. If she hadn't been nagging him to death about wanting a family, he wouldn't have been drinking too much, and his damn secret never would have come out.

"I told her that perhaps I had a child."

"With this other woman." The detective did not sound surprised. Then again, in his line of work, he'd probably seen just about everything.

"Yes." Jack's hands were sweating. He rubbed them on his thighs. "I don't know. . . . Crystal Harper was a secretary in the parts department of one of my dealerships. I had to let her go after a few weeks because she proved unreliable."

"Which didn't stop you from fucking her."

He felt his cheeks burn beneath his tan. He was a pillar of the community, dammit. No one talked to him this way.

"My point is that she could have been lying."

"Or not."

"Which is why I'm hiring you. I need to find out if she was telling the truth. And if she was . . ." He took a deep breath and finally found the strength to spit it out. "I need you to find my child."

52

It rained for the next three days, keeping the campers indoors much of the time. Which wasn't the worst thing that could happen, Charity decided as she and Gabe worked together helping the kids put the photos into a scrapbook.

Since many of the campers hadn't grasped the concept of editorial choice, she and Gabe had stayed in the workroom while the kids went off to paint scenery and work on the songs and skits they'd be performing with the counselors on the closing night.

"Have you heard from the judge yet?" he asked as they sat in the lodge office, culling through at least a hundred photos of ducks.

"Unfortunately not. But he did check in with his office. The court clerk assured Mom that he hadn't been attacked by pirates or anything dire."

"Your mother seems to be doing okay."

"She's hurting." After the ducks came

several dozen of Gabe's dog, who in one was wearing one of the glittery cardboard tiaras Amanda had picked up at a local party store. "I think it's unusual for her because typically I hear a litany of complaints when a marriage goes south. This time she's being strangely closemouthed."

"Maybe because she wants things to work out. And if they do stay together, family get-togethers would probably be more uncomfortable if she dumped a lot of personal stuff about her marriage on you."

"That's very perceptive for a guy who doesn't have any family."

"I may not have one now."

Just when Charity had thought Angel Harper only knew how to take photos of animals, Gabe paused on a shot of the girl's brother swinging over the lake on a rope Fred had hung from a tree limb.

"But I did," he said. He zoomed in on the photograph. "Who knew that kid could laugh?"

"Not me. He's not nearly as sullen as he was last year, but except for the photography, which he really seems to be into, thanks to you, he hasn't exactly been the poster boy of a happy camper."

"Something's weighing heavily on his mind."

"Not surprising, given his circumstances."

"True. But one of the reasons I'm still alive is that I've learned to trust my spidey sense. Which is telling me that this is something different. Something more recent."

"Something that's happened since he arrived here?"

"Yeah. He might have arrived with the cloud of doom hanging over his head, but whatever's on his mind has him a lot edgier. He keeps looking around like he expects Bigfoot to leap out of the woods and take his sister away."

"Do you think he's having a problem with some of the other campers?"

"It doesn't feel like that." Gabe rubbed his chin as he considered her question. "But I suppose it could be, although Fred and Ethel seem to have everyone pretty well supervised, so it's unlikely, if he was dealing with a bully or anything like that, that no one would have noticed. I thought he might tell me the other day —"

"When you were both standing by the lake. During the swimming lessons."

"You saw that?"

"I was in the kitchen and glanced out the window." She didn't want to reveal that she spent way too much time watching him. Or

that she, Kara, and Sedona had been discussing him.

Although they'd spent the past two nights
together — after Amanda had insisted she'd
really prefer to be alone to read a book
about women and blue-water cruising she'd
bought at Tidal Wave Books — she and
Gabe had remained determinedly casual
during the day.

Which didn't mean that she didn't think
about him during the times they were apart.
Because she did. All the time. And couldn't
help hoping that he was thinking of her, too.

"Your conversation looked serious."

"I was sharing a bit of my checkered past."

None of which he'd shared with her.

It was just sex.

She could tell herself that until doomsday,
but dammit, the one thing they'd overlooked
when they'd made that deal was that sex,
by its very nature, was personal. At least for
her.

"That was a good idea," she said. "By not
coming off like Mr. Perfect Marine, he
might be more encouraged to open up
about whatever it is that's bothering him."

"That's what I thought," he said absently.
"Damn. Look at this." He zoomed in even
closer, going to a pixel view of Johnny Harper's chest.

438

"It's your tattoo," she said.

"Yeah," he muttered. "He was standing in the line the first day, when I was putting those stick-on ones on the kids, but he said he didn't want one."

"Well, he has one now."

"Seems to." He tucked his tongue in his cheek. He'd done it again. Gone to that walled-off place inside himself.

"Do you think he's been smoking?"

"I wouldn't be all that surprised, but it's not as if he's got a lot of time to himself around this place. Why do you ask?"

"I thought I caught a whiff of smoke in his hair."

"They roasted marshmallows last night. It was probably from the campfire."

"Probably."

They worked in silence a bit longer. Charity printed out a photo Gabe had taken of Johnny and Angel Harper onto a square piece of fabric that was going to be the front of a pillow. She'd come up with the idea so the campers could feel their siblings' presence in their beds after the camp had ended and they'd returned to their separate homes.

"I told him my parents were drunks."

"I'm sorry."

"So was I. I might not have landed in the system, the way these kids did. But I pretty

439

much raised myself."

"Well, you certainly did a pretty fine job of it, from what I can tell," she said mildly, not quite sure where he was going with this.

"They died my freshman year of college."

"That must have been difficult." At the same time? In an accident? Or worse? she wondered as the murder-suicides that showed up on the nightly news from time to time flashed through her mind.

"Actually, I was relieved. The two of them were textbook enablers. I spent a lot of time while I was growing up worrying that one of them might die and I'd be left to take care of the survivor."

"That's sad. That a boy would think of his parents that way."

Charity might not have had that much stability — okay, hardly any — growing up herself, but at least she'd always known that her mother, father, and Lucas had honestly loved her.

He lifted his shoulders. "As it happened, they died together. Which was undoubtedly just the way they would've wanted it. In an accident."

Myriad possibilities flashed through her mind. None of them pretty.

"The bitch was that they'd gone on the wagon a few weeks before. I doubt it would've lasted, but my mother called to tell me that they'd 'found Jesus' and were going off with a mission group to spread the gospel in Central America. They were in a bus that went off a cliff."

"That is tragic. Did you share this with Johnny?"

"No. There didn't seem any point. Especially since I have no idea what his parental situation is, so I didn't want to risk bringing up bad memories."

"He's been eligible for adoption for several years. So has his sister."

He angled his head, studying her even as he hit the print button. "That's not in his camp records," he guessed.

"No." She straightened her shoulders, refusing to let him make her feel defensive. "I called his social worker."

"Why would you do that?" She watched as comprehension dawned. He shook his head. "Hell. You're thinking about taking in two more strays, aren't you?"

"That's a terrible way to put it." She set her teeth when she wanted to grind them.

"How would *you* put it?"

"Anyone can see those children belong together," she said. "I wasn't fortunate enough to have any siblings, except for Lucas, my stepbrother, but I can still imagine how horrible it must be to be separated from your sister or brother. To only see each other for a few days a year. And as lovely as this camp is, it's still an artificial environment. It's not the same as if they actually lived together all the time."

"What they've undoubtedly gone through is a bitch. And unfair. But even you can't save the entire planet. And you can't treat those Harper kids like you do that polar bear of a dog you rescued."

"That's not what I'm suggesting doing." She was on her feet now. And, dammit, trembling.

"Isn't it?" He kept his eyes on hers as he stood up, as well. They were toe to toe and he didn't look happy. "Look, I know you want a family —"

"And I know *you* don't. You've made your point loud and clear, but I don't see how my feelings, or what choices I might make in my own life, have anything to do with you."

She wrapped her arms around herself, wondering where this conversation had taken a wrong turn. All she'd wanted was to know some personal thing about Gabe. And suddenly she was having to defend her behavior, which wasn't any of his damn business, since he'd made it clear that he wasn't into complications. Or baggage, which a woman and two kids would definitely involve.

"I have a big house," she repeated what she'd been telling herself the past two days. "I'm financially stable. I work from home, so I'd be around all the time. And everyone knows dogs are good for children. It seems applying to be a foster parent makes sense."

"Look, I'm not sure how the system works, but I'm pretty sure being a foster parent is usually a temporary situation. Again, sort of like what you do with the strays that wander through your shelter."

"That's usually the case, but —"

"Shit." He dragged a hand through his hair, and for a man who claimed to be into this relationship just for the sex, he seemed awfully frustrated by her life choices. "Tell me you're not thinking about adoption."

She could have told him that once she'd started following her intuition, instead of planning everything to the nth degree, her life had improved exponentially. She'd moved out west, into a house she'd fallen in love with the first moment she'd seen it on the Internet.

Her clinic was thriving; she had more friends than in Chicago, where the few friends she'd made were mostly Ethan's.

She was ready — financially and emotionally — for a family. Having grown up jumping rope to the old jingle "First comes love, then comes marriage, then comes Charity with the baby carriage," she'd always just assumed that she'd follow the traditional route.

But that hadn't happened. At least not yet. So, what would be wrong with mixing up the order?

She lifted her chin. "Excuse me, but again, I fail to see how any plans I may or may not have for my future are any of your business. It's not as if my life will have an effect on yours, since you're going to be in Washington. Or Alaska. Hawaii. And God knows where after that."

She was surprised by the razor sharpness of her voice, which definitely wasn't her usual tone. Even when she'd informed Ethan she was calling off the wedding, she'd stayed calm and collected. At least on the outside. Inside she'd been shaking like a leaf. But her weasel of a former fiancé hadn't realized that.

Apparently Gabe was equally surprised by her flash of temper. He scrubbed both hands down his face.

Charity knew he was frustrated by her possible plan, but couldn't understand why.

Granted, she hadn't known him all that long, but from what she'd witnessed, he didn't seem to be the type of controlling male who felt the need to dominate a woman's life. In fact, if she was to be perfectly honest, she hadn't had to work all that hard to push the dog on him, despite his earlier protest that he didn't want it.

He was leaving, she reminded herself.

In just days.

Did she really want to risk running him off sooner just because he'd mentioned some negatives to an idea that still hadn't fully formed in her mind? Cutting off her nose to spite her face, as the old saying went? As her mother had done so many times in the past. Including during this latest storm with Judge Benton Templeton.

"I think," she said slowly, gathering up the scattered threads of her composure as she felt the anger leaving like air from a deflating balloon, "that it's possible we've just had our first fight."

"I think you may be right. But don't worry about it." That bad-boy grin that had been making more and more frequent appearances since the first night they'd made love flashed. "We'll spend tonight making up."

445

53

Charity couldn't tell if her mother had suddenly begun filling up a social calendar because she'd truly decided to move on with her life, or was so heartbroken over what seemed to be a seriously shattered marriage that she was attempting to keep busy so she wouldn't have to think about the future.

Or there was always the possibility that she was merely trying to give Charity and Gabe as much private time as possible before he left town.

Last night Amanda had eaten dinner at the Douchetts', returning home with knitting needles and some sunshine yellow yarn for squares she'd signed up to make for Project Linus, a charity Adèle was active in that made blankets for ill, traumatized, and otherwise at-need children.

"So at least something positive can come out of this debacle," she'd said proudly as she'd shown off the first few rows of her first evening's work. "I'm going to knit the squares. Then Adèle's going to link them together for me."

"That's a really lovely idea." And the last thing she'd ever imagined her social butterfly of a mother doing.

"I thought so. Adèle told me there's also a chapter in Washington, so if my marriage survives, hopefully I'll be able to help them, too."

Tonight she was playing bunco with Doris, Dottie, Adèle, and Maureen Douchett, Adèle's daughter-in-law and Sax and Cole's mother.

Her mother's 180-degree turnaround only added to the local lore that there was, indeed, something in Shelter Bay's water.

Gabe was standing in the doorway when she arrived but was at the car before she got out of it.

"It's about time you showed up." He scooped her off her feet and carried her up the metal steps into the motor home.

"I got stuck on the other side of the bridge," she said.

His dog, overjoyed to see her, began jumping up and down like a jack-in-the-box. "Hello, sweet boy," she said, reaching down to pat its head on one of the jumps.

"I'm obviously not the only one happy to

see you."

Gabe managed to grab a training cookie from a jar on the counter without so much as bobbling her, reminding Charity again how strong he'd have to be to carry not only all his Marine military gear but his body armor and camera equipment over those Afghan mountains.

"Sit," he said.

The dog obediently plopped its fuzzy butt down on the floor.

"Good boy." He tossed a cookie, which disappeared with a snap of the small, square jaw.

"Now stay."

Amazingly, it did.

When he shut the bedroom door behind them, Charity could hear it jumping up on the couch. Which was the same thing Peanut, who believed himself to be a lapdog, tended to do when left alone.

"That's very impressive," she said.

"We've been working on it." He covered her mouth with his and gave her a long, deep kiss that stole her breath and set her head to spinning. Then he put her on her feet. "But can we table the dog-training discussion for later? Because it seems like I've been waiting forever for you to show up."

"I felt it was taking me forever to show up. That damn bridge took ages to go back down. But now that I'm here . . ."

Grabbing the bottom of his T-shirt, she pulled it over his head. Her hands grazed over the hard muscles of his chest, his ribs, her fingers playing with the line of dark hair arrowing down to the waist of his jeans.

When she pressed moist kisses against his warming skin, she could feel his heart beating wildly beneath her lips, matching the rhythm, the beat, of her own runaway pulse.

"You do realize that you're making me crazy." Gabe took her hand and pressed it against his lower body.

"My . . ." Charity bit her lip, trying not to grin as she looked up at him. "Did I do that?"

"What do you think?"

"I think," she said, struggling with the cumbersome buttons on the fly of those faded jeans, "that the first thing I'm going to do when the stores open in the morning is buy you a pair of pants with a zipper."

"Perhaps I can help."

His dark, deft fingers dispatched the row of metal buttons. Just the sight of him was enough to send thrills skimming beneath her skin. But when he slid first the jeans, then his gray boxer briefs, over his hips and down his legs, Charity forgot the vow she'd made while waiting for the damn bridge to go back down, to take things slowly.

Unlike her, who'd always felt a little uncomfortable taking showers with all those girls at boarding school, Gabe appeared to have no problem with nudity. He seemed totally at ease in the magnificent male body that made her mouth go dry.

She wondered for a fleeting moment how many women had seen Gabriel St. James this way. Worse, how many would see him after he'd left Shelter Bay.

Don't go there.

Sticking to her recent vow of living in the moment, she turned her mind to the now.

He was tall and lean, with the power and endurance of a long-distance runner. His deeply tanned skin was smooth and tight over his bones and muscles. Although definitely, relentlessly male, he was beautifully formed, and if he'd been around in the days of Michelangelo, the sculptor wouldn't have been able to resist immortalizing him in marble.

No, she decided. Marble was too cold.

"Bronze," she decided, realizing she'd spoken out loud when he arched a dark brow. "Have I mentioned that I love your body?"

450

His laugh was rough and strained. "It's all yours."

"Oh, goody." Because it had been too long since he'd kissed her — at least a minute — she cupped her hand at the back of his neck and dragged his mouth to hers.

The power was volcanic, erupting with a force that nearly buckled her knees.

Desire. Need. Want. All were too weak to describe the powerful sensations surging through her.

"You know those things I said I wanted to do to you?" He'd murmured them in her ear after they'd gone back to photo editing, hot, sexy, mind-reeling suggestions of ways they could make up after their brief fight.

"I seem to recall something about that." Her legs were going weak. She dug her short, filed nails into his shoulders to keep her balance.

"That was just for starters."

Charity's head spun as she pressed her palms against his chest. He'd already brought her to levels of passion she'd never imagined. And yet now he was telling her there was more?

"Promises, promises," she said on a ragged laugh.

He cupped her chin, holding her gaze to his. "That sounds a lot like 'Bring it on.' "

Just as she'd never been all that comfortable parading around naked, Charity had never felt all that confident about her sexual skill set. After all, it was difficult to be proficient at something you didn't practice. It wasn't that she didn't like sex. She just had never understood why sensible, rational people made such a big deal of it.

Now she knew.

She also knew that Gabe knew things she'd only ever dared dream of. She'd witnessed it in his hot, hungry eyes when he looked at her. She'd felt it in his hands, which revealed a familiarity with the female body that caused needs to well up inside her even as she hated all the women he'd ever touched.

"I want you." She skimmed her fingertips down the side of his face, over the raised scar bisecting his brow, down the five-o'clock shadow that felt like the finest-grade sandpaper against her fingertips. "I want everything."

"Then hold on, sweetheart." His fingers went to the buttons of the pretty white blouse she'd bought for their first date. "Because it's going to be a bumpy ride."

Before she could sense his intention, he ripped the blouse open, sending the white buttons skittering across the floor.

Speed. Fury. Heat. Gabe's hands were everywhere, sending her torn blouse and lacy ivory bra flying.

His mouth was hot and hungry as it fastened on a bared breast while his roving hands yanked her jeans down her thighs.

Caught up in the storm she'd invited, Charity was as helpless as a raft caught in a tsunami. She heard herself cry out, heard her heart pounding like the surf in her ears, the sob that escaped her lips as he ripped away the bit of lace between her thighs, pressed her back against the bedroom door, and plunged his fingers into her.

The orgasm, quick and sharp, and bordering on pain, shot through her. Even as she struggled for air, before she'd even caught her breath, those rough, sinfully wicked hands were taking her up again.

Surely it wasn't possible to feel so much and survive, she thought as he used his mouth and teeth and tongue on her, driving her beyond reason.

She heard her own cry of shocked release as her body rocked from the hot explosion of pleasure. Destroyed, her bones turned to sand, Charity sagged against the door.

But her surrender only fanned the flames.

She'd never been ravished. Never imagined she'd want to be. But as the forbidden thrill of being overpowered shot through her, she wrapped her legs around his hips as he lifted her off her feet and impaled her.

"Stay with me," he said as his mouth ground against hers.

As if she'd had a choice. As if either of them had from the beginning.

He carried her, half-walking, half-stumbling, to the bed. And when he tumbled down onto the mattress, Charity clung tight as she fell with him.

54

"Are we still alive?" Charity asked when she could finally speak again.

"I think so." He touched his mouth to hers. "But I'm not that certain about anyone else in town, because either that was an earthquake, or we've just logged a personal best."

"And here I always thought that was a literary cliché. Making the earth move."

She laughed lightly at that and snuggled against him, loving the way he could make her burn one moment and feel so amazingly lighthearted the next. She'd never laughed in bed. Though there had been times when she'd nearly wept.

Ethan had always assured her that sexual compatibility was something that took time. That the passion they were lacking in their relationship would inevitably come. She'd wanted to believe him, even though deep down inside, she'd always secretly blamed

455

herself for her inability to respond as she sensed he'd wanted. The way the woman he'd cheated on her with must have done.

"My wedding was supposed to be the highlight of the social season."

"Not surprising. Since you mentioned your fiancé's blue blood."

"Blue as ice," she muttered. "Anyway, all the newspapers sent their society reporters. They were gathered together on the sidewalk, like vultures, when I arrived at the church."

"Which isn't exactly the casual, anonymous life you're living now."

"Hardly. One of them, a reporter from a tacky little supermarket tabloid, managed to slip into the church before the ceremony, posing as a flower-delivery guy. He caught me at one of the rare moments I was alone — which makes me think he'd been lurking in the corners waiting for my mother to leave the room — and asked me to comment on the story of the lawsuit that had been filed against Ethan."

"Someone was suing Douglas?"

"Apparently so. Since it was the first I'd heard of it, I told him I had no comment, and asked him to leave."

Charity realized that just as it no longer hurt, she didn't care enough to harbor even the slightest bit of anger anymore.

"It was a paternity suit."

His hand, which had been idly playing with her hair, stilled. "Ouch."

"Ouch, indeed."

"So, I guess the fiancé admitted it was true?"

"Actually, he denied it."

"He wouldn't be the first guy to deny screwing around."

"Ah!" She held up a finger. "But he didn't deny having had sex with the woman. Just that it was his child."

"Which you didn't believe. Which is why you called off the wedding."

"Actually, I *did* believe him. And not just because I'm gullible, which I'm not. Well, maybe a bit, since I had no idea he even liked sex enough to be having it with two women, one of whom he was supposed to be marrying, during the same period of time."

"Shows he was an idiot. Because any man lucky enough to have you in his bed sure as hell wouldn't need anyone else."

"Thank you." She smiled and pressed her lips against his.

He lifted his right hand. "It's the God's honest truth."

"It's different with you," she said. "*I'm* different with you."

"Lucky for me the guy turned out to be a dud. Or you might be living in some Mc-Mansion in a gated suburb in Chi-town and we never would've met."

"I'm beginning to wonder about that," she murmured. She'd been wondering about fate ever since he'd brought it up the first night they'd made love.

"Anyway, it turned out that he had proof that although apparently they'd been having an affair for several months, he couldn't possibly be the father because he'd had a vasectomy."

"I see." But Charity could tell from his tone that he didn't. Not really.

"Since the woman in question filed a paternity suit, I take it he hadn't told her about his little snip job," Gabe said.

"Actually, he hadn't let either of the women in his life know about his surgery."

He looked down at her. She liked the surprise on his face because it revealed what she'd already figured out for herself. That Gabriel St. James truly took the Marine code of honor seriously.

"Are you saying —"

"I'm saying that Ethan knew I wanted children. We'd discussed it. We'd even put a down payment on that stone McMansion with lots of bedrooms and a big backyard for a swing set. And he purposefully chose, for whatever reason, to deceive me. Which is why I didn't go through with the marriage."

"That's a damn good reason."

Tenderness. Gabe felt it and fought against it. He tried, instead, to focus on his anger that the cheating bastard had hurt her.

Like you're not going to?

If he had half the sense of that mutt he'd somehow ended up adopting, he would've left town before they'd gotten this far.

Because as much as he cared for her, and he did, more than any other woman he'd ever met, there was no way he could see this ending well.

Even knowing he was being selfish, and in his way as much of a bastard as her fiancé, Gabe wanted Charity.

And because he also needed her, more than he'd ever thought possible, more than was comfortable, he made love to her again.

And again.

He'd always been a loner. Even during his short-lived marriage, as his ex had pointed out to him on numerous occasions, he never let anyone else in.

How many different beds had he slept alone in over his lifetime? How many mornings had he awakened alone?

Countless.

Which had been just the way he'd liked it.

But now, as he lay awake long into the dark of night, stroking the silk of Charity's hair and listening to her quiet breathing along with the sound of the surf hitting the cliff below, Gabe wondered if he'd ever be able to recapture that sense of solitary contentment.

55

The Lab proved a hit. Leia behaved like a perfect lady, charming Kelli and even impressing Cole, who Charity imagined would be willing to move heaven and earth to give his bride anything she wanted.

Professing a need to show her new furry baby off to her in-laws, Kelli dashed out the door before Charity had gathered up the adoption paperwork to take back to the clinic.

"She's certainly excited," she said.

"She is. But she also has an ulterior motive. I'm supposed to talk with you."

"With me?" Charity looked up from the manila folder she'd been about to put in her laptop bag. "About what?"

"Gabe."

"What about him?"

"She says that I should tell you about him."

"Oh, I don't know if that's such a good

idea." It was what she knew she should say. But Charity was also so curious.

"Kelli says that Kara told her that you two have gotten pretty involved."

He gave her that same long, steely-eyed look she'd grown accustomed to getting from Gabe. The one that looked right into you. Charity wondered if the Marine drill instructors taught it at boot camp, or if it was something warriors were born with. "I suppose you could say that."

"Then it's not serious?"

"I can't speak for him."

He laughed at that. "I can't think of many people who'd dare. He's a tough nut to crack. At first I thought that the reason he always seemed to be different from the rest of us is because he was a photographer instead of a real Marine, whatever the hell that is. Then Fallujah happened and I watched him switching back and forth between his M4 and his camera during a firefight without blinking an eye, and I realized that he was actually the kind of gung ho Marine they made all those old World War Two movies about. The guy actually believed he was bulletproof."

"Yet he wasn't," Charity said, thinking of the scars.

Cole sobered. "No one is. I've always been

pretty good at reading people, but when he first joined our unit, I've got to admit that I didn't have a clue what makes him tick."

"Join the club." Although she didn't know Cole all that well, she was close with Kara and his brother, which allowed her to feel more comfortable than she might have been having this discussion with a stranger.

"You have to understand how it is in war," he said. "It's a lot like being in a movie, but the script's being written minute by minute. And there aren't any do-overs. If you screw up, you can end up going home in a body bag with a flag draped over the coffin.

"Adrenaline can help keep the fear of dying away while fighting — otherwise even the toughest Marine, unless he was flat-out crazy, would probably be hunkered down behind a wall crying for his mama. But afterward, there's this need to talk about what happened. To hash it over and over again." He shrugged. "Because if you get it out in the open, you can kind of put it behind you and move on."

"I suppose that makes sense."

"But Gabe wasn't like that. You'd have to drag things out of him. The guy flat-out never talked."

"He doesn't much now." Charity thought how Johnny Harper might actually know more about Gabe's childhood than she did.

"Yeah. Kelli figured that might be a problem." He dragged his hand over his dark hair, which, although he'd left the military, he still wore in a Marine high and tight cut. "Because the guy pretty much lives in his own head."

"Maybe that's not so surprising," Charity said. She'd been thinking about it a lot as she'd looked at the photos in his book over and over again, searching for even the smallest piece of the man behind the lens. "Given what he's witnessed."

"Yeah." He blew out a breath. "There was this one time when a mob was chasing a woman who'd been accused of adultery. Which even in post-Taliban days in Afghanistan could mean a stoning sentence.

"We couldn't do anything because we were supposed to be turning that town over to the local police, and if we *had* fired, we would've ended up killing a bunch of civilians. Like most days downrange, it was pretty much an express elevator to hell.

"Since all the men in the mob were armed, anyone with any sense would have gotten the hell out of the way. I've seen other war photographers who've been more than willing to see people killed, just to get the photo they wanted."

"But not Gabe." It was not as much question as statement. Perhaps she'd come to know him better than she'd thought.

"No. Not Gabe. He was right there running in the middle of the crowd, reaching out to grab her hand, maybe just for human contact, maybe because the crazy son of a bitch thought he could actually get her out of there, but then she fell and they were on her like a pack of wolves. . . .

"Meanwhile, Gabe's literally on his knees, pleading with them not to kill her."

"But they did."

"Yeah. And somehow he managed to take the photo. Not because he thought it would win him any prizes —"

"Which it did."

A Pulitzer, she remembered. She'd been riveted by the photo when it had come out in all the papers, never realizing that someday she'd meet — and fall in love with — the man who'd taken it.

"He's never cared about that. The funny thing about Gabe is that after all he's seen and all he's been through, you'd think he'd be cynical. And he comes off that way. But he's not. He had this crazy idea that eventually good would actually triumph over evil, if only enough people saw the violence others are forced to endure. If his photos could somehow shake the world out of its indifference to suffering.

"And I think the only way he can endure what he's witnessed and do the work as well as he does is be relentlessly single-minded and totally centered inside himself."

He'd just described the man to a T.

"Thank you," she said, not exactly encouraged by what she'd learned. "And please thank Kelli for me."

"No problem." Cole's dark eyes held compassion, and, she feared, a bit of pity.

He walked her out to her vehicle and insisted on holding the door open while she climbed into the driver's seat. Then, before she could close it, he said, "There's just one more thing."

Terrific.

"What's that?"

"I agree with my bride. If there's anyone who can get the guy to open up, it's you."

As she drove out to the camp, Charity only wished she could believe that.

56

"Are you sure we have to spend the night here?" Gabe complained.

"We all have to leave at dawn," she repeated what she'd already told him. "Having everyone stay at the lodge only makes sense."

"Maybe because *everyone* doesn't have something better to do. How am I supposed to sleep if you're sharing a damn dorm room instead of being with me?" *Where you belong,* he thought, but did not say.

"It's not a dorm room. It's a double."

"With another woman in the second bed."

"It's only one night," she soothed.

He looked down at the slender hand, which looked as if it should be pouring tea from a gilt-rimmed cup in some Victorian parlor. Having watched her wrestle a balky bulldog into its crate for the drive back to town yesterday, he knew her hand, like the rest of her, was a lot stronger than it looked.

"Camp's almost over." Which of them was he reminding? Her? Himself? Both? "We don't have that many nights left."

"Your choice," she reminded him.

Since there was nothing to say to that, Gabe didn't respond. At least not to her.

"Women," he complained to his dog later that evening.

Although Charity's vet assistant had taken the other dogs back to the shelter, Peanut and the mutt had stayed behind and were going along on tomorrow's adventure. At the moment the dog, who still didn't have a name, was lying on its back offering up its stomach for attention.

"Why do they have to complicate every damn thing?"

The dog, wiggling in ecstasy as Gabe rubbed its belly, either didn't know, didn't care, or wasn't telling.

57

The alarm shattered the night silence. At first, shaken from a dream of making love to Gabriel beneath Rainbow Falls, Charity was disoriented.

"It's the fire alarm," Sedona, who was already out of the other double bed and throwing a T-shirt over a sleeveless undershirt, said. The boxer shorts she'd gone to sleep in were printed with cupcakes, which Charity would have found faintly humorous under any other circumstances.

"I don't smell any smoke," she said as she hurriedly dressed and shoved her feet into her running shoes without bothering with socks. "I wonder if we're supposed to do like in a hotel. And stay put until we hear differently."

As if on cue, her cell phone rang, followed a moment later by Sedona's.

"It's one of the cabins," Gabe informed her. "Fred says they're all wired to ring here.

469

They also trigger a call to the fire and police departments."

"Which cabin?" she asked.

He hesitated.

"Gabe? Which cabin?" Her nerves tangled like seaweed.

"It's the one the Harper kids are in," he said with obvious reluctance as her heart cratered.

"It'll take twenty minutes for the fire department to get here," she said.

"Fred and I are on it. You stay put."

"The hell I will," she shot back. But she was already speaking to air. He'd hung up.

The smoke was burning his lungs and blinding him. Desperate, Johnny groped around in the dark for his sister.

"Angel! Where are you?"

"I'm here," a small, frightened voice called out.

"Where?" He was madly ripping away at the bedding on the lower bunk. Which felt empty.

"Here," the little voice, trembling with fear, answered. "Under the bed."

"You've got to come out."

"I learned in fire drill at school that you're supposed to stay on the floor when there's a fire," she argued.

"That's so you don't breathe in smoke." Which he was definitely doing. It scorched his throat and burned his lungs. "But we can't stay in here. We've got to get out."

"I'm scared!" she wailed.

She wasn't the only one. As the sirens blared and the smoke made his nose run like a faucet, Johnny remembered what the Marine had said about managing fear, and tried to reassure them both.

"It'll be okay," he said. "I'll get us out of here."

He crawled the few feet and put his hand against the door. It was hot as an oven. And if he lay down right next to the crack at the bottom, he could see orange flames dancing from the living room.

"We're going out the window," he said as he crawled back. He swept his hands beneath the bed, as far as he could reach. "Dammit, Angel, I can't fucking find you!"

"You're not supposed to use the *f* word." She'd begun to cry, big, deep, gulping sobs that were probably pulling more smoke into her lungs. "And don't yell at me!"

"I'm sorry. But can you *pretty please* come out?"

"I want to wait for the firemen. They'll save us. Like Fireman Ted."

"Fireman Ted?" Jesus, could this get any worse?

"He's a b-b-bear who becomes a fireman when his toast catches on fire one morning. He puts it out with a fire extinguisher, then rescues puppies and kittens all before he gets to school. Which makes him late and the principal gets so mad his pants catch on fire. But F-F-F-Fireman Ted saves him, too."

"That's a great story."

Okay. Yelling wouldn't help. Neither would scaring her any more than she was already scared. But tiny fingers of flames were starting to lick beneath the door. The entire place could blow up any minute.

"When we get out of here, you can read it to the dog." Just this afternoon he'd watched them sitting together beneath a tree, the mutt seeming to actually look at the pages as she'd read to him about the grand adventures of a paper-bag princess who foiled an evil dragon and rescued Prince Charming. "I'll bet he'd like that a lot."

"I got it at the library. That's where I get all my books, but they don't let you keep them for longer than two weeks."

Inside Johnny was screaming even louder than the fucking alarm. Outside, he struggled for the calm necessary to get his sister out of here and keep her safe.

"I'll bet they have a library in Shelter Bay." Lying down on his stomach, he wiggled beneath the bed, making wide sweeping actions with his arm. "We'll check it out."

He could hear a roar coming from the living room. Had the other kids in the cabin gotten out? Or were they stuck in their rooms, too? Though they probably weren't having to suffer through such a stupid, time-wasting conversation.

He usually hated it when one of the foster parents would drag him to church, because he'd long ago decided that if God really did exist, he wouldn't allow such bad things to happen to kids, who hadn't done anything to deserve getting thrown into the fucking system. But now, as the smoke continued to fill the room, Johnny began wildly making deals with God.

If only he could get hold of Angel, he'd never swipe another cigarette again.

If only he could talk her into crawling out from beneath the bed before the place went up in flames, he'd quit bucking the system and be the most obedient foster kid anyone had ever known.

"Angel?"

She didn't answer.

"Angel?" he tried again.

Again, no answer.

What if she'd died of smoke inhalation? He'd read somewhere that was a bigger danger than dying in flames.

If he could only get her out the window and into the fresh air, safe and sound, he'd even become a priest. First he'd have to become a Catholic, but for Angel, he'd be willing to do that, too.

His eyes were tearing. He took a deep breath and felt as if he'd swallowed a chestful of burning coals from last night's campfire.

Finally! His fingertips brushed hers. *Thank you, God.*

Johnny's relief was short-lived. Just as grabbed hold of her limp hand, the door literally exploded off its hinges.

"Jesus Christ!"

He yanked hard, but pulling deadweight from a prone position wasn't easy. Especially when he was half beneath the bed himself.

Flames were racing up the walls, licking greedily at the ceiling.

Please, God.

Proving that sometimes prayers really were answered, he'd no sooner said the words in his head than the window glass shattered.

"Don't worry, kid," the familiar deep voice

said, sounding awfully calm considering they were all seconds away from being turned into crispy critters. "The Marines have landed and the situation is well in hand."

58

"I've never been so frightened in my life," Charity said to Gabe as she paced the ER waiting area.

Less than two minutes after Gabe had dragged the little girl through the window and run clear of the cabin, the entire building had burst into a fireball.

"If you hadn't been there . . ." She closed her eyes and dragged her hands through her hair, dislodging bits of soot, which fell to the green tile floor like flakes of blackened snow.

"But I was. And I didn't do it alone. Fred sure as hell did his part by helping get those other kids out." Fortunately, unlike Johnny and his sister, they'd already been climbing out the window on their own.

"Poor Johnny. He must have been frantic."

She could see inside the emergency unit where he and Angel were both receiving oxygen for smoke inhalation. The paramedic

476

who'd arrived with the fire truck had also found that Johnny's nasal hairs had been singed and although both children's mouths and throats were reddened, other than sore throats and possible coughs, he'd believed that the prognosis for a full recovery would be good.

"I'd say that's a good word for it. But they're fortunate kids, that's for damn sure."

"I wonder what started the fire."

"From what Johnny and the older kids in the other rooms said, it seemed to have started in the living room. Could've been the wiring."

"The cabins are only a couple years old."

He shrugged. "I imagine the investigators will come up with something. They've got lots of ways to discover points of origin."

"So I've heard."

She'd also seen *Backdraft.* Three times. Not because she'd enjoyed the fire scenes, which she hadn't. But because the lonely teenage boarding-school girl she'd been back then had had a major crush on Kurt Russell.

"I hate that they won't let us in," she muttered as she watched the DHS caseworker talking with one of the doctors who'd first examined the children when they'd arrived at the ER.

"We're not official," he reminded her.

"But I care." She felt the moisture sting at the backs of her lids as she looked up at him.

"I know." Instead of criticizing her for that, as he had yesterday, Gabe stroked her hair. "And you know what I said? About you taking in strays?"

"Yes, and if you're about to warn me again —"

"No. I'm about to say that your warm and open heart is what makes you who you are. And if more people in this world were like you, there wouldn't be any kids without parents and stray dogs that need you.

"Damn." He pulled a tissue from the box on the table next to a pair of ugly vinyl chairs and dabbed at the tears that had begun to trail down her cheeks. "I'm sorry. I didn't mean to make you cry."

If her emotions weren't in such a turmoil, Charity might have laughed at the fact that the big bad Marine could fight battles and run into burning buildings without a second thought, but sounded on the verge of panic when forced to deal with a woman's tears.

"I'm going to try to take them home with me," she said.

"I'd expect no less."

He bent his head and brushed his lips

478

against hers. The kiss, while soft as a feather, and all too brief, was the sweetest they'd shared. It also, when she realized that it could well be their last, now that the camp had closed for the season, threatened to shatter her heart.

59

The doctor and the nurses had all told Johnny that his sister would be fine. They'd also prided him on keeping her calm, but he knew that if the Marine hadn't shown up when he did, Angel would be dead.

Which meant that the guy was a hero. But he sure hadn't acted like one. In fact, he'd brushed off any attention, and when the TV-station van arrived with the pretty blonde in the pink suit who'd raced around sticking microphones in front of everyone — even him, though all he'd been able to do was cough — the Marine had picked up his dog and disappeared. Like Batman.

But then, when he could have bailed on the whole thing, he'd shown up at the hospital. Johnny had watched him talking with the vet through that glass window. He'd figured out at the very beginning that they were probably sleeping together. The way they looked at each other when they didn't think anyone was watching was a giveaway.

But although he didn't know all that much about relationships, having never been in a stable one of his own, he could tell that whatever it was between them was serious. And just watching them together tonight caused a painful lump to grow in his already fire-red throat.

He was so busy watching them, and wondering why the vet had begun crying, that at first he didn't notice the sheriff arrive in the ER with one of the firemen. So many of the people in whose homes he'd been forced to stay had threatened to call the police and have him arrested if he didn't toe the line. Which, lots of times, had meant that he'd pretty much been like a slave. Or at least an indentured servant. They'd known they could get away with it because it wasn't like he had a lot of other places to go.

So he'd never really liked cops. But the sheriff was cool. She was pretty, which was a surprise. And she'd told him, while she'd been showing him how handcuffs worked, that she had a son the same age as Angel. She'd also said that maybe she'd bring her kid to the camp so he and Angel could swim together during the free swim.

He'd figured that was just another false

promise, like adults were all the time making, but then the next day she'd shown up with this freckled-faced blond kid, Trey. Later that night, before she'd finally fallen asleep, Angel had told him that she was going to marry Trey Conway when she grew up.

Although some of the older kids talked about Sheriff Conway having caught a killer in Shelter Bay, which meant she had to be tough and knew how to use that gun she wore in a black holster on her belt, he'd never seen her not smiling.

Until now.

She was talking with the DHS lady, the two of their heads so close together he couldn't read her lips. Every so often the fireman would add something. Then they'd look over at him and Angel. Then talk some more.

He could tell that it was serious and worried that they thought he'd started the fire. Lots of angry foster kids tried to get back at the system by setting fires.

Johnny might be angry, but he'd never been one of those kids.

But that didn't mean that the sheriff knew that. And the DHS worker, who was the third he'd had in eighteen months, didn't know anything about him, either. None of them ever did. The few caseworkers who actually tried to become personally involved mostly burned out after a couple years, because the system was nearly as depressing for them as it was for the kids they tried to help.

Maybe his mom had been arrested again. Maybe the voices had taken control. From the furrowed brows, he could tell that the social worker hadn't come to announce that everything was peachy keen, that his mother had conquered the whisperers once and for all, and he and Angel were going to move into that apartment in town with her and they'd all walk on the beach, eat saltwater taffy, laugh until their sides ached, and live happily ever after.

No. That was not going to happen. Because the more he thought about that surprise meeting with Crystal, the more he realized that the only thing that had changed during all their years apart was that she'd gotten better at lying and hiding what was really going on in that buzzing wasp nest of a brain.

Whatever it was about, it was getting worse. Because now the three of them were in that room talking to Charity and the Marine.

Johnny braced himself for the worst when

Charity lifted a hand to her mouth, which had the Marine putting his arms around her. You'd have thought someone shot that big white dog of hers. But then they were looking through the window, straight at him, and he knew.

A nurse pulled the white curtain shut around his bed, closing him off from Angel, who, exhausted from all the stress, was dead to the world. First he'd worried she might be unconscious again, but a pretty nurse wearing pink scrubs had assured him that she was fine. Just sleeping.

Which was a good thing. She'd already been through enough today.

It was the Marine who came through the curtain. Which had Johnny winning the bet he'd made with himself while waiting to see whom they'd choose to break the news.

"Hey, kid," he said. But not in any fake cheery way, which Johnny appreciated. The only thing he hated more than the system was some of the people in it who always pretended that his life didn't suck. That being a foster kid was actually a good thing.

"Hey." Johnny waited.

"The doc said you're doing okay," the Marine said.

"Yeah. Thanks." He tilted his head over toward the other side of the curtain. "For saving my sister. And me."

"No problem."

The Marine shrugged broad shoulders that reminded Johnny of Paul Bunyan. He'd read a lot of the stories about the mythical lumberjack when they'd lived in Akeley, Minnesota, where Paul Bunyan was supposed to be buried and there was a huge statue of him wearing a black and red checked shirt, jeans, and lumberjack boots, kneeling down and holding his oversized ax.

For a long time he'd carried the photo of his mom sitting on the statue's hand, but then it had disappeared from his duffel bag. Which had taught him never to keep anything he cared about, because somebody would steal it.

They'd moved to Akeley after Crystal had taken them off in the middle of the night from Nevada, crying the entire drive. It was where Angel was born, but they hadn't stayed long because his mother claimed snow could freeze a baby's blood.

More silence as the Marine looked down at him, and Johnny looked back up, focusing on the scar to keep from seeing the trouble in the guy's eyes.

"I've done this more times than I'd want to count," the Marine said. "And there's no way to do it easy, so here goes."

Johnny decided to help him out. "It's my mom."

"Yeah." The Marine cursed beneath his breath. "I'm sorry, kid. But she died in the fire. No one knows what she was doing there, but —"

"She was trying to keep us alive." The irony wasn't lost on him. Surprisingly, the news didn't hurt as bad as he would've guessed. Maybe because he'd lost his mother a long, long time ago. He met the Marine's eyes as he said out loud what he'd never told anyone before. "Because God told her to."

Instead of the pity he'd expected to see, Johnny viewed empathy. Like just maybe the guy knew something about what he was feeling.

Which for some weird reason triggered something inside him, like breaking open a rusty padlock. And for the first time since that long-ago night that Buck had stabbed Crystal and got shot himself, the night that his and Angel's already very bad life got really horrible, Johnny put his face in his hands and bawled like a damn baby.

60

It rained the day they buried Crystal Harper. Charity stood beside the grave in the hilltop cemetery, beneath a huge black umbrella, with Johnny and Angel, who were temporarily staying with her, at her side. She'd already begun the process to get certified to be a foster parent and been assured that the paperwork was merely a formality.

Angel had settled into the princess-decorated guest room Amanda had fixed up for her as if she'd been born in the big sprawling house. Granted, Johnny — whose room shared a Jack and Jill bath with his sister's — would take a little longer to feel at home, but Charity had no doubt she'd be able to wear him down. Eventually.

The next step, to her mind, was adoption, but Crystal's children had already been through so much that she wanted to give them time to adjust before springing the idea on them.

After that brief breakdown in the hospital, when he'd talked with Gabe and her about his mother's mental illness, he'd barely spoken. He wasn't sullen. Just distant. And troubled, which was understandable, given that Crystal had died in such a horrific way.

What Charity had no way of knowing was that the fifteen-year-old boy, who'd already taken on so many burdens, was blaming himself for his mother's death.

It wasn't a large turnout, but more people showed up than she'd expected. Sedona and Kara were there. As were Sax, Cole, and Kelli Douchett. And Adèle and Bernard, their son, Lucien, and their daughter-in-law, Maureen, and Amanda, who'd proved a rock during these days, fussing over the children as if they were her own grand-children. Which, if Charity had anything to say about it, and she hoped she did, they soon would be.

Although she would have liked to believe that he was still in Shelter Bay because he couldn't bear the idea of a future without her, Charity knew that Gabe had stayed to help Johnny achieve closure. Though, from what the case file had told her about the children's unstable life with their mother, she wondered if that would ever truly be possible.

Out at sea, draped in a shimmering pewter mist, a tall-masted fishing boat chugged its way along the horizon, reminding Charity that the world kept spinning, and life continued, even in the face of death.

Due partly to the weather, but mostly due to the tragic circumstance of Crystal Harper's death, the graveside service was brief, lasting less than ten minutes, ending with a bagpiper from the VFW playing "Amazing Grace."

"I want one of those," Angel said to her brother.

"A bagpipe?" Johnny asked.

"No. A purse like that." She pointed toward the black leather bag with silver thistle top and three tassels the bagpiper was wearing on his belt. "It's pretty."

Her high child's voice carried on the breeze, drawing a ripple of laughter. Charity thought she saw just a hint of a smile twitch at the corners of Johnny's lips.

A long black limo glided up to the black wrought iron gates of the cemetery. A moment later, a man climbed out of the backseat.

"Oh, fuck," Johnny muttered.

"What's wrong?" Charity asked. Gabe's arm, which had been around her waist, tightened. The energy radiating reminded her of a guard dog on alert.

"It's that dickhead car dealer."

"Car dealer?"

"My mom worked for him for a while when we lived in Nevada. Before Angel was born. He didn't like me, which was okay, because I felt the same way about him. He fired my mom. Then we moved to Minnesota."

The car dealer was not alone. He was accompanied by a younger man and one of the women Charity had met yesterday when she'd been jumping through all the hoops the state required for temporary custodial approval.

Sharon Greene, Angel's caseworker.

Seeming not to notice, or care, that he was interrupting the service, the car dealer strode between the mourners and the open grave, stopping right in front of her.

"You would be Charity Tiernan," he said flatly. His gaze skittered over Johnny's face, lingering for a brief moment. Then he stared at Angel in a way that sent alarm bells ringing inside Charity.

"I am. And you would be?"

"Jack Craig." He gestured toward the younger man, who was wearing a Burberry raincoat. "This is my attorney, Kenneth Cunningham. And, of course, you know

490

Mrs. Greene."

"Of course." The social worker looked decidedly uncomfortable. As if she'd rather be anywhere but here. "May I ask you what you're doing here, Mr. Craig?"

He cleared his throat. "I've come for my daughter."

A sound, like what might have been ripped from a wounded wolf, came out of Johnny's mouth. Before Charity or Gabe could do anything to stop him, he launched himself at the interlopers.

He hit Jack Craig in the middle of the chest, knocking him off-balance on the wet, rain-slick grass.

As the onlookers gave a collective gasp, boy and man tumbled into the open grave, landing with a horrible thud on the casket Amanda had insisted on buying.

61

"I don't understand," Charity complained.

Seeking neutral territory, Charity, Gabe, the social worker, the lawyer, and Jack Craig had gone to the courthouse. Amanda had taken both children back to the house, but only after Johnny had sworn to Gabe that he wouldn't do anything rash, like try to run away with his sister until they could get things settled. Charity thought Johnny's reluctant willingness to make that deal reflected how close Gabe had managed to get in such a short time.

Which, she considered, as she turned down the coffee the court clerk had offered, made sense since it sounded as if the two of them had more than a little in common.

"It's very clear," the lawyer said. The voice, which he might use to speak to a particularly slow kindergartner, was the same one Ethan had always used on her. That superior attitude had annoyed her then. She hated it now.

"Mr. Craig has every reason to believe that he's Angel Harper's father. And now that her mother has died, he's come to take custody of his daughter."

"She's not an item that can be traded, like some velvet Elvis paintings on eBay," Charity snapped. She shot the car dealer a skeptical look. "She's eight years old. If you're that concerned about playing the role of her father, where have you been all this time?"

"My client has been in Las Vegas," the lawyer began.

"I was talking to your client," Charity snapped. Oh, yes, he was reminding her of her former fiancé more with every word. "Who, I would think, could speak for himself."

"I didn't know where my daughter was," Craig asserted.

"So you did know there *was* a daughter."

"Crystal mentioned something about being pregnant." The lobes of his ears turned as scarlet as a boiled crab, giving Charity the impression that Angel's mother had done a lot more than merely *mention* it. The poor woman probably would have felt desperate. "But then she left town and I couldn't find her."

"Yeah, I'll bet you looked really, really

hard, too," Charity muttered. "How did you find her now?"

"I hired a private detective, who saw Crystal's obituary online, on your local newspaper's Web site. Naturally, I got on the first flight I could book out of Las Vegas. To come here, meet my daughter, and bring her home."

Damn. Charity suddenly hated the Internet.

There was more to the story. More he wasn't telling her. Charity exchanged a look with Gabe, whose expression told her that he was thinking the same thing.

"Do you have any proof Angel even *is* your child?"

"Ms. Harper listed my client as the father of record on the child's birth certificate." Once again answering for his client, the attorney reached into an alligator briefcase and pulled out the piece of paper, which bore an official-looking state seal.

"From what your client has said, the woman wasn't exactly a credible witness," Gabe entered the conversation. "She was mentally ill. According to what Johnny told us, she seldom stayed on her medication."

"She firmly believed God spoke to her," Charity added.

The conversation with Johnny Harper

about the years he'd lived with the woman had been one of the most difficult of her life, making all those announcements from her own mother that their family was breaking up again seem practically benign.

She suspected he'd just skimmed the surface of what he'd survived, but refraining from weeping in front of the boy, who, although he was nearly as tall as her, was still just a child, had taken every ounce of her self-restraint.

Yesterday, the day after the fire, inspectors had ruled that the blaze that had destroyed the cabin had started from a cigarette in the cushions of the sofa in the communal living room. Which verified Johnny's claim about his mother believing God had instructed her to protect them from evil.

The thought of the tortured woman, who'd been fighting her own demons for what sounded like most of her life, chain-smoking as she'd held vigil over her children to the very end broke Charity's heart.

"Unfortunately, that's true about her hallucinations." The lawyer's cool voice broke into her unhappy thoughts. "Which is why my client also didn't believe her when she told him that she was pregnant. She was, after all, known to be a habitual liar. Even by those who'd been given the responsibility to protect the children from her."

"She was ill," Charity repeated, more sharply this time. Crystal Harper had died in a misguided, confused attempt to protect those same children. There was no reason to attack her when she wasn't here to defend herself.

"Whatever." The lawyer shrugged and reached into the monogrammed case yet again. "We also have an order for a blood test."

"Blood tests aren't conclusive," Gabe said.

"Which is why we're also requesting a DNA test." Craig's attorney was starting to remind her of a magician pulling rabbits out of a hat as he revealed yet another document. "Meanwhile, Mr. Craig's wife is staying at an inn in Shelter Bay, where the girl will join them until the blood test results are in. Then, unless it negates the possibility of paternity, they'll be taking the girl back to Las Vegas."

"The *girl* has a name," Charity said. "It happens to be Angel. And how can you just take her out of state without a hearing?"

"Mr. Craig's credentials are very strong," the social worker finally spoke. "He's a respected member of his community. We have no problem giving him temporary custody while this matter is sorted out."

"I don't believe this," Charity flared. "These children have already spent too many years in a system that offered benign neglect at best. They've been apart for most of Angel's life. Now not only could they have died — they lost their mother. This is no time to uproot them."

"Yet isn't that precisely what you were planning to do?" the lawyer asked. "Mrs. Greene here" — he nodded toward the social worker, who looked as if she'd spent her morning sucking pickles — "tells me that you've applied to foster the children, which would involve taking the girl, Angel," he corrected at her glare, "from her current home."

Although she'd never hit a person in her life, as Gabe straightened out her fingers and smoothed his hand down the back of hers, Charity realized she'd actually made a fist.

"So Johnny and Angel could be together," she said between gritted teeth. "You're threatening to permanently separate them."

"The boy isn't my son," Jack Craig said. "I don't see where I have any responsibility toward him."

"How about a moral responsibility?" Gabe asked.

When the man's face turned blank at that

question, Charity swore that there was no way in hell she was going to let this horrid man separate those children yet again.

"My mother just happens to be married to a judge," she said. "A Washington State Supreme Court justice with powerful friends in Oregon legal circles."

She had no idea if that was true, but surely after all these years on the bench, Benton had connections he could call upon. "One phone call and he'll stop this travesty of justice from taking place."

"Do your best." Not appearing all that intimidated, the lawyer closed the briefcase with a decisive snap. "Meanwhile, Mrs. Greene will be at your home to retrieve the girl and take her to my client and his wife at three this afternoon. Please have her packed and ready."

He walked out the door, the heels of his Italian loafers clicking on the tile floor, the other two members of his unholy trinity trailing like sheep behind him.

"The idea of handing Angel over to that man, even for a short time, makes me want to cry," Charity said as she blinked back tears more born of anger than sorrow.

"I know." Gabe drew her close and pressed his lips against her hair. "But we're going to beat the guy. Somehow."

She wondered if he'd even noticed that he'd said *we*. As if they were a team.

Which they were.

She needed him. So much, Charity thought.

And he needed her. Along with the family she intended to create. Gabe was too alone. Had been too long. And the saddest thing was that he didn't even know it.

Yet.

62

It was brutal. That was the only word Charity could use to describe it. Angel screamed bloody murder at being told that she was going to be taken away to live with a father she'd never known, away from her brother.

She struck out, swinging wildly at the sour-faced Mrs. Greene, one small fist connecting with the woman's jaw. Apparently prepared for resistance, Craig and the lawyer had brought along Kara, who looked as if she'd rather be anywhere else.

"It's going to be all right," Kara repeated what Charity had said countless times since she'd returned to the house to find Angel in tears. "This is just a temporary situation, darling."

"But it is rough," Charity admitted. She went down on her knees and took hold of the small, trembling shoulders. "And unfair. But here's the deal. My mom's husband is a very important man. He'll figure out a way to fix this. But right now, you have to go with Sheriff Conway and meet your father." She tried to put a positive spin on this situation that was anything but positive. "Your father's been waiting to meet you for a very long time."

"I d-d-don't want to be with him." She reached out and grasped Gabe's hand, which was so much larger that her hand disappeared inside it. "I want Gabe to be my daddy. And I want Shadow to be my dog. And I want to live here and marry Trey."

Well. No one could accuse her of not knowing her own mind. And actually, Charity thought it all sounded like a lovely plan.

"Shadow?" she asked.

Angel looked up at Gabe. "He needed a name. So I decided that Shadow would be a good one because he's black and because he always sticks with you and me. Just like a shadow." Her lower lip, which had been stuck out in a stubborn pout, started trembling. "I hope you don't mind."

"I think Shadow is a perfect name," he assured her.

"Me, too," Charity said, purposefully ignoring the fact that whatever happened with her foster-care application, by the time Angel was back home under this roof, the dog would probably be in Washington State.

501

With Gabe.

Since the tantrum had stopped, for now, Gabe scooped her up into his arms. "How about I give you a piggyback ride out to Sheriff Conway's car?" he suggested.

"The police car?" She perked up a bit at that suggestion.

"We brought the limo," the attorney said.

"I'll drive her to the inn," Kara said in a no-nonsense, don't-even-try-to-mess-with-me cop tone Charity had never heard from her, but bet it had worked really well on perps back in Southern California, where she'd been a cop before moving home to take over her father's job as sheriff.

They all walked out with her.

Gabe's hand rested on Johnny's shoulder as they stood on the sidewalk, watching the black limo glide down Harborview, followed by Kara's police cruiser. Then both disappeared around the corner.

"This is one more suckfest in a truly rotten week," Gabe told the teen. "But you can help set things right."

"Like, yeah. That's worked real well these past years," he muttered.

"No. Seriously. Listen to me."

Charity couldn't imagine anyone not. His Marine voice, like Kara's cop one, radiated quiet authority.

502

"I know what you're thinking. That you might as well just split. Run to Portland. Or maybe Seattle."

Johnny scuffed the toe of his sneaker on the concrete. "I was thinking Seattle," he admitted.

"You've been carrying all this crap all by yourself for too long. You've got yourself a dream team now. Charity, her mom" — he gestured toward Amanda, who'd been a blessing during this difficult time — "her husband, who's a big-shot judge, and me.

"We're going to get your sister back and the two of you are going to move into this house and someday down the road, you might even have to warn Trey Conway that if he ever dares to drink and drive with your sister in the car, or treats her with anything less than the respect she deserves, you're going to have no choice but to rip his heart out and feed it to Peanut as a midnight snack."

That drew a hint of a smile, which Charity had known was his intent.

"Just because that lawyer is a creep doesn't mean he's not good at his job. He's going to try to find some reason why his dirtbag client would provide a better home for your sister than Charity. Which is where you come in by toeing the line because no way is Angel's dad's new wife going to be anything like the supermom this woman was born to be."

He smiled up at Charity. With his mouth and his eyes.

His words shouldn't cause her such a rush of pleasure. And, dammit, hope that just possibly Gabe might be including himself in that family portrait. But they did.

"I'll try," Johnny muttered.

Gabe squeezed his shoulder. "That's all we can ask, son."

63

Charity couldn't think of anything but what might be going on at the Sea Cottage Inn.

She'd tossed and turned all night long. Despite having claimed that he didn't want complications in his life, instead of escaping while he could, Gabe had not only stuck around and spent the night; he'd taken Johnny out for the day of fishing and whale watching with the Douchett men on Cole's crab boat. She knew that the teen was every bit as distracted as she was, but took it as a positive sign that he trusted her when she promised to call Gabe's cell if there was any news of Angel.

Amanda, meanwhile, was on the phone, calling every one of the judge's friends and acquaintances, trying to track down her errant husband.

Knowing that her distraction wouldn't be fair to any animal she might be treating, Charity arranged to have two other vets rotate for her for the next few days until her life hopefully settled down into something resembling normal.

Her nerves already on edge, when her cell phone rang, she scooped it up without even bothering to check the caller ID.

"Hello?"

"Charity?" a familiar, sonorous voice boomed. "It's Benton."

"Benton? Where the hell have you been?"

She hardly ever cursed. It was a sign of her mental state that she did now.

"Sailing back from Maui. Is your mother there?"

"Yes, I'll go get her —"

"Don't do that," he cut her off.

"Why not?" Surely he wasn't leaving her to tell his wife that their marriage was over?

"You'll see soon enough. Bring her down to the yacht-club dock in fifteen minutes."

The way he'd stated it, as a directive rather than a request, might have annoyed Charity had it not spoken to the fact that he was a man used to getting his own way. A judge she was counting on to help give Johnny and Angel Harper the family they deserved.

"This had better be good," she muttered.

"It's better than that," he promised before leaving her talking to dead air.

"Are you sure you feel up to going out?" Amanda asked ten minutes later as they walked down Harborview toward the harbor on the south end of the bay. "You know I'm always up for lunch, but you do realize that after what happened at the cemetery, you're going to end up answering a lot of questions from everyone."

Assuring herself that the ends justified the means, Charity had lied and told her mother that she was craving the Sea Mist's smoked clam chowder. Helping her in the ruse was the fact that the restaurant was located right next to the yacht club where she'd been instructed to show up.

"I'm going to have to deal with them someday." And wasn't that the truth? "Might as well get it over with sooner than later."

Amanda nodded, her hair gleaming like polished copper in the sun-shower streaming through the fog that was finally beginning to burn off. "I suppose that makes sense."

Charity was not surprised when the judge's timing proved right on the money. The billowing white sails were approaching as they reached the dock.

"Oh, wow," she said. "That's one gorgeous sailboat."

"It's a sloop," Amanda said. "You can tell by its single mast, jib, and mainsail."

"That's impressive you know that."

"I told you, your grandfather was a sailor. And since this is supposed to be a fun lunch to take our minds off our troubles, I don't want to think of any damn boats, because it only makes me think of Benton. I swear, if he ever does show up, I won't know whether to kiss him or kill him."

"Well," Charity said as the man behind the gleaming white yacht's wheel began waving his arm, "I'd say you have about a minute to decide."

As it happened, there was no decision to be made. Because Amanda kicked off her pricey Prada heels and took off running, barefoot, hair flying in the salt-tinged breeze, to where her husband was pulling the *Amanda* up to a slip at that floating dock.

Leaving them to their reunion, despite all the problems she still had left on her plate, despite the fact that her heart was still aching for Angel and Johnny, Charity was smiling as she walked back to the house.

64

Gabe had found Charity's mother dramatic but amusing when they'd first met. As the days had passed, he'd discovered that, just like her daughter, she was a woman of contrasts. Of hidden depths. Which was what, he assumed, more than her still amazing looks, had so attracted the judge.

He liked Judge Benton Templeton. Who, despite having a reputation for a clear and cool head on the bench, had shown he could be as clueless as the next male when it came to dealing with a woman.

Deciding that he needed to do something drastic to get his mind back to where it had been before his heart attack, he'd cleared his court calendar and flown to Maui, telling Amanda he was attending a legal conference.

What he hadn't told her, and what he admitted over dinner had been a mistake, was that he'd also left a first-class plane ticket in the study. The plan, which failed big-time when she'd discovered the Viagra in his luggage, had been to call her from Hawaii and instruct her to fly down and join him.

By the time she arrived, he'd have accepted delivery of the blue-water sloop and together they'd take a leisurely cruise back to Washington State, where they'd begin preparing for their grand around-the-world adventure.

"Best-laid plans," the judge said, shaking his head as he beamed at his wife sitting next to him. Who beamed back like a besotted schoolgirl. Since Charity had reported it had taken them more than two hours to show up at the house after the *Amanda* had docked, Gabe suspected they hadn't spent that time sampling the chowder and crab cakes at the Sea Mist.

"Well," Charity said as she rose from the table to answer the kitchen phone. "All's well that ends well. I'll be right back."

She turned toward the teenage boy, whose face held a touch of sunburn, but much less strain than it had when he'd left the house this morning. "Johnny, I'm dying to hear all about your fishing adventure."

She was gone less than three minutes. When she appeared in the doorway, she was

510

white as a glacier.

Gabe jumped up, was at her side in two strides, and took her in his arms. What the hell had gone wrong now? "Sweetheart? Who was that?"

"That was Mrs. Greene." She was trembling. "Angel's gone missing."

65

Johnny jumped to his feet so fast, he knocked over the chair. It nearly landed on the newly named Shadow, who'd been lying beneath it, happily receiving the bits of crab he'd been sneaking to the mutt.

"I know where she is."

"I'd assume she's on her way here," Charity said. "To be with you."

"You already sent her away once," Johnny said. "She'd never trust you not to make her go back." He realized, from the stricken look on the vet's face, that his words had hurt. But he figured he could make up for that later. Once his sister was safe.

"I asked the social worker how that could have happened," Charity said. "You know what she said? That Angel stole a bike that was in the rack outside the inn."

Johnny could tell she was even more angry than when the dickhead car dealer had said he was going to take Angel away.

512

"Forget about the bike," Gabe said. "How about the fact that they weren't watching her? After turning her life upside down, they didn't even care about her that much."

"That's *exactly* what I told her." She no longer looked like the warm and friendly veterinarian who'd offered his sister and him a home. What she looked like, as she turned toward the judge, was some super-heroine from a comic book.

"We're going to find her," she said. "Then, Benton, when we do, you're going to make sure those horrid people never get near her again."

"Sounds like a plan," the old guy, who'd taught Johnny how to tie rope knots while they'd been out on the boat, said.

"I know where she is," Johnny repeated. Then he suddenly remembered the tide charts Fred had taught about. "Oh, fuck! Fuck! Fuck!"

"Take it easy," Gabe said, putting his hand on Johnny's shoulder.

"Fuck that!" Johnny couldn't take it easy. Not when his sister was about to die. "She's in the cave. The one she said she wanted to run away and live in. I talked her out of it, but she'd know I'd come there."

"The tide!" Charity said.

"It'll be coming in," Gabe said, looking

grimmer than Johnny had seen him. "We'd better haul ass." He turned to Amanda. "Call Kara. And have her call the rescue squad."

They were out the door in a flash. As Johnny piled into the Jeep with Gabe, Charity, and the judge, he realized that as shitty as this day was turning out to be, for the first time in his life, he had a clue what it would feel like to have a real family.

66

The sun was quickly setting. In just a few minutes they'd be working in the dark. Kara was sending out a crew with klieg lights, but Gabe feared by the time they reached the beach and got them set up, it might be too late for the little girl.

"There's a ledge," Johnny said. "Halfway up the wall. But I don't think she could climb up there by herself."

"We'll make it in time," Gabe assured him.

"Absolutely," Charity said.

Fortunately, having learned the necessity for backup, Gabe had two flashlights in the Jeep. Which, with the emergency one Charity had grabbed from the clinic, at least assured they'd have some light.

"You wait here," Charity told Johnny as Gabe stopped the Jeep about twenty yards from the sand. He was unfamiliar with this strip of coastline, and didn't want to risk the vehicle being washed away.

"Hell I will." Johnny bailed out of the backseat before the judge could grab him.

"It's his sister," Gabe said. "He needs to be along."

She was clearly torn as she looked back and forth between him and the teen. "I understand, but if anything were to happen —"

"I can take care of myself," Johnny insisted.

"I'd say he's proven that," the judge said.

"Meanwhile," Gabe pointed out, trying not to grind his teeth at the delay, "we're wasting time."

"I give up." She literally threw up her hands. "But I'm coming, too."

"There's a surprise." Gabe figured it would be impossible to keep her away.

Their flashlights cut through the fading light and fog as they made their way over the low, grassy dunes to the water. Every few seconds the sea would brighten from the flash of the lighthouse beam.

Like so many Marines he'd served with over the years, Gabe had a GPS in his head. Fortunately, having come looking for the kids when he'd realized they'd left the others during their beach day, Gabe knew exactly where the cave was located. Unfortunately, the trek over wet, moss-draped rocks was proving the longest of his life.

Not encouraging was the fact that the tide was knee-high when they reached the opening.

"Angel!" Johnny shouted over the water that had begun surging into the cave.

"J-J-Johnny?"

Gabe knew that the relief that flooded through him was shared by everyone.

"It's me, Angel!" Johnny called. "We came to get you."

"I knew you'd come! But I was beginning to be afraid I was going to drown."

"No way we'd let that happen," Gabe said. The cave lit up in the glow of the flashlights as they entered through the roiling water.

"Wow," Charity said.

"They're d-d-diamonds," Angel said. "Johnny and I were going to sell them to get money for an apartment. Before that mean man took me away."

"Well, you're not going to have to do that," Charity said with the self-confidence that Gabe found as sexy as everything else about her. "Because you and your brother are going to live with me."

"But what about Mr. Craig?" Angel asked.

"Screw him," Johnny said as Gabe scooped the little girl up and deposited her on his shoulders, the same way he'd carried her out to the police car that had taken her away.

"Not exactly the words I would have chosen," Charity said. "But I totally agree."

"What about the lawyer?" Johnny asked, as they made their way back to the Jeep. Kara and Benton had arrived with klieg lights, as promised. They were shining out toward the water, turning the beach nearly as bright as day.

"Don't worry about him," Benton said. "He's a nonissue. Because you and your sister have friends in high places."

"Friends like you?"

"Absolutely," the judge assured him. "I've always wanted grandkids, and from what Amanda's told me, I'd say I hit the jackpot with you two."

Johnny's head whipped around, a lot like the kid's in *The Exorcist,* and shot Charity a look. "You're going to adopt us?"

"I was hoping to. If that's okay with you," she tacked on.

"Yeah. Sure. That'd be cool." His tone might be trying for teenage nonchalance, but Gabe could see the tears welling up in his eyes.

"Well then," she said, "I'd like to see anyone try to stop me."

She'd no sooner spoken than her jeans

518

pocket began playing "Dancing Queen."

"Hi, Mom," she said as she answered her iPhone. Hearing the ringtone she'd assigned to her mother, Gabe wondered what she'd given him. Or maybe she hadn't bothered to give him his own signature song, since he wouldn't be sticking around that long. "Your timing's perfect. We've got her."

There was silence as she listened to whatever her mother was saying.

"Okay," she said finally. "Thanks for letting us know."

She put the phone back in her pocket. "Mother received a call from the Craigs' lawyer. His client doesn't want us to bring Angel back to the inn. Not that we would have, of course. But apparently Craig and his wife have changed their minds."

Johnny's hoot could probably have been heard all the way to Portland.

As he pumped a fist in the air, Gabe met Charity's gaze. And as her eyes brightened with moisture, and his own began burning, as well, Gabe felt something inside him, like the fault line that ran beneath the town, shift.

67

It turned out to be amazingly easy in the end.

After Johnny and Angel were safely in bed, Mrs. Greene had arrived at the house and explained to Charity something that had not been included in Angel's official records. Every time over the years, whenever numerous caseworkers had found what they'd hoped would become a permanent placement for the seemingly adorable little girl, the families she'd been placed with had called back within days, usually in a panic, insisting that there must be something very wrong with her, because the terribly violent temper tantrums she'd suffered made her seem possessed.

Despite her mother's long-diagnosed schizophrenia, MRIs, CT scans, and examinations by a host of neurologists and psychiatrists could find no medical reason for Angel Harper's abrupt change in behavior.

So caseworker after caseworker had kept trying.

And each time Angel would get herself thrown back into the system. Charity and Gabe realized that the out-of-character behavior was the only way the little girl had been able to think of to keep from becoming forever separated from her big brother. Who, to her mind, hung the moon.

She'd been at Charity's house for a week now. With Amanda and the judge back in Washington, and Johnny and Angel settled into their new home with what appeared to be amazing ease, proving the resiliency of children, Charity thought, life would have been perfect. Except for one shadow hovering on the horizon.

Each night she went to sleep in Gabe's arms, afraid the next morning she'd wake to find him gone.

Which didn't happen. But on the seventh morning, when she woke and found him sitting hunkered over a mug of coffee at the kitchen table in the stuttering early-dawn light, she knew they'd run out of time.

"You're leaving."

He looked up at her. His eyes were deeply shadowed, suggesting he'd been awake all night.

Tough, was her first thought. Her second

was that he was making the biggest mistake of his life and she couldn't think of any way to stop him.

"We both knew I would."

"Yes." That was the deal, after all. One she'd signed on to. But they'd packed so much into the past weeks, surely he considered her more than simply another girl in another town.

"You could always stay," she suggested as she went over to the counter and poured a cup of coffee for herself. The pot was nearly empty. He'd been up a long time. "The photos you've taken while you've been here have been amazing."

They'd also shown a depth of emotion that had been missing from all his others, which, he'd told her, hadn't gone unnoticed by his agent, who was excited about his apparent change in direction. What Charity had realized was that he'd begun to let his own emotions break out of that strongbox he'd locked them into so many years ago, when he'd been even younger than Johnny was now.

He just needed a bit more time to understand that himself.

She just needed a bit more time to help him see that his life could be so much more.

"I've got a contract that calls for three

more states," he reminded her.

"I'm sure other photographers don't live like nomads."

"A lot do."

"But not all."

"No."

He sighed, obviously sensing where she was going with this.

Like her mother, Charity had followed her heart, which had led her into love. Unlike what her mother had done, on so many occasions, she was not going to give up this relationship without giving it her best shot.

"Surely some have spouses. Children. Families who wave them off and welcome them back home. This isn't the eighteen hundreds. People travel for their careers all the time. That doesn't mean they also allow work to define every moment of their lives."

"Some do. Others end up in so many serial relationships they make your mother look like a cloistered nun."

"That's very good." Because she wanted to pace, she forced herself to sit down and at least appear reasonable. Because if she gave in to instinct, she wouldn't have a dish left in the house. "Focusing on the extremes. Rather than what I'm sure are the majority."

He shrugged again.

"Would it make a difference if I told you I love you?"

Sighed again. "I know you do. And I love you, too."

She'd known that, but wasn't sure that he was that in touch with his own feelings. Oh, he'd shown her in countless ways. But this was the first time he'd said the words out loud. And instead of sounding like music, they fell dark and heavy between them. Like a death knell.

"And it's because I feel that way —"

"Love me." She was going to make him say it again. And again, if that's what it took to pound some sense into that rock-hard Marine head.

He nodded, accepting the correction. "It's because I love you that I'm leaving."

Charity didn't scream as she wanted to. Refused to cry as she desperately needed to. She'd already seen that, like most men, Gabe would rather face down a horde of terrorists than female tears.

She would not use that weapon, because if he stayed, and God, how she wanted him to, she wanted him to do it not because of any feminine ploys but because he wanted, needed, to stay for himself.

"You realize that doesn't make any sense."

"It does to me. You've made a terrific life

here, Charity." He waved his hand, encompassing the kitchen, the house, the entire town that gleamed in the rays of morning like a romanticized scene from a postcard. "I wouldn't have any idea how to be a husband and father."

"Join the club. Because I don't have any idea how to be a wife and mother. But I'm willing to give it my best shot."

"Yeah. Well, anyone could tell that you're going to be great. I'd just screw things up and you'd end up hating me. And neither one of us want that."

His tone was flat. Final.

You knew it was coming. So suck it up and try to get out of this with some dignity intact.

"Have you packed?"

"Last night." He gestured toward the duffel bag sitting by the door that she hadn't noticed when she'd come into the kitchen.

He traveled light. No complications, no baggage. At least, she thought with a deep, inner sigh, he would no longer be totally alone. Because now, thanks to her, he had Shadow.

"Well then. I have a lot to do today." That was a lie. The only thing she'd planned was a day at the beach with Gabe, the kids, and the dogs. "I guess I'd better get at it."

He was letting her go. Part of her had

known it would end this way. But another, stronger part had believed that when push came to shove, he wouldn't be able to walk out the door.

Charity was headed toward the back staircase when he called her name.

"What?" She glanced back. Hope was a hummingbird, fluttering its delicate, brightly colored wings in her chest.

"Have a good life."

One of Kara's favorite movies, which she'd made Charity and Sedona watch countless times, was *Casablanca*. It crossed her mind that for a parting statement it sure didn't come up to what Bogie had told Ingrid Bergman just before he'd put her on that plane.

Wanting to leave him with some pithy, parting words of her own, she nearly shared that thought with him.

Then, instead said, "You'll think of me. You might be able to run, Gabriel. But I'll be with you. Everywhere. And always. Wherever in the world you go, you won't be able to get me out of your mind. Or your heart."

As she swept from the room with a flair she suspected even Amanda would admire, she heard him mutter, "I may be an idiot. But I already figured that part out."

68

"I thought Marines were supposed to be so fucking brave."

Gabe glanced down at the glowering teenager, who was straddling the black mountain bike he'd bought him two days ago at the Magic Spoke.

"You're not a foster brat anymore," Gabe said mildly as he finished hooking up the Jeep to the back of the motor home. "You're going to have to clean up your language. Make Charity proud."

"Fuck that." If the kid's eyes were as deadly as they looked, Gabe would be six feet under. "*You* made her cry."

"I'm sorry about that." And wasn't that the understatement of the year? Decade. Century.

"Don't tell me, dude. Tell her."

"It's better this way." They were both studiously ignoring Shadow, who had dropped onto his back the minute Johnny had ridden up and was doing his wild, you-know-you-want-to-rub-my-belly wiggle.

"It's because of me, isn't it?"

"What?" Startled by that question he hadn't seen coming, Gabe looked up from the hitch. "Where did you get that idea?"

"I heard you say you love her."

"That would mean you were eavesdropping."

"So sue me. Is it true? Or did you just tell her that to get in her pants?"

"Christ." Gabe stood up and wondered, not for the first time since he'd arrived in Shelter Bay, what he was doing to keep landing in these minefields. "First of all, show the lady the respect she deserves by not talking about her in such a crude way."

"I respect *her.* You, I'm not so sure about."

"Don't feel like the Lone Ranger. And no, dammit, my leaving doesn't have anything to do with you. Or your sister. You're both great kids, she's fucking lucky to have you in her life, and you're all going to make one dynamite family."

"You just said *fuck.* And we need a dad."

"Maybe you do. But I'm not dad material."

"Says you." It was a sneer.

"Yeah. Says me."

The kid flinched, just a bit, at that, but

528

showing himself to be the fighter Gabe had already seen him to be, he came out swinging again. "You're making a big mistake."

"It won't be my first one."

"Okay." He reached into his backpack and pulled out a manila envelope.

Not quite trusting his surrender, Gabe took the envelope.

"Wait till you're out of town to open it," Johnny said.

Then, after bending down to give the dog the rub it had been begging for, he took off, pedaling furiously, toward the bridge leading back to town, taking a little bit more of Gabe's heart with him.

"Okay," he said to the mutt. "Let's get this show on the road."

69

"Men," Sedona said as she placed the pink box on Charity's kitchen counter. "You can't live with them. And unfortunately you can't shoot them."

"Not without me having to take you in," Kara, who'd shown up right behind Sedona, agreed. After a moment's deliberation, she plucked a red velvet cupcake from the box.

"Maybe you could arrest him," Sedona said. "For expired plates."

"His plates are current. I already checked that," she admitted when Charity gave her a surprised look. "I was holding it back as a possible option. . . . Damn, this thing is going to go straight to my hips."

"Like you have to worry," Sedona said. "How about speeding?"

"That's merely a ticketable offense. Unless he's caught committing some other crime."

"There has to be something we can do."

Sedona bit into a lemon coconut cake, chewing with such relish Charity had the impression she was imagining biting off some vital part of Gabe's anatomy. Of the three of them, Sedona was the most given to watching violent movies, which was ironic since she'd grown up on that commune with pacifist parents.

After swallowing, she looked at Charity. "I don't suppose you left anything in that motor home."

"No." Nothing but some buttons and torn underwear, which she wasn't quite prepared to share with even her closest friends.

"Too bad. If you had, you could call in and report it stolen."

"That'd be an offense," Kara said. "Filing a false police report."

"It's a moot issue," Charity said. "Since I wouldn't do it."

After much deliberation, she selected a better-than-sex chocolate cupcake. Which she'd always thought lived up to its name. Until she'd had sex with Gabriel St. James.

If he didn't come back, she was probably destined to spend the rest of her life as a celibate. Because unless the military had done top secret experiments and cloned warrior Marines, there wasn't another man on the planet who could make her feel the way Gabe did.

And wasn't that a fun prospect?

He'd be back.

She'd give him a week. Maybe two, Charity decided.

Then she was going after him.

70

It didn't take two weeks. Or even two days.

Two hours after leaving Shelter Bay, Gabe pulled into a scenic turnout to take a long shot of the Shelter Bay lighthouse. Admittedly lighthouse photographs were a dime a dozen. Go to any royalty-free stock company's Web site and you'd find hundreds taken by rank amateurs. Most were vacation shots, taken solely to capture a special time apart. A time worth remembering.

Which was why he was taking this shot. To have one last memory of Charity Tiernan. Not that he'd ever forget her smile. Or her rain-forest eyes, her smooth hands, and the soft little sounds she made when they were making love.

He snapped the photo just as the light, which had been guiding sailors into the harbor for two hundred years, flashed a brilliant yellow.

He was getting back in the motor home

when he saw the envelope he'd tossed on the dashboard. He'd been so caught up in thinking about her, reliving every moment of their time together, that he'd nearly forgotten all about it.

He took out a penknife and slit the end.

Unsurprisingly, it was a photo. But not one Gabe had seen on Johnny's camera. It was an eight-by-ten photo of Charity and him, taken unawares three days ago on a day's outing at the beach. Continuing to show talent, Johnny had caught some great shots of Peanut jumping up into the air to catch a red Frisbee that was a bright contrast to the blue of the water, the silver sand, and the soft misty hue of the sky. There were others of Angel making sand castles, and a strangely poignant one of the sea beginning to wash the castle away, as if to show that, in the end, all things were fleeting.

Including relationships, Gabe thought, as he looked at Charity laughing up at him, and him looking down at her with so much emotion in his eyes it was almost painful to see.

But it was more than desire, or even love, which was also so obvious. It was amazement. Like a mortal man who'd somehow found a mermaid washed up on his beach. A mermaid who, rather than return to the sea, had chosen to stay and love him instead.

He looked, he thought, exactly the way Cole had gazed at Kelli while they'd been dancing at the reception. In the photo the new bride had informed him during the dinner she'd cooked for Charity and him at her house, that she'd chosen for the cover of her wedding album.

"Idiot."

If there was one thing all those years in war zones had taught Gabe, it was that lives were too brief, too fragile, and too fleeting, and the unpalatable fact was that most people died alone. And a helluva lot sooner than they thought.

"Come on," he said to the dog as he twisted the key in the ignition. "We're going home."

Charity was sitting in one of the chairs on the porch when he drove up. She didn't jump up and come running toward the motor home, like one of those love-struck women in shampoo commercials. But the fact that she didn't go into the house and slam the door behind her was encouraging.

Gabe took his time walking toward her, his brain madly scrambling to remember all the clever, contrite words he'd thought up on the drive back to town designed to worm his way back into her good graces.

They were good words. And a clever plan. At least he'd hoped so. Because this was, hands down, the most important mission he'd ever been on in his life.

But then, damn, she'd smiled up at him and his mind was wiped as clear as glass.

"Knitting?" Great opening line, fuckhead.

She arched a dark brow, appearing as surprised as Gabe was by his opening gambit. "My mother talked me into it. We're making blankets for kids in difficult situations."

"Sounds like a great idea," he said as the two dogs began chasing each other as if it had been years rather than a few hours since they'd seen each other.

"Project Linus is a national organization. Adèle's spearheading the Shelter Bay group."

"Good for her."

"Yes." She tilted her head. "But surely you didn't come back to discuss my new hobby."

"No." His knees were shaking as if he'd been going into battle. He considered locking them but, having witnessed too many fellow Marines passing out during inspection by cutting off the flow of blood to their head, forged on.

"I came to grovel. To crawl naked down Harborview over shards of broken glass to

536

beg forgiveness for acting like an ass."

"That naked glass crawling is my mother's idea," she said. Another slight smile played at the corners of that luscious mouth he knew he'd still want to taste when they were in their nineties, sitting on this porch, watching their grandkids windsurfing on the bay. "I also thought, at the time, that perhaps it was a bit excessive."

"How about this?" He dropped to one knee on the porch. "I love you. I'm not real good at saying the words, but maybe that's partly because I don't know any words strong enough for how you make me feel. You make me believe that I'm a better man than I know I am."

"A better man than you sometimes think you are," she corrected softly.

Oh, hell. She was beginning to mist up. Was that a good thing? Or bad?

"Whatever. The fact is that when I'm with you, I want to be the kind of man who'd make a good husband. The kind that would be a good father to Johnny and Angel. And any other kids you might want to consider having.

"Down the road," he tacked on quickly, not wanting her to think he was putting any pressure on her. But she had said she wanted a big family. "If you want, that is. If you don't —"

She placed a finger against his lips, cutting him off. "I can't think of anything I'd rather do than make a child with you."

"You know that movie. Where Tom Cruise tells that actress that she completes him?"

She nodded. "*Jerry Maguire.*"

"That's it." Romantic comedies would never be his first choice, but they'd shown it at the theater in the Green Zone during one of his tours in Iraq. "I always thought that was a cheesy line."

"You wouldn't be alone in that."

"But the deal is, I understand it now." He took hold of her hand and linked their fingers together, and, lifting them to his lips, pressed a kiss against her knuckles. "You fill a hole in me, Dr. Charity Tiernan. One I didn't even know was empty. Until I met you."

"Damn." Her eyes were glistening now, the tears starting to flow. "I never cry."

"I promise, if you just forgive me for being the world's biggest idiot, I'll spend the rest of our lives trying to make you never cry again."

"You *are* an idiot." It was a half laugh, half sob. She hit his shoulder with her free hand. "Because these are happy tears."

Cooling relief flooded over him. It was going to be okay. *They* were going to be okay. And she wasn't even going to make him crawl naked over broken glass. Which he'd been totally willing to do, if that's what it had taken.

As he took her into his arms, all Gabe could think about was that, after all these years wandering the world, he was home. With Charity.

Home where he belonged.

Later that evening
They were all gathered together on the porch, sitting in the white Adirondack chairs facing the harbor. Was there a more clichéd shot than a family photo?

Probably not.

Was there a better shot?

Not in Gabe's view.

"Okay," Johnny instructed as he set the timer on the camera he'd placed on the porch railing, "no one move." He shot a hard look at the dogs, who were sprawled in front of the chairs. "And that includes you mutts."

He started the timer clicking, then dashed back and was in his chair, sitting in front of Gabe and Charity, right beside his sister, with time to spare.

"On the count of three everyone has to

smile," he said.

"That's an easy one," Gabe said as he put his arm around Charity's shoulders.

"One."

"Two."

"Three," the teenage photographer called out.

And as the camera clicked, freezing this perfect moment in time, Gabe smiled.

ABOUT THE AUTHOR

JoAnn Ross lives with her husband and three rescued dogs in the Pacific Northwest. Visit her Web site at www.joannross.com for a video tour of Shelter Bay.

The employees of Thorndike Press hope you have enjoyed this Large Print book. All our Thorndike, Wheeler, and Kennebec Large Print titles are designed for easy reading, and all our books are made to last. Other Thorndike Press Large Print books are available at your library, through selected bookstores, or directly from us.

For information about titles, please call:
  (800) 223-1244

or visit our Web site at:
  http://gale.cengage.com/thorndike

To share your comments, please write:
Publisher
Thorndike Press
10 Water St., Suite 310
Waterville, ME 04901